## "Even if we tried, we'd never work," I whispered.

"Shut up," he whispered back.

"You live in a different zone than me," I shared again and watched his head descend. "The upper zone. I'm the lower zone. Never the twain shall meet." I said my last against his lips which had found their way to mine.

"Shut up," he repeated, his lips moving against mine.

"Mitch—"

"All right, baby, I'll shut you up."

Then he did, his head slanting and his lips taking mine in a repeat performance of the open-mouthed, knock my socks off, rock my world, best kiss in the history of all time...

# Praise for
## KRISTEN ASHLEY

"[LAW MAN is an] excellent addition to a phenomenal series!"
—ReadingBetweentheWinesBookclub.blogspot.com

"[LAW MAN] made me laugh out loud. Kristen Ashley is an amazing writer!" —TotallyBookedblog.com

"Run, don't walk...to get [the Dream Man] series. I love [Kristen Ashley's] rough, tough, hard loving men. And I love the cosmo-girl club!" —NocturneReads.com

"I adore Kristen Ashley's books. She writes engaging, romantic stories with intriguing, colorful, and larger-than-life characters. Her stories grab you by the throat from page one and don't let go until well after the last page. They continue to dwell in your mind days after you finish the story and you'll find yourself anxiously awaiting the next. Ashley is an addicting read no matter which of her stories you find yourself picking up."
—Maya Banks, *New York Times* bestselling author

"I felt all of the rushes, the adrenaline surges, the anger spikes...my heart pumping in fury. My eyes tearing up when my heart (I mean...*her* heart) would break."
—Maryse's Book Blog (Maryse.net)
on *Motorcycle Man*

"There is something about them [Ashley's books] that I find crackalicious." —Kati Brown, DearAuthor.com

# LAW
# MAN

# LAW MAN

## KRISTEN ASHLEY

FOREVER

NEW YORK   BOSTON

Forever
Hachette Book Group
237 Park Avenue, New York, NY 10017
www.hachettebookgroup.com
www.twitter.com/foreverromance

Printed in the United States of America
Originally published as an ebook
First Mass Market Edition: December 2013
10 9 8 7 6 5 4 3 2 1

OPM

Forever is an imprint of Grand Central Publishing.
The Forever name and logo are trademarks of Hachette Book Group, Inc.

The publisher is not responsible for websites (or their content) that are not owned by the publisher.

The Hachette Speakers Bureau provides a wide range of authors for speaking events. To find out more, go to www.hachettespeakersbureau.com or call (866) 376-6591.

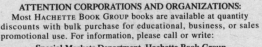

# Acknowledgments

To Chasity Jenkins, who originally proofread this book and does many things to keep me sane. Gratitude, sister.

To my cousin, Detective Amanda Giannini, MSW (Domestic Violence Investigations, Child Development Community Policing Liaison, Crisis Intervention Team Officer), who gave me the skinny about how it would go down with Child Protection Services. I took artistic license, of course, but my brave cousin charted my way. You're the best, Mandy, so proud of you, all you've accomplished and what you do.

And to my readers, thank you for making a dream come true at the same time you keep that dream alive. You rock my world!

# Author's Note

Upon asking a friend to give me names of the male and female offspring of a loser, he asked, "What's their dad's name?" I answered, "Bill." He immediately replied, "Billy and Billerina." I found this so hilarious, Billy and Billie were born. Hopefully, you can tell them apart. As for me, every time I read their names, I giggle. But still, I fell in love with them.

# LAW
# MAN

# PROLOGUE

## Law Man

I walked out of my apartment into the breezeway and saw her.

At least a Seven, maybe an Eight, to give her a score, I put her at a Seven Point Five.

She was standing outside the open apartment door smiling inside at someone.

I knew who she was smiling at.

Detective Mitch Lawson.

I also knew that my neighbor Detective Mitch Lawson was at least a Ten, maybe an Eleven, so to give him a fair score I put him at a definite Ten Point Five.

In other words, he was beyond perfect from the top of his dark brown-haired head to his usually boot-clad feet.

He was the man of my dreams.

I was in love with him and I didn't know him and he definitely didn't know me. This was not in a sick-stalker-type way because I was too shy to be a stalker and I liked him too much to put him through something like that. This was in an ohmigod he's got the perfect body, perfect bone structure, perfect smile, most beautiful eyes I've ever seen way. It was a totally benign, admiring from afar love.

Except that we lived across the breezeway and one apartment down from each other so it wasn't that far.

I turned and made certain my door was locked. When I turned back Detective Mitch Lawson was out in the breezeway, his Seven Point Five standing so close she was pressed against his side. He too was checking to make certain his door was locked.

It was morning and I was going to work. I suspected that he was going to work too. I also knew Seven Point Five had spent the night. I'd noticed, since I ran into them on occasion, he had a lot of Sevens to Tens who spent the night or who came over in the evenings, the afternoons, or other times. Being a Two, maybe a Three, so placing myself at a Two Point Five, there was no way in hell I'd ever be standing out in the breezeway pressed to Detective Mitch Lawson.

In this world, Sevens to Tens gravitated to each other and rarely, if ever, dipped below the Seven mark. They might try a Six or even go slumming with a Five, but they'd settle in for the long haul with someone in their zone. Then the Fours to Sixes gravitated to each other. There was more workability here for those under Four to get in but it was also rare. And my zone, Ones to Threes gravitated to each other. If you were of my zone, only the foolish aimed higher than a Three. Higher than a Three equaled heartache.

I walked toward them since I had to get to the stairs that led down to the parking spaces at the side of our unit. As I did, my heels clicked and echoed loudly on the cement landing of the breezeway. Four apartments were off that breezeway, two by two next to and facing each other. Detective Mitch Lawson's was closer to the stairs that led to the parking. My apartment was closer to the stairs that led to the greenbelt and creek that ran through our complex.

Unfortunately, as he always did when I ran into him in the many years we'd been living in the same unit, when he noticed me, his head came around, his dark brown, soulful eyes caught mine and they warmed.

This was another reason I knew I loved him. His eyes warmed anytime he saw me. I was shy and therefore not overtly friendly, at least not to him. I was very friendly with Brent and Bradon, the gay couple who lived next to me. I was also very friendly with Derek and LaTanya, the not gay couple who lived next to Detective Mitch Lawson and across from me. But he scared the hell out of me, so I tried to give him a wide berth.

Even so, anytime he saw me his eyes always warmed and right after he'd smile.

Just like he did now.

*God.*

That smile. I felt it in my belly. His eyes were the most beautiful eyes I'd ever seen, but when they were warm and his beautiful lips turned up into a smile making his whole face warm, it was too much to take. Four years ago, when he first moved in and I first experienced that smile, it nearly brought me to my knees. Luckily, I'd practiced my control, and now it only made my knees wobble.

"Hey," he said as I got close to passing them.

This sucked. Not only did he have beautiful eyes and beautiful lips, he also had very broad shoulders and was very tall and dressed really well. He also had a nice, rich, deep voice.

"Morning," I muttered. My eyes slid to his Seven Point Five, who was looking at me for some reason like I'd slithered out from under a rock (it was my experience sometimes that when a Seven or higher looked at a Three or lower they got this look). To be courteous I repeated,

"Morning," to her. She returned a partial chin lift and did it in a way that made that minimal effort seem taxing.

Then I looked to my feet mainly because I needed to concentrate on not tripping and also because if I caught sight of him again I might start to stare. I knew if I stared at him too long my eyes might burn out of my head.

To focus on something that did not include him or his Seven Point Five, I lifted a hand to capture the thick tendril of hair at the front of my face that always escaped the chignon at the nape of my neck and tucked it behind my ear. Then I scurried past them and down the stairs, praying I wouldn't tumble down. Mostly I didn't want to look like a fool, but I also didn't want a broken neck.

I successfully made it to my car and focused on getting myself sorted by stowing my purse and travel coffee mug. I connected my MP3 player, found a good song that would put me in the mood to work and hooked my seatbelt. I did this so I wouldn't look at Detective Mitch Lawson and his Seven Point Five coming down and driving away. I could watch him for hours. I knew this even though I'd never done it. Doing that would make me a sort of stalker and even insignificant stalker-type behavior was creepy.

It took me a while to get sorted. And by the time I had Grand Funk ready to shout out "We're an American Band," I was belted, the ignition was turned and I looked up to back out, Seven Point Five was gone.

But Detective Mitch Lawson remained. I knew this not because I looked for him, but because I couldn't miss him. There was an empty spot next to mine and his SUV was in the next spot. He was also in that spot, standing outside the driver's side door to his truck, his hips to it, his arms crossed on his chest, and his eyes were on me like *he* was watching *me*.

This had never happened before and was also against all the laws that ruled my universe. Therefore, I may have stared for a second before my mind started tripping over itself trying to figure out what to do.

I decided on a little wave, which was what I did. This earned me another smile from Detective Mitch Lawson that I felt whoosh through my belly in a *really* good way.

Okay, that was it. That was all I could take.

I looked away, hit play on my MP3 player, Don Brewer started beating out the intro to "We're an American Band," and I did my best to back out without hitting anything.

And I just managed to drive away without looking again at Detective Mitch Lawson, his perfect body, his great hair, his fabulous lips, or his beautiful eyes.

# CHAPTER ONE

## Doohickey

"HELLO, THIS IS Mara Hanover in unit 6C. I've called three times today and I really need someone to come over and look at my bathroom tap. It won't turn off. Can you please have the maintenance guy come around? Thanks."

I shut down my cell after leaving my voicemail message and stared at my bathroom faucet, which hadn't turned off after I was finished with it that morning. I had called the management office of the complex before going to work and left a message. When I didn't get a call back, I called at lunch (leaving another message). Now I was home after work and it was past office hours, but someone was supposed to be on call all the time. I should have had a callback. I needed a callback. What I didn't need was a water bill out the roof or to try to go to sleep listening to running water while thinking of my money flowing down the drain.

I sighed and kept staring at the water running full blast out of my faucet.

I was a woman who had lived alone her entire adult life. I'd once had a long-term relationship with a Five Point Five that got nowhere near living together. This was because I was a Two Point Five and he was a Five Point Five who wanted a Nine Point Five. Therefore, we were both destined for broken hearts. He gave me mine. He later found a Six Point Five that wanted a Nine Point Five. She got herself a breast enhancement and nose job, which made her a firm Seven (if you didn't count the fact that she thought she was a Ten point Five and acted like it, which really knocked her down to a Six) who broke his heart.

Regardless of the fact that I was now thirty-one and had lived alone since I was eighteen, I knew nothing about plumbing or cars. Every time something happened with my plumbing or my car, I vowed to myself that I would learn something about plumbing or cars. I would get that said something fixed and I'd totally forget my vow. Then I'd lament forgetting my vow in times like I was experiencing right now.

I walked out of my master bath, through my bedroom, down the hall into my open-plan living-slash-kitchen-slash-dining area and out the front door. I crossed the breezeway and knocked on Derek and LaTanya's door.

Derek knew something about plumbing. I knew this because of two things. First, he was a man and men had a sixth plumbing sense. Second, I knew this because he was a plumber.

LaTanya opened the door, and her big, dark eyes widened with LaTanya Delight.

LaTanya Delight was different than anyone else's delight and therefore deserved a capital letter. It was louder, brasher, brighter and cheerier. The look on her face communicated her joy at seeing me like she and I had been separated at birth and were right then being blissfully reunited. Not like she'd just seen me the night before when she came over to watch *Glee* with me.

"Hey girl!" she squealed through a big smile. "Perfect

timing. I'm about to mix a batch of mojitos. Get your ass in here and I'll pour us some cocktails!"

I smiled at her but shook my head. "Can't," I told her. "Something's up with my faucet, the office hasn't returned my calls, and I really need Derek to look at it. Is he around?"

I sensed movement at my side and LaTanya did too. We both looked that way to see Detective Mitch Lawson walking up the stairs carrying four plastic grocery bags.

If I were a Seven to Ten and in his zone, which meant I could be in his life, I would lecture him about plastic grocery bags. Considering the state of the environment, no one should use plastic grocery bags, not even hot guys who could get away with practically anything. Since I was not in his zone and I didn't know him and *couldn't* know him for fear of expiring from pleasure should he, say, speak more than a few words to me, I'd never get the chance to lecture him about plastic grocery bags.

"Yo Mitch!" LaTanya greeted him loudly with Delight.

"Hey LaTanya," Mitch greeted back, then his beautiful eyes skimmed to me and his lips tipped up further, "Hey."

"Hey," I replied, locked my legs, ignored the whoosh I felt in my belly and looked back at LaTanya. She was checking out Detective Mitch Lawson—as any woman should or she would be immediately reported to then thrown out of the Woman Club. I heard the rustling of bags, but I ignored it and called her name to get her attention. When I got it, I repeated, "Is Derek around? I wouldn't bother him but my faucet won't turn off and I really need someone to look at it."

"He's not here, Mara, sorry, babe," LaTanya replied. "You said the office hasn't called you back?"

"No," I told her and was about to ask her if she would send Derek over when he got home when I heard from my side:

"You want me to look at it?"

This came from Detective Mitch Lawson, and I sucked in breath and turned my head to look at him. He was standing outside his open apartment door still carrying his bags and his eyes were on me.

My mind went blank. I lost the lock on my legs and my knees wobbled.

God, he was beautiful.

"Mara," I heard from far away, and even though I heard it and it was my name, I didn't respond. "Mara!" I heard again. This time louder and sharper, my body jolted and I turned to LaTanya.

"What?" I asked.

"Mitch'll look at it, that cool with you?" she asked me.

I blinked at her.

No. No it was *not* cool with me.

What did I do?

I couldn't have him in my apartment walking through my *bedroom* to look at my faucet. That would mean he'd be in my apartment. That would mean he'd walk through my *bedroom*. And that would mean I'd have to speak more than one word to him.

Crap!

I looked to Detective Mitch Lawson and said the only thing I could say.

"That would be really kind."

He stared at me a second then lifted the bags an inch and muttered, "Let me get rid of these and I'll be over."

I swallowed then called, "Okay," to his closing door.

I watched his door close and then I kept watching his closed door wondering if the weird feeling I was having was just panic or a precursor to a heart attack. Then La-Tanya called my name again, so I looked at her.

"You okay?" she asked, studying me closely.

I had not, incidentally, shared my love for Detective Mitch Lawson with LaTanya, Derek, Brent, Bradon or anyone. This was because I thought they'd think I was a little insane (or a stalker). They often invited him to parties and such, and if he came, I would usually make my excuses and leave. They'd never cottoned on. I figured mostly because he didn't often attend their parties due to his being a police officer with long hours, but also because he had his buds over for games and his babes over for other things. He wasn't the type of man who went to gay men's parties or LaTanya's cocktail extravaganzas. The ones he went to I suspected he did just to be neighborly. Though Derek, more often than not, went to his place to watch games. Usually in order to escape LaTanya's cocktail extravaganzas, which were frequent occasions.

"Yeah, I'm fine," I lied to her. "Just had a tough day at work," I continued lying. "And I'm not happy the management office didn't call me back. They don't pay my water bill." I wasn't lying about that.

"I hear you," LaTanya agreed. "Service around here has taken a turn for the worse even though they upped our rent three months ago. You remember our fridge went out last month?"

I remembered. I also remembered it took three weeks to get it replaced. Derek had been none too happy, and LaTanya had been loudly none too happy.

"Yeah, I remember. That sucked."

"It sure did. Buyin' ice all the time and livin' outta coolers. I don't pay rent for that shit. Fuck that."

Fuck that indeed.

Detective Mitch Lawson's door opened, and I realized my mistake instantly. I should have run to my house and done something. I didn't know what. Nothing needed tidying because I was freakishly tidy. There was nothing I could do with my appearance, but I figured I should have tried to do *something*.

He started walking our way asking, "Now a good time?"

No, no time was a good time for the Ten Point Five I was secretly in love with to be in my apartment.

I nodded and said, "Sure." Then I looked at LaTanya and said, "Later, babe."

"Later. Remember, a mojito is waitin' for you, when Mitch gets your faucet sorted out."

"Thanks," I muttered, smiled and then glanced at Detective Mitch Lawson before looking down at my feet, turning and walking the short distance to my door. I opened it, walked through, and held it open for him to come inside.

He did and I tried not to hyperventilate.

"Which one is it?" he asked as I closed the door behind him.

I turned, stood at the door and looked up at him. He was closer than I expected and he was taller than he seemed from afar, and he seemed pretty tall from afar. I'd never been this close to him and I felt his closeness tingle pleasantly all across my skin. I was wearing heels and I felt his tallness in the depth of the tip of my head, which didn't tip back that often to look at someone seeing as I was tall.

"Pardon?" I asked.

"Faucet," he said. "Which one? Hall or master?"

I didn't have any clue what he was talking about. It was like he was speaking in a foreign language. All I could focus on were his eyes, which I was also seeing closer than I'd ever seen before. He had great eyelashes.

Those lashes moved when his eyes narrowed.

"You okay?" he asked.

Oh God. I had to get a hold on myself.

"Yeah, fine, um...the faucet's in my master bath," I told him.

He stood there staring at me. I stood there staring at him. Then his lips twitched and he lifted his arm slightly in the direction of my hall.

"You wanna lead the way?" he asked.

Ohmigod! I was *such* an idiot!

"Right," I muttered, looked down at my feet and led the way.

When we were both in my bathroom, which, with him in it, went from a normal-sized master bath to a teeny-tiny, suffocating space, I pointed to the faucet and then pointed out the obvious.

"It won't turn off."

"I see that," he murmured. Then I stood frozen with mortification as he crouched and opened the doors to my vanity.

Why was he opening the doors to my vanity? I kept my tampons down there! He could see them! They were right at the front for easy accessibility!

Ohmigod!

He reached in, I closed my eyes in despair and wished the floor would gobble me up and suddenly the water turned off.

I opened my eyes, stared at the faucet and exclaimed, "Holy cow! You fixed it!"

He tipped his head back to look at me then he straightened out of his crouch to look down at me.

Then he said, "No, I just turned the water off."

I blinked up at him. Then I asked, "Pardon?"

"You can turn the water off."

"You can?"

"Yeah."

"Oh," I whispered then went on stupidly, "I should probably have done that before I left for work this morning."

His mouth twitched again and he said, "Probably. Though you can't do somethin' you don't know you can do."

I looked to the basin and muttered, "This is true."

"There's a valve under the sink. I'll show it to you after I take a look at the faucet," he said, and I forced my eyes to his. "You probably just need a new washer. Where are your tools?"

I blinked again. "Tools?"

His stared at me and then his lips twitched again. "Yeah. Tools. Like a wrench. You got one of those?"

"I have a hammer," I offered.

One side of his mouth hitched up in a half smile. "I'm not sure a hammer is gonna help."

It took a lot of effort but I only glanced at the half smile before my eyes went back to his. This didn't do a thing to decelerate my rapidly accelerating heartbeat.

"Then no, I don't have tools," I told him, not adding that I wasn't entirely certain what a wrench *was*.

He nodded and turned to the door. "I'll go get mine."

Then he was gone, and I didn't know what to do, so I hurried after him.

I should have stayed where I was. I'd seen him move, of course, I just hadn't seen him moving around in my apartment. He had an athlete's grace, which I had noticed before. But it was more. He had a natural confidence with the way he held his body *and* the way he moved. It was immensely attractive all the time, but seeing it in my apartment was not going to be conducive to peace of mind. Something it was difficult for me to find on a good day, much less a day when my faucet didn't turn off and I was forced to endure an evening that included Detective Mitch Lawson having to be in my apartment.

He stopped at the door and turned to me. "I'll be right back."

I nodded, and he disappeared out the door.

I stood in my living area in my heels, skirt and blouse from work. Then I wondered if I had time to change before he got back. Then I wondered if he'd notice it if I'd spritzed on perfume when he got back. Then I wondered if I should do a shot or two of vodka before he got back. Then he knocked on my door, which meant he was back.

I ran to the door, looked through the peephole (you couldn't be too careful) and saw him looking to the side. I sucked in a calming breath then opened the door.

"Hey," I said, "welcome back."

I was such a dork!

He grinned. I stepped aside, and he came through carrying a toolbox. Learning from my mistakes, I immediately led him through the living area, down the hall, through my bedroom and to the bathroom. He put the toolbox on the basin counter and opened it. He pulled out what I figured was a wrench and went right to work.

I watched his hands, which I'd never really noticed before. They were a man's hands. There were veins that stood out that were appealing. His fingers were long and strong looking. He had great hands.

"So your name is Mara." His deep voice came at me. My body jolted and I looked to his head, which was bent so he could watch what he was doing.

"Yeah," I replied, and my voice sounded kind of high so I cleared my throat and stated, "And you're Mitch."

"Yeah," he said to the faucet.

"Hi, Mitch," I said to his dark brown-haired head, thinking his hair looked soft and thick and was long enough to run your fingers through.

That head twisted so I was looking into dark brown eyes whose depths were so deep you could lose yourself in them for eternity.

Those eyes were also smiling.

"Hi, Mara," he said softly, and my nipples started tingling.

Oh God.

I scanned my memory banks to pull up what underwear I'd put on that morning. I thanked my lucky stars that my bra had light padding, all the while thinking maybe I should leave him to it.

Before I could make good an escape, his head bent back to the tap and he asked, "How long have you lived here?"

"Six years," I answered.

Shoo! Good. A simple answer that didn't make me sound like an idiot. Thank God.

"What do you do?" he went on.

"I work at Pierson's," I told him.

His neck twisted and his eyes came back to me. "Pierson's Mattress and Bed?"

I nodded. "Yeah."

He looked back at the faucet. "What do you do there? An accountant or something?"

I shook my head even though he wasn't looking at me. "No, I'm a salesperson."

His neck twisted, faster this time, and his eyes locked on mine. "You're a salesperson," he repeated.

"Yeah," I replied.

"At Pierson's Mattress and Bed," he stated.

"Um...yeah," I answered.

He stared at me and I grew confused. I didn't tell him I was a pole dancer. I also didn't tell him I spent my days in my den of evil masterminding a plot to take over the free world. He appeared slightly surprised. I was a salesperson. This wasn't a surprising job. This was a boring job. Then again I was a boring person. He was a police detective. I knew this because I'd seen his badge on his belt on numerous occasions. I also knew this because LaTanya told me. I reckoned, considering his profession, he'd long since figured out I was a boring person. In my mind police detectives could figure anyone out with a glance.

"You good at it?" he asked.

"Um..." I answered because I didn't want to brag. I *was* good at it. I'd been top salesperson month after month for the last four years after Barney Ruffalo quit (or resigned voluntarily rather than face the sexual harassment charges that Roberta lodged against him). Barney had been my nemesis mainly because he was a dick and always came onto me, along with every woman that worked there or walked through the door, and because he stole my customers.

Mitch looked back at my tap, muttering, "You're good at it."

"Pretty good," I allowed.

"Yeah," he said to the faucet and continued, "put money down that ninety percent of the men who walk in that place go direct to you *and* make a purchase."

This was a weird thing to say. It was true. Most of my customers were men. Men needed mattresses and beds just like any other human being. When they came to Pierson's, since we had excellent quality, value and choice, they'd not want to go anywhere else.

"Why do you say ninety percent?" I asked Mitch.

"'Cause the other ten percent of the male population is gay," he answered the faucet. I blinked at his head in confusion at his words. He straightened, putting the wrench down and lifting his other hand. Between an attractive index finger and thumb was a small, round, black plastic doohickey with a hole in the middle that had some shredding at the edges. "You need a new washer," he informed me.

I looked from the doohickey to him. "I don't have one of those."

He grinned straight out, and my breath got caught in my throat. "No, don't reckon you do," he told me. "Gotta go to the hardware store." Then he flicked the doohickey in my bathroom trash bin and started to exit the room.

I stared at his well-formed back, but my body jolted and I hurried after him.

"No," I called. "You don't have to do that. The water is off now and I have another bathroom." He kept walking and I kept following him and talking. "I'll pop by the management office tomorrow and let them know what's up so they can come fix it."

He had my door open. He stopped in it and turned back to me, so I stopped too.

"No, *I'll* go by the management office tomorrow and tell them how I feel about them lettin' a single woman who pays for their service and has lived in their complex for six years go without a callback when she needs somethin' important done. And tonight, I'll go to the hardware store, get a washer, come back and fix your faucet."

"You don't have to do that," I assured him courteously.

"You're right, but I'm doin' it," he told me firmly.

Okay then. Seeing as his firm was very firm, I decided to let that go.

"Let me get you some money." I looked around trying to remember where I put my purse. "You shouldn't be out money on this."

"Mara, you can buy about a hundred washers for four dollars."

My head turned to him. I stared at him then asked, "Really?"

He grinned at me again, my breath caught in my throat again and he answered, "Yeah, really. I think I got it covered."

"Um . . . thanks," I replied without anything else to say.

He tipped his chin and said, "I'll be back."

Then I was staring at my closed door.

I did this blankly for a while, wishing I'd shared with *someone* that I was in love with my Ten Point Five neighbor so I could call them or race across the breezeway and ask them what I should do now.

It took a while but I decided to act naturally. So *Mitch* had been in my house. He'd grinned at me. I'd discovered he had beautiful hands and beautiful eyelashes to match all the other beautiful things about him. He actually was a nice guy in a way that went beyond his warm smile, what with turning off my water, going to get his tools, finding my shredded doohickey, planning to have a word at the office on my behalf and then heading out to the hardware store to buy me another doohickey. So what? After he fixed my faucet, he'd be back in his apartment and I'd be alone in mine. Maybe I might say something more than "morning" to him in the mornings. And maybe he'd say my name again sometime in the future. But that would be it.

So I did what I normally did. I changed my clothes, taking off my skirt, blouse, and heels and putting on a pair of jeans and a Chicago Cubs T-shirt. I pulled the pins out of my chignon, sifted my fingers through my hair and pulled it back in a ponytail with a red ponytail holder to go with the red accents in my Cubs tee. Out of habit, I lit the scented candles in my living room and turned on music, going with my "Chill Out at Home Part Trois" playlist, which included some really good tunes. After that I started to make dinner.

I was cutting up veggies for stir-fry when there was a knock on the door and my head came up. I spied the candles, heard The Allman Brothers singing "Midnight Rider" and immediately panicked. I burned candles and listened to music all the time. I was a sensory person and I liked the sounds and smells. But now I wondered if he'd think he'd walked into a Two Point Five setting the mood for an illegal maneuver on a Ten Point Five.

Crap!

No time to do anything about it now. The scent of the candles would linger even if I blew them out, and he had to hear the music through the door.

I rushed to the door, did the peephole thing and opened it, coming to stand at its edge.

"Hey," I greeted, trying to sound cool. "You're back."

His eyes dropped to my chest and I lost all semblance of cool. There wasn't much to lose but what little existed was quickly history.

Then his eyes came back to mine. "You're a Cubs fan?" he asked.

"Yes," I answered then declared, "They're the best team in the history of baseball."

He walked in and I closed the door. Through this neither of us lost eye contact. This was because he was smiling at me like I was unbelievably amusing and this was because I was staring at him because he was smiling at me like I was unbelievably amusing.

He came to a halt two feet in, and I turned from the closed door, which meant I was about a foot away from him.

"They haven't won a pennant since 1908," he informed me.

"So?" I asked.

"That fact in and of itself means they aren't the best team in the history of baseball."

This was true. It was also false.

"Okay, I amend my statement. They're the coolest, most interesting team in the history of baseball. They have the best fans because their fans don't care if they win or lose. We're die-hard and always will be."

His eyes warmed like they always did before he'd smile at me, and I felt my knees wobble.

"Can't argue with that," he muttered.

I pressed my lips together and hoped I didn't get lightheaded.

"Colorado bleeds black and purple in spring and summer, though, Mara. Careful where you wear that tee," he warned.

"I like the Rockies too," I replied.

He shook his head, turning toward my hall.

"Can't swing both ways," he said as he moved into the hall.

I watched him move. I liked watching him move. I liked it more as I watched him move down my hallway toward my bedroom. I knew I liked it so much I would fantasize the impossible fantasy that such a vision would happen so often it would become commonplace.

I wondered if I could call out to him that I really needed to run an errand. Like say, take care of an old relative who needed me to get her out of her wheelchair and into her bed. Then read her a bedtime story because she was blind. Something I couldn't get out of that would make me seem kind and loving but would really be an excuse to escape him.

Then I realized that would be rude and I followed him.

When I hit the bathroom, he said, "This shouldn't take long and you can get back to making dinner."

Oh boy.

Should I ask him to stay for dinner? I had plenty. He was a big guy, but I still had enough. I just had to cut up another chicken breast or two. Add a few more veggies.

Could I survive a dinner with him? Would he think candles, music and dinner was a play he had to somehow extricate himself out of without seeming like a dick? Or would he know it was just my way of saying thanks?

Crap!

I listened as "Midnight Rider" became America's "Ventura Highway," and I did what I had to do.

"Would you like to stay for dinner as an, um...thank-you for helping out?" I asked. "I'm making stir-fry," I went on.

"Rain check," he told the faucet, not even looking at me, and I was immensely disappointed. So much so I felt it crushing my chest at the same time I was relieved, because his answer meant all was right in Mara World.

Then he continued talking, making Mara World rock on its foundations.

"Knock on my door when you're makin' your barbeque chicken pizza."

I blinked.

Then I breathed, "What?"

"Derek tells me it's the shit."

I blinked again.

They talked about me?

Why would they do that?

Derek was definitely a firm Nine. LaTanya was too. Nines could be friends with Two Point Fives, but male

Nines didn't talk to each other about Two Point Fives. They talked about other Sevens to Tens. If they were younger or were jerks, they made fun of Ones to Threes. But they never talked about Two Point Fives and the really great pizza Two Point Fives could make. *Ever.*

His head tipped back and his eyes hit mine. "Derek tells me your barbeque chicken pizza is the shit," he repeated and explained, "as in, really fuckin' good."

Derek was right. It was really good. I made my own pizza dough and marinated the chicken in barbeque sauce all day and everything. It was awesome.

Seeing as I was unable to respond, I didn't. Mitch looked back at the faucet and carried on rocking my world.

"Or when you're makin' your baked beans. Derek says those are even better. But tonight, I gotta take a rain check because I gotta get back to work."

They talked about my baked beans too? This meant they talked more than a little about me. This was more than a passing comment, "Oh you gotta try Mara's barbeque chicken pizza. It's the shit," or something like that. This meant more than a few sentences. My baked beans were so good they *had* to be a whole other topic.

*Ohmigod!*

I remained silent and tried to level my breathing. Mitch kept working. Then he kept talking to the tap.

"You got great taste in music, Mara."

Oh God. I liked my music. I liked it a lot. I played it a lot and sometimes I played it loud. Damn.

"I'm sorry, do I play it too loudly that it bothers you?" I asked. His neck twisted to the side but his head was still bent so his eyes were on me but he wasn't exactly facing me, yet he was.

"No, at least not so it's annoying. I can hear it now

'cause I'm in your house. The Allman Brothers' "Midnight Rider," America's "Ventura Highway," great taste."

God, of course. I was an idiot.

"Right," I whispered, "of course."

Something happened to his eyes. Something I didn't get but something that made a whoosh sweep through my belly all the same. It was stronger than normal and it felt a whole lot nicer.

"Better than your taste in baseball teams," he stated, and it hit me that he was teasing me.

Holy crap! Detective Mitch Lawson was in my bathroom teasing me!

"Um…" I mumbled then bit my bottom lip and checked the impulse to flee the room.

"Relax, Mara," he said softly, his eyes going super warm. "I don't bite."

I wished he did. I really, really did. Just like I wished I was at least a Nine. He'd never settle for anything lower than a Nine because he didn't have to. As a Nine, I might get the chance to find out if I could *make* him bite me and I'd get the chance to bite *him*.

"Okay," I whispered.

"But I am serious," he went on, his eyes holding mine captive in a way I didn't get but I still couldn't look away no matter how much I wanted to.

"About what?" I was losing track of the conversation.

"I expect a knock on my door, you're makin' pizza or your beans."

"Um…okay," I lied. There was no way I was knocking on his door when I made my pizza or beans. No way in hell. In fact, I was moving the first chance I could get.

"Or just anytime you feel like company," he kept going, and I felt the room teeter.

What did he mean by that?

"Um... I'm kinda a loner," I lied again and he grinned.

"Yeah, I noticed that. Your imaginary friend who was over watchin' TV last night sounded a lot like LaTanya though. Now *she* sings loud and it skates the edge of annoying. Luckily it's more funny than annoying and it only lasts an hour."

Oh damn. He'd called me out on a lie. And double damn because I also sang with the kids on *Glee*. Hopefully he couldn't hear me but he wasn't wrong. LaTanya thought she was Patti LaBelle's more talented sister. She diva'ed her way through every episode of *Glee* that we'd watched together. And we'd watched every episode of *Glee* together.

"Um..." I repeated, my eyes sliding to the mirror, but I wish they hadn't because I could see his broad shoulders and muscled back leading to his slim hips. I could also see him straightening, which meant I had his full attention. Not that I didn't have it before, just that now I *really* had it.

"Mara," I watched him call, my eyes at the mirror and they slid back to his then he kept talking. "What I'm sayin' is, I get it that you're shy..."

Oh God. Totally a police detective. He had me figured out.

He moved his body closer and kept speaking. I held my breath as he held my gaze. "But what I want you to know is that I'd like you to come over, but because you're shy, you gotta walk that breezeway, sweetheart. I'm tellin' you you're welcome, but I made the first move, you need to make the next one. You with me here?"

No. No, I wasn't with him. He'd made the first move? What move?

And he'd called me sweetheart, which made the belly whoosh move through me like a tidal wave.

I was pretty certain I was going to die right there, totally swept away.

Then it hit me as I stared into his beautiful eyes. They were so dark brown they seemed fathomless, and if I wasn't careful, I would drown in them. But I was careful and I knew who I was and what zone I lived in. So when it hit me, I understood.

Derek and LaTanya were both Nines. Brent and Bradon were firm at Eight Point Fives in the gay world, the straight world or an alien world (both Brent and Bradon were gorgeous, very cool and very, very nice). But they all liked me. We were not only neighbors, we were good friends. And Mitch had been living across the way from me for four years. He was a good guy. He fixed faucets. He smiled warmly.

Therefore, he was trying to be a good neighbor and maybe even a friend.

"I'm with you," I whispered.

He came closer and when he spoke his voice dipped lower. "That mean you're gonna knock on the door tellin' me you're makin' pizza sometime soon?"

"My barbeque chicken pizza takes planning and preparation," I explained. His eyes flashed and I finished, "It'd have to be this Saturday, when I have a day off."

He got even closer. I pulled in a breath because he was now *really* close. His head had to tip down *really* far, and if I moved up on my toes, just a tiny bit, I could actually touch my lips to his.

I felt another belly whoosh.

"Works for me," he murmured.

Oh. Wow.

"'Kay," I breathed.

He stood where he was. I stood and started drowning in

his eyes. He didn't move. I didn't either. I felt my body lean toward his a centimeter, such was his hot-guy magnetic pull, at the same time I licked my lip. His eyes dropped to my mouth but not before I saw them get even darker and more fathomless. My heart started to beat in my throat. His cell rang.

Then his eyes closed and the spell was broken as he moved a bit away growling, "Fuck."

He pulled his cell out of his back jeans pocket, hit a button and put it to his ear as his gaze came back to mine.

"Lawson," he said into his phone, and I moved farther away, thinking distance was a good thing. He was a good neighbor. He didn't need to be being neighborly and have the person he was being neighborly toward throw herself at him. That would be wrong. "Yeah, right," he continued. "I said I'll be there, I'll be there. I got somethin' I gotta do. When I'm done I'm on my way. Yeah?" He paused and kept hold of my gaze. "Right. Later."

He shut down his cell and shoved it back in his pocket.

"Work?" I asked.

"Love it most the time, hate it right about now," he answered.

"Uh-huh," I mumbled like I understood what he meant when I didn't. Changing a doohickey wasn't the height of entertainment that you didn't want to be torn away from to do work you loved.

"Gotta get this done, Mara," he told me.

"Okay," I replied.

He stared at me and didn't move. I did the same.

His grin came back and he repeated, "Gotta get this done."

"I know," I said. "You have to get to work."

"Yeah and I gotta get this done."

I blinked then said, "So, um . . . can I help?"

"You can help by lettin' me get this done."

What did he mean? I wasn't stopping him.

"Please," I motioned to the sink, "carry on."

His grin became a smile. "Sweetheart, what I'm sayin' is," he leaned in, "you're a distraction."

I was?

Oh God! He was saying he didn't need me hanging around chatting with him.

I was such a dork!

"I'll, uh … go make dinner."

"Good idea."

I nodded. "And thanks, um … for, you know," I motioned to the sink again, "helping out, especially when you're so busy."

"Any time."

"Well, I hope it doesn't happen again," I pointed out the obvious. "But thanks anyway."

A sound came from deep in his chest. I realized it was an immensely attractive chuckle, and he said, his voice deep and vibrating with his chuckle, "Mara."

There were many things I wished in my life. Many. Too many to count.

But the top one at that moment in time, scratched at the top of that list in a way I knew it would stay there a good long while, was that I wished with everything that was me that my life would lead me to a new life. One where I would hear Detective Mitch Lawson say my name in his deep voice that vibrated with his laughter time and time and time again.

"I'll just go," I whispered and turned to leave.

"I'll show you the valve to turn off the water another time," he offered to my back.

"Thanks," I said to my bedroom.

Then I was out the door.

Detective Mitch Lawson left not ten minutes later. He was carrying his toolbox. He lifted a hand in a wave as he walked through my living-room-slash-dining-room space. But he stopped at the door, his eyes leveled on mine and he said two words.

"Saturday. Pizza."

Then all I saw was my closed door.

# CHAPTER TWO

## Pizza

I SPRINKLED THE cheddar cheese liberally around the edges of the pizza dough to be certain when it cooked the dough would puff up, those edges would be thick and soft, like they always were, *and* crusted with yummy cheese. Then I stood back, swiping grated cheddar cheese residue from my hands.

I stared at the pizza. It was a work of art. My barbeque chicken pizza was great, but I could tell this one was better than any I'd made before. I'd put the chicken in to marinate yesterday morning, poking the breasts with the tip of a knife so the barbeque sauce would sink deep. I hadn't broiled it in the broiler. Instead I'd grilled it on my cast-iron grill pan, which had been seasoned with much use, so the chicken pieces had deep charcoal grill marks. It was kind of a pain in the ass to do it that way but I knew it would taste a whole lot better. I'd bought the expensive black olives and taken time to chop the mushrooms fine. I used twice as much cheese, and I'd bought the expensive kind of that too.

Just looking at it, not to brag or anything, I knew this particular pizza could win awards. This particular pizza

was fit for a king and it was definitely fit for Ten Point Five
Detective Mitch Lawson.

* * *

My faucet had broken on Wednesday.

On Thursday, I'd gone to work, and because I was brimming with excitement over my encounter with Mitch, I
had to tell someone. In a moment of quiet at the store, I
grabbed Roberta and we curled up on one of the display
beds. There, I told her everything (except my classification
system of Ones to Tens and the fact that I was secretly in
love with him, now more than ever).

* * *

I had been at Pierson's for seven years, and Roberta had
worked there for five.

She started out as a part-timer, doing something to
bring in a little extra money for the household and to get
herself out and about so she didn't spend 24/7 with her
kids. After that her husband decided he was in love with his
best friend's wife. He moved out. Then he moved from the
suburbs of Denver to Portland, and suddenly Roberta was
the primary breadwinner for herself and her three kids.

Our boss and the second generation Mr. Pierson
who owned Pierson's Mattress and Bed was a top-notch guy.
He was a family man, loyal to his family *and* to his family
of workers, so he put her on full time even though it was a
hit for all his salespeople. We didn't need another full-time
salesperson and we worked mostly on commission.

Barney lost his mind and bitched about it all the time to
anyone who would listen. But I figured Mr. Pierson knew
Barney's time was short since Barney was a dick and, like
anyone, Mr. Pierson didn't like dicks. But since Barney

was a good salesperson Mr. Pierson didn't really have a reason to get rid of him that was legal. That was, until Barney tried to make things so difficult for Roberta that she'd have to leave. He did this by being an even bigger dick to her. I talked her into lodging a complaint, then Barney was gone and all was well in the world of Pierson's Mattress and Bed.

Roberta had been a Seven when I met her because she was pretty, petite, with thick brunette hair and a little extra weight that she held well. She was also happy with her family and her husband in their suburban house with two cars and vacations to Disney World. She'd slipped down to a Five Point Five when she got angry and moody and hated the world and mostly all the men in it after her husband left. Now she was back up and surpassed the Seven to be an Eight because she'd settled into her new life; her kids were great kids and came through the divorce really well because she was a great mom. She'd realized her husband had always been a big jerk, she just hadn't noticed it so much because she loved him. Therefore, she had come through to the other side stronger. An independent woman with a happy non-nuclear family who was secure in the knowledge that she was a good mom and better off without her jerk of a husband.

Oh, and she had a new boyfriend and he was really cool.

When she heard about Mitch, it was Roberta who talked me into making the pizza.

"You *have* to!" she'd nearly shrieked. She did this because I'd waxed on perhaps a little too enthusiastically about Mitch's looks, his warm smile and his neighborly behavior.

I shook my head. "I don't know. He freaks me out."

"Yeah, I get that. Johnny Depp came in and fixed my faucet then told me he wanted to try my pizza; that would freak me out too. But I'd still make him my freaking pizza."

Johnny Depp was hot, very much so, but he was no comparison to Mitch. Too skinny, not tall enough and I doubted when he said my name it would sound as good as it did when Mitch said it.

"That's easy to say," I returned. "Johnny Depp is never going to fix your faucet. Mitch is my neighbor." I leaned in closer to her. "You should have seen me, Roberta. I was a total dork. I made an absolute fool out of myself. I don't need to sit down to pizza with him. I might drop some on my shirt or something worse. I might talk with my mouth full. I could do anything, say anything, he freaks me out that much."

She examined my face and stated, "Seems to me he didn't think you were a dork."

"He did, I'm sure he did. He's just nice. You don't come right out and tell someone they're a dork, especially not if you're nice," I returned.

"If he thought you were a dork and that was a turnoff to him, he wouldn't ask for your pizza," she pointed out.

I leaned back sharply and stared at her because this point held merit.

She kept speaking. "Maybe he likes dorks. Especially cute ones, because *if* you were a dork, I bet you were a cute one."

I kept staring at her. No one liked dorks. Even cute ones. Did they?

She grabbed my hand. "Mara, make him pizza. I know Destry jacked you around because Destry's a jackass and that's what jackasses do. But not all men are jackasses. It took me a while to learn that but I'm here to tell you it's true."

She *was* there to tell me it was true. She'd been seeing her boyfriend, Kenny, for seven months. He was a really nice guy and wasn't hard on the eyes. He had two kids of his own and he was a good dad.

But I didn't understand why she was talking about Destry, the Five Point Five who broke my heart.

Pizza with Mitch wasn't a date. First he'd never ask me out on a date. Second Mitch was the kind of guy who, if he wanted a date, he'd ask for one. If he wanted anything from a woman, he'd ask for it and get it. I knew that from the number of Seven to Tens who frequented his apartment. A date with Mitch would be a *date*, not coming over for pizza.

"I don't know," I hedged.

"Make him pizza," she urged.

"Really, Roberta, I'm not sure," I told her.

"Make him pizza," she pushed. "You aren't pledging your troth. You're making a nice, handsome guy pizza. So you drop barbeque sauce on your shirt. It wouldn't be the end of the world." She squeezed my hand. "What *would* be the end of the world is if you stuck yourself in that apartment with your candles and music, having LaTanya over for *Glee,* going over to B and B's for tarot card nights, coming to my place for action movie marathons and that was it in your life. No risks. No chances. Nothing that made your heart beat faster. Nothing that made your toes curl. Nothing that was exciting. Nothing that gave you a thrill. That, honey..." she gave me another hand squeeze, "would be the end of the world."

"I don't need a thrill, or not that kind of thrill. Mitch Lawson is not the kind of thrill for the likes of me," I explained, and her face turned funny as she looked at me.

"Everyone needs that kind of thrill, Mara, and I don't understand what you mean 'the likes of you.' The likes of you should be having those kinds of thrills all the time. Honestly, I've wondered. LaTanya has wondered. B and B have wondered. Even Mr. Pierson wonders why you aren't living a thrill a minute."

I didn't understand what she was saying, but explaining to her what the likes of me meant was explaining to her my One to Ten Classification System. I didn't want to do that, especially explaining where I felt I came in on the scale.

I'd learned not to share this information, because friends who cared about you always tried to talk you into believing you were so far up that scale it was unreal. My oldest friend, Lynette, who still lived back in Iowa, was the only person I'd told about my system. She even tried to talk me into believing I topped the scale at Mitch's rank of Ten Point Five. She was convinced of it and tried to convince me. I knew she was wrong and I knew she was convinced I was a Ten Point Five because she liked me. I liked her too. She was a definite Eight Point Five. When she was in a good mood and her sunny disposition shone even more brightly, she soared up to a Nine Point Five, so she had nothing to worry about.

I couldn't wander around in a daze of thinking I was in another league, which meant making the mistake of making a move toward someone out of my league. This, as I had learned the hard way, only led to a broken heart.

Therefore, I didn't explain because friends could be convincing. That was why I got messed up with Destry, who had the looks of a Seven but was a Five Point Five since he was a jackass. Friends could be very convincing. I'd been convinced of other things due to friends. Some of them good, like when Lynette talked me into getting the hell out of Iowa and away from my crazy mother. Some of them bad, case in point Destry.

Because I couldn't tell Roberta all this, I gave in on the pizza. Since Mitch had moved in, I had managed to go from nearly fainting every time I saw him to being able to say good morning. I'd survived him in my place being nice and teasing me. Perhaps I could have pizza with him. Maybe if he came to another one of Brent and Bradon's parties or LaTanya's cocktail extravaganzas, I could chitchat with him *before* escaping. Maybe it wouldn't be so bad.

Because of this I went to the grocery store after work, got the ingredients for the pizza, two bottles of red, two bottles of white and two six packs (one of fancy beer, one of good old American beer) so Mitch would have choice. Friday morning I set the chicken to marinate and Saturday morning I went back out to the grocery store so the salad fixings would be fresh. If I was going to make pizza for Ten Point Five Mitch Lawson, it was going to be a pizza feast fit for a king.

*    *    *

I slid the pizza in my fridge, turned on the oven in preparation for baking, grabbed my phone, hit the three for speed dial and Bradon picked up.

"Hey girl, what's shakin'?" he asked, having caller ID on his phone and knowing it was me.

"Can you do me a favor, look out your window and tell me if Mitch's SUV is there?"

I heard silence before I heard Bradon ask, "Why?"

"He fixed my faucet and payback is me making him barbeque chicken pizza. The pizza is ready and I just want to check if he's there before I go over and knock."

I heard more silence then, "You made him your pizza?"

"He asked for it."

I heard even more silence before Bradon shouted, "Brent! Get this! Mara made her barbeque chicken pizza for Mitch. He fixed her faucet. He's going over there tonight for pizza!"

Ohmigod!

B and B lived right across from Mitch! He might be able to hear Bradon shout.

"You're joking!" I heard Brent shout back then I heard a closer-to-the-phone shout of, "Excellent!"

"Bray!" I hissed. "Stop shouting!"

"I love this," Bradon said in my ear.

"I love it too!" I heard Brent shout.

"Why?" I asked.

"Because it's cool *and* because it's about time. I don't know what your deal is, girl, but he is *hot*. I was a girl and I was straight, I would have made my move a *long* time ago," Bradon told me.

"This isn't a move. This is a thank-you pizza," I informed him.

"Uh-huh," Bray mumbled. "I hope you're wearing that little camisole, the sage-y gray one that's satin. It's hot. You're hot in it. And if I was straight and you made me pizza and I came over and you were wearing that top, I'd jump you…" he paused, "*before* the pizza."

See what I mean? Friends always thought you were in a different zone than you truly were.

"It's just a neighborly thanks-for-fixing-my-faucet pizza," I again explained.

"Right. Wear that top," Bradon returned.

"Definitely wear that top," Brent said loudly in the background.

"With those jeans, the tight ones that are faded and have the split in the knee," Bradon added.

"Oh yeah," I heard Brent put in. "And the silver sandals. Not the wedges. The ones with the stiletto heel."

"Absolutely. Those silver sandals are beyond hot. They're *smokin' hot*," Bradon continued.

"I can't wear those sandals with those jeans. Those jeans are knockabout jeans. Those sandals are fancy sandals," I argued. "You don't put those together."

"Oh yeah you do, especially since those jeans do things to your ass that would knock the gay out of Elton John," Bradon retorted.

These guys.

"Whatever," I muttered and got back to the matter at hand. "Can you just tell me if his SUV is out there?"

I didn't want to wander over there and knock if he wasn't there and I didn't want to have to go out there to see if his SUV was there. If I had to take time out to do anything that scary, I'd lose my nerve. I'd made the pizza. I'd gone all out. I was psyched up. This had to go smoothly. Anything going wrong could put me off.

There was nothing for a second from Bradon and I figured he was going to his living room window then I heard, "Yeah, his SUV is there."

Damn. Suddenly I decided that was bad news.

"Change into that outfit, girl, and go, go, *go*," Bradon encouraged. "Then call me tomorrow morning when he's out buying you a bagel and let us know if he's as good with that fabulous body as the way he moves promises."

I felt these words all over my body, but my scalp, nipples and points south tingled the most.

Would that I lived in a world where Detective Mitch Lawson ate my pizza, spent the night and left my bed the next morning to buy me a bagel. I loved bagels. I'd love Mitch leaving my bed to buy me one more. Mostly because that would mean he was coming back.

"Shut up. You're freaking me out," I told Bradon.

"*You* shut up, change and go get him, tigress," he returned and then disconnected.

I hit the off button on my phone. Then I sucked in breath. Then my feet took me to my bedroom and for some fool reason, I changed into the camisole, the faded, tight jeans and slipped on my silver sandals. I put on lip gloss (I'd already put on makeup, not heavy, just enough to lift me from a Two to my Two Point Five) and spritzed myself with perfume.

Why I did any of this, I didn't know. I just did. Maybe it was because hope springs eternal. Maybe it was just because I was stupid.

But I did it and I really shouldn't have.

Before I lost my nerve, I hoofed it over to Mitch's and before my mind could talk me out of it, I knocked on the door.

I stood outside thinking I was an idiot, wishing I'd kept on my nicer jeans and semi-nice tee and flip-flops. I wished this so long that it was a moment before I realized that he hadn't answered the door.

My head turned to the side and I looked to the parking lot. His SUV was definitely there.

Maybe I didn't knock loud enough.

I knocked again, louder but not insistent and not long. Just three sharp raps. If he didn't open the door in ten seconds I was going back to my place. I could eat the whole pizza by myself. It would take days but I could do it. I'd done it before. He was probably taking a nap. He worked all hours. He probably needed naptime so he'd be alert when he was bringing criminals to justice.

The door opened, not all the way, and Mitch stood in it.

I stopped breathing.

"Mara," he said softly, his eyes moving the length of me. The lack of oxygen and the intensity of which I liked it when he said my name made me feel faint.

With effort I pulled myself together, shot him a smile that I hoped looked genuine and not scared out of my brain and I said, "Saturday. Pizza time."

"Who's that?" a woman's voice came from inside his apartment and she sounded ticked.

I stopped breathing again. The warmth fled Mitch's face and his jaw clenched.

Then he said, "Mara, Christ, I'm sorry but now's not a good time."

Damn. Shit. Damn. Shit, shit, *shit*.

"Right," I whispered then tried and failed to rally. "Okay then, um..."

God! I was a dork! Why was I such a dork? Being a dork knocked me down to a One Point Five.

"Mara—"

I talked over him. "I'll just," I jerked my thumb over my shoulder, "let you go."

I turned. I didn't want to but I couldn't stop myself from running across the breezeway, my heels clicking triple time on the cement.

I didn't make it to the door. I was brought up short and this happened because Mitch's hand caught mine and tugged. I had no choice but to whirl to face him.

"Mara, just give me—"

I pulled at my hand but didn't succeed in freeing it. His hand was big. It engulfed mine. It was strong and so warm. Unbelievably warm.

"Some other time," I told him.

"I asked," a woman's voice came at us. I looked around his body and saw a stunning Nine Point Seven Five standing in his doorway, arms crossed on her chest, face pissy. Even so, nothing could change how incredibly beautiful she was. She was wearing an outfit that cost about five times what mine did, and my shoes were pretty expensive. "Who's *that*?"

"Give me a minute," Mitch growled, and my eyes went to him to see he was looking over his shoulder and he didn't seem very happy.

"Baby, you don't have a minute," she shot back, all attitude.

"Give me a minute," Mitch clipped and I knew from the way he spoke he *really* wasn't very happy.

"Mitch," I called and his eyes came back to me. "Some other time," I repeated but it was a lie.

I'd learned my lesson. I'd chitchat with him at LaTanya and Derek's and B and B's should they have get-togethers but no more pizza. No more. No thrill or belly whoosh was worth this. This was humiliating.

"I'll be over in fifteen," he told me and I blinked.

"You'll *what*?" the Nine Point Seven Five snapped.

"No, really, that's okay," I said quickly. "Some other time."

"You made pizza," Mitch stated, squeezing my hand. His eyes moved down the length of me, telling me he knew what the camisole meant, what the sandals meant, that I'd aimed high. He was a good guy and he wasn't going to shoot me down. Not now. Not in front of her.

I felt like crying.

"Promise, it's okay," I told him.

"I'll be over in fifteen," he repeated.

I couldn't take any more. With a rough twist, I pulled my hand from his and took a huge step back, my shoulders slamming into my door.

"Some other time," I whispered, whirled, turned my doorknob and flew into my house, slamming my door.

I wished I didn't slam my door but I couldn't help it.

My momentum was such I couldn't stop it. Then I ran to my oven and turned it off. Off to my bedroom, where I changed clothes and shoes, grabbed my bag. I checked my peephole and listened, opening my door a crack to look. When I saw the coast was clear, I ran into the breezeway, down the stairs and to my car.

I took off and I wasn't home in fifteen minutes. I wasn't home after an hour. I went to Cherry Creek Mall and bought a ticket for a movie that started in an hour and a half. I got myself a pretzel for dinner. I kicked around in a few stores not seeing anything, not allowing myself to feel much of anything and then I watched the movie.

I didn't get home until late.

Even so, I'd barely walked in and turned on the lights when I heard the knock on my door. I closed my eyes, went to the door, and looked through the peephole.

It was Mitch.

God.

I put my forehead to the door and stood there, not moving. He knocked again. I still didn't move.

"Mara, open the door," his deep voice called.

God!

I moved, opened the door a bit and stood in it.

"Hey," I said, and the minute my eyes hit him, I again felt like crying.

They needed to separate the zones. Mandatory boundaries. Ones to Threes got Canada (because there were a lot of us and we needed the space). Fours to Sixes got the US. The fewer numbered Sevens to Tens got the sultry, tropical beauty of Mexico. If they separated us, things like this wouldn't happen and therefore hurt like this wouldn't be felt.

"Can I come in?" he asked.

"It's late," I answered.

His whole face warmed. God, he was beautiful.

"Sweetheart, let me in," he said gently.

He was also nice. *So* nice. Why did that suck? Why couldn't he be one of those arrogant Ten Plusses? Sure, if he was, it might knock him down to an Eight but he'd still be an Eight and out of my league.

"Mitch, it's really late."

He studied me. Then he nodded.

I thought I was off the hook, but then he said, "Does your pizza keep?"

I blinked at him. "Pardon?"

He asked a different question. "Did you eat it?"

"Um . . . no," I answered.

"Does it keep?"

"I think so," I told him, though I didn't know. I made it. I baked it. I ate it. I'd never tested to see if it would keep in raw form prior to baking.

"Tomorrow night. Seven thirty. I'll be back."

My breath left me.

When I sucked some back in, I told him quietly, "You don't have to do this."

His brows drew together and he replied, "I know that. What I don't know is why you'd think I'd think I do."

There was no way I was going to explain it to him, especially since I knew he knew; he was just being nice, so instead I said, "I'm just saying."

"What?" he asked when I said no more. I didn't respond so he continued, "What are you just saying?"

"I'm saying you don't have to do this."

He started to look impatient before he said, "Mara, let me in."

"I'm tired and I need to work tomorrow."

"I'm thinkin' we need to talk right now."

I shook my head. "There's nothing to say. I should have maybe slipped you a note or something to tell you when I'd be over. I'm sorry that I put you in that—"

He cut me off, definitely impatient, "Mara, just let me in."

"Mitch, really. Sundays are crazy at work. I need to sleep."

"That wasn't what you thought it was," he told me.

I shook my head again. "There's no need to explain."

"Jesus, Mara, just let me in."

"I'll knock on your door next time, leave you a note, give you a warning, make sure you're free."

"Mara—"

I stepped away from the door and started closing it, "'Night, Mitch."

"Damn it, Mara."

I closed the door, locked it and ran to my room, closing that door too.

Then I got in my nightgown, slid into my bed and finally let myself cry.

A long time later, when I was done, I wiped my face, and then I went to sleep.

Alone.

Like many Ones to Threes did every night.

# CHAPTER THREE

## Messes

IT WAS A week after the Mitch Incident.

My candles were lit and I was lying on my couch listening to my Chill Out at Home Premier Edition, the first of the Chill-Out playlists I'd created. Al Green was singing "How Can You Mend a Broken Heart," and I was doing nothing but listening to him sing and drinking a glass of red wine.

I didn't know if Mitch had come over Sunday night because I wrapped up my pizza and took it to work. I put it in the fridge in the break room and took it to Roberta's after work. I cooked it in her oven, and both Roberta and I managed to eat a piece before her children decimated it. I hung out with Roberta watching action movies until it was way late, and I needed to get home before I was too tired to operate a motor vehicle.

Incidentally, this proved my pizza kept prior to baking.

Roberta asked about pizza with Mitch mainly because she was curious, but also because it didn't bode well that she was eating Mitch's pizza. I told her that Mitch hadn't been able to make it. She looked about as disappointed as I felt.

Okay, maybe not that disappointed. Since I felt the need

to scan newspaper ads to find an apartment somewhere on the other side of Denver—far away from Mitch. But not before I became an alcoholic in order to numb the pain.

But she did look really disappointed.

Luckily, I'd worked the next two days and found reasons to get home later than normal. Both nights this effort proved unnecessary, as his SUV wasn't there when I got home.

Wednesday, however, I was off, and that night at five thirty there came a knock on my door. I went to the door and looked through the peephole to see Mitch standing outside. He didn't look happy. He looked impatient and maybe a little angry. When I kept looking and he kept looking angrier, I stopped looking and put my forehead to the door again. He knocked again. I didn't move or make a noise.

He stopped knocking, and when I pulled in a breath and chanced a look through the peephole, he was gone.

There was no more from Mitch. He didn't come back even though for the next three nights when I got home, later than normal each time, his SUV was in the parking lot.

It was now Sunday, my day off. Since I ran all my weekly errands after work, I could hole myself up in my apartment, clean, putter around and avoid even the possibility of running into Mitch. I also avoided the phone that day and the many times throughout the week that Brent *and* Bradon *and* LaTanya (who, clearly, B and/or B told about Mitch and pizza) had phoned, left messages and texted—all asking about Mitch.

I definitely had to move.

On that thought, my phone rang and I really wanted to ignore it but I didn't. It might be Lynette, and I could use talking to Lynette. I'd known her since seventh grade. She'd get it about Mitch. She wouldn't *agree* with it but she'd get it. I was toying with calling her anyway. We talked once a week at least and we were due.

When I got to my phone, I saw my caller ID on my house phone said *Stop 'n' Go—Zuni*.

I felt my brows draw together at the same time I felt my heart speed up. I picked up the phone, beeped it on and put it to my ear hoping B and B or LaTanya hadn't headed out to some Stop 'n' Go to wangle a conversation with me. I was hoping more that whatever it was wasn't about Billy and Billie.

"Hello," I greeted.

"This Mara?" a gruff male voice asked.

"Um . . . yes," I answered.

"You know some kids named Billy and Billie?"

I felt panic seize my chest.

Just as I feared, it was about Billy and Billie, my stupid, lame, petty criminal cousin Bill's kids.

Bill had followed me out to Denver, which was something I didn't need. When we were kids, I loved Bill. He was fun and funny and we got on great.

When he got older, he wasn't so easy to love. Mainly because the way he had fun and the way he dragged me into it and got me into trouble was no longer so great. He'd never stopped liking hanging with me. I'd stopped liking hanging with him. I left Iowa to escape my crazy mom (whose sister was Bill's crazy mom) but also to escape Bill and his antics.

Unfortunately, Bill followed me.

Also unfortunately, in the ensuing years, Bill had two kids with two different women. Both women wisely took off. Both women were the kind of women who, when they took off, they left their kids behind. And these were precisely the kinds of women with whom Bill would hook up.

So Bill had Billy, his son, who was nine. And also Billerina, his daughter, who was six.

Yes, he named his daughter Billerina. Seriously, he was stupid, lame, a petty criminal, a joke and so much of all of these that he didn't realize he was also cruel. Bill called her Billie, thinking it was funny because he was stupid, lame and not very funny.

I loved those kids and I spent as much time with them as I could. They were the reason I was able to get home late twice that week since I went to go visit them.

Unfortunately this time came with spending time with Bill. But I loved them enough to put up with their father. Seeing as I was the only solid adult in their life whose love came unconditionally and without a shitload of dysfunction attached to it, they loved me.

Also seeing as Bill was the idiot to beat all idiots, sometimes shit happened, and during those times, I was always dragged in. I didn't want Bill's shit hitting the fan and splattering his kids. Unfortunately shit was happening more frequently lately and my normal concern was escalating to panic.

"Yes," I answered the gruff voice.

"You their ma?" he asked.

"No...I'm a family friend," I answered. "Are they okay?"

"The boy said you're his guardian. You his guardian?" the gruff voice asked.

"Um...yes," I lied. "Um...we, uh...got separated—"

"Right, whatever. You need to come get 'em. They're hungry. Stop 'n' Go. Zuni."

Then he hung up.

I closed my eyes, beeped the phone off and flew into action.

Billy and Billie ran away a lot. Well, Billy did and he took his sister with him.

Billy had somehow managed to get himself a smart gene in the gene cesspool he'd been offered. At nine, he knew the life he'd been born into was not a safe life to live. Maybe he got this gene from me, for I'd also figured my shitty life out early (around the age of four) and felt the same way. Billy had also somehow managed to get himself a loyal and sweet gene, which meant he took care of his sister.

Billie had managed to get mostly adorable little girl genes, which apparently were strong and coated you with Teflon so that your shitty life could bounce off you and you could only see the wonders of the world. She thought I was wonderful. She thought her father was wonderful. But mostly she thought her brother was wonderful.

Two out of three weren't bad.

I blew out the candles, turned off the music, grabbed my purse and hightailed it out of my apartment. I was rushing hell-bent for leather, my head down, my mind consumed with this problem.

This was the fourth time in half as many months that Billy had tried to run away taking Billie with him. In other words, Billy's great escapes were escalating. Something was not right in the Bill, Billy and Billie household, more than the normal not right. It was becoming clear that I was going to need to wade in. I didn't want to wade in with Bill. Wading in with Bill meant that shit might get stuck to me. But I couldn't leave Billy and Billie in a situation that was worse than the normal not right. The normal not right was already pretty freaking bad.

"Whoa, Mara, Jesus!" I heard right before I slammed into Detective Mitch Lawson near to the top of the stairs.

He went down two steps, me going with him. He threw

his arm out and grabbed the railing. I was moving so fast I couldn't stop, so my body collided with his. To steady myself my hands automatically lifted to clutch his shirt at his chest. His other arm wrapped tight around my waist. He managed to stop us from both tumbling backward down the steps to possibly break bones or crack open skulls when we hit the cement sidewalk.

When we teetered to a stop, I looked up at him.

A week away and he was no less gorgeous. Indeed, that close, he was even more gorgeous than ever.

"Sorry," I whispered.

"You all right?" he asked.

"Yeah, sorry," I said again, trying to take a step back.

His arm around my waist tightened and not just a little, a lot. So much that even though my torso was already resting against him from chest to belly this tightening made it so my torso was *plastered* against him from chest to hips.

"What's the hurry?" he asked.

"I..." I hesitated, not wanting to share anything with him. But I really did not want to share that I had a hick, stupid, lame, petty criminal for a cousin. And I further did not want to share that Bill was the definition of Not A Great Father whose kids I had to rescue *again*. "Need to be somewhere," I decided to say.

His eyes moved over my face and their movement was doing funny things to my belly at the same time my heart was tripping over itself due to our proximity. This was because I'd just discovered his body felt as hard and muscled as it looked, while my two precious second cousins were hungry at a Stop 'n' Go.

"Is everything all right?" he asked.

"Yeah," I lied. "Fine, I just need to be somewhere."

"Your face doesn't say everything is fine," he replied.

"It is," I lied again.

"It isn't," he returned.

I stopped clutching his shirt and pushed against his hard chest.

"Really, Mitch, I have to go," I told him.

"Where?"

"I need to pick something up."

"What?"

I stopped pushing and glared at him, beginning to lose my temper mainly because the gruff-voiced guy said Billy and Billie were hungry.

"Would you let me go? I've got to be somewhere."

"I'll let you go when you tell me where you've got to be and why your face is pale and you look freaked."

I lost a bit more of my temper. "It's none of your business," I said. "Really, let me go."

His arm gave me a squeeze and his face changed from looking kind of curious and definitely alert to still definitely alert and kind of pissed.

"Four years I see you and every time I see you, you're in your own world. Goin' to work, comin' home with groceries or from the mall. You're never in a rush but you're always in your head, and I can see that's a decent place to be."

I blinked at him, shocked he paid that much attention.

"Now you're sprinting down the stairs, not lookin' where you're goin' when you're always careful to look where you're goin', and you're in your head but wherever you are in there, it is far from a decent place to be." I was still staring up at him but now unblinking and I felt my lips had parted. He went on, "You got a problem?"

"I—" I started to lie but stopped when his arm gave me another squeeze, pressing the breath out of me.

"And don't lie," he warned.

I took in a breath. Then I thought of the kids. Then I decided I probably shouldn't lie because, clearly, I was right about police detectives. Even though he didn't know me, he had finely honed skills where he could totally figure me out and know when I was lying. He wasn't going to let me go until I told him the truth. And I needed him to let me go for a variety of reasons.

"Family problems," I explained honestly.

"Bad?" he asked.

I shook my head. "Annoying."

That was a fib rather than a lie since I wasn't certain it was bad. I just figured it was getting there.

"You need me to come with you?" he offered.

"No!" I blurted too fast and too loudly and on a desperate pull against his arm, which made him give me another squeeze, keeping me right where I was.

When I calmed enough to register the look on his face I realized my mistake. I should have kept cool and paid attention to him. Close attention. For he still looked very alert, he now looked very pissed and he'd added a narrow-eyed, alert, angry disbelief, which I knew for sure was not a good addition.

"Now, sweetheart," he said in a soft, dangerous voice, "I'm thinkin' you just lied to me."

Oh boy.

Mental note: If given the chance again, never but *never* lie to Detective Mitch Lawson.

"Not really," I evaded (not a lie). "This happens sometimes."

"What happens?" he asked, and I figured he was good at his job, especially in the interrogation rooms.

"I have a cousin, he's ... well, he's kind of a mess and he's got two kids. I'm close with his kids and sometimes

I need to..." I searched for a word, found it and said, "intervene."

"What kind of mess is he?" he asked.

"What kinds are there?" I asked back.

"Lots of kinds," he answered.

"He's all those," I answered too.

He studied me. Then he muttered, "Shit."

I took in a breath, put minor pressure on my hands at his chest and whispered carefully, "Mitch, I really need to get to the kids."

He studied me again. Then he said, "Right."

Finally he let me go and stepped down another step. Again I felt that crush of disappointment at the same time I felt relief.

I felt these for about half a second. Then his hand curled around mine and he tugged me down the stairs toward his SUV.

I followed because if I didn't, the determined way he was moving, I knew he'd start dragging me.

"Um...Mitch?" I called, he lifted his other hand and I saw the lights and heard the beep of his locks opening on his SUV.

Oh boy.

"Mitch?" I called again as he led me to the passenger side.

He didn't answer. He pulled me around the door and opened it.

"Uh...Mitch," I said again, and he used his hand in mine to maneuver me into the door.

Then he spoke.

"Climb up."

I twisted to look up at him. "But, I—"

Mitch cut me off, "Climb up."

"I think that I—"

Suddenly he was in my space, and there wasn't a lot of it seeing as he was a big guy and we were wedged between his truck and the door. I had to put my hands up again in an automatic effort to fend him off. But they only made it to his (rock-hard, by the way) abs before his face was all I could see, and my body, heart and lungs all stilled as I stared into his eyes.

"Mara, climb...the fuck...up."

Oh *boy*.

I was in trouble and I was in trouble because Detective Mitch Lawson, close, pissed off and bossy was *hot*.

"I can take care of this on my own," I assured him. "I've done it before."

"I'm a cop," he announced suddenly.

"I know," I told him.

"I know you know. What you might not know is I've been a cop a long time. That means I know all the kinds of messes people can be. You're not a cop," he informed me. "So, you tellin' me your cousin is all the kinds of messes *you* know means he's probably all the kinds of messes *I* know and there is no fuckin' way I'm lettin' you get in your car and drive into a mess. Now, Mara, climb...the... fuck...*up*."

"Okay," I agreed instantly because close, pissed off, bossy Detective Mitch Lawson was also pretty freaking scary.

He slammed the door behind me. I buckled up as he rounded the hood and swung up beside me. He'd backed out and we were motoring forward when he spoke again.

"Where are we goin'?"

"The Stop 'n' Go on Zuni."

Mitch nodded and guided us through the complex.

Mitch and I lived in a middle income apartment

complex east of Colorado Boulevard. It had a fantastic pool, clubhouse and gym. All of the people who rented units in our complex, along with all of the people who owned the built very close together, middle income homes in the gated community across the street, used these as an added benefit to their HOA.

Our complex was known throughout Denver as the singles hotspot of apartment complexes, and I had to admit, it was kind of the truth. Rent was high enough to keep out the riffraff. Everyone who lived there was a professional working their way up the ladder or someone who did pretty well at whatever their job was. The complex was attractive, attractively laid out and attractively landscaped. It was a haven for the active suburban single. The greenbelt and creek had jogging-slash-bike trails, plus stations where they had sturdy equipment that you could do decline sit ups, pull-ups and stuff like that. The pool had a gorgeous, nearly unfettered view of the Front Range. It also had two hot tubs; the clubhouse bar was close and you could drink around the pool. All highly conducive to the singles scene.

Since what normally happened was that you hooked up with someone while in the apartment complex (as B and B and LaTanya and Derek did), lived with them there then moved to the housing development across the street when you got married, the community was also kind of incestuous. If you lived there long enough, everyone knew you and you knew everyone.

I didn't move there to be a single in a singles nirvana. I moved there because I liked the look of the place. It was quiet, close to the mall and downtown, the apartments were spacious and the units had lots of green space between them. I also moved there because I loved pools and had a freakish need to be tan for as long as I possibly could be, weather permitting. Me tan slid me up to a Three Point Five, or at least I fancied it did.

"You wanna tell me what we're walkin' into here?" Mitch broke into my thoughts to ask a pertinent question.

"My cousin's name is Bill," I answered. "And he has a nine-year-old son and a six-year-old daughter and their names are Billy and Billie. Billy, the boy, with a 'y' and Billie, the girl, with an 'ie'."

I felt Mitch's eyes on me before I felt them leave me and he flipped on the turn signal.

"You aren't laughing," he remarked after he'd turned out of the complex and I'd said no more.

"I'm not laughing because it isn't funny and it isn't funny because I'm not joking," I replied.

"Shit," he muttered, already knowing exactly what kind of mess Bill was.

And Mitch was right. Bill, Billy and Billie's names said it all.

"Anyway, Bill isn't a great dad, so occasionally Billy packs up his sister and they run away. They usually don't go very far and once they get there, they talk someone into calling me. I go get them. We have a chat. I get them food because their dad doesn't remember to feed them. I take them back to their dad. Then I have a chat with Bill, leave and come home."

This was most of it, not all of it. I didn't share that every time I left, I considered kidnapping my cousin's kids. I also considered a phone call to Child Protection Services. And lately, I considered that I lamented the fact that I hadn't kicked their drunk, stupid, lame dad's ass before I left.

"So they ran away, they're at the Stop 'n' Go and they called you," Mitch deduced.

"Yep."

"Where's their mom?"

"Moms, plural, and they're both long gone."

Mitch had no reply to that.

I decided since he'd been pretty angry and I wasn't certain if he was still angry, but I was guessing he was, that I would share a little more. Maybe being forthcoming would shear the edge of his anger.

"I'm their only family here. That's why they call me."

"That isn't why they call you," Mitch returned immediately, and I turned my head to look at him.

"Pardon?" I asked.

"That isn't why they call you," Mitch repeated.

"I heard what you said," I told him. "I just don't know what you mean."

"I mean, you're a brother and sister with two different moms, both who took off, a dad that's such a mess at nine years old you're runnin' away, and your dad's cousin is a woman whose smile lights up her whole face and her laugh ignites a room, you want that in your life. So you run away and call her in hopes that she's gonna give you that light and warmth to fill your life."

I stared at his profile as he drove and I felt my heart beating in my throat, but my stomach had clenched so hard I found I couldn't breathe.

I didn't recall ever smiling at him, not a real, unabashed smile and I definitely never laughed around him.

"I've never laughed around you," I blurted stupidly.

He glanced at me then back at the road before saying, "Sweetheart, you're with Brent and Bradon or LaTanya and Derek, I can hear it through the walls."

Ohmigod!

"So you're saying I have a loud laugh," I noted.

"No," he said with what sounded like extreme patience.

"What I'm sayin' is you have a gorgeous laugh. I've heard it. I like it."

*Ohmigod!*

That couldn't be true. He was just being nice, and since I couldn't deal with him being nice...*er* we needed to move on.

"My smile doesn't light up my whole face. It's wonky," I informed him.

"It isn't wonky."

"It is."

"Mara, it isn't. You don't smile at me like you mean it, because you're always too freaked out to let yourself go. But I've seen you at Derek and LaTanya's smiling like you mean it. I'll take your smiles even when you don't let yourself go because they work really fuckin' well. But I'll tell you, when you let yourself go, they're fuckin' fantastic."

I forced my eyes to look ahead and I forced my brain to find an explanation for this madness.

"You're just being nice," I whispered.

"I'm a nice guy," he agreed. "But I'm not bein' nice. I'm bein' real. And now what I'd like to know is why every time I give you a compliment, you freak out and twist it into something bad."

"I don't do that," I denied.

"I told you, you had good taste in music and you immediately jumped to the conclusion that it annoyed me because you played it too loud. How do you go from someone saying you have good taste in music to it being a complaint about you playin' it too loud?"

I had to admit that sounded absurd.

"Um..." I mumbled.

"Same with your laugh. I say I like it, you take it as me sayin' it's too loud."

He needed to quit talking.

"You need to quit talking," I blurted and wished I could clap my hands over my mouth because I sounded like a fool.

I should have lied to him earlier. I should have kicked him in the shin and run away. I shouldn't be in his SUV with him. I shouldn't be anywhere near him.

"Yeah," he muttered, "I bet you need that."

My head jerked to face him. "What does that mean?"

He didn't answer. Instead he asked, "Why'd you stand me up on Sunday?"

Uh-oh.

"I didn't stand you up."

He glanced at me again and I felt his anger, which had dissipated, start to fill the cab again.

He looked back to the road and said, "Mara, we had plans. Pizza at seven thirty."

I looked back to the road too and said, "I don't really want to talk about this."

"Yeah, I bet you need that too."

I ignored what he said and told him, "I need to focus on what I'm going to do with Billy and Billie and what I'm going to say to Bill."

"Yeah, I know, you need that too. You need to focus on anything other than what's goin' on with *you*."

I fought back the urge to clamp my hands over my ears and chant "la la la" and decided to stay silent.

"Why'd you stand me up?" he repeated into the void.

"I didn't. You said you were coming over but I didn't agree."

"You stood me up."

"I didn't."

"Mara, you did and you did it, essentially, twice."

My head jerked to face him again and I snapped, "No, I didn't!"

He shook his head and muttered, "Jesus, you got your head so far up your ass it's a wonder you can breathe."

"Pardon?" I hissed.

"You heard me."

"Yes," I bit out, "I did, and what you said was not very nice."

"No, baby, it wasn't but it *was* the fuckin' truth."

Was I sitting in Detective Mitch Lawson's SUV fighting with him? Two Point Fives didn't fight with Ten Point Fives. It was against all the laws of the universe. How did this happen?

"I don't have my head up my ass!" I snapped somewhat loudly.

"You live in a whole different world," he retorted.

"Do not!"

"Oh yeah, sweetheart, you do."

I crossed my arms on my chest, looked forward and announced, "Well I'm glad to know you can be a jerk. It's easier to deal with a hot guy who's a jerk than it is to deal with one who's unnaturally nice."

Of course I sounded like a fool but I didn't care. I always sounded like a fool, and anyway, he'd told me I had my head up my ass. What did I care that he thought I was a fool?

"Finally, I'm getting somewhere," Mitch returned. "All I gotta do is be a dick to you, you let go and a little of that Mara Light shines through. What now, Mara? I keep bein' a dick to you, you let me get my hands down your pants and the only way I can keep that privilege is continue to treat you like shit? Then eventually you'll kick me to the curb, and it's a self-fulfilling prophecy that all men are dicks? Is that how it goes so you can retreat into that cocoon you've built around yourself and rest safe in the knowledge that you're makin' all the right moves?"

My head swung to face him again. I was breathing heavily because he was, indeed, being a dick *and* he'd intimated he wanted to get his hands down my pants, which was insane.

"Are you insane?" I asked with my voice pitched high.

"This is what I know. I'm nice to you, you're scared as shit, you barely speak without ums and uhs and at one point you ran away from me, literally. I'm a dick, you got no problems communicating with me. Is that an insane conclusion?" he asked, shook his head at the windshield and answered his own question. "Fuck no."

"Can you explain *exactly* why you were so all fired up to take me to Billy and Billie? Is it so you could be an asshole about not getting to taste my pizza?" I asked acidly and with very bad timing.

We'd come to stop at a red light, which meant he could turn his full attention to me. This he did, with his arm draped on the steering wheel and his eyes locked to mine.

Then he said, "I hope I got a little window into Mara World and this gets through because it's really fuckin' important," he growled, at least as angry as I was, maybe angrier. "I don't want to taste your pizza, Mara. I don't give that first fuck about your pizza. Clue the fuck in, sweetheart, before you wake up at eighty-five years old and wonder where your life has gone."

I stared at him, or more like glared at him, and shot back loudly, angrily and with a fair amount of exasperation, "Then why'd you make such a big freaking deal about the pizza?" I hesitated then finished on a near shout, *"Twice?"*

He glared back at me and his glare was pretty scary. Luckily I was so angry I didn't care.

Then he closed his eyes, turned his head away and muttered, "Jesus Christ."

I faced forward and informed him, "The light's green."

I heard him pull in a deep breath.

Then we were moving forward.

# CHAPTER FOUR

## Exactly the Kind of Friend I Intend to Be

MITCH HAD BARELY come to a halt in the parking space outside the door to the Stop 'n' Go before I had the door open and was jumping out.

This was because I wanted to get to the kids, but it was also because I was freaked out and really, *really* pissed off.

It was late April, nearly May. We were having a warm spell, so I was in flip-flops, jeans (unfortunately the jeans that Bradon told me to wear last Saturday, which even I had to admit did great things for my ass) and a tee. My flip-flops were thin-strap Havaianas and a nice, muted-gold color, and my tee was cream with a square neckline, cute, pleated ruffles as sleeves, and it clung to my breasts and ribs fairly provocatively. Not exactly skintight but it stated its case. My hair was in a ponytail at the back of my head, and that fat, stupid lock at the front had fallen out. I shoved it behind my ear as I yanked open the door.

Billie ran screaming straight at me before I cleared the door. I stopped and braced because I knew she wouldn't stop.

She didn't. She slammed into me with all her six-year-old, happy it's a wonderful life no matter what exuberance, and I started to go back on a foot. The thing was I didn't and this was because Detective Mitch Lawson wasn't only beautiful and a big, fat jerk who moved really well, but he apparently moved really *fast*. He was right behind me, so when Billie slammed into me, I slammed into Mitch.

One of my hands went to her head, one to her shoulder as I twisted my neck to glare at Mitch. He absorbed my glare and hurled back his own. His was more effective, so I scrunched my face at him in an added effort to tell him nonverbally I thought he was a big, fat jerk. His eyes dropped to the vicinity of my nose and mouth, and his glare instantly evaporated. He pressed his lips together in a weird way as his eyes lit with what appeared to be amusement.

Jerk!

"Auntie Mara!" Billie screamed, and I looked down at her to see she'd tipped her head back to look up at me. "I want burritos!" she was still screaming.

Whenever I saw them, I always took them out to a meal. This was because Bill filled the house with junk food (when he remembered to buy food at all) and forgot to make certain his children ate and never made certain they ate well. Therefore, Billie was conditioned that seeing Auntie Mara meant a full belly.

"All right, baby, let's see what your brother wants," I said softly to her. Then I felt Mitch's hands at my hips and he was shuffling us in and to the side, the front of his body still in contact with mine at the back.

I noticed belatedly that a customer was wanting out the doors we were obstructing, and I tried to sidestep for the customer *and* to get away from Mitch. I didn't succeed in this because Mitch's hands clenched my hips and he kept me right where I was. Plus I felt it was undignified to struggle even if we were only at the Stop 'n' Go.

He did move us out of the way and when he halted us,

Billie had forgotten about her empty belly and, like any girl, be she six or sixty, she noticed Mitch.

"Hi!" she chirped.

"Hey there," Mitch's voice rumbled in my ear, down my neck, all down my back, and I had to fight the goose bumps rising on my skin. A fight I lost.

"I'm Billie," she announced.

"Mitch," he replied.

Her eyes came to me. "Is he your boyfriend?"

Oh God.

"No, he's my neighbor," I answered.

She was still latched onto me, and since her arms were around my hips and Mitch's hands were at my hips, her eyes had a direct line of sight to his hands, including his hips, which were snug against me. She took this in then looked back up at me, her head tipped to the side in little girl confusion (and, honest to God, I felt her pain) and she smiled.

Now Billie's smile was wonky and it was one hundred percent adorable. My mom's side of the family, which meant Bill's mom's side of the family, had all the dominant characteristics. This meant Billie looked a lot like me. Except on Billie, it was cuter: long, thick, lush, shining dark brown hair, beautiful, wide cornflower blue eyes, flawless skin and long limbs. If you didn't know, you'd think she was my child, except she was going to be a knockout because she was already a mini-knockout.

"Auntie Mara," I heard and I looked beyond Billie to see Billy.

Billy was a slightly older, male version of Billie, and I figured Mitch probably looked like him as a kid. There was no mistaking it; Billy was going to be gorgeous when he grew up because he was already a mini–hot guy.

Bill, their father, could have been all of this. But a

hard-living, hard-drinking, stupid-decision-making life meant he was tall, not built but reed thin. His skin was sallow, he had dark marks under his once shining blue eyes, and his hair was too long, lank, lifeless and often dirty.

This hit me harder than normal when my mind took that moment to fast forward to the future and I didn't like what I saw. I wanted these two beautiful kids to be able to be all they would be. Not just gorgeous but Billy to have the chance to use his brains, loyalty and sweetness to find a good life and Billie always to have a bit of that lively, innocent girl somewhere inside her.

It was definitely time to make a decision about what I was going to do with Bill but more, what I was going to do about his kids.

"Hey, buddy," I greeted Billy. "You hungry?"

His eyes flicked to Mitch then back to me. He'd stopped throwing himself in my arms a while ago. He was too grown up for that now. I missed it. But he wasn't usually this distant, and I could see he didn't know what to make of Mitch. Billie had adored Destry because Billie adored everybody. Billy not so much.

"Yeah," he answered.

"You want burritos?" I asked, knowing he would say he did because he knew that was what his sister wanted. I'd never know what *he* actually wanted because he'd do what he could to give his sister everything her heart desired.

"Yeah, burritos sound good," he replied, then his eyes flicked up to Mitch again and back to me.

"This is my neighbor Mitch," I told Billy.

"Is he gay like Bray and Brent?" Billy asked, and I heard and felt Mitch's chuckle again.

"No," I answered.

"Is there a reason he's touching you?" Billy asked

straight out, and I noticed his nine-year-old face had gone nine-year-old boy hard and protective.

"Um…" I answered

"We're not just neighbors, we're friends," Mitch put in.

"Goodie!" Billie cried and did a couple of jumps up and down, shaking me against Mitch. "I like all your friends!" she declared.

"That's good, honey," I said to her.

"Bray and Brent and Derek are your friends and they don't touch you," Billy, keeping his distance and his hard expression, pointed out.

"Well—" I started.

"I'm not that kind of friend," Mitch said over me.

"What kind of friend are you?" Billy asked.

"A different kind of friend," Mitch answered.

"What kind of different?" Billy shot back.

"A good kind of different," Mitch replied.

What on earth was he talking about?

No, no, I didn't care. Moving on.

"Let's get food," I butted in. "You ready for dinner?"

"Yes!" Billie shrieked, jumping up and down again, which meant I moved against Mitch's body again.

I didn't know what it meant when his fingers tightened their grip at my hips. Did this mean he was holding me still or something else?

I decided against trying to figure that out. Mostly because I probably never would. Also because, suddenly, I was hungry too.

"All right, everyone out to Mitch's truck," I ordered.

Billie let me go and raced to Billy. She grabbed his hand and hauled him with fake, hilarious grunts to the doors, all the while Billy dragged his feet and eyed Mitch, who still hadn't taken his hands off me.

They made it to the door, and I was about to pull away to follow them when one of Mitch's hands moved and I froze. I froze because it slid from my hip to my belly and pressed in just as I felt his lips at my ear.

And it was there he whispered, "You jump outta my truck again before I've come to a complete halt, swear to God, baby, I'll turn you over my knee. You with me?"

My chest was rising and falling swiftly. I'd lost the ability to see, everything went blurry and I'd also lost the ability to think.

His fingers at my hip gave me a squeeze at the same time his hand at my belly pressed in again and he prompted, still whispering, "Mara, you with me?"

I nodded.

I got another squeeze and belly press then, *I kid you not*, I felt his lips *against* the skin of my neck where he murmured, "Good."

His hands dropped away. My body realized it had its opportunity and it started to take flight. I got one step away before I was hooked with a strong arm and turned before I was hips to hips with Mitch again, this time full-frontal. His arm locked around my waist while his other hand lifted to curl around the side of my neck.

"Now a couple more things we're gonna get straight," he said quietly.

Oh God. He was close. He looked serious and he was talking quietly, but he was also talking in that bossy voice that was very firm. All of this equaled trouble for me, I just knew it.

I was not wrong.

"Mitch, the kids—" I breathed.

"First, we're goin' to Lola's and giving them a good meal."

I blinked at him.

Lola's?

*Lola's?*

Lola's was awesome and had absolutely fantastic food, but it was also not what the kids were used to. It wasn't fancy, but it wasn't Taco Bell, either, and it wasn't exactly inexpensive. I hadn't actually asked Mitch to accompany me, but since he did, I thought we'd pop to the nearest fast-food joint, go through a drive-thru and get the kids home. After, I would do whatever it was I was going to have to do at Bill's, then get home and *away* from Mitch.

Lola's meant sitting down. Lola's meant time. Time spent with Mitch and time Mitch spent with me *and* the kids.

What man wanted that? Kids he didn't know and a woman who he thought had her head up her ass.

Maybe he *was* insane.

"But—" I started and Mitch talked over me.

"I'm payin', and if you even open your mouth to argue with me, I'm gonna be forced to find a way to stop you speaking, and the way I'll pick means Billy's gonna get an eyeful of exactly the kind of friend I intend to be."

My mouth dropped open and I felt my eyes get wide.

"We straight?" he asked.

No. No, we were not. We definitely were not. We *absolutely* were *not* straight.

"Um…" I mumbled.

"Yes or no, sweetheart," he prompted.

"Uh…" I muttered.

He grinned and I swallowed. Then my throat closed when his face dipped closer to mine.

"Um and uh aren't options, baby," he told me softly.

"Mitch—"

His grin built to a smile, I clamped my mouth shut, and he declared, "We're straight."

Then he grabbed my hand, hauled me to the doors the kids were standing at, both of them staring at us with polar opposite expressions on their faces (Billie happy, Billy not at all happy). He led the three of us to the SUV. I opened the door for Billy to climb in. Mitch opened the door and hefted Billie into her seat, something that made her giggle, but then a lot made Billie giggle. I got in the passenger side while Mitch folded in behind the wheel.

"We all buckled in?" Mitch asked into the cab.

"Yes!" Billie shrieked.

"Yes," I whispered.

"Bray, Brent and Derek don't touch Auntie Mara in *any* of the ways *you* touch her," Billy stated on a clear accusation instead of answering Mitch's question.

"No, they don't," Mitch agreed. "You buckled in?"

There was no response until I twisted in my seat to look at him. He glared at me.

Then he crossed his arms on his chest, turned his glare in Mitch's direction and grunted, "Yeah."

# CHAPTER FIVE

## A Strong Hand to Hold Onto

I DIDN'T WANT to have to ask. I really didn't want to have to ask, but there was a waiting list at Lola's. They said fifteen minutes, and I had to ask.

Mitch was standing at the hostess station. I got as close to him as I dared, went up on my toes and with my mouth near his ear, I whispered, "Can you do me a favor and look after Billie while I take Billy outside for a chat?"

His neck twisted, his eyes leaving the hostess, who was staring at him like she wanted to pounce, which was probably how most women stared at him (including me). I'd only ever been in public with him this once. I wasn't looking forward to it and that was one of the *many* reasons. He tipped his head down and his eyes caught mine. They scanned my face. Then he nodded once.

"Thanks," I murmured, moved away and looked down at Billie. "You stay with Mitch. Billy and I are going outside for a sec."

"Okay," she agreed readily, skipped to Mitch immediately and grasped his hand.

I watched with utter fascination as his big, strong, attractive hand closed around her little girl's hand without even an instant's delay. Then my eyes lifted to his as I felt something warm slide through my insides.

His eyes caught mine, and when they did they went warm like I felt inside right before he gave a gentle jerk of his head to the door, prompting me to do what I needed to do.

I nodded, tore my eyes from him, shoved the warmth resolutely aside and looked down at Billy.

"Got a second to talk, buddy?" I asked.

Billy was glaring at Mitch. He kept glaring at Mitch even as he approached me and grabbed my hand. This surprised me. He hadn't grabbed my hand in a while. He looked away from Mitch to tug me down the ramp that led to the front door. When we were outside, I took over the lead and we went to a bench. I climbed up it so I was sitting on the back, my feet on the seat, and Billy climbed up too and settled in beside me.

"Talk to me," I encouraged gently.

"Dad's a dick," Billy replied.

I closed my eyes. This was true, but nine-year-olds shouldn't talk like this. Sure, with their friends they could be naughty but not with adults and not so casually. Billy talked like this because Bill didn't teach him better. In fact, Bill egged it on because he thought it was funny.

"Billy, buddy, do me a favor, don't say that word," I said softly.

"You know he's one, Auntie Mara," Billy returned, and he was right.

"What did he do now?" I asked and looked at my little cousin to see his eyes were pointed angrily at the road in front of us. His jaw was set.

"He's still got that guy comin' over all the time, and I don't like him. He's a creep. And I don't like him around

Billie. He's sugar sweet to her and it freaks me out. Gives her candy. Tells her she's pretty. It's weird."

Billy had been telling me about "that guy" for a while, and Billy had good instincts, so I figured whoever "that guy" was, he wasn't a good guy. And what he said about how "that guy" treated Billie made my stomach clench and my mouth taste sour.

More indication I really, *really* needed to do something about what was happening at Bill's.

Billy kept talking. "And we didn't have any food. *And* he was passed out. *And* he didn't have any money in the whole house so I could go get us something to eat. Billie was hungry." His eyes turned to mine. "We have to eat."

"Like we talked about last time, you don't have food, you need something or you get freaked out, you call me," I reminded him.

"Yeah, right, I'll call you but on what phone? His cell didn't have any charge and he hasn't paid the bill so even if it did, it wouldn't work. And they turned off the house phone months ago. You know that."

Shit. I did. Damn. I knew about the house phone, though it was news about Bill's cell.

Damn again.

"I'll get you a cell phone," I told him. "You can hide it and—"

He straightened, looked me right in the eye and I braced for what he was going to say next because he had that look about him that always made me brace. "Auntie Mara, Dad *steals* from *us*. You know that locket you gave Billie for her birthday last month?"

Oh no.

He read my face and nodded. "It's gone. I didn't want to tell you, because I knew you'd be upset, but it was gone like *the next day.* Dad convinced Billie she lost it, and she cried for like *an hour.* She loved that thing. Said it was the prettiest thing she had."

It *was* the prettiest thing she had. Bill barely kept the kids clothed. All the clothes they were wearing, including their shoes, I bought them before school started months ago. And I'd noticed both of them were growing out of them.

I clenched my teeth and looked away.

"He stole it," Billy went on, "because he's a big dick."

I looked back at him. "Billy—"

He suddenly and uncharacteristically lost it, slammed his fists into his knees and shouted, *"He is!"*

My heart started beating wildly, my eyes filled with tears I blinked away and I lifted my hand to curl it around the back of his head.

I knew how he felt. *God.* I knew exactly how he felt. I hadn't felt it in a long time, but if you knew that feeling, you never forgot it.

I knew that feeling. It lived in me.

I pulled him to me as I bent to him and rested our foreheads together. Shockingly, he let me do this but I figured he did because he was suddenly breathing heavy and concentrating on fighting it.

"Billy, honey," I whispered.

"I hate him, Auntie Mara," Billy whispered back. I heard his breath hitch and I understood the breathing heavy. He was close to tears.

"I know." I was still whispering.

And I *did* know.

"I *hate him*," he said quietly and passionately while his breath hitched again.

Oh God. God, God, *God.*

I knew what I had to do.

God!

"You know I love you?" I asked him.

His eyes slid away. He pushed against my hand at his head. I let him move away, but I wrapped my arm around him anyway and slid him across the back of the bench so the side of his body was pressed against mine. Shockingly, he didn't fight this either and leaned into me.

"I know," he replied.

"And you know I love your sister?" I asked.

He didn't answer. His eyes were again on the street and he just nodded.

I looked to the street and made my decision.

"I don't know what I'm going to do, honey," I said softly on a squeeze. "But I'm going to try to figure out something. I promise you. Do you believe me?"

I looked down at him and he nodded again.

"You're going to have to give me time, okay? In the meantime, I'm going to buy you a cell and I'm going to go to the grocery store tomorrow after work to get you guys some food. And I'm going to give you some emergency money. You've got to find a good hiding place for the phone and money. But if he gets it, don't worry about it, okay? Just tell me the next time you see me and we'll try again. Okay?"

He nodded and whispered, "Yeah, okay."

"And Mitch is a police detective. I'm going to talk to him and see what my options are."

Billy's head shot up, he looked at me, and for the first time in the short time he knew Mitch his eyes lit with a positive light.

"That guy's a cop?"

I nodded. "Uh-huh. He'll know who I need to talk to."

"Will he help us?" Billy asked, and my heart clenched as I looked into his hopeful yet sad and defeated eyes, like he wanted desperately for me to say yes but expected me to say no. I found this odd, I found it disturbing and I also found it heart wrenching.

"That's what he does, buddy," I told him. "He does it for a living, helping people, protecting them, keeping them safe. He'll help you and Billie and he'll help me help you. I'm certain of it."

I gave him another squeeze to allay his fears and to hide the fact that I really didn't want to ask for Mitch's help. But I had no choice. Billy and Billie had no one but Bill. Bill's sister was a mess and living her own dysfunction back in Iowa. Bill's mom was arguably crazier and meaner than mine and she didn't do a great job raising Bill and his sister; she'd suck at raising Billy and Billie.

It was only me. And me it was going to be.

"Can we stay with you tonight?" Billy asked.

I pulled in breath and nodded.

Apparently, I *was* going to need to get a different apartment, one with three bedrooms rather than two. A lot of things were going to need to change.

"We need to stop by your house to get your stuff and tell your dad, though," I informed him.

"He won't even know we're gone," Billy replied.

This was probably true.

"We still have to do it," I replied. Billy's face got hard and I gave him another squeeze before I let him go and bumped his side with my own, smiled at him and stated, "At least to go get your stuff. You can't go to school tomorrow wearing the same clothes."

"We got nothin' clean," Billy told me.

My teeth clenched again.

Then I forced myself to smile before I said, "Lucky I have a washer and dryer at my house."

"Right," Billy muttered then he smiled back.

I felt him before I saw him but not fast enough. His hand still holding Billie's, who was skipping in place by his side, Mitch was right behind us, and Billy and I both twisted. I looked up at the same time Mitch's hand swept my ponytail to the side. That hand rested warm and strong at the back of my neck in a familiar and intimate way which was a complete shock. A shock I liked way too much but freaked me out even more.

"Table's ready," he told me.

"Burritos!" Billie shouted.

"Awesome," Billy muttered, jumped down and raced around the bench.

I was frozen in place. Mitch's hand hadn't moved even as Billie let his other one go and raced up to and through the front doors with her brother.

"What's the story?" Mitch asked, his eyes tipped down to me.

"I need to figure out how to get custody of my second cousins," I answered and watched his eyes flash.

"That bad?" he murmured.

"They've had nothing to eat all day. There's no food in the house. Their father was passed out. He had no money. They couldn't call me because they have no phone. And Bill stole the gold locket I bought Billie for her birthday a day after I gave it to her," I told him, watched his eyes flash again as his hand tightened at my neck and I kept talking. "And there's a mysterious man who visits the house that freaks Billy out and Billy reports he's creepy around his sister."

Mitch's gaze didn't leave mine as he muttered, "Fuck."

I nodded then went on, "Billy hates his dad. A lot. I don't know how bad it has to get, but that's bad enough for me."

He took his hand from my neck. I missed it even though

I didn't want to, but I didn't have to miss it long. He leaned forward and rested his weight in his hand on the back of the bench, which brought the rest of his torso and definitely his face close to me.

When his eyes locked back on mine, he asked quietly, "You need me to help?"

There it was. The offer I needed. An offer that terrified me, but I had no choice but to take it.

"Since I don't know the system and you do, and I love those kids and I need to get them away from that mess, yes. Any advice you can give me would be appreciated," I answered, and I did it fast before I lost the courage to do it at all.

His eyes kept mine captive, but they changed. I couldn't put my finger on how, but however it was made a whoosh sweep through my belly.

"I can do more than advice, sweetheart," he said, still talking quietly.

"Whatever you could do, Mitch, like I said, would be appreciated."

His eyes moved over my face, and when they caught mine again, he noted, "You care about them."

"I love them."

"Family?" he asked probingly.

"They're great kids," I answered, telling him it was much more than blood ties.

"They love you," he said softly.

"I know," I replied just as soft.

"You've struggled with this a while," he surmised.

"Yeah," I whispered.

He stayed leaned into his one hand; his other hand came up to curl around the side of my neck, and his thumb swept my jaw as he said, "Makin' the decision is half the battle, sweetheart."

I sucked in breath through my nose, pulled my lips between my teeth and closed my eyes. When I opened them, I'd slid them away so I wasn't looking at him.

I did this so I could admit, "If that's true, then why am I scared to death of what's to come?"

"'Cause it might get ugly. 'Cause any change in life is scary. 'Cause you avoid risk like the plague and this is a big one that's gonna have a long-lasting effect on three lives. And 'cause you're not stupid."

My eyes went back to his and I remarked, "Don't sugar-coat it, Mitch. Give it to me straight."

He chuckled and his fingers curled deeper into my neck before he said, "You're gonna be all right, Mara, and they're gonna be all right, which is why you're doin' this in the first place. You gotta believe in that."

"Right," I muttered, my eyes sliding away again.

I got a squeeze at the neck and my eyes went back.

"Right," he whispered.

He was looking at me with his serious, firm face, but his eyes were warm and it hit me that it wasn't the same friendly neighbor warmth but something deeper. Something more important. Almost like he respected me. Like he was proud of me.

My breath caught, and then the warmth in his gaze shifted to something else. His fingers pressed into my neck, bringing my face closer to his as his moved closer to mine, and that was when we both heard Billie yell, "Sillies! What are you doing? It's time for burritos!"

Mitch closed his eyes slowly as his fingers flexed into my neck.

I pulled free quickly, jumped off the bench, told myself I *was* being silly and rounded the bench to get myself and my soon to be legal charges (hopefully) some food.

I didn't make it to the door without Mitch catching my hand. It was crazy to let him keep hold of it as we walked in, walked up the ramp and by the hostess station and to our table, but I let him keep hold of it. First, because his hold was strong and firm and it would take some effort to get my hand away. And second, and most important, because I'd just made a life-altering decision that was going to have a long-lasting effect on three lives, it scared the living daylights out of me and I needed a strong hand to hold onto.

*       *       *

It happened after the three-course meal Mitch bought us.

It was after Billy had melted toward Mitch and they were thumb wrestling across the table. Billy was laughing, which was something I hadn't seen in a good long while. And Mitch was smiling at him like he knew it was something the boy didn't do often, and he liked it a lot that Billy was doing it now.

Mitch and I were side by side on a booth bench; the kids sat across from us on chairs while we were eating. But now that we were done, Billie had left her seat to crawl in close to me, wrap herself around me, play with my ponytail and whisper girlie stuff to me.

It was at this time, after Mitch had asked for the bill and we were waiting for it, that the elderly woman walked to our table.

Mitch's head turned and tipped back to look at her, and when his did, so did Billy's. I twisted my neck to look at her as well, and Billie pressed deep to look around me so she could see her too.

But the woman only had eyes for me.

"Sorry to disturb you, but I just wanted to say, you have the most beautiful family I've ever seen." My heart stopped. She smiled big, touched Billy's hair, a Billy who was staring up at her with his mouth wide open, and then she looked back at me. "Kids are usually grouchy, everyone's always snappy, fighting, loud, kids racing around. It's nice to see a polite, happy, beautiful family for once." She nodded to me and finished, "Keep up the good work."

"Uh..." I mumbled.

"Thanks." Mitch's deep voice sounded.

She smiled at Mitch then Billie then Billy. She nodded to me again, turned and walked away.

I blinked repeatedly at her departing back.

"She was nice!" Billie declared exuberantly, and my head turned to look at her smiling face.

"Yeah, baby, a very nice lady."

"I've never been part of a beautiful family," Billie stated.

I stared at her, my heart wrenched, my head turned again, and I caught Mitch's eyes just as his arm wrapped around my shoulders. He pulled me into his side, and since Billie was in my arms she came with me.

Mitch leaned into us both so his face was close to Billie's before he advised, "Live it up, gorgeous."

"Yippee!" Billie cried.

"Hush, honey, that's a little loud," I whispered to her.

"I can't live it up quiet," she whispered loudly and logically back to me.

"She's got you there, sweetheart," Mitch murmured, gave my shoulders a squeeze and then turned to the waitress, who was there with our bill.

I scooted a bit away and sucked in breath. Then I let it out. For the next few minutes I allowed myself to pretend this table with Billy, Billie and Mitch *was* me and my beautiful family. Something I never had. Something I always wanted. Something that wasn't for the likes of me.

Then we left the restaurant to go deal with Bill.

# CHAPTER SIX

## Butterflies and Flowers

MY ALARM WENT off. I opened my eyes and saw it was an hour and a half earlier than it was normally set to go off. I blinked at it and then I remembered.

I reached out a hand to turn it off and rolled carefully.

Billie was dead asleep next to me, sprawled out on my bed, the fingers of her right hand clutching a new, little, fluffy, pink teddy bear. She was sprawled yet she was so small she didn't take up much of the bed. And she was also apparently oblivious to alarm clocks.

I moved into her, kissed her forehead then exited the bed and went to my bathroom, yesterday evening playing out in my head.

Suffice it to say things at Bill's did not go well. In fact, they went worse than I could have imagined because things at Bill's *were* worse than I ever imagined.

This was not because I lost it or Bill lost it when I shared with him that I intended to get custody of his kids. Though he did lose it, but not because I told him I intended to take his kids from him.

This was because Mitch lost it. I knew I didn't want him to know about Bill, Billy and Billie and how all that reflected on me, and him losing it only proved I was very, *very* right.

Even so, this had been surprising. I didn't know Mitch very well, but I'd seen him get angry. I'd heard him get angry. And he could be a jerk when he was angry.

Then again, I didn't know just how bad things were at Bill's.

And they were bad.

You see, when we walked into Bill's, he was on the couch and he was high as a kite. His eyes were glassy, his body limp and his limbs not in his control. There was an open bottle of half-drunk vodka next to some drug paraphernalia on the dirty, cluttered coffee table in front of him.

I stared at my cousin, frozen in shock. I'd never seen him like this. I'd seen him drunk, of course. I'd even seen him drunk around his kids, though infrequently. I'd also seen him high, back in the day, and guessed he still partook, but my guess was he partook of weed. Not what would necessitate him having the kind of drug paraphernalia he had right then. I'd never seen him high like this and *definitely* not high around his kids

He didn't hide his liquor from me or his kids, which was something I didn't like. I knew how weird and uncomfortable it was seeing a parent drink all the time, drink until they were fall-down, crazy, stupid and sometimes mean drunk. And I didn't want that for Billy and Billie. But it wasn't illegal, and to my knowledge it didn't happen very often.

I'd never seen the drug paraphernalia. Not ever.

Seeing Bill sitting on his couch getting stoned, not worrying that his kids were gone and not out searching high and low for them, but instead getting drunk and high pissed me off to no end.

Also, I'd tidied their house that week, *twice*, and it

looked like it hadn't been picked up or cleaned in the last decade. How it could go from relatively clean and tidy to a disaster in a few days was beyond me, but it did. The proof was spread out before me.

But I couldn't think about any of this. I had to think of the kids who I didn't want to see this. So I turned to them saying, "Kids, go to your room."

To this Billy, his eyes on his dad, his lips in a mini-nine-year-old-kid sneer, replied, "This is no big deal. We've seen this before, Auntie Mara. We see it like, *all the time*."

I froze again for half a second at learning this knowledge before my eyes moved to Billie to see she didn't seem overly perturbed by the state of her dad, although she was standing very close to her brother in a way that it appeared she was seeking some sort of protection. The only hint she gave that she was uncomfortable was her ankle twisted to the side and her little-girl hand was clenched in her brother's. I turned back to my cousin, and on my turn I saw that Mitch was examining Billy and Billie and his jaw was rock hard.

Then Mitch, too, turned back to Bill and growled in a voice that sent a chill up my spine, "Your kids are gone, you got no food in the house, but you can get your hands on smack and vodka?"

Bill blinked up at Mitch then blinked at me, grinned a wonky (*not* adorable) grin and slurred, "Hey, beautiful Mara."

"Bill—" I started, but Mitch interrupted me.

"Get their shit," he ordered tersely, my head whipped to him, and that was when I noticed he was losing it. He was holding on but only by a thread. I knew this because it wasn't only his jaw that was rock hard, his entire face was.

"Pardon?" I whispered cautiously.

He was digging into his back jeans pocket, but his eyes never left Bill when he said to me, "Get their shit."

"Mitch—" I began, and his gaze sliced to me.

"Get their *shit*," he snarled. "*All* of it."

He then pulled out his phone, and I thought maybe I should make an effort to tame the suddenly savage beast.

"Maybe while I talk with Bill, you could help them—" I started to suggest, and Mitch leaned into me and I stopped speaking because at that moment the thread on his control snapped, and he roared, *"Mara, get their shit!"*

I blinked in the face of his anger as my heart stuttered in my chest.

I thought this was my scene, my struggle, my fight and Mitch was along for the ride. What I realized in that moment, staring in the face of his fury, was that I was not in control of this situation, and there was no way I was going to gain control. No way at all.

That was why I whispered, "Okay, Mitch."

He stabbed his phone with sharp, angry movements, holding his entire body tense while he did it, like if he didn't he wouldn't be responsible for what his body would do.

Then he hit some buttons as Bill said on a wince, "Dude, keep it down. What the fuck?"

"Shut your mouth," Mitch ground out, eyes to his phone, face hard.

Bill looked to me. "Who's this fuckin' guy and what's his fuckin' problem?"

"Right now, I'm *your* problem, assclown," Mitch bit off, his eyes cutting to Bill.

I glanced at Billy and Billie. Billie was staring wide-eyed at the proceedings. Billy was fighting back a grin.

Oh boy.

Maybe I *should* try to gain control of the situation.

"Mitch," I said, sidling closer to him, "maybe you should—"

I didn't finish again because his eyes cut to me again, and he asked on a dangerous whisper, "What'd I tell you to do?"

I stared up at him, frozen to the spot. Okay, that answered that. Mitch was in charge.

I nodded and turned to the kids. "All right guys. Let's go get your stuff." I moved to them. "Come on, let's go."

Billy grinned at me then tugged his sister's hand and they moved down the hall. They shared a room, which was okay for now considering their ages, but it was just okay. Billy was getting old enough he needed his own space, and it wouldn't be long before it was borderline inappropriate for a brother and sister to share a room.

I wondered what the rent on the three-bedroom town-houses at the complex was as I searched for some kind of luggage or bags. Though I knew this would be fruitless as I knew there were none and I was right. They didn't even have garbage bags, something I discovered upon tidying one of the million times I tidied. I always meant to remember to buy some and, being me and being a dork, I always forgot.

I found a load of plastic grocery bags (Bill clearly not the kind of person to worry about the environment). By the time we filled these with Billy and Billie's not so abundant collection of clothes, shoes and toys, I found they barely had any soap or shampoo. I added a quick pit stop to the store to my evening's agenda. Then we trudged out to the living room carrying the bags only to find there were two police officers in the room.

"You brought a cop here!" Bill shouted when the kids and I hit the room, and I looked at my cousin to see he'd lost his drugged lethargy. He was pacing agitatedly and awkwardly while he eyed the cops and me.

"Bill—" I started.

"Mara," Mitch called, and I stopped talking and looked to him. He was holding out his keys. "Load up the truck."

"But—" I began again.

"I can't believe you brought a fuckin' cop here!" Bill yelled, he was up, but his coordination was not so good and he was mostly fumbling around. I didn't figure he was much of a threat, what with him being drunk and high and three cops being in the room.

"I'll deal with this," Mitch caught my attention. "Load up the truck."

My eyes went to the uniformed police officers before going to Mitch. I was thinking this was not good. Bill was an idiot, but he was my cousin and he was the kids' dad. There was good in him somewhere, I knew it. I just needed to stop screwing around living in denial and find a way to jumpstart him by pulling out the good so he could get himself sorted. I needed to remind him how we used to talk about how we wanted our lives to be and how we'd dreamed and schemed of making them something better. I just needed to make sure Billy and Billie were safe while Bill sorted himself out, and I was thinking my plans might be foiled if Bill was thrown into jail because of me.

"I think—" I started to say to Mitch.

His eyes narrowed before he clipped, "Baby, load up the *fuckin'* truck."

The uniformed police officers were both studying me with what appeared to be weirdly intense interest, but I was again frozen in the face of Mitch's fury. It was then that Billy moved forward, calmly grabbed Mitch's keys and headed to the door carrying four bags full of clothes and shoes. Billie followed her brother.

There it was again. I was not in charge.

Damn.

I glanced at Bill and followed Billie.

After the first round, I made the kids sit in the truck while I got the rest of their stuff. When I opened the door and walked in, Bill was ranting, flailing and struggling with the police officers. He did this while Mitch glared at him, his phone to his ear, his other hand to his hip. I scurried through the house to go and grab some more bags.

On trip three, the last of the trips, I heard Mitch say in his phone, "Give me a second." Then he called, "Mara," and I looked at him. "That it?" he asked, dipping his head to the bags I was carrying.

I nodded.

"Don't come back," he ordered. "Stay in the truck with the kids."

"Okay," I whispered.

"You freakin' *bitch*!" Bill shouted at me. I tried not to look at him, but I had to look at him, so I looked at him to see he was cuffed and sitting on his couch, bouncing clumsily around. His eyes were shooting daggers at me. "You *freakin' bitch*!"

"Mara, out to the truck," Mitch demanded.

"I can't believe you'd do this to me!" Bill yelled. "My fuckin' family. Flesh and blood! You *bitch*!"

"Out to the truck, Mara, *now*," Mitch clipped.

"Fuck you, Mara!" Bill screamed at me. "Fuck you! You just bought yourself trouble, you bitch!"

I looked at Bill and explained, "Bill, they hadn't eaten all day."

"I'll fuck with you!" he shouted.

"Mara, out to the truck," Mitch ordered but I ignored him.

"Somewhere inside you, you have to know they deserve better. You know how you're making them feel. You know you don't want to make them feel that way," I said softly to my cousin.

"Fuck you! *Fuck* you! Fuck *you*!" Bill yelled loudly to me.

"They've been gone for hours. They came in, Bill, and you didn't even look at them. Now you're not even asking about them," I pointed out, and Bill scowled at me.

Mitch started toward me with a warning, "Mara."

My head jerked to him then I looked to my cousin, who was glaring at me, too far gone to let anything penetrate. Then I nodded and turned to the door.

And as I walked out the door, I heard Bill shriek, "You'll regret this, you bitch! You'll regret it! I swear to fuckin' *Christ* you'll fuckin' regret this!"

I closed my eyes hard and walked swiftly to Mitch's truck, luckily making it there mostly blind.

Mitch came out before the officers led Bill out and we were away.

"Everyone okay?" Mitch asked into the silent cab when we'd made it to Speer Boulevard.

"Oh yeah," Billy answered with a smile in his voice, which made me feel slightly better.

"I'm okay," Billie answered uncertainly, which made that slightly better fade away.

I stared out the side window. I was terrified out of my head for a lot of reasons and wondering what on earth I was going to do next.

"Mara?" Mitch called.

I kept staring out the side window, focused on my terror.

Mitch's fingers curled around my knee and squeezed. "Sweetheart?"

"I'm okay," I lied to the window.

We got home and Mitch and Billy unloaded the truck

while Billie and I (well, mostly I) separated darks, lights and whites before we started loading up the washer.

When they had it all in, I announced, "Billy, you're in the second bedroom. I'll pull out the futon later. Billie, you're with me."

"Yippee!" Billie cried, that Teflon fortress clearly having clamped tight around her, and life was no longer scary and uncertain, it was wonderful again. She was on an adventure, on Billie vacation. She'd always liked visiting her Auntie Mara's house.

I ignored Mitch, who scared me normally, but his behavior at Bill's scared me more than normal, and I continued my pronouncements.

"Before we deal with sleeping arrangements, we have to go to the drugstore." I turned to Mitch. In an effort to dismiss him politely from his self-appointed duties, I told his shoulder, "Thanks for everything. Uh... we'll talk tomorrow?"

"What do you need at the drugstore?" Mitch asked, and my eyes slid to his.

"We're okay now," I assured him. "I'll pop by tomorrow—"

"I didn't ask if you were okay. I asked what you needed at the drugstore," Mitch replied.

"Um—" I mumbled.

Mitch, who was standing at the mouth of the hall, walked to where I was standing in the middle of the hall by my stackable washer and dryer. He did this while Billie, who was standing beside me and Billy, who kept his place where he had been standing beside Mitch at the mouth of the hall, watched Mitch move.

When Mitch made it to me, he got close, my head tipped way back, his chin dipped way down and softly he said, "Mara, sweetheart, I asked what you needed at the drugstore."

"The kids need shampoo," I whispered because with him that close it was all I could do.

"Right," Mitch whispered back, immediately turned and asked the hall at large, "Who's comin' with me to the drugstore?"

I blinked in surprise at his back.

"Me!" Billie shouted and skipped after him.

"I am too," Billy added and fell in step beside him.

The kids shot out the door and turned left toward the parking lot. Mitch turned at the door and gave me a warm grin. Then he was gone.

I stood in the hall among a bunch of piles of kid laundry on the floor and I stared at the door long after they left.

They came back over an hour later, when I had the futon out and made up for Billy to use. Load one was in the dryer and load two was in the washer.

There was a drugstore not five minutes away, so by the time they got back, I was worried. I was in the kitchen inventorying my grocery supplies as I didn't think, leaving Bill in cuffs with two officers of the law, that the kids were heading back there anytime soon. And kids needed food.

When they came back, I didn't have to wonder what took them so long, considering both kids raced in carrying a big plastic Target bag each. Mitch was carrying four, not to mention he had a brand-new car booster seat.

I watched Mitch set the booster seat on the floor by the wall next to the front door. Then my eyes moved and I stared at the kids, who ran directly to my couch and dumped their bags. After witnessing that, I turned my stare back to Mitch.

"That looks like a lot of shampoo," I remarked, but a new kind of whoosh was surging through the region of my belly. This had to do with the Target bags, the booster seat and the warm look on Mitch's face as he followed the kids into the house.

"Look Auntie Mara! Look! Look! Look!" Billie shrieked, digging frantically through her bag. Finding what she was looking for, she turned. Her arms were straight up in the air. I saw she held a piece of plastic on which dangled supremely girlie ponytail holders with what looked like plastic butterflies attached to them. They were clenched in one little-girl fist, and equally girlie barrettes, with what looked like hearts and stars, were clenched in the other. *"Mitch bought me butterflies!"* she screeched.

The idea of super-hot, super-gorgeous, super-*masculine* Detective Mitch Lawson buying girlie hair shit made my mouth drop open. My gaze slid back to super-hot, super-gorgeous, super-masculine Detective Mitch Lawson, who was dumping his bags on the bar.

I managed to hide my shock before his gaze came to me.

"Please tell me you bought shampoo," I said to him.

His eyes smiled and he opened his mouth to speak, but Billie tossed her prized hair shit aside and started digging through her bag again. She was pulling stuff out at random, all the while informing me, "He got me girl shampoo and he got Billy boy shampoo and he bought Billy new jeans and he bought me a jeans *skirt* and it has a pink ruffle at the bottom!" she shouted breathlessly and then kept going. "It matches the pink T-shirt with the flower on it." She pulled out the T-shirt, whipped around to me, stretched the tee out on a muddled diagonal across her front and gave me a wonky grin. "Isn't it *pretty*?"

It was. It was adorable. Furthermore, I didn't know there were such things as *girl* shampoo and *boy* shampoo. Shampoo was shampoo. Wasn't it?

My eyes slid back to Mitch. He was leaning against the

bar that separated the kitchen from the living room and he was watching Billie while smiling.

Oh God.

"It's very pretty, baby," I said to Billie, as she clutched the shirt to her chest like she wanted to graft it to her skin, leaned forward and breathed, "I *know*!" Then she whirled back to the bags.

I decided to get some order, so I told the kids, "All right, sort out what's what. Billy, take your stuff to your room, help Billie get her stuff to our room and anything that needs to go in the bathroom, put it in there. All right?"

"Yeah, Auntie Mara," Billy agreed, looked to his sister and said, "Come on."

Thus started bag rustling and running back and forth into various rooms. This I ignored because I needed to get something straight with Mitch.

So the minute the kids' attention was on their chore, I called, "Mitch."

He turned to me, leaned into his forearms on the bar and his gaze leveled on mine. I instantly forgot what I needed to get straight when I started drowning in the depths of his soulful brown eyes.

"These are groceries," he dipped his head to the bags. "The kids told me what they liked to have around the house and I got some shit I figured you'd need."

"Mitch—"

He kept talking. "Colorado law says kids need to be in car seats until they're eight." He tilted his head behind him. "That's for Billie. Got an extra one for my truck."

An extra one for his truck?

I didn't get a chance to ask, Mitch kept speaking. "You need to give me your numbers and you need to get your phone so I can program mine in yours."

"Mitch—"

He pulled out his phone and talked over me. "Get your phone, Mara."

"Mitch—"

"Get your phone."

"Mitch!"

Suddenly, he reached his long arm out, caught my wrist and used it to pull me forward. This made me lean across the counter toward the bar attached to it and he was leaning across the bar toward the counter where I was. Then his hand slid down my wrist and his fingers closed around mine.

"Sweetheart, get your phone."

I swallowed then whispered, "Um...you're being very cool and I really appreciate it but, uh—"

"Get your phone."

"Mitch, I appreciate it, but this isn't your problem. You can't buy the kids—"

"Mara, phone."

I tried to pull my fingers from his, his only tightened, so I gave up and said softly, "I'm not comfortable with—"

He moved around the bar, my arm moving with him as he did this because he didn't let my hand go. Suddenly he was in my space, our arms bent, our hands pressed to his chest and his other arm was around my waist. This meant he was pressed to me, I was pressed to him and our faces were super close.

"Mara, baby, get...your...phone," he ordered gently.

"'Kay," I whispered because, really, what else could I do?

He let me go. I got my phone. He programmed my numbers into his then he programmed his numbers into mine. When he was done he called out to the kids to tell them he was going, and they raced from wherever they were in the apartment to say good-bye. He lifted Billie up and kissed her cheek, which made her giggle. He shook Billy's hand solemnly, which made Billy's chest puff out and his shoulders straighten.

Then he opened the door, looked at me but said to the kids, "See you guys tomorrow."

Tomorrow?

Before I could ask, I was staring at a closed door.

"I like him!" Billie shouted. "He's nice and he bought me butterflies and flowers!"

I liked him too. In fact, I was back to loving him even though he thought I had my head up my ass.

He wasn't just a nice guy. He was a really, freaking great one.

When he wasn't being a jerk or scary, of course.

I was in trouble.

The rest of the evening was taken up with washing and folding laundry and me trying to get the kids sorted. Mitch bought Billy more than jeans. He bought him three pairs of jeans and also bought him some T-shirts and a baseball mitt. Billie's flower T-shirt and jeans skirt with cute pink ruffle was only the favorite of the three outfits Mitch bought her. It was her favorite because it was the cutest and girliest but only by a small margin. There were also two more plastic cards filled with girlie hair shit and a tiny, fluffy pink teddy bear.

Yeah, I was back to loving him.

Crap.

It took a while to get to sleep. This was not only because I was used to sleeping alone and having the whole bed to myself. The entire day, and every encounter I'd had with Detective Mitch Lawson, was dancing in my head. These thoughts alternated with Bill threatening me, and neither was conducive to peace of mind.

Finally, I slept. Which brought me to now.

I did my bathroom thing, went to the kitchen, made a pot of coffee, had a shower and did my after-shower thing. I got Billy up so he could take a shower while I did my makeup thing. Then I got Billie up so she could take a shower in my shower while I kept my eye on her and did my hair drying thing. We had a drama when Billie changed her mind about which was her favorite new outfit that she wanted to wear that day. Then she changed her mind again, which necessitated her changing her outfit.

We finally had that sorted and I was in the kitchen, the kids on the stools opposite me with glasses of milk in front of them. I was drinking a cup of coffee that, by this time, I desperately needed, while talking to the kids about what they wanted for breakfast. Breakfast groceries were part of what Mitch bought, including pancake mix, eggs, bread and three types of jelly.

I was also eyeing the living room, which had stacks of kids' folded clothing on every surface. Most of it, I'd discovered, didn't deserve to be laundered because it was worn or stained and should be thrown out. And I was thinking that my being able to be freakishly tidy and having a modicum of peace of mind because I was able to control my surroundings was a thing of the past. Then there was a knock at the door.

I blinked at the door. I was stuck in my head because I was scared to death about my future, the kids' future, Bill's threats and how I was going to clothe, feed and house three humans. Not to mention all things Detective Mitch Lawson. So the knock at the door coming so early in the morning threw me.

It didn't throw Billie. She jumped off her stool and raced to the door shouting, "I'll get it!"

"Billie, don't." I moved out of the kitchen, taking my coffee cup with me. "Let me check the peephole."

She was turning the door handle desperately this way

and that, ready to welcome whoever was out there whole-heartedly. These efforts were to no avail as the door was locked and chained.

I looked out the peephole and saw Mitch.

Oh God.

His hair was partially wet, the drying ends curling around his ears, neck and collar. I knew he was ready for work because he was wearing a light blue chambray shirt and a dark olive-green kickass sports jacket. Detective Mitch Lawson work clothes.

Jeez, he was hot.

"Who is it?" Billie asked.

"It's Mitch," I mumbled, gently moving her out of the way and unlocking the door.

"Yippee!" she cried and then shouted to the door, "Hi, Mitch! I'm wearing my new outfit!"

I opened the door to a smiling so much he was nearly laughing Detective Mitch Lawson.

Full-on belly whoosh.

"Hey," I said, standing between the doorframe and the door.

"Hey," he replied, not standing but moving *toward me*.

Seeing as I didn't move, his hand went to my belly at the last minute. He gently shoved me inside as he came inside with me.

"Hey, Mitch," Billy, who'd kept his seat at the bar, called.

"Hey, Billy," Mitch answered, shutting the door behind him. "Did I miss breakfast?" he asked, and my lungs seized.

"No!" Billie shouted. "We were just deciding what to have!"

"Eggs," Mitch decided for everyone, and I stood where

I was, watching him move into the kitchen. Then I stayed where I was as I watched him move around the kitchen talking to the kids, pouring himself a cup of coffee, opening and closing cupboards, getting stuff out and, lastly and most scarily, *making himself at home.*

Woodenly, I walked to the kitchen, stopped by the end of the counter and asked, "What are you doing?"

He had the eggs, bread and a bowl out and he didn't even look at me when he replied, "Makin' breakfast." I opened my mouth to protest, but he kept talking. "Do me a favor, sweetheart, put in some toast."

My mouth was still open. I started to form words when his beautiful eyes came to me, and my breath got caught in my throat.

"What hours do you work today?" he asked.

I blinked then answered, "I'm on late shifts this week. Noon to nine...now, Mitch—"

"I'm takin' the kids to school," he announced, cutting me off and looking down at the bowl into which he started cracking eggs. "I gotta talk to the people in the office. I'll pick them up this afternoon and take them to Ma."

"Ma?" I breathed, and he tossed some eggshells into the sink and looked at me.

"Yeah, my ma. She works part time at my sister's shop. I called her last night. Her schedule is flexible. I'll pick them up, take them to her place, get them after I'm done at work and I'll hang here with them until you get home. You'll need to give me a set of keys."

I swallowed. Then I whispered, "Keys?"

"Keys," he nodded, his eyes swept me up and down and then quietly he said, "Baby, toast."

My body jolted, my gaze slid to the kids, who were

watching this avidly, before I went to the bread, put down my mug and pulled the toaster away from the wall.

Then I pulled myself together and started, "Mitch—"

"You need to talk to your boss," he told me.

"I know," I replied. "But Mitch—"

"And friends," he interrupted. "Child Protection Services are gonna talk to everyone you know. They should have a heads up. You'll need to get school runs sorted and have somethin' set up for after school and weekend days you work. I'll do what I can. Ma said she'd do what she can. LaTanya only works twenty hours a week and she'll probably pitch in. Bray's hours are like yours so he can probably help out if we need him to. But this is all short term. Long term, you're gonna need to get childcare sorted out. With me?"

Wow, he'd thought about this more than I had.

"Um..." I mumbled.

"They'll also inspect this place," Mitch went on. "You'll need beds. They'll talk to you and they'll set you up with foster parent classes. I'll stop by the management office and see if they got any open townhomes in that block across the creek. The kids need more space but you do this, you need to be close to your posse."

"Mitch—"

He dumped the scrambled eggs into the waiting melted butter in the skillet and looked at me. "Get the butter and jelly, baby."

I moved to the fridge and I did this mostly because if he told me to throw myself in front of a train but did it adding the word "baby," I would have done it. I put the butter and all three jars of jelly on the bar in front of the kids and turned to Mitch just as the toast popped up. So I slid down the counter to open a drawer and get a knife. I pulled out the toast, put in more bread and started spreading butter.

"Maybe we should talk about this when the kids—" I began.

"They gotta eat and they gotta get to school," Mitch cut me off again, moving the cooking eggs around the skillet. "You also gotta look into changing their school when all this is formalized. They'll need to be moved to a school closer to home."

"Are we movin' in with you, Auntie Mara?" Billie asked, her tone slightly confused, and I turned to her.

Then I pressed my lips together because her face looked slightly confused too, and I preferred Billie looking happy and carefree.

"Yeah, honey, I hope so. Your daddy needs to sort a few things out," I told her quietly.

She stared at me uncertain and I didn't like that either.

"I think it's cool," Billy put in. "Auntie Mara's house is clean. Bray and Brent and Derek and LaTanya and Mitch all live close by and she's always got food."

Billie's teeth started worrying her lip as she studied her brother. Then she asked, "But who's gonna stay with daddy?"

"Who cares?" Billy asked back, and I moved to the counter.

"Billie," I called, and her worried eyes moved to mine.

I leaned into my forearms on the counter.

"I know you're worried about your daddy, but he's an adult so he needs to worry about himself," I told her. "You're a kid, and that means, while you're a kid, someone's supposed to worry about you, take care of you, make sure you have food in your belly and shampoo for your hair."

I got up on my toes and leaned closer to her as my voice dipped quiet.

"I love you, baby, and I want that person to be me. I want to make sure you're always okay and not have to worry that you aren't eating and your clothes aren't clean. And the only way for me not to have to worry about that is for me to take care of you myself. If your daddy gets himself sorted out, we'll see. But in the meantime, will you let me do that for you? Make sure you have shampoo, food and someone to look out for you? Is that okay with you?"

"But daddy will be all alone," she replied in a small voice.

"I know, sweetie," I whispered. "But I can't help him, he has to help himself. What I *can* do is look after you." I reached out a hand and set it flat on the bar in front of her. "And I *want* to. I want you here with me, Billie. Will you stay with me?"

"You want me here with you?" she asked.

"Yeah," I answered.

"Do you want Billy?" she asked.

"Definitely," I answered.

She stared at me then her eyes moved beyond me to Mitch before she looked back to me. "I like my new shampoo, it smells pretty."

I smiled at her. "Is that a yes, baby?"

"Are you lonely without us?" she whispered.

"I worry about you when I'm not with you," I told her. "If you're with me, I don't have to worry anymore."

"I don't want you to worry." She was still whispering. "But I don't want daddy to worry either."

"Dad won't worry," Billy muttered, and Billie's head swung to him.

"Look at me," I called quickly as her lip started to tremble and Billie's eyes came back to mine. "You don't have to make a decision now. Just have Mitch's eggs. Go to school and you can think about it. We'll talk about it again when you're ready. Is that a deal?"

She took in a breath then nodded. "Deal," she whispered.

"Okay, baby," I whispered back.

Then I felt heat at my back as Mitch leaned into me to set two plates filled with fluffy scrambled eggs and buttered toast, with cutlery resting on the sides of the plates, in front of both of the kids. Once he'd done this he stayed where his was, both fists on the counter on either side of me, his body pressed to mine.

"Eat up, we gotta get on the road," he ordered.

Billie looked down at her food. Billy looked down at Mitch's fists on the counter. I tried to straighten and slide away, which meant one of Mitch's hands left the counter and his arm curled around my belly.

"You want toast, sweetheart?" he asked quietly in my ear.

I figured I'd throw up if I tried to eat anything. But I nodded because I was hoping he was offering to make me some, and he couldn't make me toast pressed into and holding me. Therefore, I nodded.

I was right. He let me go and I heard the bread bag rustling.

Billy's eyes came to my face and he studied me, looking about fifty years older than he actually was. Then he started eating.

Billie was already wolfing her food down at the same time inspecting the unusual plethora of jelly at her disposal.

I was thinking of school runs, Child Protection Services, buying new beds, when I'd have time to take foster parent classes and Mitch's "ma." I was thinking about this so hard Mitch was in front of me holding a plate of buttered toast before I knew it.

I looked down at the toast then up at Mitch. The instant my eyes hit his, I knew it was definitely time to take control.

I took the plate, set it on the counter and asked him quietly, "Can we talk?"

He studied my face, and I watched his eyes grow guarded. Then he nodded.

I walked around him, saying to the kids, "I'll be right back." Then I walked to the front door and out into the breezeway.

Mitch followed and closed the door behind him.

I sucked in breath and pulled up the courage to look him in the eye.

"Can you take a minute to explain to me what's happening?" I asked.

"Thought I did that inside, Mara," Mitch, eyes still guarded, answered.

"No, I mean from here on in. With Bill and the kids and Child Protection Services," I explained.

He kept watching me and finally he nodded.

"Bill's been arrested," Mitch answered. "I'll know more when I get into the station. Child Protection Services have been called. Normally, Bill would decide who looks after his kids. Considering the state we found him in, I made that decision. They'll be contacting you and they'll do it soon because usually they'd decide who was an appropriate guardian if Bill was incapable of making that decision, which I deemed he was. While Bill stays incarcerated, they'll stay with you. If Bill gets out, then you'll need to convince Child Protection Services he's unfit and then prove to them you are. If the last happens, it won't be difficult from what I've seen. But to be awarded guardianship, you'll have to take foster parent classes." He paused and finished, "So that's where we are."

I nodded then asked, "Why was Bill arrested?"

Mitch stared at me a minute, his expression shifting quickly to one that said he didn't know what to make of me.

Then he answered, "Mara, he was in possession of illegal substances and I'm a police officer. We tend to do something when we see someone in possession of something illegal. That's kind of our job."

This was true. Shit. I was such a dork!

Though possession of illegal substances wasn't *that* bad unless you were in possession of a lot of them and, from what I saw, Bill wasn't. That said, he'd been arrested twice that I knew. The first time he got community service. The second time wasn't a big deal; his jail sentence was six months and he'd been paroled after three. It was only Billy then, Billie hadn't been born yet, and I'd looked after him those three months. It had been tough but I did it. Then again, Billy was a toddler, so he hadn't been able to dress himself. And now both of them could dress themselves, so maybe it wouldn't be that tough this time around.

But three strikes wouldn't be good. And I'd walked a police officer into his house.

Damn.

"Right," I whispered and noted Mitch was studying me closely, which made me feel weird and it reminded me I needed to get this done. "Can I ask why you need to talk to the office at school?"

His head tipped slightly to the side, like he was confused, before he replied, "In order to introduce myself, tell them I'm a cop, explain what's going on and get my name on the list of who they can expect to drop the kids off, pick them up and who they should call in case of emergency."

"My name is already on that list," I informed him.

"I guessed that, but now my name needs to be on it," Mitch informed me.

"Why?" I asked.

"Why?" he repeated.

"Yes, why?" I reiterated.

It was then his head straightened and his eyes slightly narrowed. "Were you in there with the kids and me just now?"

"Um...yes."

"So you know why."

I shook my head. "No, I don't."

He took in a breath that appeared to be an effort to remain calm then explained, "While you get shit sorted, Ma and I are gonna help out."

No. No, he and his mother were not. His mother was probably a Ten Point Five too, and Ten Point Fives didn't help out Two Point Fives. That was law in Mara World.

I straightened my shoulders and said firmly, "Thank you, that's very kind. In fact, um...all you've done is, uh...very kind, but I've got it now."

This time his eyes fully narrowed. "You've got it now?"

"Yes," I answered.

"You've got it now," he said disbelievingly.

"Um...yeah," I repeated.

"You work twelve to nine," he reminded me.

This was true, this week. The other shift was nine thirty to six thirty, which wasn't much better. How I was going to pick them up, look after them *and* sell beds so I could keep them fed was unknown to me, but I'd figure something out.

"Yes, I know," I told Mitch.

"So explain to me, when you gotta work, how 'you've got it now'?" Mitch demanded to know. He looked like he was getting angry.

"I just do." I provided no information and then decided to be polite but move this on so I could move onto whatever was next for me, Billy and Billie. "Really, I want to thank you because you've been really cool about all this and um... with the kids and everything, but I'll take it from here."

"You'll take it from here," he repeated, and I wished he'd stop repeating after me because it was freaking me out.

"Yes," I replied.

He studied me again. Then he said, with what seemed like strained patience, "I don't think you get it, sweetheart. I told you I'd help out and I'm helping out."

Jeez, I wished he wasn't so damned nice.

"Yes, I understand that, but what I'm telling *you* is that you don't have to, um... get involved. I'm good. The kids will be good. I've got it now."

"You're a single woman who works full time selling mattresses, Mara, and suddenly you got two kids on your hands. There is no way you've got it now."

My freak-out was beginning to melt to anger. I crossed my arms on my chest and informed him, "We'll be perfectly fine."

"Not without help you won't," he shot back.

"Mitch, I've got this."

"Mara, there is no way in hell you've got this."

That was when I lost it and I threw up my hands, hissing, "Jeez!" I leaned in. "I'm letting you off the hook! You don't need to wade in Mitch. We'll be fine. You can go..." I hesitated, looked at his door then back at him and finished, "Do what you do, enjoy your life, whatever."

"I didn't ask to be let off the hook," he pointed out.

"Yeah, nice guys don't but they still want to be," I replied.

"Don't tell me what I want, Mara. I'm seein' with this shit that, again, you have no clue what I want."

"Okay, then I'll tell you what *I* want. What I want is not to be standing out in the breezeway arguing with you when

I've got a million things on my mind. What *I* want is for you to stop butting into *my* life by getting out of it!"

My anger had built up so quickly I didn't realize his had too and his surpassed mine. But I noticed this when he leaned into me, his face hard, his eyes flashing with a muscle jumping in his cheek.

"I was right. Your head is right up your ass, but the problem now is you got two kids you gotta worry about and you can't stumble through life with your head up your ass at the same time taking care of two kids."

In our anger race, at his words, I pulled ahead and leaned into him too.

"Stop telling me I have my head up my ass, Detective Mitch Lawson. I've got my eyes wide open. I've *always* had my eyes wide open."

"You're totally fuckin' blind."

"You don't know me enough to say something like that," I snapped.

"Mara, I know you a lot more than you think, and you're not only blind, you're clueless."

"I'm not clueless!" I hissed.

He clenched his jaw and stared at me. Then he leaned back and swept me from top-to-toe with his eyes before they locked on mine.

"Thought it was worth it," he muttered like he was talking to himself. "Totally fuckin' wrong. Not fuckin' worth it."

I knew what he was saying. I knew exactly what he was saying. I should have been ecstatic that he figured it out. Instead it felt like he'd shoved a knife in my heart and twisted.

Before I could get used to the pain, Mitch concluded, "You got it, baby? Go for it." Then he turned and sauntered through the breezeway.

I saw him lift a hand and his chin slightly, and my

horrified eyes went to Bradon and Brent's door to see Brent standing there. His head moved back and forth between Mitch jogging down the steps and me standing, breathing heavily outside my door.

"Hey Brent," I called, my voice trembling just as the tears that I felt were in my eyes were doing.

"Hey girl, you okay?" Brent asked.

"Perfect!" I lied, trying to sound chirpy and totally failing, so I decided to escape. "See you!" I said and I turned to my door, opened it and dashed inside.

Billy and Billie looked at me.

"Mitch can't take you to school today, but I can. After school you're going to hang with me at the store," I informed them. "Won't that be fun?"

Billie's arms went up in the air. I noticed she had grape jelly smeared on her face, and I also noticed more than a little of it was smeared on the bar and her hands, and she shouted, "Yippee!"

Mental note: Do not leave Billie alone with the jelly.

I looked to Billy to see his eyes go to the door and he stared at it contemplatively for several seconds before his eyes came back to me. Then his face went hard.

Then he said, "Okay, Auntie Mara."

I closed my eyes. Then I sighed. Then I hustled the kids through the rest of their morning and took them to school.

# CHAPTER SEVEN

## People Like Me

I LOOKED THROUGH Mr. Pierson's office window to the cavernous space that was filled with bed and mattress displays.

Yesterday, my first day with the kids, I'd finally pulled myself together enough to remember that Roberta had the day off. So I'd called her and told her all that went down (well, most of it, I left out all things Mitch). I asked if she could help out, and she'd instantly said yes. So I took my lunch hour to pick up the kids from school, took them to Roberta's and went to go get them after work.

Now they were out in the store. Billie, luckily being quiet for once, was standing next to Roberta, who was with customers. Billy was sprawled on a bed playing a video game that Roberta brought in to help him fill the time.

Yesterday I'd also told Mr. Pierson about my change in life circumstances and asked for some leeway while I got the kids sorted. Not surprisingly, he'd agreed.

"Can't make it a habit, Mara, honey, but until you set them up, do what you need to do," he'd said. He then asked, "Now, how can Mrs. Pierson and I help?"

That was Mr. Pierson. Totally a nice guy.

Therefore, today the kids were in the store with me until

I could sort out afterschool childcare. But first I had to sort out how I was going to pay for afterschool childcare. I'd called a couple of places and what they'd quoted, especially since the hours I needed them ran late, was a resounding strike to my budget for just one kid. Two was crippling.

I had a nest egg, which I had carefully built up so any unforeseen emergencies wouldn't crush me. Once I had that at five thousand dollars, I let it sit in a savings account and started to build up my "I'm Going to Own My Own House One Day, Damn It" account. This was building up too and was relatively healthy. Not to the point I could buy my own house, or even close, but it wasn't anything to sneeze at.

Pierson's Mattress and Bed was a big warehouse store. We had all your mattress and bed needs. Including entire bedroom suites and contracts with contractors who would build built-in wardrobes and units that surrounded beds and stuff like that. Our price range fit everyone's budget. I didn't do too badly. We moved a lot of product because everyone knew they could find something at Pierson's and buy it from friendly, helpful salespeople. Then, after purchase, they had their wares delivered on time, during an unheard of two-hour window, instead of having to wait all day for the guys to show up whenever they showed up. Mr. Pierson guaranteed it on all of his commercials. That two-hour window set him above all his competitors. No one wanted to hang around waiting for mattresses all day.

This meant I lived well. I had a nice car. Great furniture. Decent quality clothes. A nest egg. The money to be able to afford to buy my friends really, freaking great birthday and Christmas presents.

But I didn't live large. No way.

And I didn't want Billy and Billie to live small. Just taking on afterschool childcare, living small was exactly where life was leading us, and I didn't know how to do anything about that.

Then again, they'd been living small for a while—tiny, so anything I could do was better than what they were used to.

"You need beds," Mr. Pierson announced behind me, and I turned to him.

He was a couple inches shorter than me when I was in heels. He was also very skinny and had white hair sprinkled not very generously with black cut short around the sides and back of his head. The rest was bald. On the looks scale, he was around a Three. Add his cheery personality, his kindness and his generosity and he was totally an Eight Point Seven Five.

He was sitting behind his desk, smiling at me.

"Yes, Child Protection Services are coming around on Friday and I need to get their room sorted before they do."

"Right," Mr. Pierson nodded. "Take two of the Spring Deluxe Singles. I'll give them to you wholesale, with a twenty percent discount, plus your employee discount added on to that."

My mouth dropped open. The Spring Deluxe mattresses were the best of the best. The cream of the crop. I had one and I loved it. It was ultracomfy.

But they were expensive. I'd had to save for three months *and* buy mine during a store-wide sale. I could only afford it because Mr. Pierson let us use our employee discounts, even during store-wide sales.

"I—" I began.

He waved his hand in front of his face. "Otis overordered. For months we've been sittin' on an inventory of Spring Deluxes we can't move. They're pricey. People don't often spring for the Spring Deluxe, not even when *you're* sellin' them." He grinned at me and continued, "Why he ordered that many, I do not know."

I didn't either, but then again, this was Otis. It was my experience that everyone had an annoying cousin, and Otis was Mr. Pierson's. I figured Mr. Pierson kept him working in the warehouse because no one else would keep him working for more than a couple of days due to the fact that Otis wasn't all that smart. He was a nice enough guy (although I had to admit I thought he was creepy and Roberta agreed) but he wasn't all that smart. It wasn't a nice thing to say, but it was true.

"They're just takin' up space in the warehouse. Space I need. You'd be doin' me a favor," Mr. Pierson finished.

He was full of it. He was losing money on the deal he offered me. Big time. He was just being nice.

"Mr. Pierson—" I started but stopped when his eyes caught mine.

"Kids need good beds," he said softly.

He was right. They did.

God, I loved my boss.

"I love my boss," I told him, and his face melted into a smile, the whole of it, just like he always smiled. I loved my boss and I also loved his smiles.

"You're off tomorrow. I'll set up delivery," he told me.

"Thanks," I whispered.

"Mitch!" I heard Billie screech from the showroom floor. I whirled around to look back out the window only to see Billie tearing through the maze of beds in a direct trajectory to Mitch.

She aimed, she fired, she hit her target, throwing her arms around his hips and giving him a big hug.

I watched Mitch's hand settle on her hair. Then I looked at all that was Mitch and I really wished that I wasn't still kind of in love with him.

What on earth was he doing there?

I turned back to Mr. Pierson, who was also looking out the window, undoubtedly at Mitch.

"That's my, um…neighbor. I think I need to go talk to him," I said to Mr. Pierson.

His body visibly jolted and his eyes slid to me. "Neighbor?"

"Look!" I heard Billie shout, and I turned back to the window. "I'm wearin' one of the outfits you bought me!" She had let him go and was yanking her T-shirt out at the bottom hem to show him.

I watched Mitch smile at her, and he said something I couldn't hear because, unlike Billie, he wasn't shouting.

Then I felt a whoosh surge through my belly at witnessing his smile.

I forced myself to turn back to Mr. Pierson, who was now standing with his eyes back at the window.

"Yes, my neighbor. Do you mind…?" I trailed off, and he looked at me. Then he looked to the window. Then back at me, and his eyes quickly darted the length of me.

Then he grinned a grin I'd never seen him grin before, and he advised, "Don't forget to ask him if he needs a bed."

I nodded, knowing there was no way in hell I was going to ask Detective Mitch Lawson if he needed a bed, and moved quickly from the office.

The instant I hit the showroom Mitch's eyes came to me. The instant his eyes came to me, my eyes went to Billy. He was still sprawled on the bed, the video game in his hands but now his gaze was on Mitch and his little face was hard. He didn't, I noticed, throw himself at Mitch, and I wasn't certain he'd even said hello.

My head swung the other way, and I saw Roberta with her customers. She was trying to pay attention to them while at the same time eye up Mitch. It was a name she knew, and now that she had a handsome face, fabulous hair, fantastic body and great clothes to put with that name, she was obviously having trouble listening to her customers.

I made myself look back at Mitch just as Billie ran to me, grabbed my hand and tugged me toward Mitch, telling me, "Look, Auntie Mara! Mitch is here!"

"I see that, honey," I murmured to her as I got closer and closer to Mitch.

She kept tugging at me. "Isn't it *great* that he's *here* so he can see my *outfit*?" she asked.

"It's awesome," I muttered as we stopped in front of Mitch.

*"I know,"* she breathed.

"Mara," Mitch greeted, and his face was closed, no warmth, no smile, nothing.

Yep, he'd figured it out. Ten Point Fives didn't give Two Point Fives warmth. Disdain, often. Shared breathing space, yes, but only because everyone needed oxygen. Warmth, no.

That knife that I hadn't had time to pull out of my heart twisted.

"Mitch," I replied.

"You got a place we can talk privately?" he asked.

I stared up at him wondering what this was all about. Then I decided my best bet was to find out and get him on his way as fast as I could. So I nodded.

"Break room," I answered and bent to Billie. "Do me a favor, baby, and go sit with your brother." She nodded up at me, and I added, "And no jumping on beds or racing through the showroom. Just sit quiet with Billy until I come back. Can you do that for me?"

"Sure, Auntie Mara," Billie chirped, grinned at Mitch then skipped toward Billy, who was still staring at Mitch with his hard face. Billie climbed up on the bed then landed full body on her brother.

She was so totally not going to do that favor for me.

I looked back at Mitch to see his eyes were on Billy. "If you'd like to follow me," I invited, and he tore his gaze from Billy to nod at me.

I led the way to the door of the back hall, punched in the code, opened it, moved through the back hall with Mitch following me and then I turned us into the break room.

I flipped on the light, and Mitch closed us in.

I sucked in breath when my eyes hit his no longer soulful, now expressionless, still beautiful ones.

Fast. I needed to do this fast.

"Is everything okay?" I asked.

"We got a problem."

Oh boy.

He kept talking before I even had time to brace.

"Remember I said that if your cousin was all the kinds of messes you know then he was probably all the kinds of messes I know?"

This wasn't starting out so great.

"Yeah," I replied hesitantly.

"Well it's confirmed. He's all the kinds of messes I know."

I felt my body grow solid, my eyes locked on his and I whispered, "Oh shit."

"That about covers it," Mitch agreed.

"Tell me." I was still whispering.

"Bill's had a bad coupla days. He's detoxing and it hasn't been pretty, mostly because he's hooked on smack *and* he's hooked on speed *and* he's a drunk and there's likely other shit he's hooked on. He's a user and he's a dealer. He's real good at the first, sucks at the last. Not popular with the suppliers in Denver mostly because he's fucked half of them over and the other half he owes money. He also owes money to a variety of other people, none of them people you wanna owe shit. He's recently devolved to selling information, which makes him even *less* popular, and he was already pretty fuckin' unpopular. And if that wasn't enough, when they went through his house they found a shitload of H *and* E, enough that he's been charged with intent to distribute. And proving he's not just an assclown but a serious fuckin' assclown, they also found stolen property that we reckon he either stole himself, he stole from someone else who stole it or he was gonna fence it for somebody."

"This doesn't sound good." *Still* I was whispering, but now it was because I was more than a little scared for my cousin.

"It isn't," Mitch confirmed. "The good news is, you got the kids out in time, and we got to him in time." He hesitated, studied me a moment and then continued, "But you should know, Mara, once he detoxes and goes to lockup, he's got so many enemies, it isn't likely he'll be real safe there. That said, we know this, and he'll be placed in protective custody so at least he's safer there than he was out on the street. And Billy and Billie are a fuckuva lot safer with you than they were with him because there was a good chance they'd be in the wrong place at the wrong time. Their home was the wrong place to be and, until you intervened, they had no way to avoid it."

"Great," I muttered, looked away and bit my lip.

"Look on the bright side, Mara," Mitch's voice came at me, "right now everyone is safe."

I nodded, trying to find the bright side. "Okay."

"Got more to tell you."

I looked up at him and scrunched my nose not wanting to hear more, but I still repeated, "Okay."

He watched my nose scrunch and didn't speak, not for

a long time, long after I'd unscrunched my nose. In fact, he seemed to lose focus as his eyes settled on my mouth. Then his eyes moved to mine and he regained focus.

"That guy that Billy said was visiting?" he asked.

"Yeah," I replied.

"Got a feeling his name is Grigori Lescheva. He's Russian mob, and when I say that I mean he's the top guy in the Russian mob."

This didn't sound good. On all the television shows the Russian mob guys were the worst.

"That doesn't sound good either," I pointed out when Mitch said no more.

"Nothing about this shit is good. Lescheva's just the worst part of it. Sources say Lescheva's settin' up a power play to claim new territory. Bill was passin' him info about competitors. At first he was doing this because Lescheva was paying him. In the end he was doing this because Bill owed Lescheva. You do not want to deal with Lescheva at all. But if you gotta deal with him, you want him to owe you for whatever you got, not the other way around. Your cousin knows every scumbag in town. He's sold to them. He's bought from them. He's partied with them. He owes them money. They've fucked him over or he's fucked them over. He's been busy since he hit the city and therefore he's a good informant. But there's only so much he has, only so much he can give. Especially now that no one likes him, no one trusts him and most everyone wants something from him. And some of them, him not breathin' is what they want. His usefulness to Lescheva was diminishing, which means Lescheva would be calling on the debt. Bill is an assclown and a nuisance and not worth the effort for most unless the opportunity presented itself. That is, he was until he started feedin' Lescheva information. But

Lescheva doesn't like debts and he'd call it, one way or the other. If Bill couldn't pay, Lescheva'd get creative in finding a way to get it."

I stared at Mitch, wrapped my arms around my ribs and focused on not crying and/or freaking out.

"That *really* doesn't sound good," I whispered so quietly *I* could barely hear me.

"The good news for you is Bill's being held without bail. He's considered a flight risk."

"Okay," I whispered, though his good news was relative.

"That means the kids will remain with you if CPS approves you fostering them after they visit, which they'll do."

I nodded.

"The other good news is that with the evidence they have and the fact that this is strike three, it's unlikely he'll be breathing free for a while."

Damn. He knew this was Bill's strike three. Of course he would. It was the computer age. He probably discovered that in, like, two seconds.

Bill's blood flowed through me. No wonder he had no more warm smiles for me.

I nodded again even as I felt the knife twist.

"That means, while he's inside, you can work to make that permanent."

Yet again, I nodded.

"I'll text you names and numbers of lawyers who can help you out with that. You might as well start now."

"Thanks," I whispered, wondering where I'd find the money to pay a lawyer.

He stared at me. Then he turned his head and looked at the wall that separated the break room from the showroom. Then he looked back at me.

"They doin' okay?" he asked.

"Um...yes," I answered. "Billie asks after him. Billy seems fine with everything."

It was his turn to nod.

Okay, it was nice of him to come all the way out to Pierson's to tell me this, but I had to shut this down and move on. Again.

So I went about doing that.

"Um...thanks for coming all the way out here to, uh... keep mc in thc loop."

I watched his jaw clench. Then he looked to thc side and muttered, "Clueless."

Oh boy. Here we go.

"Mitch—" I started to shut it down, and his eyes sliced back to me.

"You workin' this weekend?"

My head did a little shake at his confusing question. "Pardon?"

"This weekend, you workin'?" he repeated with slight amendments.

"Um...yes."

"Both days?"

"Yes, Mitch, but—"

"Who's lookin' out for them while you work?"

I straightened my shoulders and admitted, "I haven't got that far."

He glared at me and muttered, "Right."

I sucked in a breath through my nostrils and started, "Mitch—"

He cut me off. "Twelve to nine?"

My head tipped to the side. "Pardon?"

"Your shifts this weekend. Twelve to nine?"

"Yes, but—"

"I'll be at your place at eleven," he declared, and I blinked.

"Um...what?" I whispered.

"Mara, I'm speakin' English."

"But, I—"

Mitch finished for me. "Need right now to get your head out of your ass."

Oh hell. Not this again.

My arms uncrossed and my hands went to my hips.

"Mitch—"

"And, I'll add, clue in," Mitch went on.

"Seriously, that is not nice, and you have no right to speak to me that way," I snapped.

"You got a living, breathing, responsible human being standin' right in front of you offerin' to do you a favor. Not a small one, like changin' a washer, but a big one, like makin' sure those kids are safe, they eat somethin' and they get to bed on time. Now any person who does not have their head up their ass and isn't entirely fuckin' clueless would take up that offer 'cause kids need to eat, be safe and get to bed on time. You, for whatever twisted, fucked up reason, are gearin' up to throw that offer in my face. So, even though I know I'm wastin' my breath, I'll still advise you to get your head outta your fuckin' ass, clue in and accept my offer."

I glared at him, and before my temper caught up to my brain, I bit out, "Fine."

His eyebrows went up. "Fine?"

"Yes, fine," I clipped. "Although I'm not all fired up to let a big, fat jerk look after them, you're right. I haven't been able to sort out anyone to look after them while I'm working. I need someone to look after them while I'm working and although you're a big, fat jerk to me, you aren't to them and Billie likes you. So, fine. Thanks," I expressed my gratitude acidly. "If you could watch them this weekend that would be a huge help."

After I finished he stared at me. I glared at him.

Then he said, "Great. I'll be there at eleven."

"Perfect." My tone was still injected with acid.

He didn't move. I didn't either.

Then for some reason the blankness went out of his face and his eyes started to warm.

"Mara—"

I shook my head and started to the door, saying, "Oh no you don't. You can't be mean to me and then be nice because being mean makes you feel shit because you're usually a nice guy." I stopped and put my hand on the handle of the door and my eyes hit his. "It's okay to be mean to me, Mitch. Even people that are nice all the time are mean to people like me. I'm used to it. Go with it. Just don't ever be mean to them." I jerked my head toward the showroom, so caught in executing my dramatic tirade that I didn't notice his expression had changed completely. Thus I didn't notice how it had changed. "They don't deserve it, and the reason I took all this on is to make certain they don't ever get to the place that they do. Now, are we done here?"

He was again studying me closely.

Then he said quietly, "I don't think we are."

"Well, I disagree," I retorted, turned the handle and, without looking back, I marched right out.

# CHAPTER EIGHT

## Spring Deluxe

I WAS NO more than two steps into the showroom when Mr. Pierson materialized out of thin air, arm extended to some point behind me.

I stopped and turned as he passed me, and I watched him capture Mitch's hand and pump it zealously.

"Hello there!" he cried with manic sociability. "I'm Bob Pierson, owner of Pierson's Mattress and Bed." He let Mitch go while I blinked because Mr. Pierson wasn't a stranger to the showroom floor, but he'd never acted like *this*. I was so deep in my surprise, I wasn't able to do anything about Mr. Pierson curling an arm tight at my waist and hauling me into his side before he continued, "And I've been this delightful little lady's very lucky boss for the last seven years!" He turned his head to look at me then back to Mitch before he finished grandly, "My Mara could sell a mattress to a bat, she's so good at it." He gave me an affectionate squeeze that was so affectionate it rocked my whole body. "Aren't you, dear?"

"Um . . ." I mumbled.

"Mitch Lawson," Mitch saved me by introducing himself in return.

Mr. Pierson nodded. "I hear you're Mara's neighbor."

"Yeah," Mitch replied, his eyes no longer expressionless but now filled with amusement.

"Good neighbor to have, the po-lice detective who worked with the FBI to sweep the streets of Denver clean," Mr. Pierson declared, my head turned slowly to him and he kept talking. "Read all about that triple bust in the papers, son, saw your picture too. Bet your parents are real proud. I know I was them, I would be."

What was this? Triple bust? FBI? Mitch in the papers?

I looked back at Mitch. I did this making a mental note that after I got the kids beds, clothes that fit and weren't stained or worn out, shoes of the same caliber, kept them fed, got them decent afterschool childcare and gave them a life that would lead them directly out of the One to Three Zone and straight to the Seven to Ten Zone they deserved to live in that I would buy some tools, learn about plumbing and cars and also start reading the paper.

"You worked with the FBI?" I heard coming from my side, and I looked there to see Billy, keeping his distance behind a mattress, eyeing Mitch with his face semihard, semicurious.

"Hey, Billy," Mitch replied.

Billy's eyes darted to me then back to Mitch then he said, "Hey." Pause, then, "You worked with the FBI?"

"Yeah, Bud," Mitch answered.

Billy pressed his lips together, for some reason having difficulty making up his mind about what to think of this.

At this point Billie careened into our conversation. She did this by careening directly into Mitch's hips at the side, wrapping her arms around them, looking up at Mr. Pierson and announcing, "He bought me butterflies and flowers!" Then she pointed at the barrette I put in her hair that morning, which had a heart on it, not a butterfly or flower. Then she pointed at her chest before she held out her hand with three fingers up. "And *three* pretty outfits!" Not done, she concluded on a shout, "And a fluffy, pink teddy bear!"

My eyes slid to Mr. Pierson to see, for some unhinged reason, he looked about ready to burst with joy at this news.

"Well isn't that just fantastic!" Roberta took this moment to join us, pushed right in and also pumped Mitch's hand exuberantly, saying, "I'm Roberta. I work with Mara. And let me just say, you *totally* missed out with her pizza."

Oh God, no. Not the pizza.

Roberta, please shut up!

Before I could open my mouth to say something that might make my friend shut up, she kept going. "Trust me, *nothing* is worth missing Mara's barbeque chicken pizza. Nuh-*thing*. Next time, make certain you don't get called away."

Mitch's eyes cut to me.

Oh crap.

"Uh…" I mumbled.

"I love Auntie Mara's pizza!" Billie screeched.

Oh *crap!*

"I should probably get back to work," I put in, unfortunately sounding just as desperate to escape this new and excruciating personal life crisis as I was.

"Oh no, no, take your time, dear," Mr. Pierson said magnanimously. "Or, actually," he looked at Mitch, "what kind of mattress do you have?"

Damn.

"What kinds are there?" Mitch unwisely asked, and Mr. Pierson's face melted into a smile.

"Son, you walked into the den of a master. If you aren't able to extol the virtues of your mattress, Mara will guide you to one that you are. So, while you're here, you *need* to let Mara show you our Spring Deluxe."

No! I was not going to show Mitch mattresses!

I stepped out of Mr. Pierson's arm and slightly to the side, saying quickly, "Mitch is really busy. He has things to do. You know, the streets of Denver never stay clean for long." I looked at Mitch and prompted, "Right?"

"I have time to look at the Spring Deluxe," Mitch drawled.

My eyes narrowed.

"Excellent!" Roberta exclaimed. "It's my dinner break, Mara, so I'll just take the kids with me to Kentucky Fried Chicken." She looked down at Billie. "You want chicken?"

"Chicken!" Billie yelled which meant yes.

"Billy?" Roberta asked.

"Sounds good," Billy replied, slinking toward the front door, trying not to look like he was watching Mitch while watching Mitch.

Roberta grabbed Billie's hand and said to Mitch, "Great meeting you."

"You too," Mitch replied.

"Bye, Mitch!" Billie cried, moving away with Roberta and waving at Mitch so hard her hand was a blur.

"Bye, Billie," Mitch called to her waving, retreating form then his eyes went to Billy. "Later, Bud."

"Later," Billy mumbled and hurried after Roberta and his sister.

"I'll just leave you in Mara's capable hands," Mr. Pierson said, his hand suddenly at my back giving me a none-too-gentle shove, which made me take two steps in Mitch's direction. Then he started moving away, saying, "Remember, two-hour window on delivery freeing you up for the rest of your day."

I watched his departing back at the same time I took a calming breath. Then I tipped my head up to look at Mitch.

"I think the coast is clear for you to go now," I told him.

"Before you show me the Spring Deluxe?" he asked, the warmth back in his eyes, and it hit me that he was teasing me.

That knife twisted even as it sunk in deeper.

"This isn't funny," I whispered.

His eyes roamed my face as the warmth left his. It grew thoughtful, then he took a step toward me.

I stepped back.

He stopped and looked at my feet. Then he looked back at me and took another step toward me.

I stepped back.

He kept coming, and I had to stop when the backs of my legs hit a mattress. That was when he got in close.

Damn.

I tipped my head way back to look at him. "Mitch—"

"Actually, that whole thing was funny," he replied to my earlier comment.

"No, actually, it wasn't," I retorted. "Now, you don't want to be around me and this is your chance to escape so," I tipped my head to the front door, "go."

It was like I didn't even speak. "Except your friend saying I got called away from pizza. That wasn't funny." His head dipped closer. "You lie to your friends, Mara?"

I stared into his eyes and realized he wasn't amused or teasing anymore. I didn't know what he was, but I knew he wasn't amused or teasing. Not even close.

"I don't often share my personal life," I told him. "Now—"

"That's because you don't have one," he told me.

I clamped my mouth shut and fought the tears that suddenly stung my nose because him saying that and *knowing it* really hurt.

Then I tried, "Listen, it's only Roberta and me on the floor, so I really need to get back to work."

His head lifted. His eyes scanned the cavernous space, which was empty except for him and me, a bunch of furniture and mattresses. Then they came back to me. "Now you're lying to me."

Damn. Why was I such a dork?

"Mitch—"

"And not very well either."

"Um..."

"What are you afraid of, Mara?"

I bit my lip and then answered, "Uh..."

"What scares you so fuckin' much?" he asked.

Totally a police detective and therefore totally figuring me out. I hated that.

I looked at his shoulder.

"And what did you mean, people like you?" he pushed.

Oh boy.

I looked back into his eyes. "Um..."

"What kind of people are you?"

I took a quick step to the side and then another step back and blurted, "Would you like to see the Spring Deluxe?"

He turned to face me again. "No, I'd like to know why you think I don't want to be around you."

I ignored him and stated, "It's an exceptional mattress."

He closed the distance between us. When I started to move back, his arm shot out and curled around my waist, halting my progress even before it began. His other arm came around me, caging me in.

In Mitch's arms again. This time at work. Great.

"Have I ever given you the impression I don't want to be around you?" he kept at me.

Yes. He had. There was the time he told me I had my

head up my ass and all the other times he said it. And the times he told me I was clueless. And not ten minutes ago when he was in the break room with me which was also a time when he shared he thought I was clueless *and* had my head up my ass.

I didn't remind him of this. Instead I said, "It's our highest-end model but it's worth the price. Trust me. You try it, you'll want to buy it, and there's a possibility that Mr. Pierson will let me give you my employee discount."

"You're not gonna answer any of my questions, are you?"

"Lumbar support is very important, and the Spring Deluxe provides excellent support while affording ultimate comfort," I stated instead of answering. And I knew this to be true not only because I'd experienced it, but also because I was quoting verbatim from their brochure.

He stared down at me and I pushed carefully against his arms, hoping he'd get the hint, drop his arms and let me step back.

He didn't.

Instead he said quietly, "Billy's lookin' at me like I told him there's no Santa Claus."

I closed my eyes.

"You did that," Mitch told me, and I opened my eyes.

"Billy knows there's no Santa Claus. Bill already told him so he wouldn't have to buy him presents at Christmas," I shared more information that cemented the fact that my cousin Bill was indeed an assclown. Not that Bill needed it. His assclownedness was carved in marble.

Mitch shook his head and muttered, "Priceless."

I pressed my lips together.

Mitch leaned in closer. "I broke through with him. He doesn't trust anyone except you, and I broke through. Then you broke that. *You* did that, Mara."

"I'm sure you'll break through again this weekend, Mitch," I said softly.

"I'm not, considerin' Billy doesn't give much of a shit who treats him right. What he does give a shit about is who treats his sister right and who treats *you* right. And he thinks I walked away on Monday and left you to fend for yourself. And he might only be nine years old, but he still knows exactly the load you took on takin' on him and his sister. So now he thinks I'm a dick. And you did that."

He was right. I did do that. Crap.

"I'll explain things to him," I assured.

"Right, bet you'll be good at that since Billy's more clued into what's goin' on than you are."

My body stiffened and I whispered, "Can we not go there again?"

Mitch grew silent, and he did this to study me again. Then he returned to his earlier theme and asked softly, "What kind of people are you, Mara?"

Mitch was using a soft voice. Mitch's voice sounded nice soft. If Mitch talked to me soft for long, the jig would be up, as in, I'd throw my arms around him and declare my undying love for him. Therefore I decided it was time to give him an answer.

"Not your kind, Mitch."

His brows drew together and he asked, "What's my kind?"

"Not my kind."

"There it is," he whispered.

"There what is?" I whispered back.

"I was wrong. When you're in your head, it isn't a decent place to be. It's a twisted, fucked up place to be, but you're so shit-scared to leave it, it's the only place you're willin' to be."

I put gentle pressure on my hands at his biceps before saying, "I know you're smart and I know you're a detective, but I also know you don't know everything. I especially know that you think you've figured me out, but you don't know everything about me."

"Then prove me wrong," he returned instantly.

"You don't know it, but you don't want me to do that," I advised.

"Why? Because you're not my kind?"

I nodded.

"Then you're wrong and I'm right. I do know everything about you. Because out here in the real world, there aren't 'kinds' and only someone twisted and fucked up or just plain stupid thinks there are. Since I don't think you're the last one, that only means you're the first two. But you waste your life thinking that way, then you're all three."

With that infinitely successful verbal strike, he quickly let me go. I teetered as I turned and watched him walk out of the store. I did this with my nose stinging again, but this time I wasn't able to hold back the wetness that hit my eyes and my vision went blurry.

"You didn't even get close to the Spring Deluxe!" I heard Mr. Pierson call after the door closed on Mitch.

I sucked in a shaky breath. Then to hide my tears, I called back without looking, "Mitch is set with his mattresses, Mr. Pierson!"

"Shame," I heard Mr. Pierson mutter as a tear slid down my cheek.

It was. A crying shame.

# CHAPTER NINE

## I Could Work with This Mara

I PULLED INTO the complex listening to Nick Drake's "Pink Moon," which was on my Premier Chill-Out playlist, the first one I'd made.

I needed to chill out.

It was Saturday, nine forty-five at night, and I was driving from work to home, a home where Mitch was. I was exhausted beyond any exhaustion I'd ever felt in my life. My exhaustion crept deeper just knowing I'd be facing Mitch and everything else I would be facing in the coming days and weeks, and I didn't even know what that would be. I just knew it would be exhausting.

On my day off Wednesday, I'd taken the kids to school and then went home and dragged all of my stuff out of the second bedroom. I found places for some of it in my room, my storage unit and the living room. Then the delivery guys delivered and set up the beds and two dressers I bought from Pierson's. They also took away my futon because I gave Jay, one of the delivery guys, a screaming deal on it. During this, I did laundry. After it, I went to the grocery store.

Kids were little, but I found they made more than their

fair share of laundry and they also went through more than their fair share of food.

I dragged the food home, tidied the house, and after this, I found the day was already gone and I was nearly late leaving to get the kids. I ran back out to my car, picked up the kids and took them to the mall so they could pick their bedclothes for their new beds. Then we went to get them some shoes. Billy's tennis shoes were falling apart and Billie's shoes were scruffy and didn't match the cute outfits Mitch bought her, which, every girl knew, wouldn't do.

While we were getting Billie shoes, we found more shoes Billie had to have (this was Billie's idea, but I had to admit I agreed, they were adorable little girl shoes and she *had* to have them). Then I decided that both Billie and Billy needed more than a few decent outfits, and they definitely needed new pajamas and underwear, so we got more clothes. Then I decided to quit spending money or we'd be eating canned soup until my next payday. So we went home and we had dinner. I made up their beds and put their clothes in their new dressers. Then I helped them with their homework, which luckily, considering their ages, wasn't too taxing. Finally they went to bed, and I cleaned up after dinner.

Then I called Lynette to fill her in on everything. As in *everything*. Including Mitch. Before she could wind herself up into lecture mode and try to convince me I was the Ten Point Five I was *not*, I told her I was tired and had to crash. She let me go because she was nice and because she knew after years of trying, her lecture wouldn't get her anywhere.

LaTanya had the day off on Thursday and watched the kids for me that day. Since LaTanya wasn't on the pickup and drop-off list, this necessitated me driving the twenty minutes to their school, the half an hour to the complex to drop them off at LaTanya's, then the half an hour back to Pierson's, which meant my lunch hour went long. Mr. Pierson didn't say a word, but I knew I couldn't do that often or the kids and I wouldn't be eating canned soup. We'd be dumpster diving and living under a tarp.

Friday I had off. After dropping the kids off in the morning, I rushed home and started to clean the house. Child Protection Services were an hour late showing up, which was good because this allowed me to deep clean, as if surgical cleanliness proved my ability to raise children. The guy who showed up gave the house a cursory look through, proving that surgical cleanliness didn't mean much and it seemed nothing actually did. He checked some stuff off on a clipboard and informed me that my boss, Bradon, Brent, LaTanya, Roberta and "one Detective Mitch Lawson" gave me stellar references "the like we never see."

He then declared the kids were mine as long as Bill was in jail and I successfully completed foster parent classes, but CPS would be calling around frequently to make sure all was well.

Finally good news.

I went to get the kids, and off we trudged to check out childcare centers. The kids liked the more expensive one, of course. Or at least Billie did. Billy just agreed with Billie. I signed them up and told them my schedule for the next week: nine thirty to six thirties, with Tuesday off. I also had Saturday off, but the childcare center didn't care about that since they weren't open on weekends. I had no clue what I'd do with the kids next Sunday.

As I pulled into the spot beside Mitch's SUV, I added that to tomorrow's to-do list.

Tonight, I was getting a glass of wine, lighting candles, putting my Premier Chill Out on low and relaxing.

That was after I got rid of Mitch, who showed at eleven just like he said he would. I'd had a chat with Billy to try to rectify my mistake, but I'd made a muddle of it. The fact that he didn't come out of his room to greet Mitch (the way Billie did, enthusiastically) proved I made a muddle of it. This made an already not happy to see me Mitch look less happy. Luckily he was good at hiding it when he lifted up Billie and gave her a kiss on the cheek while she giggled.

I quickly explained his choices for lunch and dinner for the kids and told him to make himself at home. I then went to say good-bye to Billy with another word to him to be cool to Mitch because Mitch was cool. And from the hard way Billy stared at me, I figured I made a muddle of that too. Then I had a cuddle and kiss session with Billie. Finally I said good-bye to Mitch, he lifted his chin at me and I skedaddled.

Now I was back, climbing the stairs and after executing that herculean task, deciding no wine, candles or music, just bed.

I unlocked my door, opened it, walked in and saw Mitch stretched out on my couch watching a baseball game.

God, he looked good stretched out on my couch.

His eyes came to me and did a head to toe.

"Jesus, you look wiped," he announced, but other than that, he didn't move a muscle.

Great, I looked wiped. Undoubtedly attractive.

"That's because I am," I replied, walked in and dumped my bag on the coffee table. "Were they okay today?"

"Billie thinks I hang the moon, but then I think Billie thinks everyone hangs the moon. Billy still thinks I'm a dick."

So then, batting five hundred. Could be worse. Though, probably not fun spending the day with a nine-year-old who thought you were a dick.

Mental note: Have another chat with Billy.

I pressed my lips together and stared at him stretched out on my couch. Since he looked so hot stretched on my couch that prolonged watching could conceivably burn out my retinas, and I needed my retinas, my eyes drifted to the TV. I stared vacantly at the action on the screen. What I didn't know was once I started, I was so zoned out and tired, I did this for a while.

"Shoes off, Mara," I heard Mitch order, and automatically I put my hand to the back of my armchair to steady myself. I put my toes to my other heel and flipped off one shoe and then repeat on the other.

*Nice.* That felt better.

Mitch's voice came to me again. "You mind if I finish the game?"

I did. I did mind. I wanted to go to bed. I wanted hot Detective Mitch Lawson off my couch before I did something in my extreme exhaustion that I'd regret, like jump him. I was tired, but I reckoned I'd never be too tired to do that.

But after he watched the kids all day, if he didn't want to miss the mere seconds he would miss walking from my apartment across the breezeway to his, who was I to say no?

"Be my guest," I muttered, still staring mindlessly at the screen, then asked, "Want a beer?"

"You got enough energy to get me one?" he asked back.

"Just," I mumbled, turned and wandered into the kitchen. I opened the fridge and called, "Bud, Coors, Newcastle or Fat Tire?"

"Coors," Mitch called back.

I decided against wine and went for beer. Wine required a corkscrew and a glass. Beer you just popped the cap and sucked straight from the bottle. I didn't have the energy to fiddle with a corkscrew and a glass. And anyway, wine didn't go with baseball. Even Cubs fans who accepted everybody might look down on someone drinking wine while watching baseball.

I popped the caps, wandered back to my living room and got close enough to Mitch to stretch out an arm so he could take the bottle from my hand. He took it, and I moved to the armchair and collapsed in it.

I sucked back beer. A lot of it. It tasted good.

"Ah," I breathed after I was done. I lifted my feet and put them on the coffee table.

"Your feet hurt after you're on those heels all day?" Mitch asked, and I looked down at the high, spiked heels next to my chair.

Then I looked at the TV.

"Yes," I answered.

Even though I wore heels every day for years, this was no lie. They still hurt.

I sucked back more beer and watched a Dodger strike out.

I vaguely sensed Mitch moving and I equally vaguely heard his beer bottle hit the coffee table. What was not vague was his hands capturing my feet to pull them into his lap, thus twisting me in my seat.

My head jerked toward him to see he was no longer stretched on my couch. He was sitting at the end closest to my chair, my feet were in his lap and he was lifting his to set them on the coffee table.

"Um..." I mumbled when I'd regained the ability to speak. "What are you doing?"

His fingers on both hands dug into one of my feet, his palms wrapped around, the warmth, the pressure, the power, holy crap... *heaven.*

"Massaging your feet," Mitch belatedly replied, long, muscled legs stretched out in front of him, eyes to the TV, his hands working sheer magic.

"Uh…Mitch, my feet are fine," I told his profile.

"They'll be better when I'm done," he told the TV.

He was not wrong.

"I think—" I started to protest, I lost his profile and gained the full beauty of his face when he looked to me.

"Shut up, Mara, and relax."

"'Kay," I murmured.

He stared at me a second, shook his head and looked back to the TV, his hands not for a moment ceasing in giving bliss.

I drank beer and watched baseball while I tried to force myself to relax. Mitch finished with one foot and started on the other. I drank more beer, watched baseball, and Mitch's talented hands did what I could not do and forced me to relax.

I was in the zone. Beer done, bottle on the floor by the chair, eyelids half-mast, probably close to drooling when Mitch's hands left the foot he was working on and went back to the other one but up, starting to massage my calf.

"Uh…Mitch?" I called.

"Quiet, baby, and relax," he said softly.

"'Kay," I whispered. I did this because he called me baby, because he said it softly and because his hands felt so good. Then I slunk down in the seat to give him better purchase on my legs.

I stared at the TV, Mitch rubbed the tension out of my legs, and together we watched the Dodgers win by a bottom-of-the-ninth, two-run homerun.

My head tipped back when Mitch's hands stopped moving on my flesh. His feet came off the coffee table, and he gently set mine back on it. Then he was up and I watched that too, my head pressing into the back of the chair to keep my eyes on all the magnificence that was him. I watched him bend toward me and put his hands on the armrests on either side of me, his face close to mine.

"I like this Mara," he said quietly. "I could work with this Mara."

I didn't know what he was talking about.

"I'm always this Mara," I whispered, unable to talk louder not because I was exhausted and relaxed, but because I liked his face that close to mine. I liked the way he said my name in that quiet voice. And it was taking everything I had not to lean in two inches and kiss him.

"No, sweetheart, the usual Mara has got herself wrapped so tight in that cocoon she's woven around herself, she'll never break free."

Oh no. Not this again.

"Please, Mitch, I'm worn out. Can we not go there?"

"All right," he replied without hesitation. "We won't go there, but I'm gonna take advantage of you bein' worn out and point out that you are. And if you'd let me in, I could help and maybe you wouldn't be."

I was never letting him in.

"I'll get used to it."

"You might, or it might wear you down."

"I'll be fine."

He shook his head, and one of his hands left the armrest. It lifted and I held my breath as he took that lock of hair that always escaped the twist at the back and tucked it behind my ear. A whoosh surged through me because his being so close, looking so good and his touch being so tender was something I'd never had.

Not in my whole life.

And it was beautiful.

Then he was speaking as his fingers trailed from behind my ear down my jaw. "I'm sensing, baby, you're not a fighter. You're a survivor. You need to be a fighter not to get worn down by all this shit." His hand cupped my jaw, his eyes roamed my face, his face warmed and he whispered, "What I'd pay money to know is what you survived."

Stupidly, I replied, "It wasn't that interesting."

His eyes instantly cut to mine. "So it was something."

Oh shit.

Mental note when dealing with Mitch: He was a police detective and he had ways of getting information, therefore never let your guard down.

"It's just normal, everyday life stuff. Lots of people have been through worse than me," I told him. When his eyes didn't leave mine and his thumb swept my cheekbone and that felt so freaking nice, I repeated, "Lots of people."

"Normal everyday stuff does not make someone retreat from life like you do."

"I don't retreat from life. I have a job. Friends. A car—"

Mitch's hand left my face and planted itself back on the armrest as his next surprising words cut me off and totally flipped me out.

"You're into me," he declared.

My breath froze in my throat.

I pushed past it to whisper, "Pardon?"

"You're into me," he repeated.

I straightened in my chair, and since he didn't move I, firstly, had no escape and I, secondly and stupidly, brought my face even closer to his.

"I'm not into you," I lied.

"Liar," Mitch called me on it. "You're so into me you're shit-scared of me."

God! I hated it when he figured me out.

"I am not!" I lied again.

He ignored me. "A woman like you, who looks like you, dresses like you, and who's into me does not run away from me. She does not push me away and she does not lie to her friends about me unless she's, for some secret reason, shit-scared of me."

Okay, we were done.

"You need to leave," I told him.

He continued to ignore me. "What a woman like you who's not got some secret that makes her shit-scared of me does is make me pizza. She tells me about her life. She asks me about mine. And she doesn't get pissed as all hell any-time I get close to figuring something out about her."

"Well, you would know. You've had plenty of women 'into you' parading in and out of your apartment," I fired back.

"So, you paid attention," he returned.

"It was hard to miss."

"No, Mara, you paid attention."

He was not wrong about that.

Moving on.

"I will remind you, Mitch, that when I made you that pizza, which you said you didn't care much about but bring up all the time, you had a woman in your apartment."

"And I'll remind you, Mara, that I told you I'd be over in fifteen minutes, which meant I intended to get rid of her in fifteen minutes so I could be with you."

"So you could have my pizza!" I snapped.

"No," he growled, visibly losing patience, "so I could be with you."

I glared at him. He kept talking.

"And I was here in fifteen minutes, but you were gone.

And when you got back, I came to you and tried to explain, and you shut the door in my face."

"It was late," I reminded him.

He ignored me again. "I had no idea she was comin' over. I didn't want her over. I wasn't happy she was over, because she and I have been over a while and she just doesn't get it. But mostly I wasn't happy she was over, because I wanted...to be...*with you*."

"Can I ask that we have this conversation another time like...*never*?" I requested sarcastically.

Mitch ignored me yet again. "Why do you find it so difficult even to consider the fact that I want to be with you?"

"Mitch, please, would you just shut up and leave?" I snapped.

"Yeah, I'll shut up when you give me an honest answer."

"I already have," I lied.

"What was that everyday-life thing that you survived?" he asked.

"It wasn't a big deal," I answered.

"If it was an everyday-life thing that wasn't a big deal, why won't you tell me?"

"Because it's not your business, now will you shut up and go?"

"It isn't because it's not my business. It's something else."

"God! Will you just shut up and go?"

"Yeah, I will, after you fuckin' *talk to me*."

"Why are you pushing this?" I bit off.

"Why do you think?" he shot back.

"I've no idea."

"Could it be, Mara, because *I'm* into *you*?"

I pushed back against the armchair, staring at him, stunned.

Then I felt the shutters snap closed on my soul as I whispered, "Shut up."

His eyes roamed my face then captured mine and he whispered back, "Christ, you won't even let that penetrate."

"Shut up," I whispered.

"What happened to you?" he whispered back.

"Shut up, Mitch."

His hand came back to my jaw, and he asked gently, "Baby, what happened to you?"

"Shut up."

His thumb swept my cheek again, God, so sweet, so tender, then his fingers sifted back into my hair.

"Did someone hurt you?"

Still gentle.

God. Beautiful.

"Please, shut up."

"Who hurt you, baby?"

"Shut up."

His fingers curled around the back of my head, his face moved to within an inch of mine and his soulful eyes were so close. So, so close.

"How did they hurt you?"

That was when I lost it. I couldn't take any more. Not with him that close, his deep voice that sweet, his hand on me, his eyes looking into mine like he could see into my soul.

I had to stop the questions. I had to shut him up.

So I did. I lifted both my hands and put them to both sides of his head and I moved up as I pulled him down to me. Tilting my head at the last second, I pressed my lips against his and I did this hard.

Immediately, his arms wrapped around me tight, pulling me to him, locking me close as he lifted up, taking me with him as he straightened. My body tight to his, his head slanting, his mouth opening, mine following suit and his tongue swept inside.

Oh God.

My hands left his head so I could wrap my arms around his neck. He tasted good, he felt good against me, and it had been a long time since I'd been kissed. Destry and I broke up over two years ago. I hadn't even had a date, much less a lover, and definitely no kisses.

And this kiss was a *great* kiss. Not because Mitch was a Ten Point Five and the impossible was happening and he was kissing a Two Point Five. It was just because it was a *great* kiss. He knew what he was doing, and I liked what he was doing, *all of it*.

This must have been why one of my hands curled around his neck and went up. My fingers slid into his hair, and I was right, it was soft. It was also thick. It felt as beautiful as it looked.

I pressed myself to him to get more of him, more of his kiss. His arm at my waist slid down, his hand curling around my hip and, thankfully, he pulled me into him. This made me make a noise in the back of my throat. My other hand went down to press under his arm to wrap my arm around him and my fingers encountered the hard muscle of his back. At the feel of it, which I liked a lot, I pressed deeper. My chest into his, my hips into his and my tongue tangled with his as my hand held his head to mine and our heads moved. Switching position, then back, then again, and again, our lips locked, our tongues dancing, drinking, our bodies pressed deep, our arms caging each other in.

It was the best kiss I'd ever had, it could have been the best kiss in history, and I never wanted it to end.

But everything ended, though the way our kiss did rocked my world.

Mitch tore his mouth from mine but I felt his forehead rest against mine before I heard him growl on an arm squeeze that took what little breath I had left, "Jesus fuckin' *Christ*, baby, you can kiss."

My eyes opened slowly to see his *right there*, and I didn't think, because I couldn't think, and therefore I didn't stop myself before I blurted stupidly and breathlessly, "Oh my God, that was the best kiss I've ever had."

His fingers tensed against my scalp, and his shocking reply was, "Damn straight."

It was then I noticed we were both breathing heavily. Our breaths mingled against our lips, which were still close. We were looking into each other's eyes, and neither of us had moved even a smidgeon away, so we were pressed deep and wrapped in each other's arms.

"Yeah," he whispered, his arms going tighter, one side of his mouth inching up and his eyes going warm. "I could work with this Mara."

I closed my eyes slowly.

Oh God. Now what had I done?

I opened my eyes and whispered back, "Mitch—"

Before I could say another word, there was a pounding at the door.

Then I heard my mother shout, "Marabelle Jolene Hanover! Open this fuckin' door!"

That was when my body and face froze in terror.

# CHAPTER TEN

## Mom and Lulamae

I WAS FROZEN in Mitch's arms. I felt his body go solid against me and his head jerking up. Everything left my head as I heard the pounding at the door, my mom shouting, my aunt Lulamae, Bill's mom, shouting with her.

Aunt Lulamae, arguably crazier and meaner than Mom. Double trouble.

I hadn't seen them since I left home. I hadn't seen them in nearly thirteen years.

God! What were they doing at my door after ten at night? In fact, why were they here at all?

"Open this goddamned, fuckin' door!" Mom screeched.

"Fuck me," Mitch muttered, his eyes looking over my shoulder at the door. He let me go and started moving that way.

I came unstuck, focused and sprung forward, grabbing his hand, tugging back hard and desperate. His neck twisted and he looked down at me.

"Don't," I begged on a whisper. And my face must have expressed exactly the panic I was feeling because his fingers flexed around mine and his eyes narrowed on me.

"Marabelle!" Aunt Lulamae shrieked. "We're not

leavin' until you open this door and give me my god-damned grandbabies."

At her words, I instantly let Mitch go, retreated with quick steps, running into the coffee table and stopping as my terrified eyes shot to the door.

Bill. Bill had called them. Fucking, *fucking* Bill!

"Open the door!" Mom screamed, but suddenly Mitch was in my space and in my face.

"Talk to me fast," he whispered.

"My mom and Bill's mom. Aunt Lulamae."

"Bad news?" he asked.

I nodded. "The worst."

"I thought you said you were the only relative local," Mitch observed.

"They're not local. They live in Iowa. I haven't seen them since I left. It's been thirteen years."

His eyes flashed. "That assclown called them," he muttered.

I nodded again.

"Marabelle!" Mom screeched.

"Seriously, keep it down or I'm callin' the cops." I heard Derek's voice enter the cacophony.

"Fuck you!" Aunt Lulamae shot back.

"You're not close," Mitch noted, and my gaze went from his shoulder to him to see his eyes looking deep into mine.

"Things weren't good at home," I whispered, and Mitch's jaw went hard.

More pounding on the door then Aunt Lulamae, "Get your fat ass outta bed and open this door!"

"Stop shouting!" Derek shouted.

"The kids?" Mitch asked.

I shook my head. "Bill hates them just as much as me. The kids have never met either one of them."

"Marabelle!" Mom shrieked.

"Get outta sight," Mitch ordered, and I blinked up at him.

"What?" I asked.

"Right, I'm callin' the cops," Derek stated.

"Go right ahead! I hope you do. You live next to a fuckin' kidnapper!" Aunt Lulamae shouted.

"Mara, now," Mitch clipped urgently, "outta sight."

"I don't—"

His hand came up to cup my cheek. "Now, baby."

I nodded. Then I raced to the end of the hall, where the door to the kids' room was. I pressed against the side wall, prayed they slept deeply and didn't wake to hear this.

I knew this was wussy behavior, but I didn't care. There were reasons I left Iowa and both of them were standing at my door. Mitch was a big guy and he was a cop. I didn't want him to be confronted with what he'd be confronted with but in that moment of sheer panic, all I could think was that it was better him than me. He could walk away from it. It was in my blood. It lived latent in me, and I didn't need that part of me waking up.

Therefore, I watched Mitch open the door just enough so he could stand in its frame but not enough for them to see me.

Then I heard my mom say, "Well fina—who the fuck are you?"

"I'm Detective Mitch Lawson," Mitch replied.

Silence, then Aunt Lulamae, "I thought Mara lived here."

"Mara does live here," Mitch stated very unwisely, then, equally unwisely, he went on to lie. "We're seein' each other."

"Mara's seein' a *cop*?" Mom asked, voice filled with shock, disbelief and revulsion, like he'd said I was seeing a serial rapist.

"Yeah, she is, and she's explained you're estranged, so I think maybe it's best that you go," Mitch explained.

"Estranged! Right. That's good. Fuckin' hilarious. Marabelle Jolene 'My Shit Don't Stink' Hanover is estranged from her momma. I'm laughin' my ass off," Mom stated.

Why this would be, I couldn't fathom, since we very much *were.* Not seeing or speaking to someone in over a decade had to be the definition of *estranged.* Except, of course, my mom probably didn't know what that word meant.

"Like I said, I think it's best that you go," Mitch repeated.

"You give me my grandbabies, I'll go," Aunt Lulamae entered the conversation.

There it was. The reason they were here. Just what I feared. Shit!

"Mara has temporary guardianship of your grandchildren, so I'm afraid I can't do that," Mitch replied.

"Temporary guardianship, my ass. They need to be with their grandma, not some uppity bitch. You let me in and let me get my grandbabies," Aunt Lulamae returned.

"I advise you not to force entry or I'll need to call units to the scene," Mitch warned, shifting to cop speak, and I knew they were trying to push in.

Damn.

*"You can't keep me from my grandbabies!"* Aunt Lulamae shrieked.

"I know your grandchildren pretty well, ma'am, they've not once mentioned you," Mitch replied in a calm voice on a semi-lie then went on to flat-out lie. "Their teachers and principal have not mentioned you." Then he started to tell the truth. "The emergency contact on their school records is Mara. Bill Winchell is currently incarcerated. He was not offered bail because he's a flight risk. He can't afford representation, and the evidence they have is substantial. Regardless, he's not fit to raise those children, and the evidence to support that is even more substantial. Mara's temporary guardianship will likely be full guardianship soon, and you don't factor into that equation. I suggest if you'd like to see your grandchildren, you phone Mara at a decent time and arrange to have a meeting where you talk civilly about your wishes and she can decide when and how you'll see your grandchildren. Now, if you wish to see them and not give Mara ammunition to keep you from them, I suggest you quiet down, go to your car, leave the premises and phone Mara to set a time to talk about this amicably."

"Well, *officer*, considerin' I didn't understand half of them fancy-ass words that came outta your cop mouth, you can go spit for me quietin' down and leavin' *the premises* before I see my grandbabies," Aunt Lulamae shot back, and I closed my eyes.

"Why do cops talk like that?" Mom asked Aunt Lulamae.

"Search me," Aunt Lulamae responded.

God. It was like Idiot Skank and her sidekick Skanky Moron do Denver.

"Dispatch?" Mitch said, my eyes shot to him to see he had a phone at his ear and then Mitch continued. "Yeah, this is Detective Lawson. I need a couple units at the Evergreen. Unit C. Upper floor. There's a disturbance."

"You did *not* just call the cops!" Aunt Lulamae screeched.

"Fuckin' shit!" Mom shouted. "Just let her see her grandbabies! How hard is that?"

"Yeah? Thanks. Later," Mitch said, then he hit a button on his phone and stated, "You shout one more time, pound on the door, wake those kids or Mara's neighbors, I'll cuff you both, haul you down to the sidewalk myself and get creative with what to charge you with. And what I pick won't be somethin' easy like disturbin' the peace. Don't try me, I'm not joking. I'm being very serious."

This was met with silence, and I suspected this was because Mitch was looking as serious as he sounded, and he sounded *very* serious. Mom and Aunt Lulamae weren't the brightest bulbs in the box, but they also weren't strangers to a jail cell, and as often as they'd tried it, they'd never liked it.

Then Mitch said, "I think we're done here." A pause, then another lie, "Ladies." And Mitch closed the door.

Then, somewhat muted, "You did *not* just shut the door in my face!"

That was Aunt Lulamae.

*"Pig!"*

That was Mom.

I watched Mitch move toward me. When there was silence outside, I turned to the kids' door and cautiously opened it, peeking in.

Billie was sprawled, covers half on, half off, Mitch's pink teddy bear firmly in hand, dead to the world. Billy was on his side curled into a tight ball, hands shoved under the pillow. Both were asleep.

Thank you, God.

I moved back, closed the door carefully and turned to see Mitch close.

"All good?" he whispered, and I nodded.

Then I moved quickly down the hall to the front door and checked the peephole. I couldn't see anything, so I put my ear to the door and I couldn't hear anything.

I moved to the wall beside the door and banged my head on it. This I did repeatedly. This was what I was doing when Mitch made it to me.

His hand wrapped around my upper arm, and his mouth muttered, "Sweetheart," as he pulled me away from the wall.

My eyes went to him.

"Case in point," I declared.

He pressed his lips together, looking amused and knowing exactly what I was referring to. My eyes narrowed on his mouth then shot to his.

"Do you want to have that discussion again about there not being different kinds of people out there in the real world?" I asked.

"Mara," he whispered.

"You want to call *your* mom here?" I asked. "Stand her beside *my* mom? Do a comparison?"

He used my arm to guide my body toward his, and when he got my body close enough both his arms closed around me.

"Yeah," he replied. "We can have that discussion because you're still wrong. But I'd rather take this opportunity to point out that you're also wrong about bein' able to take all this on your own. Now I know I'm right more than I was before, and before I was already right," Mitch stated. His hands had started traveling up and down my back in a soothing way, which, even though I was strung out emotionally, I had to admit felt really good.

"I *am* right. You live in a totally different zone than me," I asserted.

"Sweetheart," he murmured, lips twitching, for some reason finding this funny, which it was *not*.

"Your mother probably wears twinsets," I told him.

"I don't even know what that means," Mitch told me.

"Pretty matching sweaters and cardigans," I explained.

"And?" Mitch asked, which proved I was right about the twinsets.

"She also probably adds scarves," I added for good measure.

"And?" Mitch repeated.

Yep, she also wore scarves.

"I'm sure she picks very pretty scarves that accessorize her twinsets perfectly."

"Mara," he said on a rumble that communicated he was close to laughing.

"Was my mother baring cleavage?"

That did it. All humor fled, and I watched him wince. It was a strong one which meant he'd seen my mother's cleavage and it was now an ugly memory burned on his brain instead of him not seeing it and it was simply an ugly concept.

"She was baring cleavage," I muttered to his shoulder, mortified because it was likely she was baring lots of it and it was also likely Aunt Lulamae was too.

"Mara," Mitch called, and my eyes slid to him.

"Even if we tried, we'd never work," I whispered, and his hands stopped soothingly traveling my back; one clamped around my waist, and the other one slid up my neck into my hair.

"Shut up," he whispered back.

"You live in a different zone than me," I shared again and watched his head descend. "The upper zone. I'm the lower zone. Never the twain shall meet."

I said my last against his lips, which had found their way to mine.

"Shut up," he repeated, his lips moving against mine.

"Mitch—"

"All right, baby, I'll shut you up."

Then he did, his head slanting and his lips taking mine in a repeat performance of the open-mouthed, knock my socks off, rock my world, best kiss in the history of all time.

I was holding him to me and pressed tight to him when his lips released mine. My hand was in his hair. He had really, freaking *great* hair.

"You have great hair," I breathed against his mouth.

Mitch smiled against mine.

Then he kissed me again, and it was so fantastic, when his mouth broke from mine I couldn't hold my head up anymore. I had to bend my neck and rest my forehead against his shoulder while I fought to steady my breathing.

"Shit, but you can fuckin' kiss," he whispered in my ear.

He was wrong. He did all the good stuff. I was just an avid participant in the festivities.

This was not a favorable turn of events that was conducive to peace of mind. Mitch being the best kisser in history on top of all the other fabulous things that were Mitch, his being my neighbor and his asserting he was "into me," all equated to the exact opposite of peace of mind.

"What are you still doin' here?"

Mitch's torso twisted, I looked around his body and we both saw Billy standing in his pajamas at the mouth of the hall. His face was slightly sleepy and slightly ticked.

Great. Caught in Mitch's arms by Billy, who apparently was playing possum five minutes ago.

I pulled from Mitch's arms and walked toward my cousin, saying, "Billy—"

His angry eyes went from Mitch to me and he asked, "Who was that shoutin'?"

I stopped and did a knees-closed squat in front of him. "We'll talk about it in the morning," I said softly. "Now you need to do me a favor, go back to bed and get some sleep."

"Why's he still here?" Billy asked, ignoring my request and jerking his head to Mitch.

"He—"

Billy cut me off, "He's around then he's gone, then he's around again and touchin' you. Tomorrow will he be gone again?"

"He's spending the day with you tomorrow, honey, you know that."

"What about the next day?" Billy asked.

"I—"

Billy's eyes tilted up to Mitch and he informed him, "We're okay without you. I can watch Billie when Auntie Mara has to work. I did it all the time at home."

I reached out, curved my hand around his jaw and brought his eyes to me.

"All right, buddy," I said gently. "First, you're not okay to be on your own with Billie. You're a smart kid and you take good care of your sister, but your dad leaving you alone was not the right thing to do."

Billy started glaring at me.

I dropped my hand and went on, "Second, I told you now twice that Mitch is being cool, he's helping out, and he is. You don't get into the faces of people who help you out." I scooted closer to him and my voice got softer. "And that was my mom and your grandma at the door." His glare got intense upon hearing this news, and I continued, "We'll talk about that later, but your dad and me, we're not real close with them. And now that they're here for whatever reason they're here, I've got to figure out what to do about that. But I need time to do it when I'm not exhausted from work and it isn't nearly eleven at night. I'm lucky Mitch was here to take care of that and I'm grateful that he did."

I felt Mitch's eyes on my back as I felt the intensity of Billy's on my face.

"She said she wanted her grandbabies," Billy told me.

"Yes," I confirmed.

"Is she gonna take us away?"

"No," I said firmly.

"Is she gonna try?" he pushed.

"Maybe," I replied honestly.

His eyes slid to Mitch then back to me. "Is he gonna help you keep us here?"

"Like I said, buddy, that's what Mitch does. It's who he is. He helps people," I reminded him.

Billy's eyes moved back to Mitch. "Are you gonna go away again?" he demanded to know.

Damn. Damn, damn, damn.

I twisted and looked up at Mitch.

"I never went away before, Bud," Mitch replied. "I'm always across the breezeway."

"You went away," Billy accused, but he was wrong. I sent Mitch away. And Billy felt it. Deep.

Damn! Damn, damn, damn!

"All right, then, no. I'm not gonna go away again," Mitch stated.

*Damn! Damn, damn, damn!*

I was staring at Mitch with angry eyes because he was making promises *I* couldn't keep.

"Billie likes you," Billy told Mitch.

"I like her," Mitch told Billy.

Billy studied Mitch, and Mitch stood there letting him.

Then Billy made a decision. "I'm goin' back to bed, Auntie Mara."

Well thank goodness for that. I knew it was just a reprieve, but at that moment I needed a reprieve.

I turned to him. "Okay, buddy. I'll see you in the morning."

Billy looked up at Mitch. "You're back tomorrow?"

"I'm back tomorrow," Mitch confirmed.

Billy nodded, looked at me, then turned and walked away.

I stayed in my squat watching until the door closed behind him then I shot up, marched to Mitch, grabbed his hand and tugged him to the front door. I opened it to pull him outside so I could give him what for in the breezeway where Billy couldn't hear, but Mitch moved. His hand went to the door, he closed it, then he maneuvered me so my back was against it and he was against my front, pinning me in.

Then his hands were at my hips and sliding around to my back as he said, "Oh no, sweetheart."

"I can't believe you just did that," I hissed quietly, my hands on his shoulders pressing and his face got so close to mine it was all I could see, so I stopped pressing.

"If you think for one fuckin' second that you can kiss me like that. Then the Trailer Trash Twins darken your door, Billy comes out and gets in my face, and, I'll repeat, you can kiss me like that. Then you can haul me out to the breezeway to give me my marching orders *again*, sweetheart, you need to have your head examined."

"That isn't *your* decision," I whispered.

"Oh yeah it is. I fucked up a week ago, got pissed and walked away. I'm not makin' the same mistake twice. You're drownin', Mara, and I'm not gonna live across the breezeway and watch. Not when that means you go under, I lose my chance to find out what else you can do with that mouth. And I don't mean you usin' it to spew twisted, fucked-up shit."

"Mitch!" I snapped, getting loud, and one of his arms came from around me and lifted so his hand could cup my jaw.

"Baby," he said gently, "take a second, breathe and

think back to whatever you felt when you heard them shou-tin' at the door. And then think about Billy. And then think about that kiss. And after you do that, you tell me you don't need me, want me gone and convince me you mean it, I'll take my shift tomorrow and then I'll be gone."

"I want you gone," I said immediately.

He grinned then whispered, "Mara, sweetheart, you didn't breathe."

I glared up at him. Then I breathed. As I did I real-ized the Trailer Trash Twins weren't half done with me. Bill had threatened me and he'd also done his worst. Even hating them himself, he'd called them and he knew they could get to me. This was just the beginning and the worst was yet to come.

I thought about the last week and how I wasn't exactly certain what help Mitch was offering. But I'd be as stupid as my mother if I didn't accept it because, Lord knew, I needed it. What was more, the kids liked Mitch, and Billy had, for one shining moment, a decent man in his life and I took him away. I couldn't do that again. If I did because I was (Mitch was right) shit-scared of what I felt about Mitch, that didn't say much about me nor my ability to do what was right for those kids.

I decided against thinking about the kiss. That I was never going to do and that was never going to happen again.

I focused on Mitch. "I need to go to sleep."

"Mara—"

"But," I cut him off, "we'll talk tomorrow about how you're willing to help."

"You sayin' you need me?"

"I'm saying the kids like you. Billy needs you, and if you're willing to help, I could use it."

His grin got bigger. "You're sayin' you need me."

"Whatever," I muttered. "Can I go to bed now?"

"Yeah, sweetheart," he agreed but didn't let me go.

I waited.

"Are you going to let me go?" I asked when his not letting me go lasted a long time.

"Yeah, after you give me a goodnight kiss," Mitch answered.

"No. No more kissing. We'll be talking about that tomorrow too."

"Bet that'll be good," he muttered, still, I might add, freaking grinning!

"Hello? Detective Mitch Lawson?" I called. "Do you want to let me go?"

His eyes got dark. I liked the way they got dark and liked it so much I lost focus. And since I was paying attention to his eyes getting dark, I missed his lips getting closer. At the last minute I pulled back, my head hit the door and his lips brushed mine.

He didn't move his mouth when he murmured, " 'Night, Mara."

"Goodnight, Mitch," I murmured back, my breath starting to come hard and my heart beating harder.

He smiled against my lips.

Then he let me go.

# CHAPTER ELEVEN

## Boundaries

I HEARD DISTANT noises like the murmurs of a man's deep, attractive voice, a young boy's not-deep voice, a young girl's definitely not-deep voice and a television set.

I opened my eyes, looked at my alarm clock and saw it was nearly nine.

I blinked.

Holy crap! What happened to my alarm?

I threw the covers back, got out of bed, ran to the back of the bathroom door, grabbed my robe, pulled it on over my short nightgown and dashed to the closed bedroom door. Then I dashed back to the bathroom, grabbed a pony-tail holder out of a pretty, pink glass bowl on the shelves over the toilet that held my admittedly obsessive collection of every color of ponytail holder known to man. Then I dashed out of my room, my hands securing my hair in a messy knot at the top back of my head.

I hit the living room-slash-kitchen-slash-dining-area to see a box half-full of donuts on the coffee table, empty milk glasses *not* on coasters, cartoons on the TV. Billy was sprawled in my armchair and Billie sprawled mostly on Mitch, who was sprawled on my couch.

All eyes came to me.

"Auntie Mara! Mitch took us out and bought us donuts!" Billie cried but didn't move from her place sprawled on Mitch.

I knew this because I saw the donuts and I also knew it because she had sticky-looking chocolate frosting coating her mouth.

"I can see that, baby," I told her, and my eyes slid to Mitch, whereupon I engaged my retinal laser beam to target Mitch, who was not supposed to be sprawled on my couch eating donuts with the kids before nine o'clock. In fact, he was not supposed to be in my house at all until eleven o'clock. Unfortunately, my retinal laser beam malfunctioned, and Mitch wasn't incinerated.

"He let us get the ones we wanted," Billy informed me, and I looked at him to see he had powdered sugar down the front of the new tee he was wearing.

"Did you thank him?" I asked.

Billie's head jerked to Mitch, she lifted a hand and slapped his chest, shouting in his face, "Thank you, Mitch!"

"Yeah, thanks, Mitch," Billy echoed obediently.

I stood there, not knowing what to do, and of all the options sifting through my mind, I decided the priority was Billie's chocolate-ringed lips. So I walked to the kitchen, grabbed a paper towel, wetted it and walked to Billie and Mitch on the couch. I executed a knees-closed squat beside them, grabbed her jaw in my hand and wiped.

"You've got frosting all over you, honey," I muttered as I wiped.

"I know," she told me, her lips quirking into a wonky smile even as I wiped. "I was savin' it for later."

I finished with the frosting and my eyes hit hers. "How many donuts have you had?"

"A gazillion!" she declared.

"Right," I muttered. "How many donuts have you really had?"

She lifted her hand, I let her jaw go and saw she held up three fingers.

See? Kids totally ate more than their fair share of food. How little Billie's stomach could house three donuts was a mystery.

Her wonky smile was still fixed in place. I returned it, grabbed her jaw again, tugged her face to me as I leaned in and kissed her forehead. Then I let her go.

"I get some of that?" Mitch's deep voice rumbled at me, and my eyes went to him.

"You don't have any frosting on your lips," I informed him. His eyes smiled, and I felt his eye smile throughout my body and I decided my next move was escape.

This was thwarted after I straightened, when Mitch's warm, strong fingers wrapped around the back of my knee.

I stopped, sucked in breath and looked down at him.

"You sleep okay?" he asked.

"Yes, of course. I own the Spring Deluxe," I answered, feeling his fingers burning white hot into the skin behind my knee.

At my answer, his eye smile went full facial, and a whoosh slid through my belly.

Then I asked, "Did the kids let you in?"

"No. Found your extra key and nabbed it."

I flipped the switch on my retinal laser beam repeatedly hoping it would engage. No go.

Then I asked in an unhappy voice, "You helped yourself to my extra key?"

"You said make myself at home."

I clenched my teeth.

Then I stated, "That wasn't exactly what I meant."

Mitch made no response, and Billie, who had been looking back and forth between us as we talked, looked back at me expectantly.

It was then something occurred to me, so I asked, "Do you, by chance, know why my alarm clock didn't go off?"

"Could be because I turned it off," he answered.

My body went solid at this knowledge. I studied him trying to decide how I felt about him coming into my house and then into my bedroom while I was sleeping to turn off my alarm clock. Then I tried to decide how I felt about him getting the kids dressed and taking off with them to get donuts. Then I tried to decide how I felt about him hanging out with the kids and their donuts while I slept in.

He held my gaze while I came to a decision. And my decision was, I didn't like it much.

"Perhaps we need to have a chat in the breezeway," I suggested, and Mitch burst out laughing. For some reason, Billie did too. I yanked my leg from his hold and stepped out of reach. "Seriously, Mitch, we need to chat," I pushed.

Mitch was still smiling huge when he stated, "Happy to chat with you, sweetheart, but there's no way we're doing it in the breezeway."

"Fine," I snapped, whirled and marched to my bedroom.

It wasn't a great option, but it was the only option. The kids' room was their room and I wanted them to think of it that way. The bathroom in the hall was too small. So my bedroom was my only choice.

By the time I dumped the paper towel in my bathroom bin and Mitch made it to my room, I was in the bedroom. I had my arms crossed on my chest, a foot out and my mind focused on not tapping my toe, mostly because if my mind focused on anything else, I might be moved to acts of violence.

Mitch closed my door and then leaned against it, crossing his arms on his chest, his eyes moving the length of me.

"Cute nightie," he muttered, my head shot down and my hands moved immediately to close my robe over my little, cream, stretchy-cotton nightie with the tiny, pink flowers on it.

I tied the robe tight, rethinking my actions of rushing out of my room in a tizzy before donning seven layers. Then I crossed my arms on my chest again and leveled my gaze on Mitch.

I opened my mouth to speak. Then I closed it. I opened it again. Then I closed it.

Then I said, "I don't even know where to begin."

"How 'bout you begin by comin' here and givin' me a good-morning kiss?" Mitch suggested.

I felt my eyes narrow.

Then I announced, "I know where to begin."

His lips twitched before he invited, "Have at it."

"First, we use coasters in the Mara Hanover household," I declared.

Another lip twitch from Mitch then, "So noted."

"Second," I continued, "we have boundaries."

"Boundaries?" Mitch repeated.

"Yes, boundaries," I replied on a nod of my head. "Such as, we're in here because Billy and Billie's room is their room and I want them to feel that's their space."

"All right," Mitch agreed.

"Another example would be this," I threw out a hand, "is *my* space, and when I'm in here alone, sleeping, no one is allowed to come in here and, say, turn off my alarm clock."

"Is anyone, say, *me*, allowed to come in here when you aren't sleeping? Say, when you're awake, in that cute nightie, you lose the robe and you personally show me the exceptional qualities of the Spring Deluxe?"

I leaned in an inch and informed him, "I'm not joking, Mitch."

"Neither am I, Mara," Mitch replied.

I sucked in breath and leaned back.

All right, I'd let that go.

"Third—" I started.

"Let's go back to the second," he cut me off, pushing from the door and starting toward me. "I wanna be clear about the boundaries of this room."

I started moving back. "Mitch—"

"Just so you know, when it comes to you, I have no boundary issues about *my* bedroom."

The backs of my legs hit bed, and Mitch kept coming, so I lifted a hand to ward him off and mumbled, "Um…"

"Just so you know," Mitch repeated, his chest hitting my hand then his entire body stopping smack in my space, "I'm in my bed, sleeping or otherwise, you should feel free to, say, crawl into it with me and do anything you want."

Oh God.

I was seeing that I should have stood firm on the breezeway.

"Uh…" I mumbled as Mitch's chest pushed against my hand, and his eyes went to my bed then back to me, just as his hands settled on my waist.

Oh God!

"It looks comfortable, baby," he whispered.

"Um…"

"Though, that kind of thing is try before you buy. You gonna help me out with that?"

It took effort, but I pulled myself together.

"Are you making moves on me with two kids in the other room?" I asked.

"Billie had three donuts and Billy had four. In about five minutes they're each gonna have a sugar crash and lapse into donut comas. My guess is we have an hour."

"Mitch, seriously, we have important things to talk about."

"I agree. Setting the boundaries of your bed and my bed are very important."

I leaned into him an inch and hissed, "Mitch!"

His eyes warmed. "I promise, next time I'm in here when you're sleeping, I won't turn off the alarm."

"Fine, can we move on?"

He ignored me. "But that's the only thing I'll agree to not doing."

Argh!

I leaned into him another inch and snapped, "Fine. Can . . . we . . . *move on*?"

His hands slid from my waist to my back, one arm wrapping around, one hand sliding up to between my shoulder blades as he grinned and relented, "Fine. We can move on."

I put both hands on his chest. "I'd prefer to carry on this conversation with you *not* holding me."

His arm at my waist got tight, his hand between my shoulder blades pushed in, and I found my body pressed to his.

His face dipped closer to mine, and he said softly, "I think that answers that request. Now, moving on?"

I stared into his eyes. Then I sighed and decided to get this over fast so I could have coffee, get ready for work and get the hell out of there.

"I'm not comfortable with you having my keys, coming in and taking the kids out of the house without me knowing it."

To that, he asked, "How you feelin'?"

My head twitched and I asked back, "Pardon?"

"How you feelin'?" he repeated.

"I'm fine."

"You said you slept well."

"Yes, I did."

"You rested?"

A whoosh swept through my belly as I understood what he was asking. He'd done what he'd done so I could sleep in.

Oh my.

"Mitch," I whispered.

"I came over, sweetheart, they were up. You weren't. I told them to get dressed, I turned off your alarm, took them out but I left a note. We were gone fifteen minutes, tops. You had a rough week, a crazy night and you needed to sleep."

"Is this you helping out?" I asked quietly.

"Yeah," he answered just as quietly.

It was a nice thing to do. Intrusive and over the line, but nice.

Damn.

"We need to agree what other ways you're going to help out," I told him.

"You set up afterschool childcare?"

"Yeah."

"Then I take them to school 'cause it's off your schedule but on mine. I can get away to pick them up and take them to childcare, so I'll do that too. If I'm off before you, I get them and they hang with me until you come home. You work weekend days, if I can look after them, I will. If one of your posse can't kick in when I got something on, Ma or my sister Penny'll do it. Those are the ways I'm gonna help out."

I stared up at him. That wasn't helping out. That was doing most of the tough stuff.

"That's too much," I pointed out the obvious.

"It's not a big deal."

"You have a job, a life," I reminded him.

"I can fit this in," he told me.

I shook my head. "I'm not comfortable with that."

"Mara, sweetheart, I'm tellin' you, it's not a big deal."

"But it is. You barely know me. You barely know them!"
I was not only uncomfortable, I was getting freaked out.

"I'm gonna get to know you and the same with them."

My head tipped to the side. "What happens when you
get to know me and you don't want to get to know me anymore? What happens to them?"

He tipped his head back and looked at the ceiling, then
he muttered, "Christ, here we go again."

I gave a little shove to his chest and snapped, "Mitch!"
and his eyes came back to me. "Seriously."

"Seriously?" he asked. "I can't tell the future. All I
know is, right now I want to get to know you and I'm gonna
set about doin' that. I also know those two kids out there
have had it tough, and they need to learn the lesson that
there are good people in this world who give a shit, because
their dad sure as fuck doesn't. I'm tellin' you I'm willin' to
step in and help them learn that lesson. We're both adults.
We're both decent people. Because of that, those two,
whatever happens with us, won't feel it."

"I don't—"

"Mara," his arms gave me a squeeze, "baby, you've got
to live in the now. Not in your head. Not controlled by your
fears. You can't live for what might happen five months in
the future. You got issues you gotta face *today*. You gotta
deal with them *now*. You got two kids who count on you,
and their lives aren't gonna go perfect every day because
you weigh every decision you make and tread cautiously.

Those options are no longer available to you. You're gonna have to live day to day and make decisions on the fly. And I'm tellin' you I'm here to help. You need it and they need it. Are you honestly gonna say no?"

I pressed my lips together, finding it annoying when he was right.

I didn't tell him that. Instead I changed the subject.

"There are other things we need to talk about."

He stared at me a second then shook his head once and sighed.

Then he said, "Yeah, the Trailer Trash Twins."

"Well, actually, no," I told him. "I was referring to, um ... what, uh ... what happened last night."

He smiled and shook his head again. "Jesus, you can't even say it."

My eyes narrowed and then I informed him, "I don't need to say it to tell you it's not going to happen again."

His head jerked slightly back as he stared at me. Then he burst out laughing.

"Mitch!" I snapped, slapping his chest with one of my hands.

Still chuckling, he remarked, "Fuck, that was funny."

"I wasn't being funny," I retorted.

Now only grinning, he said, "You're tellin' me after the three best kisses you've ever had, kisses you had with me, you're never gonna kiss me again?"

"That's exactly what I'm saying."

"You're standing in your bedroom, in my arms, wearin' your cute nightie and robe, tellin' me you're never gonna kiss me again."

"Yes!" I bit out.

"You're cracked."

"I am not!" My voice was rising.

"That's okay, sweetheart, it's cute."

"I'm not cracked!"

Suddenly, his face was all I could see, and that face was serious as a heart attack.

"It's gonna happen again, Mara," he promised me. "I'm gonna kiss you, and you're gonna kiss me. I'm gonna do other things to you, and you're gonna do other things to me. No way in hell even you can share a kiss with a man like the ones we shared last night and not explore where that could go."

"Mitch—"

"Tell yourself all you want it's not gonna happen, but I'm tellin' you, baby, *it is*."

"I think—"

"That subject's closed," he announced. "Now we're talkin' about the Trailer Trash Twins."

"We need to go back to the, um . . ."

He stared at me. When I stopped speaking and couldn't start up again, he noted, "Jesus, you really *can't* say it."

Crap! I couldn't!

"Whatever," I muttered.

His arms gave me a squeeze. "Yeah, definitely cute."

I glared at him. "You know, Detective Mitch Lawson, most normal, *sane* men would run a mile from women who suddenly find themselves the guardian of two children whose father has the Russian mob after them, has trailer trash for relatives and who you think are cracked, clueless and have their heads up their asses."

"Yeah, lucky for you I think all that's definitely cute."

"Trailer trash relatives aren't cute!" I snapped the God's honest truth.

"No, those two weren't cute. You bangin' your head against the wall after they left and talkin' to me about my mother wearin' scarves was not only cute, it was fuckin' adorable."

"There it is, you aren't sane," I declared.

Mitch just grinned at me.

Moving on!

"All right," I stated then warned, "They'll be back."

"Yeah, I was guessin' that."

"I don't want the kids to see them."

"Yeah, I was guessin' that too."

"So we need a plan," I told him.

"You got any ideas?"

To that, I asked, "How illegal *is* murder, exactly?"

He burst out laughing again. Luckily this time I was joking. Kind of.

When he quit laughing, his arms gave me another squeeze and he said, "How about this? I give Bray, Brent, LaTanya and Derek the heads up that they call me if they see them. The kids and I find somethin' to do today that takes us out of the house. And since the Trailer Trash Twins have no clue I live across the breezeway, the kids and me hang at my place, and you come get them when you get home tonight. They come callin' late again, I don't hear them from my place and intervene, you call me and I'll intervene."

"If they make a ruckus, the kids can still hear them shouting."

"Yes, but I'll have a talk with Billy today and clue him in, and I'll call a unit to come get them if they make a disturbance. Billie, we'll play it by ear."

This plan held merit.

"The kids go to bed before I get home. I don't go back to nine thirties to six thirties until tomorrow."

"They can bring their pajamas and crash at my place. I'll carry them back when you get home."

This wasn't a great option, but it was the only one I had, so I nodded and said, "Fine."

"I'll call Bob Pierson today and give him a heads up," Mitch stated and my brows drew together.

"A heads up about what?" I asked.

"The Trailer Trash Twins," Mitch answered.

Oh shit. I hadn't even thought of that.

Bill knew where I worked. The very idea of Mom and Aunt Lulamae showing up at work and the antics they might dream up while doing so made me close my eyes.

My head flopped forward so it was resting on my hands on Mitch's chest.

Mitch's hand came up and started massaging my neck as he murmured, "I see you didn't think about that."

"Bill knows where I work."

"Uh-huh."

"He'll tell them if he hasn't already."

"Right."

"Shit," I whispered.

I needed to talk to Bill. I needed to get him to call off the Trailer Trash Twins. I needed to do this because I couldn't handle the Trailer Trash Twins, but mostly because I needed to stay employed. Plus I liked my neighbors and I wanted them to continue liking me.

"Mara, sweetheart, look at me," Mitch called.

I sucked in breath and tipped my head back to look at Mitch.

"Your boss thinks the world of you. He'll be cool with this and protect you," Mitch told me.

"He's mistaken about the zone I live in too, and if those two show he'll figure it out," I shared, and Mitch shook his head.

Then he remarked, "Bet you think a lot of people are mistaken about that."

He was right, therefore I made no response.

Mitch kept speaking. "Which means maybe they aren't the ones who're mistaken."

Oh no. We weren't going there again.

"I need coffee," I announced.

Mitch studied me. Then one side of his mouth went up in a grin and he muttered, "Right." He didn't move, except his hand was still massaging my neck.

Therefore, I prompted, "Like...*now*."

The other side of his mouth joined the first, his eyes went super warm and he smiled at me.

A whoosh slid through my belly, and I bit my lip and stared.

"Can I have a kiss before coffee?" he asked.

"No," I answered.

"After?" he asked.

"No," I answered.

"Before you leave for work?"

"No."

"When you come home?"

I put pressure on my hands on his chest and snapped, "No!"

"All right," he surprisingly agreed, and I jumped right on it.

"Good, let me go. I need coffee and to check on the kids."

"No."

My head tipped to the side. "Pardon?"

"No."

"Mitch, let me go."

"No."

"Mitch!"

Suddenly his hand wasn't massaging my neck. His fingers had shifted up, curled around my scalp, he tilted my head to the side and his mouth was on mine.

Crap!

I pressed my hands against his chest and my back against his arm to no avail. I felt his tongue touch my lips; I liked it, I made a grunt of effort to push him away, but my lips opened anyway and his tongue instantly slid inside. My fingers just as instantly curled into his shirt, the sweep of his tongue felt that good.

He then went on to kiss me, and he did this thoroughly. I more than let him, I participated, enthusiastically.

When his head finally lifted, my dazed eyes caught his heated ones, his arms convulsed around me and he whispered, "Told you you'd kiss me again."

I so totally *hated* it when he was right.

# CHAPTER TWELVE

## That's the Way It's Gonna Be

I CLIMBED THE stairs to my unit, exhausted not because I'd suffered more emotional turmoil, but because it had been a madhouse at Pierson's Mattress and Bed that day. The bad news was, even after a good night's sleep, I was exhausted again. The good news was, I'd sold a boatload of beds and mattresses, including two king-size Spring Deluxes. This meant Billy, Billie and I weren't facing canned soup anytime in the near future, and this made me happy even through my exhaustion.

I made it to the top and walked straight to Mitch's door, lifted my hand to knock but the door was pulled open before my knuckles could meet its surface. My body jolted in surprise, and I saw Mitch standing there; then my body moved when Mitch leaned in, grasped my hand tight and pulled me inside.

He closed the door and turned to me.

This was odd behavior, but I didn't allow it to register, because I was too busy looking around his place. What was behind his door was something I'd been curious about (avidly) for a very long time, and when my eyes hit his living room, I found the reality of it shocking.

He had fantastic furniture *and* fantastic taste. I'd worked in a furniture store before I moved to Pierson's, and I knew at a glance that his stuff was the good stuff. As in, the *really* good stuff. Huge chocolate-brown sectional couch that was both comfy-looking and well-made. A mammoth, square ottoman in front of the sectional. A dark wood wall unit that had to weigh a ton and had to have been crafted by a master. It housed his flat-screen TV, a bunch of CDs, DVDs and books.

Wow. Mitch always dressed really great and he'd traded up SUVs since he moved in, but I thought cops only did okay. His apartment said he did way better than okay.

"Sweetheart," he called, and I tore my eyes off his awesome pad and focused on him.

I held my breath at what I saw.

Something was wrong. Not wrong, *wrong*.

"Billy and Billie?" I whispered.

"They're good," Mitch whispered back, and I noticed his hand was still holding mine tight.

Uh-oh.

"What's *not* good?" I asked, still whispering.

His hand in mine pulled me closer and his other hand lifted to curl around the side of my neck. "The kids and I went out to lunch and then we went to Washington Park. Derek and LaTanya were over at her sister's place all day. Bray was workin'. Brent was at the clubhouse working out."

I stared up at him wondering why he was telling me all this.

"And?" I prompted when he stopped speaking.

Mitch didn't continue for a while, he just kept studying me. Then he closed his eyes and muttered, "Shit, I don't know how to tell you this."

Because he was freaking me out, because I had a cousin

in jail who was a marked man and because my mom and Aunt Lulamae were too close for comfort, I moved into him and placed my hand on his chest.

"Just tell me," I said softly.

He opened his eyes, and his hand at my neck gave me a squeeze. "Someone paid a visit while everyone was gone. They broke into your apartment, tossed it and they didn't go gentle."

Oh. My. God!

"No," I whispered.

"I'm afraid so, baby," he whispered back.

I didn't know what to make of this. I didn't even want to think about this. Mom and Aunt Lulamae were crazy and they were mean and they were stupid. They had certain unique skills in all those areas, but they tended to come out verbally. That took crazy, mean and stupid to a whole new level.

My hand was released so Mitch could wind his arm around my waist as he called, "Mara, sweetheart, come back to me."

My eyes focused on him. "How bad is it?"

"Bad."

"How bad is bad?"

"Shit, Mara," he muttered, and my hand slid up his chest to curl around his neck.

"How bad is bad, Mitch?"

His eyes looked deep into mine. "On a scale of one to ten?" I nodded. "Fifteen."

I couldn't hold my head up anymore. It dropped and landed on his chest because at the same time he pulled me close, now with both his arms around me.

I sucked in deep breaths and tried to process this. I couldn't process it so I asked, "Did the kids see?"

"When we got back, I saw they left the door ajar. I

brought the kids over here and then I went over there. Then I called in some uniforms. They didn't see, but they know somethin's up. Even Billie's on guard."

I nodded, my forehead rolling on his chest. At least this was good. Kind of.

"You and the kids are spending the night here," he informed me.

I nodded again.

"You need to tell me what you need, sweetheart, so I can go over there and get it."

At that, I lifted my head. "I'll go get it."

"Maybe we should tackle you goin' over there some other time. When's your next day off?"

"Tuesday."

"Then we'll go over there tomorrow night."

I stared up at him knowing with grave certainty that it was level fifteen bad if he didn't want me to see my place until I had time to react to what I saw.

I closed my eyes.

"Honey, tell me what you need," Mitch urged, and I opened my eyes.

"I need to go over there."

"I'm thinkin' now's not good."

"Mitch, I need to go over there. I can't go to sleep wondering. I need to know."

"It's late, you can know tomorrow."

"Mitch," I leaned in and got up on my toes, "please, I need to know."

He studied me again. Then he muttered, "Fuck, all right. Hang on and I'll ask Bradon or Brent to come over here in case one of the kids wakes up."

I nodded, and he let me go with one arm to pull his phone out of the back pocket of his jeans.

While he did this I asked, "Where are the kids now?"

He hit some buttons while he answered, "Billie is sleepin' on the pullout in my second bedroom. Derek and LaTanya had an inflatable mattress and that's in there too, Billy's on it."

I bit my lip as he put his phone to his ear and then said, "Bray? Mitch. Yeah, hey. Can you come over here for a few minutes while I take Mara over to her place to get some of her shit?" He paused then said, "Thanks, man." He ended the call and shoved his phone into his back pocket before his arm went back around me.

"This is a new level," I told him when he did.

"Sorry?" he asked.

"Vandalism," I explained. "It's a new level for the Trailer Trash Twins. They're stupid, crazy and mean but this . . ." I trailed off, and my eyes went to his shoulder.

It dawned on me that I'd been doing this for a while, and Mitch hadn't responded so my eyes slid back to his to see he was staring at me thoughtfully.

"What?" I asked.

"Nothin'," he answered, and there was a knock on the door.

Mitch's arms dropped, but he grabbed my hand and walked me to the door. He opened it and Bradon was there, looking worried and at the same time looking curious. Mitch guided us out of his way and Bradon walked in.

Bradon was tall, blond, slim and lean and if he wasn't gay, I'd have a faraway, freakishly shy crush on him too. Since he was an awesome guy, luckily he was gay so he could be my friend.

"Hey, honey, how you doin'?" he asked. I tipped my head to the side and felt my lips tremble. "Shit," Bradon muttered, pulled me away from Mitch and gave me a big hug. I wrapped my arms tight around him and hugged him back. "It's gonna be okay," he whispered in my ear.

"Yeah," I replied, but even I didn't believe me.

"We know this now, we'll all keep vigilant. You and those kids'll be okay," Bray assured me.

I gave some thought to my neighbors protecting me. Bray was tall, slim and lean. Brent was somewhat shorter, bulkier and more muscular. Derek was built tough and strong. All I'd encountered on Mitch was solid, hard muscle. But none of them were ninja masters.

But Mitch had a gun and the training and authority to use it. And I was pretty certain that if the Trailer Trash Twins came calling again, he'd aim to maim rather than take them out in a bloody rampage. I hated them and I had reason to, now a new reason but not a bigger one, but I didn't want them dead. I was happy with maimed. I focused on that because it made me feel slightly better.

"Thanks," I whispered to Bray then felt Mitch's hand warm on my back.

"Let's get this done, baby," Mitch said gently.

I pulled away from Bradon and returned the smile he was aiming at me. Mine was wobbly. Then I turned to Mitch and nodded.

"We won't be long," Mitch told Bradon as he opened the door.

"Whatever, Mitch, I don't need to be anywhere," Bradon replied.

Mitch nodded to him, grabbed my hand and led me out. There was yellow police tape criss-crossing my door that I hadn't noticed because I hadn't even looked that way. Something about seeing that tape made all this even more real, and I suddenly stopped halfway across the breezeway. The minute I did, Mitch was in my space.

"We should do this tomorrow," he said.

I tipped my head back, looked at the underside of the

roof over the breezeway and sucked in breath. Then I looked at him.

"I'm okay."

His hand tensed in mine and he muttered, "Survivor."

Then he led me the rest of the way, dropped my hand and dug some keys out of his pocket. He used them on a new bolt and padlock that was on my door because the doorknob and the door around it were busted to oblivion.

Oh boy.

He pushed open the door and used my hand to guide me forward, dropped it and put it in my back to force me down to duck under the crisscross tape. We walked in and he flipped on the overhead lights.

The instant my eyes saw it, my mind retreated and it didn't register on me. I saw my sofa and armchair had been slashed, the stuffing everywhere. I saw my television turned over on its face, smashed. Parts of my stereo strewn around the room. CDs, DVDs, books from my shelves everywhere, cases broken, discs broken, books torn. I saw everything in my kitchen cupboards was all over the counters and the floor. Broken crockery, even food.

Holy crap.

I wandered down the hall and reached into the hall bathroom to turn on the light. I didn't keep much in there, but what was in there was all over the place.

I moved to my bedroom and turned on that light. My Spring Deluxe was slashed too. Completely laid to waste. My raspberry sheets and blush comforter cover with its embroidered raspberry flowers, with delicate, grass-green stems and leaves was shredded, feathers from my duvet and pillows all over the place. My clothes were everywhere, my dresser drawers pulled out and tossed, broken, across the room, their contents tangled with the feathers and shreds of my sheets.

I walked to my bathroom and more of the same. Tampon boxes emptied, tampons all over the sink and floor. The plastic pulled away from toilet paper rolls, the rolls unrolled. Bottles and tubes of my toiletries open, their insides spilling out, mingled with tampons and toilet paper and staining my towels and extra sheets, which had been yanked out of my bathroom closet. My medicine cabinet looted. Even my ibuprofen capsules were littered everywhere.

"Mara, sweetheart, just grab what you need and—" I heard Mitch say from close, but I moved, drifting out of the room and down the hall where I switched the light on to the kids' room.

The same there. Their new beds where annihilated. The bedclothes slashed and shredded. Their new and old clothes scattered across the room.

I saw something and walked to it, picking up the remnants of Billie's new, tiny, pink, fluffy teddy bear that Mitch bought her. She loved that thing. It was the nicest toy she owned. She'd slept with it every night since he gave it to her. Every night. She never let it go, even as heavily as she slept.

She never let it go.

Why would Mom and Lulamae do this? Why?

As these things go, whatever fog that had drifted around me cleared, and the crushing weight of what I was seeing landed on me.

I needed new everything. The kids did too.

Everything.

Without me telling my body to do it, I folded into a deep, knees-closed squat, my ass to my ankles, my knees in my chest. I wrapped my arms around the back of my head as I pressed my face into my knees, feeling the soft fur of Billie's decimated teddy bear brushing my cheek.

"Fuck," I heard Mitch mutter.

I was sobbing into my knees, oblivious to everything but the hatred and ugliness that surrounded me. All that was hideous about the home I grew up in washing through my life, the one I'd worked so hard to build, the one I desperately wanted to give Billy and Billie. As ever, all I knew, all I was, all that was contained in the blood flowing through my veins shredding everything good that I worked so hard to have.

More fool I that I thought I'd ever get away from it, escape it. Ever.

I felt myself moving and then I was in Mitch's arms. I wound mine around his neck, pressed my face in his throat and sobbed silently against his skin as he carried me through my apartment. I vaguely heard the police tape tearing off the doorframe and we were in the breezeway. Then we were in Mitch's apartment.

"Oh fuck," I heard Bray whisper. "That doesn't look like it went too well."

I didn't lift my head, and Mitch didn't pause in walking as I heard him issue orders.

"Go get LaTanya," Mitch said to Bray. "Mara'll need stuff for a while. Tell her she needs to be careful about what she touches. She only touches what she's bringin' over. Nothin' else. Can you do that for Mara?"

"Absolutely," Bradon replied.

Then Mitch was moving funny, and I vaguely noticed he was no longer standing but sitting. I was folded in his lap, his arms tight around me. This didn't register except that I burrowed deeper and held on tighter, pressing my face hard into his neck.

One of his hands started stroking my back. I felt his head tilt down and his lips at my ear.

"It's okay, baby, everything's gonna be okay," he whispered there.

"I wah...worked so hard," I stammered back.

"I know," Mitch replied gently.

"I wah...worked so hard to be eh...eh...everything they weren't. To have duh...decent things around me," I stuttered into his skin. "Wah...wah...why do they hate me so much? What did I ever do to them except bah... bah...breathe?"

Mitch didn't respond, but he kept his head tilted to me. I could feel his cheek pressed against my hair and I felt his hand moving, warm and soothing on my back. After a while it penetrated that this felt nice, and when it did, my tears started to subside.

Mitch heard it and repeated, "Everything's gonna be okay, Mara."

I nodded against his neck, not believing him for a second.

In a cautious voice, he asked, "Do you have renter's insurance?"

I blinked at his neck. Then I pulled my face out of it, his head came up and my watery eyes went to his.

"Pardon?"

"Renter's insurance, baby, do you have it?"

Oh my God! I did! I totally did! I had maximum protection! The insurance guy was in fits of ecstasy when I signed on the dotted line. He said no one opted for my policy. He even told me that although it went against the grain, he advised I didn't need that much protection. I didn't care. It was my experience if something bad could happen, it would, and I was always planning for that day.

And that day had come.

Relief swept through me so strong, I pulled back from Mitch, but only so I could do the exact same thing I did the night before. I placed a hand on either side of his handsome head and pulled his face to me as I leaned and kissed him hard and quick on his mouth.

Then I yanked back and threw both my arms up in the air, smiling big and saying loudly, "I do! I have maximum protection!" I dropped my arms, wrapped my hands around his neck and bent my forehead to touch his, closing my eyes hard and I breathed, "Thank God. I forgot. Thank *God*." I opened my eyes and looked into his. "I'm covered. We're covered. Thank *God*!"

I watched close up as his fathomless, dark brown eyes smiled. Then I felt close up as his attractive deep voice rumbled, "That's good, honey."

I realized at that point I was in Detective Mitch Lawson's lap, my hands curled around his neck, and not only had I just kissed him (again), I had my forehead on his.

I jerked back, and one second later I found myself on my back in what was a bed, *Mitch's* bed, and Mitch's torso was pinning me to it.

Oh boy.

"Mitch," I breathed, staring up at him with what I knew were wide eyes.

"You're on a wicked roller coaster ride, sweetheart, I get that, it sucks and I'm sorry. But I saw it comin' over you, you were about to close down on me, and I'm tellin' you I'm not gonna let you do that. Not after what you just saw and not after how you reacted and especially not how you came right outta that cocoon and gave me you. For ten minutes I had the real Mara in my arms, her light shining unfiltered all around me. I liked it and I'm not givin' it back, so don't fuckin' think you can take it from me."

My heart started beating double time and I whispered, "Mitch, I can't—"

"You can, I know you can because you just did," he cut me off, lifted his hand to frame one side of my face, his thumb sweeping across the wetness still on my cheek. "I do not want to freak you more than you're freaked. And I'll preface this by sayin' that whatever is goin' down I'm in this for the long haul, for you, for those kids, you have my promise on that, sweetheart. But my guess is it wasn't the Trailer Trash Twins who did that to your place."

I gasped at this news and he kept talking.

"Someone was lookin' for somethin', Mara, somethin' they want really badly. That wasn't vandalism. That was desperation."

And that was when my heart stopped beating double time because it stopped beating altogether.

Finally I forced out a, "What?"

Mitch didn't repeat himself. Instead he stated, "Seems I'm gonna have to start diggin' a little deeper into your cousin Bill."

Oh no. Oh shit. Oh no!

"Was that..." I swallowed, "was that the Russian mob?"

He shook his head. "The Russian mob don't act desperate. I don't know what that was and I don't know who, but I'm gonna find out."

Oh boy. The way he said that made me believe he was going to do it and stop at nothing in order *to* do it.

"Mitch—"

He kept talking over me. "And while I do that, Mara, I'm keepin' you safe. I'm keepin' those kids safe, and you don't have a choice in that, sweetheart. That's just the way it's gonna be."

*Oh boy.* The way he said *that* made me believe he was going to do it and stop at nothing to do it.

"I think—" I started.

"No thinking. No discussion. Nothing. Mara, I told you that's the way it's gonna be, I mean *that's the way it's gonna be.*"

He stared down at me. I stared up at him. Then I closed my eyes tight and saw flashes of the destruction of my apartment so I opened them fast.

Then I asked quietly, "Do you think we're, um… unsafe?"

"I don't give a fuck if you are or you aren't. You're gonna be," he promised.

I stared up at him. He stared down at me.

Then I made a decision because it wasn't just me I had to protect from the forces outside I had no control over. Forces that could do that to my home, which meant they might be forces that could do worse things, such as hurt Billy, Billie or me. And I couldn't put me protecting myself against all things Detective Mitch Lawson before the safety of Billy and Billie.

So before I could chicken out, I whispered, "Okay."

Mitch stared down at me. His eyes roamed my face while his thumb did another sweep of my cheek.

When they captured mine, they were warm. A whoosh swooped through my belly, and he whispered back, "Okay."

# CHAPTER THIRTEEN

## Scawed

SOMETHING MADE ME open my eyes. I stared into the dark and was instantly disoriented. This was because I didn't know where I was.

Then I remembered.

My mind reeled back to LaTanya and Bradon, with the addition of Brent *and* Derek, all coming over with some of my clothes, makeup and toiletries, doing the best they could with the hand they were dealt. Mitch, by this time, wisely had started plying me with wine. LaTanya, Derek and Brent gave me hugs and hung out for a glass of wine and to ascertain I wasn't going to have a nervous breakdown. Then Mitch talked me into getting ready for bed, at the same time declaring in Mitch Firm Voice that I was sleeping in his while he slept on the couch. The very thought of this freaked me out, though I tried not to let it show, and I did this by arguing feebly with him.

My arguments were weak because I'd witnessed the devastation of my apartment, sobbed in his arms and agreed to temporarily move in with the man I was secretly in love with at the same time trying to get out of my life. Plus I'd had two glasses of wine. I was in no shape for anything but bed, not even arguing with Mitch, which I had proven I could do even exhausted. And anyway, I rarely won an argument with Mitch, so what was the point further exhausting myself by going whole hog?

Not to mention the fact that LaTanya and Derek, Bray and Brent were watching Mitch and my byplay with undisguised fascination. This, of course, freaked me out more.

So I gave in and went to Mitch's master bath, did my before-sleep prep of face cleansing, teeth brushing and moisturizing, and then I went to Mitch's room, sucked in a calming breath and crawled into his huge, very cool bed.

Mitch's bedroom was much like his living room and, after perusal, the rest of his apartment, which included kickass stools around his bar and an absolutely gorgeous and utterly unique wood and steel dining room table. His bedroom furniture was made of wood so dark it was nearly black. It was handsome, heavy and fabulous. He had a tall bureau and a midnight blue club chair with ottoman in front of it, floor lamp and table at the side all in the corner of his bedroom that screamed at you to curl up, relax for long hours and read.

His bed was the best part about the room. A sleigh bed with rolled footboard and high, rolled headboard. It had wine-colored sheets and a fluffy comforter covered in stripes that had a background of a mushroom with multi-width lines of wine, midnight blue, forest green, black and warm brown. The whole bed was awesome (though, he really needed the Spring Deluxe, his mattresses were okay but they weren't Spring Deluxe). In fact, the whole apartment was awesome.

If I didn't know Mitch I would think, firstly, he was on

the take and, secondly, he was gay. But I didn't reckon gay guys kissed women like he did, and I couldn't imagine that Mitch was on the take.

As I lay in his bed in the dark in the middle of the night, I tensed because I felt, weirdly, something was not right

I stayed quiet and still and listened. Then I went solid as the door to Mitch's bedroom opened.

Shit!

"Mara?" It was Mitch.

I moved, pushing up to sitting and twisted toward the light. I turned it on, and Mitch was standing in the doorway, Billie held to his chest, her little-girl arms wrapped tight around his neck, her little-girl legs wrapped tight around his waist and she was visibly trembling.

My eyes moved to Mitch. "What's the matter? Is she sick?"

Mitch moved into the room.

"Nope. Scared," he answered, walked to the bed and sat on its edge, arranging Billie in his lap. But I watched with troubled eyes as she fought this, it seemed, because it threatened to disconnect her hold on Mitch, and she only settled when he did. Then his eyes captured mine. "Not a little, Mara. A lot," he said quietly.

He didn't have to tell me that. I saw it and it was freaking me out.

"Baby," I whispered to Billie, scooting across the bed toward them. When I got close, I did what I could to wind my body around Mitch's and Billie's, lifted my hand and stroked her back. I dipped my head to hers. "What's the matter, sweetie?"

"I'm scawed," she whispered, not pronouncing her "r," which was something she'd done when she was little but conquered more recently.

"What are you scared of, honey?" Mitch asked gently.

Billie didn't answer, she just burrowed deeper into him, and I saw his arms grow tighter.

"Billie, honey, I'm here, your Auntie Mara's here, we're right here. You're safe. What are you scared of?" Mitch whispered.

"Bad man coming to get Daddy, coming to get Billy, coming to get me," Billie replied, her voice trembling.

I tipped my head back, and my eyes sought Mitch's only to see his eyes were already on me.

"What bad man, Billie?" I asked my cousin, my eyes not leaving Mitch.

"Bad man that's after Daddy," she answered, her voice small and still trembling.

Crap.

I mouthed, "Russian mob?" to Mitch, and he shook his head, not in the negative, in an "I don't know."

Mitch hitched her up higher and tighter, and her arms tensed so she wouldn't lose purchase. I bit my lip because she was so scared, I could see it and feel it.

Then Mitch said, "No bad man is going to hurt you or Bud, okay? You're safe here, Billie. Your Aunt Mara and I are gonna look out for you. Yeah?"

"Why aren't we at Auntie Mara's?" she asked, and I looked back at her.

"You're having a sleepover with me," Mitch semi-lied.

"It's not because the bad man is over there?" she asked.

"No bad man is over there, Billie," Mitch whispered. "You and your brother and aunt are just stayin' with me for a while."

"But I left my teddy over there. I can't sleep without my teddy," she stated.

"Tomorrow, we'll get your teddy. He'll be here after you

get home from school," Mitch assured her, and I hoped Target had a steady supply.

"Okay," she whispered and burrowed closer.

Mitch held her close and I stroked her back for a while. When she seemed to start relaxing, I said gently, "All right, baby, let's get you back to bed and I'll stay there with you. Will that make you feel better?"

"Can I sleep in here with you and Mitch?" Billie asked in a small, needy voice.

Me and Mitch?

My eyes shot back to his face, but his neck was bent to talk to Billie.

"How about you sleep in here with your aunt?" he asked, which caused an instant response from Billie. Her arms tightened, her back arched to get maximum contact with Mitch's powerful frame and her voice rose when she spoke again.

"You're bigger!"

"Honey," Mitch muttered.

"I wanna sleep in here with you and Auntie Mara!" she cried out against his skin.

"Billie, baby, you're safe in here with your aunt, and I'll be right out—" Mitch started, his voice soothing, but Billie was having none of it.

"You're bigger! The bad man will be scared of you!"

Oh crap. What did I do with this? She couldn't sleep with Mitch, and I couldn't sleep with Mitch.

Mitch lifted his head to look at me.

I moved closer to Billie. "Okay, sweetie, listen to me. You can stay here with me, and Mitch'll be right out in the living—"

Suddenly and violently, she twisted.

Her hand came out and latched onto my hair, tugging

so hard it hurt, and her face was red and mottled when she screamed at me, *"The bad man is coming to get me! Me and Billy!* The bad man will be scawed of Mitch! He'll be scawed! He'll be scawed *of Mitch*!"

Good God.

In the face of her little-girl terror, I gave in instantly. "All right, baby, all right, we'll all sleep in here. No one's going anywhere. We'll all stay right here."

She stared into my face then it seemed she collapsed, her hand leaving my hair, her head falling on Mitch's shoulder, her arm drifting listless down his side.

"Thank you," she mumbled.

I lifted a hand to cup her face, and her eyes closed with relief. My eyes moved to Mitch. I didn't know what to say or do. I didn't know if I could sleep beside Mitch, but I was pretty certain I couldn't. I didn't know what Mitch was thinking. What I did know was that Billie's behavior scared the hell out of me.

"Do you mind?" I whispered to Mitch, and he just stared at me.

After a while he said, "No."

"Thanks." I was still whispering.

Mitch got off the bed, and I pulled the bedclothes back. He shifted them in, rolled Billie between us then rolled back to turn out the light. Since it was dark, I heard them moving to get settled, and I reached out a hand to feel Billie was turned into Mitch, still holding on. I stroked her back for a while, then when I heard Billie's breathing turn heavy and her little body relaxed, I pulled away to lie on my back and stare at the dark ceiling.

That was when I whispered, "Mitch, you awake?"

"Yeah," Mitch replied.

"Sorry about this."

There was silence.

"Really, um . . . sorry," I said quietly.

"Don't worry about it."

"She was really scared and I, uh . . . didn't know what to do."

"Mara, don't worry about it."

"I feel badly," I told him softly. "You're being so nice and—"

I felt the bed move then I saw the shadow of Mitch's frame looming over Billie's body toward me. Suddenly, I felt Mitch's fingers on the side of my face, his thumb on my lips.

"There are far worse things than needin' to sleep in this bed with you and a scared outta her brain six-year-old. Like I said, sweetheart, don't worry about it. Yeah?"

"Okay," I whispered against his thumb.

"Go to sleep."

"Okay."

His thumb swept my lips then his shadow disappeared as he lay back down. Billie moved, nestling into him, still breathing heavily, and I hoped that meant she didn't wake up.

I lay in the dark and stared at the ceiling.

I did this a while.

Then I called, "Mitch?"

This got me a rumbly, sleepy, "Yeah?"

"Sorry, were you asleep?"

"Not yet."

I bit my lip.

"You want somethin'?" he asked.

"Um . . ."

"Mara, honey, we both got work tomorrow—"

I cut him off on a whispered, "She was freaking scared."

"Yeah."

"Not right scared," I went on.

"Yeah."

"What do you—?"

"We'll talk about it tomorrow."

I bit my lip again. Then I said, "Okay."

"Go to sleep, honey. Everything's all right right now. That's all you gotta think about."

"Okay."

" 'Night, baby."

"Goodnight Mitch."

*       *       *

# Mitch

Mara moved in the bed, curling into Billie at the same time curling into Mitch. He woke as he felt her move into him.

He was on his back, and one beautiful child female and one beautiful adult female were pressed into his side, both their arms thrown over his gut, Billie's head at his ribs, Mara's head settling on his shoulder.

Not for the first time he noticed that Mara's hair smelled unbelievably fucking great.

He stared at the dark ceiling thinking about Mara and her boundaries.

He grinned at the dark ceiling.

Then he thought about Mara's long, shapely bare legs, which he remembered seeing in shorts on a variety of occasions during the summers. He'd also seen them on a variety of occasions in a bikini when he'd been at the bar in the clubhouse or on his way into or out of the gym to work out and she'd been lounging by the pool outside. And he'd seen them the morning before, when she'd been in a short robe and that cute nightie. The nightie she was wearing right now. The nightie that clung to a lot of really fucking great places and showed most of her equally fucking great legs, which went on for-fucking-ever.

Summer was coming.

His grin grew into a smile.

Then he fell asleep.

# CHAPTER FOURTEEN

## I'll Go Gentle

MY EYES SLOWLY opened and even just upon waking, I was profoundly confused.

This was because my vision was filled with an immensely attractive, no, *criminally* attractive, smooth-skinned, defined, hard-muscled wall of chest as well as the top of Billie's head pressed to the sculpted ridges of some ribs. Then there was my arm under Billie's arm slung over a flat, carved stomach.

I blinked and the chest was still there, Billie was still there and our arms were still there.

I blinked slower and found the same when I opened my eyes.

Cautiously, I tipped my head back, and as it went I saw a familiar, corded throat, then a familiar, strong, square, dark-stubbled jaw, and then I was staring at Ten Point Five Detective Mitch Lawson's profile. Locks of hair had fallen on his forehead, and his eyes were closed. His thick, long lashes resting on his cheeks and him lying there sleeping was beyond hot. It was mega-hot. It was immeasurable hot.

He was so beautiful I couldn't breathe.

I'd been so worried about Billie last night and so out of

it about everything I hadn't realized he was bare-chested. I also hadn't really let myself think of being in his bed *with him* and with him *bare-chested*.

I liked it. All of it.

Oh boy.

I looked at the alarm clock and it was ten minutes after I usually got up to get myself sorted so I could then start getting the kids sorted. I didn't have to run them to school today since Mitch was doing it. Still, it was time to start on the day because Mitch might be running them to the school, but someone had to get them up, showered, dressed, book bags packed (wherever those were) and fed.

And that someone was me.

Carefully, I moved my head from Mitch's shoulder and bent down. Pulling Billie's dark hair out of her face and smoothing it back, I leaned in to kiss her temple. My poor girl had been scared last night of something that was very real.

That was another thing on the morning's agenda. Find some way that didn't scare the hell out of them to talk to Billy and Billie about what Billie meant.

"Sweetheart," I heard Mitch rumble.

My head tipped back to look at him. Seeing his sexy-drowsy face, his eyes warm on me, those locks of hair on his forehead, something happened to me that hadn't happened since I was four years old and learned that the world I lived in was a place I could never leave.

I got transported to a fantasy world.

"Hey," I whispered.

His hand came up and cupped my cheek as his eyes roamed my face.

Then he responded, "Hey."

"You sleep okay?" I asked quietly.

"Yeah," Mitch answered quietly.

"Good," I whispered. "I've got to get the kids ready for school. How do we do that and not interrupt your morning schedule?"

"Don't worry about me. I'll work around you."

Jeez. He was *such* a nice guy.

"'Kay," I said softly.

His eyes dropped to my mouth. They became heated, my chest heated in return and he ordered gently, "Come here."

I went there, not thinking, just moving toward him as his hand slid from my cheek into my hair. When I got close his eyes roamed my face again, all around and down to my shoulders and neck.

"Never seen you with your hair down," he murmured, his fingers sifting through it. "It's softer than I imagined."

He imagined how soft my hair was?

His hand cupped the back of my head, and his eyes locked on mine. "And I thought it would be pretty, fuckin' soft."

"Mitch," I whispered, then said no more.

His fingers put pressure on my scalp, pulling me toward him then his mouth put pressure on mine.

God. I liked this fantasy world. It was freaking *great*.

Billie shifted between us, and Mitch's hand moved out of my hair. I turned to the side and looked down to see she had her head tipped back and her sleepy, little-girl eyes were on us.

"Is Mitch your boyfriend now, Auntie Mara?" she asked.

At her question, I came crashing out of my fantasy world.

Shit!

I started to pull away, and Mitch's arm around my back tightened, his hand shifting up to between my shoulder blades, flattening and holding me close, therefore I had no choice but to freeze.

"Um…" I mumbled.

*Shit!*

I decided to shift the subject and asked gently, "You sleep okay, sweetie?"

"Miss my teddy," Billie replied.

Personally, I thought Detective Mitch Lawson was far superior to a tiny, pink teddy bear, but I wasn't six years old.

"We'll find him for you," I promised.

Mitch moved, and I watched him hook Billie under her armpit and slide her up his chest so she was face to face with him and, incidentally, me.

His arm wrapped around her back and he asked, "You eat oatmeal, gorgeous?"

Billie scrunched her face and answered, "Donuts."

I watched up close as Mitch grinned into her face, and that whoosh flowed through my belly. It was far more dangerous when I was lying in bed with him, pressed close to him (and Billie), at the same time witnessing him being so sweet to my cousin.

"Donuts are a Sunday breakfast, when you got nothin' to do but watch cartoons. Oatmeal is a before school breakfast, when you gotta activate your brain," Mitch explained.

Billie's head tipped to the side, and she smiled a mini-confused, wonky smile. "Oatmeal activakes my brain?" she asked, and Mitch's grin turned to a smile.

"Yep, it goes into your belly and gives your whole body energy, wakes it up, even your brain, so you can be supersmart," Mitch answered.

Billie lifted a hand and placed it on his neck, her eyes had grown wondrous. "Oo, I wanna be supersmart so I can grow up and be a hairdresser!" she declared.

I smiled, Mitch chuckled, and both his arms got tight, the one around Billie *and* the one around me.

"Then how 'bout while Mara wakes your brother up, you help me make you and him some oatmeal?" Mitch suggested.

"'Kay," Billie agreed.

Then, before I knew what was happening, Mitch's hand between my shoulder blades pushed me in, his head came up, his lips brushed mine and I felt another belly whoosh as well as some tingles. Mitch let me go and curled up, taking Billie with him. Then they were out of bed, leaving me in it. Luckily I was lying down so that I didn't fall down because I was treated to a view of Mitch's beautifully muscled back and equally beautiful ass in a pair of navy blue, drawstring pajama bottoms. I watched him move out of the bedroom, Billie's arms and legs curled around him, her eyes on me over his shoulder. She was waving at me as if Mitch was taking her on a vacation and not into the kitchen.

I didn't have time to marvel that only weeks ago Detective Mitch Lawson was my unobtainable dream man next door, and last night I'd slept in his bed with him. I didn't have time to commit what just happened that morning to my memory banks. And I didn't have time to remind myself where I fit and where Mitch fit in Mara World.

I had kids to take care of.

I slid to Mitch's side of the bed, got up and went to the second bedroom. I saw both the kids had their book bags in that room as well as a small pile of clothes and other necessities. I grabbed some clothes for him and Billie, took them to the hall bathroom then went back, woke Billy and guided my sleepy cousin to the bathroom.

I had exited the hall and was moving into Mitch's living room-kitchen-dining area when I realized I was wearing nothing but my nightie, at the same time I realized that LaTanya and Bray didn't bring over my robe.

I was about to turn on my heel and escape back into the bedroom to find something to put on when Mitch turned from hitting the buttons on the microwave, and his eyes caught me. They instantly dropped to my nightie. This meant I instantly felt heat hit my face. It also meant my body instantly froze. And I also instantly froze because I was staring at Mitch, bare-chested in his kitchen. Once the vision of Mitch penetrated, part of my body unfroze and that was my knees which wobbled.

Crap!

"Cranberry juice tastes funny," Billie noted, oblivious to Mitch and me staring at each other like we were in trances. She had taken her glass from her lips, leaving a cranberry juice mustache and wrinkling her nose at Mitch. She was sitting on the counter next to the stove, over which was the microwave.

Mitch tore his eyes from my nightie and turned to Billie. "Maybe, gorgeous, but it's good for you."

"Why does everything that's good for you taste funny?" She tipped her head and went on, "Or just tastes bad?"

"It doesn't," Mitch answered.

"Broccoli tastes bad," Billie parried.

"Broccoli tastes good," Mitch returned, and Billie wrinkled her nose again.

"No it doesn't," she replied.

"It's delicious," Mitch stated.

Billie studied Mitch soberly then proclaimed, "You're weird."

Mitch smiled at my cousin. My knees wobbled again.

Shit! How was I going to stay with him if I could barely stay standing in his presence?

"Do you have a robe I can borrow?" I called into their conversation, and both Mitch and Billie looked at me where I was still standing and hadn't moved a muscle.

"No," Mitch answered, his lips twitching.

"Um..." My mind whirled then I came up with, "Can I borrow one of your shirts?"

"Why do you need a shirt?" Billie queried then observed, "You don't need a shirt at your house."

"I'm chilly," I lied, which was the wrong thing to say for it caused Mitch's eyes to drop to my chest, likely in order to check the veracity of this statement.

"I'm not," Billie noted.

"Well I am, sweetie," I told her and then called, "Mitch?" whereupon his gaze shot from my chest to my eyes.

"Make yourself at home, sweetheart," he muttered, then started to turn back to the counter to do what, I did not know, because I took that opportunity to make my escape.

I went to his closet, grabbed an old, plaid flannel and shrugged it on. I buttoned some buttons on the front, just enough to cover myself, but not all the way up to my throat, which was what I wanted to do, but would make me look like an idiot.

I headed out to the kitchen, deep breathing in preparation for seeing Mitch's chest again. This didn't work, for when I hit the kitchen, Mitch's eyes hit me then slid down from head to thighs and back again. They warmed, and he smiled huge, which was a vision that was arguably better than his chest.

I ignored this and headed straight to caffeine.

Mitch didn't ignore me. "Prefer you in just the nightie, baby. That nightie's sweet."

"I do too, Auntie Mara," Billie chimed in. "It has little flowers on it, and that shirt is for boys."

I got a mug down, set it by the coffeemaker and then moved into Billie.

Putting both my hands on either side of her, I dipped my face to hers and said, "How about we stop talking about what I'm wearing and start talking about you. Are you okay?"

She nodded, grinning. "Mitch's makin' me oatmeal to activake my brain."

"Activate, baby," I said softly.

"Activake," she repeated.

I smiled at her, slid my fingers in her hair, pulling it off her shoulder and down her back before I continued in a soft voice, "You had a bad night, sweetie."

Her grin faded, and she twisted her mouth as she looked around me to Mitch then back to me.

"I'm sorry, Billie," I said quietly, "but I've got to ask you to do me a really big favor. The biggest. I wouldn't ask, but it's very important."

She untwisted her mouth and whispered, "What?"

I lifted both my hands and framed her face. "When Billy gets out here, I need you and him to talk to Mitch about the bad man that scares you. Can you do that for me?"

She twisted her mouth again, but I saw her little body get tight right along with the rest of her face. That was also when I felt Mitch's heat close to my back, then he leaned into me, putting his hands where mine had been on the counter.

"It'll be okay, Billie," he said gently over my shoulder, and I twisted my neck to look at him to see his eyes were on Billie. "You're safe, gorgeous. But Mara and I need to know so we can make you and Billy even more safe."

I looked back to Billie to see her twist her mouth the other way before she asked, "Will you make Daddy safe?"

I felt Mitch's body tense against mine. This meant he couldn't, and it also meant he didn't want to tell Billie that or lie to her and say he could.

Therefore, I stepped in. "Let's worry about you and your brother now and we'll worry about your daddy later. Does that sound like a plan?"

Her big blue eyes looked into mine and she whispered, "Where *is* Daddy?"

Oh crap. I knew this was going to happen, just as I knew I wouldn't be prepared for it. And I was right, it was happening and I wasn't prepared for it.

"Uh..." I started, and then Mitch butted right in and answered, and when he did, for some reason he did it *truthfully.*

"Jail, Billie," Mitch said carefully, and Billie's eyes got big, and not in an "isn't life wondrous" way.

Incidentally, so did mine.

"Dad's in jail?" We heard from behind us.

I let Billie's head go, and both Mitch and I twisted to see Billy, hair wet, clothes on, standing in Mitch's cool-as-hell living room.

Oh boy. I'd been avoiding this, and life being crazy and the kids adjusting to their new routine had allowed me to do it. They hadn't asked, and I hadn't offered up the information.

Now what did I do?

I stood uncertain but Mitch didn't.

I knew this because instantly he called, "Bud, come here."

Billy looked at Mitch for several long seconds, his face hard and blank, then he walked into the kitchen. When he made it close enough, Mitch put a hand in my belly and pushed me back a couple of feet. Then he bent over, linked his hands and twisted his neck to look at Billy.

"Foot in my hands, Bud, I'll give you a leg up," he ordered quietly.

Billy again hesitated for several seconds, then he put his foot in Mitch's hand, his hands on Mitch's shoulders, and Mitch hefted him up to sit on the counter by his sister.

Mitch reached out a hand to me, he tagged my shirt and pulled, necessitating my moving toward him. When I got close enough, he slid his arm along my waist, curling his hand around my hip, and he pulled me tight to his side.

Then he spoke.

"You remember a while ago we all went over to your dad's and he wasn't feelin' too good?" he asked.

Billie bit her lip.

Billy stated in a tight, angry voice, "No. I remember he was feelin' just fine, seein' as he was drunk, as usual, and shootin' up, as usual."

I sucked in breath. Billie quit biting her lip and it started trembling.

"Buddy—" I started on a whisper.

"Yeah," Mitch said over me, and I tipped my head back to look at him as he carried on. "It isn't illegal to drink alcohol, but it is illegal to take drugs. That's bad enough, but what makes it worse is doin' either of those in front of kids."

"Mitch," I whispered my warning, but it went unheeded, and Mitch kept talking.

"You do bad things, doesn't matter if you're a kid or a grown up, you get punished. Your dad has done bad and he's gettin' punished."

"Mitch," I repeated, this time in a little above a whisper, and my hand automatically went to his abs to give him a warning "shut up!" press, which, by the way, he totally ignored.

"So he's in jail because he does drugs?" Billy asked in a tone that sounded vaguely curious and not much else.

"That and other stuff that isn't too good," Mitch answered. "And you both should know, it's likely he'll be there a while."

Oh my God! What was he doing?

I watched tears fill Billie's eyes and therefore snapped, "Mitch!"

Mitch looked down at me and stated, "They should know."

"We need to discuss this elsewhere," I informed him.

"No you don't, Auntie Mara," Billy put in and I looked at him. "Mitch's right. We should know."

My eyes moved to Billie and I opened my mouth to speak. Then I saw the tears that were threatening were now trailing down her cheeks, so I closed my mouth, but Mitch moved. He let me go, plucked Billy off the counter and attached the six-year-old girl to his hip with one arm like she was a toddler and weighed no more than a large doll.

He tucked her hair behind her ear and dipped his face close to hers before he said gently, "I know that makes you sad, gorgeous. It makes you sad because it *is* sad. But maybe your daddy will take this time to sort himself out so, if he gets out, he can take better care of you. Because the bottom line is you deserve someone who'll take good care of you."

Billie looked into Mitch's eyes and the tears kept falling.

At the same time, Billy muttered, "Yeah, like that'll happen."

I put my hand on my cousin's knee to give a warning squeeze, and Billie hiccupped as her tears flowed faster.

"Bud, I get you're ticked and I get why, and you've got a right to be ticked, but you're not helping," Mitch said softly, and Billy pressed his lips together. Mitch went back to

Billie. "But right now, honey, you're in a good place. You're where you need to be with people who care about you, and you can help Mara, me *and* your daddy by telling us about the bad man that scared you last night."

"What bad man that scared her last night?" Billy asked, and I looked at him.

"Billie had a rough night, buddy," I explained. "She woke up scared and she told Mitch and me she's worried about a bad man hurting you, your dad and her."

"She should be, seein' as we can't go to your place because Dad's a dick," Billy returned, stating, as usual with Billy, that he knew exactly what was going on.

I started to call Billy on his language, and again Mitch got there before me.

"Bud, mouth," he said on a gentle growl, and Billy glared at him mutinously for a second before he looked down at the floor. Mitch then turned his attention back to Billie, who now had her head resting on his shoulder and her fist pressed against her lips.

"You okay, baby?" I asked Billie.

"No," she muttered against her fist.

Before I could say more, Billy spoke again. "How can we help you and Auntie Mara?"

Mitch lifted a hand to start stroking Billie's hair, but his eyes went to Billy.

"You know the bad man your sister's talkin' about?" he asked.

"Yeah," Billy answered.

"You see him?" Mitch went on.

"Yeah, all the time," Billy replied.

"Could you describe him?" Mitch asked.

Uh-oh. I wasn't sure how I felt about where this was heading.

"Sure," Billy responded.

"Pick him out in a picture?" Mitch continued.

Uh-oh!

"Yeah, you got one of him," Billy stated.

"Good, then when I pick you up from school today, you both will come with me to the station, talk to some of my friends, look at some pictures. You find him then we'll know who's scarin' your sister, and we might be able to do somethin' about it."

I stood there, my blood pressure accelerating, and I didn't know how to feel about this. Who was guardian to these kids anyway, Mitch or me? I didn't like the honest way he went about telling them all of this. Though they had to be told, I would have liked to have a discussion about what we intended to do about it. What I didn't like was Mitch charging in, giving the kids bad news, making Billie cry and then deciding the kids were going to the station with him without conferring with me.

I was about to suggest we retire to the breezeway, and I didn't care if Brent, Bradon, Derek and LaTanya saw us out there in our sleepwear while I gave Mitch what for, when the day's plans were sealed without me able to utter a word.

"The station?" Billy breathed, his tone not mildly curious or angry and hard, but awestruck. Clearly a visit to a police station was a treat for a nine-year-old boy.

At the same time Billie whispered, "Po-lice station?" Then, her little-girl brain catapulted her out of unhappy, criminal, drug-addled Dad in jail world into another world entirely. Her torso shot straight in Mitch's arms, her fists went into the air and she cried, "Yippee! I can't *wait* to tell my friends at school I get to go to the po-lice station!"

And equally clearly, a visit to a police station was a treat for a six-year-old girl.

I clenched my teeth at the same time I put my hands on my hips.

Then I asked Mitch in a tone that could not be mistaken, "Is the kids' oatmeal done?"

Mitch and Billy's eyes came to me, both of them not mistaking my tone.

Billie's eyes went to her brother, who she informed, "Guess what, Billy? Mitch is activaking our brain with oatmeal so we can be supersmart!"

"Cool," Billy muttered quietly, treading cautiously as I continued to glare at Mitch.

"Yeah, it's done," Mitch answered me, his eyes alert and amused at the same time.

"Excellent," I decreed, stepped back and turned to Billy. "Jump down, buddy, and take a stool." My eyes went to Mitch and I ordered, "Put Billie on a stool. She needs to eat so I can get her in the shower. Then we're chatting in the breezeway."

Mitch stared at me a brief second then started to round the counter to put Billie on a stool, saying, "Baby, maybe you haven't got this, so I'll say it straight. We gotta talk, we'll talk, but we're *never* doin' it in the breezeway."

"Fine," I snapped, yanking open the microwave door to find steaming bowls of oatmeal in there. I pulled them out and continued, "Your bedroom."

"Now that definitely works for me," Mitch muttered.

I slashed him a look as I dropped the bowls in front of the kids, who were both now at stools. I yanked a couple of drawers open until I found spoons and when I did, I grabbed two and dumped them into the kids' bowls.

Then I stomped around the counter, through the living area and right to his room. I stood with my hand on the door until he cleared it then pushed it closed. I turned around, my mouth opening to give him what for and then closing when I suddenly found myself in his arms, my body plastered to his bare-chested one.

On a normal day, this would have made me paralytic. At that present moment, it made me apoplectic.

I put my hands to his shoulders and pressed, hissing, "Let me go."

Mitch ignored my hands except to lean into them as he observed, "You're pissed."

"Uh...*yeah*," I snapped. "Your one-man show in there, um..." I shook my head, got up on my toes to get closer to his face and finished, *"No."*

"Sweetheart, they gotta know and they gotta help us out if we're gonna stop whatever the fuck is happening," Mitch explained.

"Maybe so, but *I'm* their guardian and *you* are helping out. Therefore *we* make decisions about how we communicate with them and what they'll be doing to help us out *before* we communicate with them and tell them what they'll be doing to help us out," I retorted.

"We don't have time to chat or wait for you to consider what's the best way forward, Mara. In the immediate, we got two kids to get to school. I gotta talk to the people at the school then get to work, you gotta get to work and we got a bad guy who ripped your place to shit. That's just the immediate. I don't have to remind you of all the other shit swirlin' around you and those kids."

"No, you don't," I agreed. "But that doesn't mean we don't talk before decisions are made."

"Baby," he said with what sounded like somewhat annoyed patience, "I just said, we don't have time."

I lifted up further on my toes, my face an inch from his and returned, "Honey lumpkin, when it comes to what we do with those kids, we *make* time." Then I ignored one side of his mouth hitching up at my sarcastic endearment and drove my point home by accusing, "You made Billie cry."

"She loves her dad. There was no way to avoid makin' her cry, and I get that you get that since you've had them a week and neither of them knew their father was in jail. It had to be said no matter how old they are, and there is no way to sugarcoat the fact that someone's drug-addicted, drug-dealing, thieving father is facing some serious jail time."

Damn, I hated it when he was right.

"Okay, so, you're right," I allowed, and this got an arm squeeze and a lip twitch before I went on. "But, you're also wrong. I'm not a bystander in this situation. The fact that they're told and how they were told should have been discussed and understood between us *before* they were told so we could be prepared to deal with any fallout. Or, I should say, in this instance, *I* could be prepared for any fallout. We can't do this if *you* make these decisions on your own and leave me blowing in the wind. We can only do this if *we* do this as a team so we're both prepared to offer the best support we can because, knowing Bill, my mother and Aunt Lulamae, this is only the beginning. Do you get me?"

I wasn't paying attention, and therefore his hand had drifted up my back, neck and into my hair to cup the back of my head before I clocked its movement. I also didn't notice the change that had come over him while his eyes held mine. A change that I sensed was significant, so significant it was downright important, but even so, I couldn't put a finger on it.

He took my mind off all of this when he replied quietly, "I get you."

"Good," I clipped. "And another thing, when we chat we *don't* do it with you holding me." I pressed at his shoulders again. "Now, let me go."

"Oh no, honey, no way in hell I'm gonna let you be

pissed at me, wearin' that cute nightie, your hair down and not chat with you anywhere but in my arms."

Um...what?

"What?" I asked.

"You heard me," he answered.

"I'm not wearing a nightie," I reminded him. "I'm wearing a nightie *and* a shirt."

"You could cover up that nightie with a snowsuit, sweetheart, but you in my living room wearin' nothin' but that nightie is burned on my brain in a way that I like a fuckuva lot. So all I'm gonna see is you in that fuckin' nightie no matter what you put on over it."

"That's insane," I snapped.

"You're not a guy," he replied.

"Okay, now *that's* insane," I returned.

"Maybe you don't get just how cute that nightie is," Mitch retorted.

Oh boy.

"Mitch—"

"Or just how good it fits you," Mitch kept going.

Oh God.

"Mitch—"

"Or how fuckin' great you look with your hair down."

"Mitch!"

"Or how I gotta fight against goin' hard whenever you slip outta your cocoon when you get pissed or you forget to stay shielded and that Mara Light shines out."

*That* shut me up and it made my fingers curl into his shoulders as I stared, shocked, into his fathomless eyes.

"Yeah," he murmured, his arm around my waist going tight. "Now, finally, I'm seein' *you* get *me*."

"I think we're done talking now," I whispered, and we were. We were definitely done talking.

Of course, the truth of the matter was, I was done talk-ing. Mitch was not, and I knew this when his arm got tighter just as his hand at my scalp pulled me so close to his face I felt his breath on my lips.

"Since I have your attention, baby, and I see you beatin' your retreat, I want you to take this with you when you slide back into that cocoon. Straight up, Mara, I want you in my bed. And when you're in my bed, I'm gonna be *in you*. And while I'm movin' inside you, I'm gonna make you come with your long, fuckin' legs wrapped around my back, when my hands are finally on that fantastic fuckin' ass of yours, your tongue's in my mouth and you're kissin' me as only you can kiss me. I know you got a way of twis-tin' shit so it's fucked up in your brain, so I'm hopin' if I'm direct about just what I want from you, it might penetrate and you might keep it straight long enough to give us both what we've been wantin' for a long fuckin' time."

I was trying not to listen, trying not to let what he said penetrate, but I was also failing.

What did he mean we *both* had been wanting for a long time?

"You with me?" he asked.

"Um..." I mumbled because I wasn't sure I was about some of it, but other parts I couldn't *not* be with him, and he grinned.

Then he muttered, "You're with me."

"I think—" I started, and his fingers at my scalp gave me a squeeze.

"I don't give a shit what you think, sweetheart, 'cause by the time it passes your lips, it'll probably be twisted and fucked up. But what *I* think is that we're done here...for now. I take your point and you're right. We'll talk before anything important goes down with those kids. But you need to take my point that we won't talk about it until they've both graduated from high school. Now, are you good with that?"

"You don't give a shit what I think?" I asked softly.

"Not if it's twisted and fucked up," he replied. "Now, are you good with what I said?"

"But—"

"Mara, we got kids to get ready for school," he reminded me. "Are you good with what I said?"

"I think—"

His hand left my hair to wrap around my shoulders, he gave me a squeeze and repeated, "Baby, are you good with what I said?"

"Uh...yeah. I'm good with what you said," I agreed. "Or, at least, that last part."

His eyes roamed my face and I let them because I couldn't think in his arms with the skin of his hard shoulders warm under my fingers. I needed to think somewhere else. Perhaps Canada.

"Somethin' else, sweetheart," he whispered. "Earlier, I was straight about what I want from you, but what you also need to take with you into your cocoon is that I get you more than you think I do. I get you and I like what I get. And you need to know you have nothin' to fear from me. You know what I want, but in gettin' it, I'll go gentle."

Oh my. Gentle Mitch.

Um...*yum*.

"I, uh..." I started, but stopped when his lips touched mine.

"I'll go gentle, baby," he whispered against my lips. "I promise. You'll always be safe with me."

Oh. *My*.

"Mitch," I breathed.

His soulful eyes held mine captive as he repeated firmly, "Always."

I stared into his eyes and he stared into mine. His were warm but serious. Mine were probably terrified.

Then he prompted, "Yeah?"

"Uh...yeah," I whispered.

"Good," he whispered back, dropped his head, veered left and kissed the hinge of my jaw. Then he let me go, saying, "I gotta jump in the shower."

"Um...all right," I mumbled and executed a hasty exit because Mitch was headed to the shower and my brain was headed to visions of Mitch in the shower. I didn't have time to melt into a steaming puddle at the thought of Detective Mitch Lawson naked in the shower or any other thoughts that crowded my mind after all that Detective Mitch Lawson had said to me.

I had kids to get ready for school.

# CHAPTER FIFTEEN

## He's Six Foot Three and Never Misses a Workout

"EXCELLENT," I SAID, handing the receipt to my customer who just purchased our second-highest-end model, the Slumber Excelsior. "Delivery is scheduled between ten and twelve on Saturday. This is guaranteed, and your delivery men will be…" I clicked the computer keyboard a couple of times, checking the monitor, then smiled back at my customer, "Luis and Paul."

"You even know their names?" the customer asked.

"Sure," I replied as, out of the corners of my eyes, I saw Roberta wandering our way. "Luis has been working with us for six years. Paul started two years ago."

"This really is a family place," the customer mumbled.

"Absolutely!" I declared brightly. As Roberta got closer, the customer looked over his shoulder at her then back at me quickly.

"Um…can I ask…" he started. I leaned in, raising my eyebrows encouragingly. "What are *you* doing Saturday between ten and twelve?"

I leaned back and stared at him.

I hated when this happened and it happened a lot.

"Just that…" he grinned, "you might want to come over

and have coffee. You know, make sure they get there all right."

"I'll be taking care of my two children," I blurted a semi-lie, he blinked and Roberta audibly choked down a laugh. His eyes shot to my left hand then back to my face.

"Yes, she and her police detective boyfriend will be having coffee at that time," Roberta chimed in. I turned wide eyes to her, and she joined me at the counter. "He's six foot three," she added. "And never misses a workout," she finished.

"Right," he muttered.

"Um..." I mumbled. "Still, enjoy your mattresses and if you ever need anything else in the, uh...bedroom..." God! Ugh, I hated this. "Remember Pierson's."

I smiled gamely at him.

He nodded and took off just as the door opened and LaTanya, of all people, walked in, eyes on me. But I didn't have time for a surprise visit from LaTanya. I turned to Roberta.

"Bobbie, what on earth? Mitch isn't my boyfriend!" I hissed.

"You're sleeping in his bed," Roberta pointed out, and I lamented my sharing earlier that day about what had gone on the night before.

"But—"

"And Mitch is sleeping *in* his bed *with* you," she went on.

Now I *really* lamented sharing my evening with Roberta, but mostly I lamented how much I'd shared. However, what Mitch said about lying to my friends rankled, so I shared. Now I was reminded why I didn't.

"Mitch slept with you?" LaTanya cried loudly, my eyes darted toward Mr. Pierson's office as I vowed never to share again.

"Yes—" I started to explain, but could get no further.

"Oh my God!" LaTanya exclaimed.

"I know!" Roberta exclaimed right after her.

"Calm down!" I hissed, leaning forward to push LaTanya's shoulder at the same time looking over mine toward Mr. Pierson's office again. When I saw the coast was clear, I looked back at LaTanya. "It wasn't that big of a deal. Billie was in it with us. She was scared and she wanted Mitch close."

"Uh-huh," she nodded, crossing her arms on her chest, a huge white smile on her face.

"The whole situation is extreme," I explained. "And Mitch is just being nice," I lied, because from what he said that morning (something I, fortunately, did not share with Roberta—I had told her about my evening, I had *not* told her about my morning), he wasn't being nice. He was being something else entirely.

"Mitch is a nice guy," LaTanya agreed. "So nice, he'd crawl into bed with a six-year-old..." she paused, leaned forward, her smile got even bigger, Delight shining through, "and *you*," she went on. "Not that there's anything weird about that." She leaned back, shaking her head, her sparkling with Delight eyes going to Roberta. "No, nothin' weird, seein' as you two been dancin' around each other for four years, you barely make eye contact with the guy. Then one night he fixes your faucet and *bam!*" Her arms suddenly uncrossed so her hands could clap loudly and I jumped. "You're all but moved in with him.

Hmm, it appeared I hadn't been as successful as I thought about hiding the fact I avoided Mitch.

"I'm not all but moved in with him," I informed her. "My apartment was broken into and everything in it destroyed. We had nowhere else to go."

"Um...my place?" Roberta chimed in. "Or Bray and

Brent's," she continued. "LaTanya and Derek's," she went on. "Mr. and Mrs. Pierson's," she kept going. "Or a hotel. Denver does have hotels, you know."

"I wasn't thinking. I was tired and, Bobbie, you didn't see it, it was really bad. The worst. Everything was destroyed, even my tampons were all over the bathroom. It was insane," I told her. Her face went soft, just like it had that morning (after she quit freaking out), and her hand came up to give my arm a reassuring squeeze.

"That's true, but girlfriend, you listen to me," LaTanya claimed my attention. "Mitch Lawson is not bein' nice just because he's nice. No man on this earth gets in bed with a woman and a kid just to be nice. You hear what I'm tellin' you?"

I heard what she was telling me but I didn't have to hear her. I'd heard Mitch that morning. In fact, I was pretty sure his words were etched on my brain.

I decided to change the subject and I did this by asking, "What are you doing here anyway?"

"I came to find out what's goin' on with you and Mitch seein' as one day Bray tells me you're makin' Mitch your barbeque chicken pizza, which was news enough considering he's been into you since you scraped off that jackass, and he spent years lookin' for an in that you didn't give him. Then you disappear off radar, and the next thing I know you're drinkin' wine at his place, he's actin' like you're the finest piece of crystal in the whole wide world and he'd go direct into smackdown should anyone threaten to break you. And I'm bringin' over your shit to stay awhile. And since you ain't answerin' your phone, I had to haul my black ass all the way out here to get the scoop. But I'll tell you what, I sure am glad I did. I can't wait to tell Bray and Brent you slept in Mitch's bed *with Mitch*."

"No!" I cried, reaching out again to grab her arm as the phone rang. "Don't tell Bray and Brent."

"Are you high?" she asked, her eyebrows shooting to her hairline. "There is no way I'm not sharin' this. This is huge. Half the single women in the Evergreen moved to the Evergreen because Mitch lives there. Silly bitches, since he does *not* dip his toe in his home pool. Derek told me he has a strict rule, no Evergreen babes. He doesn't need to be bumpin' into old booty calls every time he goes to the gym. Now, he's hooked up with you and you're right across the breezeway. The whole Evergreen is gonna be all over this."

I felt my heart slide into my throat, and my lungs started burning as I heard Roberta say, "Pierson's Mattress and Bed, how can I be of help?" Then she went on to say something that made my heart swell in my throat so it started choking me, "Well hey there, Mitch! How the heck are you?"

I turned woodenly to her to see she was staring at the counter and grinning ear to ear.

"Yeah, she's right here, and I gotta tell you, you called just in time. She just had another customer hit on her," Roberta informed Mitch, and my hand flew out to curl around the edge of the counter as I stared at her aghast. "Happens all the time," Roberta shared. "See, he may come back, sometimes they do, and I hope you don't mind, but I fibbed a little, told the customer she was dating a police detective who never missed a workout. You don't, do you? Ever miss a workout?" she asked curiously, settling in with a hip to the counter like she was going to gab with Mitch all day, and I heard LaTanya giggle. "Right, that's what I thought," Roberta muttered, her smile going broader, but her eyes getting a little glazed. Then she snapped out of it and finished, "So anyway, if he comes back, I can tell him she's on the phone with her man, is that cool with you?"

That was when I found my voice, but just barely, so it came out as a whisper when I demanded, "Bobbie, give me the phone."

"Oh great, glad that's cool with you," Roberta said to Mitch.

Oh God!

"Bobbie," I said louder. "Give me the phone."

"What?" Roberta asked. "Sure. You too. Hope to see you later." Pause, then, "Bye, Mitch." Then her head came up, her shining eyes came to me and shared, "He never misses a workout, just as I suspected."

LaTanya hooted with laughter.

I snatched the phone out of Roberta's hand, glared at her, pushed in front of her and gave both my friends my back as I put the phone to my ear.

"Mitch?"

"Hey, sweetheart," he said softly, I could hear laughter in his voice and I felt that familiar whoosh in my belly.

"Is everything okay?" I asked.

"It was, until your friend told me a customer hit on you. That happen a lot?"

"Um…"

"It happens a lot," he muttered.

"Uh…"

He was back to sounding amused when he remarked, "Good to know your girl's got your back."

"Um…" I mumbled, then pulled myself together and asked, "Why are you calling?"

"Wanted to give you a brief. Got the kids. We're at the station. They looked through some photos. The good news is, it isn't the Russian mob. The bad news is, we have no clue who it is. Showed the kids some photos of your cousin's known associates, nothin' sparked. Bud's workin' with a sketch artist now."

"Is Billie helping?" I asked.

"No, she had a rough night and followed that up with a rough morning. Showed her mug shots, but that's as far as I wanted to take it with her. Hank, a friend of mine, came in with his woman. Now Billie's drawing in an interrogation room with Roxie."

"Thanks, Mitch," I said softly. "I think that was the right thing to do."

"Yeah," he replied just as softly, then asked, "You'll be home around seven?"

"Just after," I answered.

"I'll get the kids fed. You got a taste for something for dinner?"

"I'll pick something up on the way home."

"No, baby, I'll cook. I need to run by the grocery store with the kids anyway. Could pick up anything you want."

I wasn't breathing nor was I listening. I was stuck on the way Mitch told me he'd cook, as if he told me he cooked for me once or twice (or more times) a week for the last ten years of my life.

And I liked the way it sounded.

"Mara?" he called, and I shut my eyes tight then opened them.

"I'm here."

"What do you want for dinner?"

"Really, uh . . . I'll just pick something up."

"We both gotta eat," he told me.

"You can eat with the kids," I told him.

"Billie's decreed she wants fish sticks, and Billy's decreed he wants whatever Billie wants. I stopped eating fish sticks when I was eleven and finally convinced my ma I hated 'em. So, I'm not eatin' with the kids, I'm eatin' with you."

"Mitch—" I started to protest, sounding exactly like I was about to protest.

"Mara, baby, quiet," he said softly, my mouth closed, partly because he called me baby but mostly because he said my name softly. When he got silence he went on. "How's this? Tell me what you don't like and I'll cook whatever I want just as long as it isn't something you don't like."

"Um…" I began then stopped.

"Not hard, baby," he whispered.

"Uh…"

"You like chili?" he asked.

"Um…" I mumbled and he chuckled.

"Mara, sweetheart, do you like chili?"

"Yes," I forced out.

"Then I'll make chili and cornbread," he decided, and the instant he did I started to get hungry because that sounded really good. What sounded better was going to Mitch's and eating dinner with him, whether he cooked it or not.

"Mitch—" I murmured, but stopped speaking and my back went straight when I heard a shouted, "There you fuckin' are!"

I whipped around just as Roberta whispered, "What on earth?" and I saw my mom and Aunt Lulamae bearing down on us.

I watched them charging through the sea of beds, noting they hadn't changed, not a bit, except for the fact that they'd aged thirty years in the thirteen that had passed. They both had dyed blonde hair. Mom's a brassy, straw blonde with at least an inch of steel gray mixed with dark roots. Aunt

Lulamae's was a mixture of blonde and chunks of brunette. She called it streaked, but she did it herself so it looked more like stripes. They were baring way too much cleavage considering not only their breasts, but also their skin were sagging. Their skin was also leathery and overly tanned even though summer hadn't quite started. They were also both wearing skintight everything. Mom: capri pants and a scoop-necked T-shirt; Aunt Lulamae: jeans and a flouncy blouse that was unbuttoned way too far down, and the buttons that were done up were straining. They both had on too much makeup, as in enough to cover the faces of the entire squad of Denver Broncos cheerleaders for at least half the season. And they were both teetering on high-heeled, platform stripper shoes.

Good God. There they were. *At my work*.

"You little *bitch*!" Aunt Lulamae shrieked when she got close.

I did nothing, said nothing, just stood there staring at them in horror, mixed liberally with fear.

"Jesus, is that the Trailer Trash Twins?" Mitch asked in my ear.

"And who are you?" LaTanya asked the Trailer Trash Twins.

Aunt Lulamae shoved her hand, palm up, about half an inch from LaTanya's face. LaTanya's head jerked back about half a foot, her hands went directly to her hips and her brows snapped together.

Uh-oh.

"I'm talkin' to you," Aunt Lulamae snapped at me. "You hear me, you too big for your britches little *bitch*?"

I started to come unfrozen when Mitch said urgently in my ear, "Mara, listen to me—"

"Gotta go," I muttered and put the phone in its cradle.

"Get yo' hand outta my face," LaTanya hissed.

"Kiss my white ass," Aunt Lulamae shot back.

I could swear I heard LaTanya growl.

Uh-oh!

"Aunt Lulamae, Mom," I said quietly, starting to move around the counter, "please, this isn't—"

I stopped talking because Aunt Lulamae's hand dropped, and both she and Mom skewered me with a glare.

"What the fuck, Marabelle? What...the...*fuck*?" Mom asked, eyes following me as I positioned myself in between them and LaTanya and Roberta. I then felt both my girls positioning themselves close to either side of my back.

As we all took our positions, I wondered, what the fuck what?

Mom didn't elucidate. She and Lulamae just kept glaring.

"This is your mom?" Roberta whispered incredulously.

"'Course I'm her mom," Mom answered. "Shit, she's the spittin' image 'a me."

That was when I heard Roberta making a gurgling strangled noise at the same time I heard LaTanya make a strangled gurgling noise. Mom and Aunt Lulamae heard the noises, and both their eyes narrowed and both their hands went to a hitched hip.

Oh boy!

"Listen," I said quickly, "I know you want to talk to me, but now is not a good time. I'm at work." Then I said what I didn't want to say at the same time I vowed that once they got gone I'd buy a new phone. "I'll give you my cell number. Call me tonight. We'll arrange to meet and talk."

"No, we're gonna talk right here, right now, about my grandbabies," Aunt Lulamae declared. "And we're gonna do it here 'cause you don't got no stick-up-his-ass po-lice detective here to get all..." she paused, then, considering she had about a quarter of the brain cells normal people have since she killed all the other ones, she went on unimaginatively, "stick-up-his-ass po-lice detective on us."

But it was with that, she made a mistake.

She'd insulted Mitch.

The Mitch who, just weeks ago, was my dream man from afar, smiling at me warmly even though he didn't know me.

Then he was the Mitch who took care of my doohickey on the sink and even paid for it, no matter that it cost a few dollars, he did it. And then he was the Mitch who fed her grandkids Lola's, which might have been the nicest meal they'd ever had in the nicest place they'd ever been. And that very night he was the Mitch who was going to feed them fish sticks. And he was the Mitch who held Billie close to him when she was scared and cared a great deal that Billy trusted him. And he was also the Mitch who handled me with care when my apartment had been torn apart—yes, exactly as LaTanya said—as if I was the finest piece of crystal in the whole wide world and he'd go directly into smackdown should anyone threaten to break me. And, lastly, he was the Mitch who did hundreds more things to kick in for a woman and two kids he barely knew just because he was a good guy, a nice guy.

Okay, so, maybe it was in part to get in my pants, but that, I figured, was a *small* part.

He was just a good, nice guy.

What he was *not* was a guy with a stick up his ass.

Therefore, as I felt my body freeze from head to toe, I also felt my lips move, and they moved to whisper angrily, "Don't talk about Mitch that way."

"And don't you tell your auntie how to talk," Aunt Lulamae shot back then looked at Mom. "Always high and mighty, always—"

I interrupted her, still whispering, but this time with a hiss giving words that had no sibilant edge a dangerous sibilant edge, "Don't you *ever* talk about Mitch that way."

"Uh-oh," LaTanya muttered from behind me.

"Mara, honey—" Roberta started.

But Mom ignored them and leaned into me. "And don't *you* tell your aunt how to talk."

I leaned into her right back. "I haven't *seen* you for thirteen years. *Thirteen years.* This is the first time I see you, you come into my place of business and you're loud, rude, bossy and you insult my ... my ..." I lost it for a second then said, "My Mitch, who's a nice guy, a *good* guy, and you don't know him enough to insult him. You don't say hello. You don't ask how I am. You just be ..." I lost it again then finished, *"you."*

"Marabelle—" Mom began, but I shook my head and raised *my* hand up in front of *her* face. Her eyes narrowed on it, but I'd made my point, she shut up so I dropped it.

"Be who you are, say what you have to say, treat me like you always treat me, but don't you dare, *don't you dare* insult Mitch," I snapped.

That was when I heard Mr. Pierson say from behind me, "Mara, dear, Mitch is on the phone."

I blinked and turned to look over my right shoulder, seeing LaTanya grinning like a lunatic and beyond her Mr. Pierson grinning like one too and holding out his cell phone.

I sucked in breath, turned my head back, blasted my mom and Lulamae with the heat of my eyes, which, unfortunately, didn't incinerate them, then I took the two steps I needed to take to get to Mr. Pierson. I lifted my hand and he put his phone in it.

I put it to my ear and whispered, "Mitch?"

"They insulted me?" he said back, but he didn't sound upset, he sounded like he was smiling.

He'd heard. How much, I had no idea, but he knew the Trailer Trash Twins had insulted him—tall, beautiful Detective Mitch Lawson.

I didn't reply. I was horrified, so much so I was immobile and speechless.

My silence lasted a while as I ignored my mom and Aunt Lulamae snapping at a murmuring Mr. Pierson, LaTanya and Roberta, and Mitch called into the void, "Sweetheart?"

"How much did you hear?" I asked quietly.

"Place of business, rude, loud, they insulted your Mitch, I'm a good guy then all the rest."

My Mitch.

I closed my eyes, dropped my head and went silent again.

Mitch again called into the void, but he used a different endearment this time, "Honey?"

I still said nothing.

That was when he said, "Honest to God, do you think I care what the Trailer Trash Twins think about me?"

"I care," I blurted, and I didn't know why I blurted it or why I cared except I did. Not about Mom and Aunt Lulamae's opinion, just that I cared if *anyone* insulted Mitch.

Mitch didn't know why either, which was probably why he asked, "For fuck's sake, why?"

Finally, I turned to see Roberta, LaTanya and Mr. Pierson in it with my mom and Lulamae, faces were red (those would be Mom, Lulamae and Roberta), brows were furrowed (that would be Mr. Pierson) and hands were on hips with head bobbing (that would be LaTanya), and I decided it was time to move on, which meant wading back in.

"They're still here and they're into it with Mr. Pierson, Roberta and LaTanya. I should go do something," I told him.

"You don't need to do anything, baby. Bob is keeping them engaged while units make their way there. I'm having them picked up. I want them brought in and questioned about what happened at your apartment."

I turned away from the kerfuffle and blinked at the carpet at my feet as I asked, "What?"

"I have a plan for the Trailer Trash Twins," he informed me.

I blinked again and asked, "You do?"

"Yeah, baby, I do. You put the phone down on me, I called Bob. He already knew to expect this, I explained things and he's instigating Operation Take out the Trash."

I couldn't help it, I giggled.

Then I whispered, "Operation Take out the Trash?"

He sounded like he was smiling again when he replied, "It's not good, but it's all I got right now. We can come up with better names tonight."

That actually sounded fun.

"And what's your plan?" I asked.

"The first part is gettin' them outta there, gettin' them in here and makin' sure they didn't do that to your apartment. The rest, I'll tell you tonight over chili."

"Okay," I said quietly, still liking the idea of having chili with Mitch at his place that night, even if it meant talking about my aunt and mother.

"And another part of the first part is Bob takin' care of this situation so you don't have to. I'm guessin' he's waded in. You let him deal with it and you hang back."

I looked back at the group and saw Mitch was right. Mr. Pierson had his arms straight out to his sides and he was herding a sniping Mom and Aunt Lulamae toward the door with Roberta and LaTanya at his back at the same time I was wondering when Mr. Pierson became "Bob" to Mitch.

I called him Mr. Pierson because he was my boss, but he was also Mr. Pierson a father figure, like your best friend's dad, who you wished was your dad. But Mitch was the kind of guy who held authority, not just because of his job but because of how he generally was, so I didn't suspect many men were "Mr." anything to him, but he was Detective Lawson to them. And he was a guy and Mr. Pierson was a guy and that was just the way of the world.

It hit me that Mitch was Mitch to Mr. Pierson and Mr. Pierson was Bob to Mitch because they'd formed a bond in order to protect me like they were doing just then and that whoosh went through my belly yet again.

So I whispered, "Mitch," and his name came out heavy with meaning.

Mitch heard it and understood it, and I knew he did when he said softly but quickly, "Remember what I said last night about the way it's gonna be?"

"Yes," I said quietly.

"Well, that's the way it's gonna be. I'm keepin' you safe. Bob is dealin' with this. You do your job, you sell mattresses, you come home, we eat chili and I deal with shit that makes you unsafe. Whatever shit that is and however you're unsafe. You with me?"

That was a good question.

Was I with Mitch?

"Baby, you with me?" he asked into my silence.

I stared unseeing at the action in front of me, considering this question, which maybe I was giving more weight than he intended it to have, and then my mouth made a decision before my mind caught up.

"I'm with you, Mitch," I whispered, and it was his turn to be silent.

From his silence, I knew that he knew the weight I'd given his question.

I held my breath.

Then he ordered gently, "Go and sell mattresses."

I pulled in breath and saw the police cruiser pull up to the front door. Then I saw my mother see it and heard her screech, *"What the fuck? Not again!"*

Mitch heard it too.

"Cruiser's there," he muttered.

"Marabelle!" Mom shouted as the cops folded out of the car. "You call that *stick-up-his-ass* cop boyfriend 'a yours *off* your aunt and me."

I took the phone away from my ear, thanked God for the first time in my life there were no customers in the store and tried to be as well-mannered as I could be when I called back, "No! And *especially* no if you keep saying that about him!"

"Is there a problem here?" one of the newly arrived police officers asked, and Mr. Pierson strode forward nodding.

"Jesus! Can't I talk to my own daughter?" Mom shouted.

"Stick up my ass?" Mitch asked in my ear, again sounding like he was smiling.

I closed my eyes.

"Marabelle! Get over here and talk to these cops!" Aunt Lulamae demanded.

"Mara, sweetheart, you stay right where you are. Those officers have been briefed," Mitch ordered.

"Right," I whispered to Mitch.

*"Marabelle!"* Mom shrieked.

"You okay for me to let you go, or do you need me to stay on the line until they're gone?" Mitch asked in my ear.

I opened my eyes and watched both Mom and Aunt Lulamae snapping at the officers, Mr. Pierson, Roberta and LaTanya, while somewhat resisting the officers' instructions and, therefore, they pulled out their handcuffs.

So my answer was, no. No, I was not okay for him to let me go while I was watching my mother and aunt get handcuffed at the same time my boss and my two best friends watched it too.

"I'm fine," I lied.

More silence, then, "You want beer or wine with chili?"

I blinked at his question as Roberta and LaTanya smiled as the officers shoved my handcuffed mother and aunt toward the doors. This happened while Mr. Pierson stared at them like he'd been talked into going to an avant-garde play he did not get and didn't much like, and I asked distractedly, "What?"

"Beer or wine with chili?" Mitch repeated.

"Um..."

"Beer goes better, baby, but you want wine, I'll get you wine. We drank all I had last night, so you gotta tell me if you want more."

"Beer's fine," I told him.

"You want me to get somethin' for dessert?"

"Uh..."

The officers were opening the backdoors to their cruiser.

"Ice cream?"

"Um..."

The officers were shoving Mom and Aunt Lulamae in.

"A frozen apple pie?"

"Uh..."

The officers were closing the doors on Mom and Aunt Lulamae.

"The kids and me could swing by Tessa's Bakery and get cupcakes."

I'd had those cupcakes, more than once, therefore I stated instantly, "Cupcakes."

"Right." And in his tone was another smile.

The officers were climbing in the front of the cruiser.

Then he said, "Got Billie another teddy bear."

The cruiser started to pull away as I asked, "Pardon?"

"Before I went to get them from school, swung by Target, got her another teddy bear."

I moved to the counter and put my hand on it because suddenly my legs were trembling.

And they were trembling because Mitch went out of his way and got Billie another teddy bear.

But they were also trembling because he knew I'd lied about being fine for him to let me go. And my guess was that he was a busy guy, but he was still taking his time to talk to me in an attempt to divert my attention from my trailer trash relatives and the mess they were making of my life. And since he was a busy guy, I knew I was sucking more of his time with all that was going on with Billy, Billie and Bill, him bonding with Bob, and instigating Operation Take out the Trash and then some.

Therefore, when I had my hand on the counter to hold myself up, I told him softly, "They're gone."

"Good," he said softly back.

I pulled in a steadying breath.

Then, still talking softly, I said, "I'm okay now, Mitch."

"Good," he repeated, also still talking softly.

I pulled in another steadying breath.

Then I whispered, "Thank you."

"You're welcome, baby," he whispered back.

"I'll see you tonight," I told him.

"Now, that makes it worth it," he replied, causing another belly whoosh, then he said quietly, "Later, honey."

"Bye, Mitch."

I heard him disconnect.

I flipped Mr. Pierson's phone shut and lifted my head to see my crew was all back and their eyes were on me.

I took them all in and said, "I'm so sorry. They—"

"Not another word, Mara," Mr. Pierson cut me off firmly. I looked to him, and his hand came up, his fingers curling around my bicep. He stepped in close and said gently, "Not another word, dear. Don't think about it. Mitch and I have it *all* sorted."

He held my eyes, squeezed my arm, smiled at me then let me go. Carefully he took his phone from my hand and walked toward the back and his office.

I turned and watched him go.

Then I turned back to see both Roberta and LaTanya staring at me.

That was when I bit my lip.

And when I bit my lip, LaTanya looked down at my mouth then up into my eyes and she ordered, "Right, the juicy stuff first, and that's what's goin' on with you and Mitch. Then we'll get to the Roller Derby Rejects. Now, sock it to me."

Roller Derby Rejects.

That was funny.

And what was funnier, but not in a humorous way, was that both Roberta and LaTanya were not looking at me like I was a Roller Derby Reject or, worse, stunned, shocked and disgusted at learning from whose loins I'd sprung. They were looking curious (very) and, well, like Roberta and LaTanya.

Not only that, Mr. Pierson didn't either. He just told me he and Mitch had it sorted in a way that sounded like he was honored to be in on Operation Take out the Trash.

And so I took in another steadying breath, looked at two women who meant the world to me, and my mouth made another decision before my mind caught up.

"Mitch is into me, I'm into him and I think I was switched at birth," I announced, Roberta and LaTanya both stared at me for several seconds, then they both burst out laughing.

And when they were done, I shared.

That's right, I shared.

Some of it I had to share between dealing with customers, but I shared it.

All of it.

And when I was done, they no longer looked curious, but they still just looked like Roberta and LaTanya.

Two women who meant the world to me.

# CHAPTER SIXTEEN

## My Mara Likes Candles

MITCH AND I didn't come up with different names for Operation Take out the Trash over chili, cornbread and cupcakes, seeing as Mitch was helping Billy with his homework and Billie was inexplicably and unusually grumpy. Billie's bad mood took all my attention between bites of delicious chili, cornbread and, finally, cupcake, as she grumbled, griped, moaned and misbehaved.

Mitch made good chili, by the way. There were four different kinds of beans. It was spicy, meaty and flavorful, but not too hot, and he topped it with grated cheese, which was all melty. The cornbread was awesome. And cupcakes from Tessa's Bakery never disappointed, partly because the cake was rich and moist, but mostly because she always topped them with a mountainous swirl of frosting.

I decided it was Billie's broken sleep last night that was making her grouchy, and I was with her. I was tired too. Except I couldn't be grouchy with a grouchy kid on my hands and Mitch close.

Finally, we got them ready for and into bed, something that was usually not a chore; they were good kids. Billy didn't put up a fuss, but Billie was whiney and recalcitrant, and I was a lot more tired when I finally got her settled. While I read to her, she dropped off, clutching her new teddy bear.

And it was after that I wandered back into Mitch's living room to see him on the sectional, beer in hand, long legs stretched out, feet up on the huge ottoman, a baseball game on his flat screen. But his neck was twisted and his eyes were on me over the back of the couch.

"She down?" he asked quietly. I was tired, worried about Billie, worried about everything else and hoping Billie got a good night's sleep, and still his question made my heart flutter.

It was simple but intimate. His concern for Billie mingled with concern for me, wrapped around a familiar kind of question a father asks a mother, a husband asks a wife.

I liked it. The simplicity and intimacy of it was beautiful, and it was more beautiful coming from a handsome man, a good man, a nice man who was sitting on his awesome sectional in his gorgeous living room with his eyes warm on me.

I thought all this.

But I said, "Yeah."

Then, tired, worried, suddenly alone with Mitch, feeling weird about where I was, what I was doing and how quickly all of it happened, not to mention what Mitch had said to me that morning, I considered my options of what was next. And this was where I should sit on his sectional.

I decided the safest bet was as far away from him as possible, so that was where I went. He was in the middle of one side of the sofa. I sat close to the armrest on the opposite side.

He watched me do this and his lips twitched, but he didn't move.

It wasn't lost on me that the last time we had a moment

of alone time in a living room while a baseball game was on TV, we'd ended up in a clinch. And I was tired, but it was still early-ish. And lastly, going to bed meant going to *his* bed.

So I had to kill time and do it so I wouldn't end up in a clinch.

To accomplish that, I blurted the first thing that came to mind, "You have good taste."

"What?"

As I spoke my eyes were on the ottoman while I shifted to curl my bare feet under me and leaned against the arm-rest but when he asked his question, I looked at him.

"You have good taste," I repeated, and his brows went up in question, so I haltingly explained, now feeling weirder, "You, um...dress really nice and your, uh... apartment is really nice too. I mean, uh...you have really nice furniture."

To that comment he asked, strangely, "You know Design Fusion?"

I tipped my head to the side and asked back, "The store in Cherry Creek North?"

"Yep," he answered.

"Yes," I answered.

"My sister Penny owns that store."

Uh...*wow*.

I'd been to that store. The furniture in that store was unbelievable and the price tags were even more so.

"Wow," I whispered, and he grinned then flicked a hand out.

"This is her shit," he told me.

"Pardon?"

"She furnished this place for me wholesale."

At that, I blinked. "Your sister furnished your apartment?"

"Yep. She's a nut. She decorates everything. The inside of her fridge is decorated."

I blinked again. "The inside of her fridge is decorated?"

Mitch nodded, grinning.

"How do you decorate the inside of a fridge?" I asked, intrigued by this concept.

"She's got decals on the sides of the fridge and fancy bowls she puts fancy shit in that isn't food that sit on the shelves. Sometimes she even puts small vases with flowers in there."

I didn't know if that was weird or cool. I also didn't share this indecision with Mitch.

Luckily, he kept talking. "When she redecorated her kids' rooms three times in a year, her husband had enough. He talked her into opening her own store so she could decorate other people's houses and make money doin' it instead of spendin' all theirs doin' it. So, when I moved in here, she took over. I let her because if I didn't, she would anyway, and if I fought it, it wouldn't be pretty."

"So you had no say?" I asked, surprised, seeing as Mitch seemed like a man in command of everything and definitely his surroundings.

Mitch shook his head. "I told her it had to be comfortable and it had to look like a guy lived here and not a gay guy. She succeeded on the first. The second is up for debate."

He stopped talking, but his eyes didn't leave me, and I got the feeling he expected me to chime in with my opinion.

So I chimed in with my opinion and stated, "It's, uh... not *totally* gay."

He threw his head back and burst out laughing. I bit my lip. His laughter became chuckles, his chin dipped back down and he caught my eyes.

"That's good, I guess," he muttered through a smile, his eyes very warm making my chest very, *very* warm.

Instead of belatedly but intelligently keeping my mouth shut and absorbing myself in the baseball game, I stupidly decided to clarify, "It looks really nice, Mitch. It suits you, since you always look really nice too."

"So you're sayin' that the way I dress is nice and not *totally* gay?" he teased, and my back straightened a bit because I knew he was teasing but I didn't want him to think I was insulting him, not even a little bit.

And furthermore, the way he dressed was *totally* nice, and not nice in the way gay guys always looked nice.

"No, I'm saying you always look nice as in, um…*nice* and, uh…that's it. You just always look really, *really* nice."

When I was finished speaking, his face changed as did his eyes. Both got warmer, but the latter got dark in a way that made my warm chest even warmer, and other parts of me got warm too. Then, suddenly, his eyes moved over my body curled into the armrest of his not totally gay, but definitely comfy and cool, sofa.

Equally suddenly he got to his feet.

I watched as he moved into the kitchen then back into the living room, and I noticed he was carrying candle jars. Then I watched as he set them in his wall unit and lit them. Then I watched as he turned out a lamp, which meant only one was illuminated, so the glow of the room changed from functional to something else entirely. Then I watched as he moved to the ottoman, nabbed the remote, pointed it at the TV and it went blank. Finally, I watched as he tossed the remote back on the ottoman, tagged another one, pointed it back at the wall unit and suddenly Journey's "Still They Ride" was playing softly from his stereo.

Great song.

And the candles were good ones. The calming scent of fresh cotton was already filling the room.

Candlelight, romantic room illumination and soft music. Uh-oh!

Frozen, I stared as he dropped that remote on the ottoman, came to me, put his hands right into my armpits and lifted me straight up.

"Mitch," I whispered, as my hands curled into his shoulders. One of his arms slid down over my bottom and he leaned into me, then it hooked behind my knees. The other one curled around my upper back; he lifted me up and maneuvered between the ottoman and the couch, taking me with him. He shifted, sat with me in his lap, twisted, leaned back so he was reclining and I was reclining mostly on top of him. Then he rolled so we were both still reclining, but now he was reclining mostly on top *of me*.

Through this, I was silenced by shock.

As he settled on top and beside me with his back to the back of the couch and my back to the seat, I repeated a now breathy, "Mitch."

"Operation Take out the Trash," he whispered, his hand coming up to curl around the side of my neck.

"Pah...pardon?" I whispered back, my hands still curled into his hard shoulders.

"I want your mom and aunt out of Denver," he announced.

I did too. I suspected he knew that, so I didn't respond and concentrated on trying not to respond to his warm, hard body pressed down the length of the side of mine, with his strong hand warm on the skin of my neck.

This got harder when his thumb moved to stroke the underside of my jaw, which felt really nice, but luckily he started talking again, and I decided to concentrate on that.

"As I guessed, they didn't know shit about what happened to your apartment. That doesn't mean I'm gonna lay off them. They're here to give you a hard time. I'm gonna give them a harder time in the hopes that they'll decide it isn't worth it and take off home."

This sounded like a good plan.

"How are you going to do that?" I asked.

"They've been here three days and been to the police station twice. If they move on you, I'll have them arrested."

I finally stopped thinking about his warm, hard body pressed down the length of mine, his strong hand warm on the skin of my neck and his thumb sweeping sweetly on my jaw and stared at him in shock.

"Isn't that police harassment?"

"No," he answered immediately. "It's the police's job to stop citizens *being* harassed. You haven't seen your mom in thirteen years. You haven't shared much, but what you've shared tells me there's a reason why. You've moved on, away from her and set up a life, a good one also away from her. Then she comes to your door shouting it down, getting your neighbors involved. Then she comes to your place of work and uses foul language, getting your boss involved. An officer of the law explained calmly to her and your aunt what the situation was and how they could communicate with you and they ignored it. They did their own thing, which was not the right thing. They change their tune, they contact you and act like decent human beings and we stall Operation Take out the Trash. They keep doin' what they're doin', they get another ride in a cruiser. They've had warnings. Two strikes. Strike three, you press charges and they sit in a cell. They get out, they have two choices. They continue on their current bent and make those charges worse, which means they'll spend more time in Colorado than they expected. Or they get their asses home and leave you and those kids the fuck alone." He paused and held my eyes for a moment before he finished, "They try to get to you one more time, Mara, I'll be explaining those choices to them through bars. That's Operation Take out the Trash."

I stared into his eyes and didn't know what to say.

What I did know was that the depths of humiliation were fathomless that this good man stretched out beside me was dealing with all that was *me*, which was to say Bill and all his garbage and my mom and Lulamae, and all the garbage that was just them.

And because of this, I closed my eyes and turned my head away.

Mitch didn't allow me to escape.

His hand cupped my jaw, turned my head back and he whispered his order, "Look at me, sweetheart."

I opened my eyes.

His head dropped an inch toward mine.

I held my breath.

Then he plumbed the fathomless depths of my humiliation by informing me quietly, "I called Iowa, pulled their sheets."

Oh God.

He went on, "I know about them."

Oh God!

His head dropped another inch so he was all I could see. "And, baby, somethin' else I know. You are *not* them."

My hand left his shoulder so I could curl my fingers around his wrist at my jaw, and I whispered, "Mitch."

"You are not them, Mara."

"I—"

His thumb moved to press against my lips, and his face got even closer.

"You...are...*not*...them, baby," he whispered.

"You..." I said against his thumb, and he moved it to sweep my cheek. "I mean, everything around you, all the stuff consuming your life right now, it's about me, Mitch. It's about where I come from. It's about who I am, and who I am is about *them*."

"You're right and you're wrong," he told me.

My other hand at his shoulder slid down to his chest, and my hand at his wrist joined it when I asked, "How am I wrong?"

"All the stuff consuming my life—as you put it—is about you, and, Mara, baby, I do not mind that. And what it's about is also about you. You being a good person. You tryin' to do right for your cousins. You puttin' yourself out there so they won't live the life I'm guessin' you were forced to live. But what's happening to you and them is about your mom and aunt and Bill and how he didn't pull himself out of that life you pulled yourself out from. And that has not one fuckin' thing to do with you."

"It does," I whispered.

"It doesn't," he returned firmly.

"Mitch, it does."

"Mara," his fingers tensed on my jaw, "why do you think I don't mind all the shit that's consuming my life?"

I blinked because this was a really good question.

"I...I don't know," I stammered, and he grinned with his mouth *and* his eyes, close up, and it was phenomenal. But he added another thumb sweep of my cheek, which made it breathtaking.

"Because you give good Christmas presents," he stated.

I felt my brows draw together as, still stammering, I asked, "Pah...*pardon*?"

"You give good Christmas presents," he repeated.

"LaTanya, Bray, Brent, fuck, even Derek, they all talk about them. And they also talk about the birthday presents you give."

They did?

"But—" I started, but he interrupted me.

"And you work hard. Your coworker thinks the world of you, and your boss thinks you're the shit so much, he considers you like a daughter."

I blinked again, my belly getting warm hearing that he got that from Mr. Pierson, and I asked, "Really?"

Mitch grinned again and answered, "Really."

"I—" I began, but his hand tensed at my jaw, and his face came even closer. So close, I could feel his breath on my lips. I closed my mouth and stared into his soulful brown eyes.

"You look nice. You dress nice. You smell nice. You have a fantastic fucking laugh. You're loyal. You're loving. And, honey, every time I'd see you in the breezeway or at a party, it was cute as all fuckin' hell—even as it was just as frustrating—how you'd tuck that hair behind your ear, avoid me like the plague and get the fuck away from me as fast as you could. Since that moron you used to date left the picture, I've been waitin' for my shot, and it sucks that it comes with you cryin' in my arms and those kids learnin' early that life can really suck. But if takin' that shot means puttin' up with that shit and comes with you bein' where you are right now rather than hiding behind your door and retreating into that world in your head, I'll put up with that shit in order to take it."

Oh my God.

Oh my *God!*

"You've been waiting for your shot?" I whispered.

Mitch nodded. "For two years, and the two years prior

to that I watched and wondered what you were doin' with that asshole who, seriously, sweetheart, even at a glance did *not* come close to deservin' to breathe your air, much less have you on his arm."

I had to admit, even though Destry was out of my zone, Mitch wasn't really wrong about that.

But he was wrong about something else.

And he was a good guy, a nice guy and he needed to know.

"Mitch, there are things you don't know about me," I told him carefully.

"You're right, but, we get time, you'll tell me."

"I don't think—"

He interrupted again, "Somethin' happened to you, and whatever that was, you'll tell me at your time, at your pace. I pulled your mom and aunt's sheets, and, Mara, seeing your cousin, your mother and your aunt, knowin' about them, I'm not turned off by it, honey. Knowin' that was how you grew up and seein' you now, miles away from that shit, having left that life behind, which isn't an easy thing to do, only makes me *more* into you, when I was already really fuckin' into you."

I stared into his dark brown eyes so close to mine and couldn't stop from blurting, "What you're saying does not fit in Mara World."

It was a stupid thing to do, stupid and revealing, and I knew this when one of his eyebrows twitched in surprise before both of his eyes lit with humor and his body shook with it.

Okay, so I sounded like a dork, but I *was* a dork. He really needed to get this for his own good, and what he needed to get was not only the fact I was a dork, but all of it.

So I kept talking. "It's against all the laws of nature."

His body started shaking more, his hand slid from my jaw to my neck and curled around, he bit his lip and I knew just looking at him that it was to stop himself from roaring with laughter.

So I whispered, "I'm not being funny."

Suddenly, the amusement swept from his features, he slowly closed his eyes and dropped his head so his forehead was resting lightly on mine, just as his fingers at my neck gave me a gentle squeeze.

Then he opened his eyes, looked deep into mine and he whispered back, "I know, but, baby, today you told me you were with me. And I'm askin' you now to stick with me, and if you do, I promise, I fuckin' *swear*, I'll guide you to a place where you get that what you just said was fuckin' hilarious."

I just *knew* he'd figured out how weighty my words were earlier.

"Mitch—" I started, but he lifted his head away an inch and shook it.

"Mara's World is fucked up and twisted, and my guess, that mother of yours and probably that aunt had somethin' to do with that. In the real world, the world everyone lives in, including you, honey, you and me make a whole fuckuva lot of sense."

That whoosh swept through my belly even as I pressed lightly against his chest and said quietly, "I don't think so and... and... I don't want you to be disappointed when you figure it out."

I watched his eyes close slowly again. When they opened I caught my breath at what I saw in their fathomless depths.

Way before I recovered (not that I *could* recover), Mitch's head descended but it veered to my right.

Then I felt his teeth nip my earlobe, then his tongue touched it and he reminded me on a whisper, "Today, you yourself said I was your Mitch."

Oh God, I forgot he heard that.

"Am I your Mitch?" he went on.

I started breathing faster, my chest so warm it was hot, my fingers clenched in his shirt, and I didn't know if it was to hold him to me or push him away.

"Am I your Mitch, baby?" he pressed.

I couldn't talk about this. I couldn't explain to him why I defended him. How I said he was my Mitch because I didn't know what to say. I didn't know how to describe who he was to me because I didn't *know* who he was to me. But I also couldn't allow them to insult him.

I had to move us on.

And that was why I told him, "The candles smell really good," awkwardly changing the subject and deciding my hands clenched in his shirt were to push him away, which I tried to do but he didn't budge an inch.

It was then I heard the song change to Paul McCartney's "My Love."

Oh God!

I loved this song! It was a great song, a sweet song, a *beautiful* song.

His nose tweaked my earlobe, then his lips slid down my neck as his hand at the other side slid over my shoulder, in over my chest then out and down my side.

While he did this, I shivered.

"If I'm your Mitch, you're my Mara," he whispered against my skin, his words making me shiver again because I liked that idea, a whole lot. Then I felt his tongue glide along my throat as his hand glided back up my side, and I shivered yet again.

Okay, it was safe to say I was losing control of the conversation (not that I ever had control of the conversation) *and* my body, and I had to do something about it.

So, somewhat desperately and not-so-somewhat breathily, I noted, "The scent is really nice, and you can tell those candles are good ones. They obviously didn't skimp with the oils."

His lips moved on my throat and I knew it was because he smiled. Then his tongue slid up the other side of my neck to my ear, where he kept whispering. "*My* Mara likes candles, so when the kids and I were at Target pickin' up food, Billie picked those candles for you."

He noticed I liked candles.

Oh God.

That was *so* nice.

His thumb started stroking my side, just under the swell of my breast.

*Oh God!*

That *felt* supernice.

I unclenched my hands and pressed lightly on his chest as I turned my head and whispered, "Mitch—"

But when I did, his head turned too, his lips captured mine and he kissed me.

He did not go all out. It was gentle. It was sweet. Probing, unhurried and soft. There were tongues, but it was nice, not invasive, giving a lot but taking nothing. And my fingers clenched in his shirt again, this time definitely to hold him to me.

Mitch broke the kiss and whispered against my lips, "Love that mouth of yours, sweetheart," and I couldn't help it, I shivered again.

He moved slightly away and held my eyes as his hands went to my wrists at his chest. He moved them around him and down, not releasing them, but still managing to pull his shirt out of his jeans and shove my hands up under so they encountered the hot, sleek skin and hard muscle of his back.

He felt so unbelievably good I involuntarily made a noise in the back of my throat.

I watched his eyes get darker. I liked the way they got darker, then his head descended and his lips captured mine again in another kiss. This one still sweet, unhurried, gentle, but not probing, giving a lot, but now taking a little, coaxing me to give. And I wanted to give to Mitch, so I did. He'd added his hands, moving on me the same way. Unhurried, gentle, discovering, and my body melted under his. My fingers explored the contours of his back. I liked what I felt so much, my hands shoved up higher so I could explore more.

He broke the kiss again, but this time his lips glided across my cheek, along my jaw. He added his tongue when they swept down my throat then back up. He added his teeth again, nipping my earlobe, and then he worked the skin behind my ear with his tongue. All slow, leisurely, taking his time as my hands moved on his back. My body yielded more under his, and my breath came faster and faster against the skin of his neck.

Then his hand moved over my rib cage, up, and I held my breath as his head came up and his lips caught mine, his tongue sliding inside as his fingers curled over my breast.

I liked the feel of Mitch's warm hand at my breast so much my back arched slightly, and a small moan glided up my throat and into his mouth.

His thumb swept over my nipple, and I liked that a whole lot more, so my back arched hard, and a long, deep moan glided up my throat and into his mouth.

That was when leisurely and gentle got lost. As my moan slid into his mouth, Mitch slanted his head and deepened the kiss. It was harder, demanding and, God, so, *so* good.

I pulled one of my hands out of his shirt so I could move it up his back, his neck and into his soft, thick hair and hold him to me. And I did this because I didn't ever want him to stop kissing me.

Not ever.

His finger met his thumb at my rock-hard nipple and rolled it over my blouse and, God, *God*, that felt so damned good I whimpered against his tongue. My hips surged up, coming into deep contact with the hardness of his, and all was lost.

He shifted so his body was more on top of me as his other hand went down my side and yanked up my skirt, even as his knee came up between my legs, forcing them open, but he didn't have to. I was already curving one leg around his thigh.

"Jesus, so sweet. So fucking, *fucking* sweet," he muttered against my lips, his voice deeper, gruff, and I felt the change in his tone rocket straight between my legs.

"Mitch," I whispered, lifting my head as my hand in his hair pulled him down to me. I kissed him, hard, demanding, sliding my tongue in his mouth, and this time I got his groan in mine in return.

That rocketed straight between my legs too.

He moved his hand at my breast to the buttons of my blouse. Swiftly and expertly he undid them as we kissed hot, wet and heavy. I pressed my body up into his and he ground his down into mine, and I loved taking the weight of him, feeling the power of him.

Then suddenly he stopped undoing the buttons halfway

down my rib cage, his fingers curled in, tugging my blouse aside, and I gasped into his mouth as my body twitched with excitement. The cup of my bra was drawn quickly aside, and I lost his mouth on mine, but his fingers curled under my breast, lifting it. His upper body angled down, his lips rounded my nipple and he sucked deep.

As in *deep*.

Oh God, *God, God*! That felt *unbelievable*.

So unbelievable, my back came off the couch, my head pressed into the cushion as my neck arched and the fingers of both my hands drove into his hair. All this as I moaned deep then whimpered as what he was doing with his mouth at my nipple shot a path of fire right between my legs.

Mitch suddenly lifted his head and twisted his neck so he was looking at the back of the couch.

I stared at him, dazedly wondering why he was doing that and how I could get him to keep doing what he'd been doing a second ago, when he muttered a harsh, low, *"Fuck."*

Suddenly his hands were moving quickly on me, pulling up my bra, drawing my blouse closed and yanking down my skirt.

Then his body quickly shifted so it was fully over mine, covering it completely, and his neck twisted the other way so he could look across the ottoman.

And it was then I heard a trembling, little-girl voice penetrate my foreplay-on-the-couch-with-Ten-Point-Five-Detective-Mitch-Lawson-addled-daze saying, "Auntie Mara, I don't feel too good."

# CHAPTER SEVENTEEN

## Keep Mitch Around

MY HEAD TWISTED around. I looked across the ottoman just in time to see Billie, standing at the opposite side of the couch, lean forward and vomit on Mitch's living room carpet.

"Shit," Mitch muttered, moved and moved me with him. Before I knew what was happening, I found myself standing on my feet by the couch.

I blinked and teetered then focused to see Mitch lift Billie in his arms, and then he was striding swiftly through the living room toward the hall.

I skirted the ottoman and her sick then ran after them, doing the buttons on my shirt. By the time I made it to his master bath, the lights were on, and Billie was getting sick in the toilet, Mitch crouched beside her, holding back her hair. His head turned and tipped back and his eyes hit mine.

"She's burnin' up," he said softly.

I moved directly to the bathroom closet hoping that was where he kept his washcloths.

"How bad?"

"Don't know. I don't have a thermometer. You got one at your place?"

"No," I answered, seeing he did keep his washcloths in the closet. I grabbed one, went to the sink and turned the tap on cold.

I heard more getting sick sounds, and then Billie whined the obvious into the toilet, "I don't feel good."

I wrung out the cloth, cooing at her, "I know, baby. Get that sick out. I've got a cold cloth coming."

I moved to Billie, Mitch shifted a bit out of the way still holding her hair, while I leaned in and flushed the toilet. Then I folded the cloth and put it on her forehead as she coughed into the bowl.

Suddenly I heard Mitch saying, "Yeah, honey, sorry to call so late but Billie's pukin' and she's burnin' up. What do we do?"

My eyes went to him to see he was on the phone, his gaze on Billie's back. I lifted a hand to stroke her there as more sick came out. I bit my lip as my heart clenched, feeling her little body working so hard to heave.

Clearly, this was why she was irritable and misbehaving.

Clearly, another woman with more experience with children would have read the signs.

Clearly, I should have been paying more attention to my charge and not freaking out about Mitch and then fooling around with him on his couch.

Clearly, I sucked as a guardian.

"No, I don't think Mara's got that, but I'll go to the drugstore. Yeah, thanks, later," Mitch said, turning his phone off, his eyes coming to me. "My sister says children's Tylenol and we should get a thermometer. If her fever is bad and stays bad, we need to take her to the ER."

"Okay, are you doing the drugstore run or me?" I asked.

"I'll go, you good here?"

I nodded and took her hair from his hand. He nodded

back and leaned across her to kiss my forehead. Then he straightened and was at the door when I called his name.

He stopped and looked down at me. "Yeah?"

"She doesn't have any insurance," I whispered.

His jaw clenched, he nodded and said softly, "Don't worry about that now, sweetheart. Let's get some medicine in her and ride it out. Yeah?"

"Yeah, Mitch."

"I'll be right back."

"Okay."

Then he disappeared.

Billie had drained herself dry, and I had her in bed with a new cool cloth on her head. I had also managed to clean up her sick in the living room without vomiting (though I did gag a lot) and had blown out all the candles and figured out his remotes to turn off the music by the time Mitch got back. He came in and I was curled around Billie in his bed. Billie was curled around me and she was whining, moaning and clearly in a state. Therefore I was inwardly in a state because her noises and the way she was clutching me was scaring me to death.

Mitch hit the door, and my eyes went right to him.

"Hurry," I whispered.

"Right," he whispered back.

He dosed her and took the cloth from her forehead because it was heated clean through while I coaxed her to hold the thermometer under her tongue. Mitch came back with a newly cooled cloth for her forehead and an extra one to put at the back of her neck. Then he took out the thermometer, read it and muttered, "Fuck."

"How bad?" I asked.

"Not good," he said, dropped the thermometer on his nightstand and pulled his phone out again. Billie pressed into me and started shivering, so I moved us both under the covers. I stretched out on my side, pulled her into me and returned the cold cloth to her head as Mitch talked. "Sorry, Penny, her fever's one hundred and three, she's shivering and she's burrowing so hard into Mara, it looks like she wants Mara to absorb her." He paused as I watched him and his eyes never left me. "Yeah, I gave it to her." Pause. "Yeah." Pause. "Right." Pause. "Yeah, I'll call you tomorrow and let you know." Pause. "Yeah, thanks, honey, later." And he ended the call.

"Your sister?" I asked.

"Yeah. She says wait it out. Give her another dose when it's safe, which is in four hours, and check her temperature. If it's worse than now, take her in."

"Mitch," I whispered with fear in my tone because I didn't know much about fevers, but little Billie's body being a hundred and three seemed bad to me.

I stared as he sat down on the bed, yanked off his boots, got up, lifted the covers and climbed into bed opposite Billie and then he slid into Billie and me.

"Mitch," I repeated my whisper, this whisper had fear too but it was an altogether different kind.

"I'll set the alarm to wake us in four hours and we'll check her."

"Um...maybe you shouldn't be in this bed—" I started.

"Want Mitch," Billie whined, somehow managing to burrow into both Mitch and me at the same time.

Shit!

His eyes locked on mine.

I tore mine away to look down at my cousin and say, "Billie, Mitch needs—"

She cut me off, "Want Mitch."

Shit!

"Okay then I'll go to the—"

"Want you. Want Mitch. *Want Mitch*!" Her voice was getting loud, and I heard her fear so I lifted my hand, stroked her hair and cuddled her close.

"Okay, he's here. I'm here. It's okay," I cooed.

"Cold," she muttered.

"You'll be okay," I whispered and tipped my eyes to Mitch.

"Don't go," she whispered back.

"I'm not going anywhere," I assured her softly.

"Make sure he doesn't go," she demanded, shifting awkwardly so she could move one of her little arms and grasp onto his shirt with her little fingers.

"I'm right here, gorgeous," Mitch murmured and started stroking her back.

"Cold," she muttered and burrowed again into both Mitch and me.

I took in a deep breath to calm my heart and my panic, panic for Billie and panic seeing as it appeared I'd be sleeping in Mitch's bed with Mitch *again*. Finally I laid my head on the pillow. Mitch rested his head in his hand and his elbow in the pillow. Through this our eyes stayed connected.

"How many kids does your sister have?" I asked quietly.

"Three," he answered.

I nodded. This was good. His sister was clearly an expert.

I pulled in a deep breath and pulled Billie closer. Billie pulled Mitch closer and then burrowed deeper into both of us. Mitch kept stroking her back and, luckily, it didn't take long before she fell asleep.

When I knew she was asleep, quietly, I shared what I thought earlier, "She was acting funny. She's rarely in a bad mood, but I didn't even—"

He knew where I was going and therefore cut me off with a whispered, "Mara, don't."

I shook my head. "She doesn't have insurance, Mitch. If this is bad—"

"Mara, sweetheart, *don't*."

I held his eyes.

Then it all hit me like a freight train. Everything that was happening. Everything that had happened. All of it coming at me so hard, I couldn't hold it back. None of the fear that was crushing me at the same time it seemed to be dragging me along somewhere I didn't know, and I was scared to go, so I had to let it out.

And I did.

"Insurance. Lawyers. A new apartment. Childcare. Mitch, honey, I've got money but not that much. If we have to take her to the hospital that might clean me out. And I didn't even *know* she was *sick* when she was acting like she never acts. I don't know what I'm doing, it's…everything, all of it, it's too much and…" I choked, swallowed, pulled it together (slightly) and then I finished in a small voice, "I didn't even know when my baby was *sick*."

I shut up when his hand left Billie's back, came to my jaw and his thumb pressed against my lips.

"Mara, baby, *don't*," he whispered again. "This is not for now. For now, she's asleep. They got a roof over their heads, food in their stomachs, people who give a shit about them and a ride to school tomorrow. Don't think about that shit now. We'll think about it later. We'll talk about it and we'll sort it out. But, for now, sweetheart, it's all good."

"Billie doesn't have food in her stomach, she just vomited it all up," I reminded him.

He grinned and reminded me, "Well, Bud does."

He held my eyes and I stared into the soulful, fathomless depths of his.

Then I heard Billie's steady breathing and felt the steadiness in Mitch's eyes communicate itself to me as his words penetrated and the freight train tossed me aside. I took a deep breath and I nodded.

His thumb swept my lips in a sweet brush, but his fingers stayed at my jaw as he ordered gently, "I got her for a second. Go, get ready for bed, come back, you take her and I'll do the same."

I kept staring at him. Then I nodded again. I carefully extricated myself from Billie and did what I was told. In my nightie with my face clean and moisturized, I slid under the sheets, and Mitch curled Billie into my arms. Then he cautiously moved out of bed and did the same (though I doubted he cleaned his face and moisturized). Barechested (again) and wearing pajama bottoms (again), he joined Billie and me and curved his big, long, warm body into us both.

Oh boy.

To take my mind off Billie, Mitch and everything, I asked, "You'll set the alarm?"

He nodded.

I curled deeper into Billie and bent my head so my face was in the top of her hair. She was right, the shampoo Mitch gave her smelled pretty.

"Go to sleep, Mara," I heard Mitch say softly.

Right, like that would ever happen with Billie having a temperature of one hundred and three, shivering and throwing up. And with me being a mother figure, but not having that first clue what to do. And me again in bed with Ten Point Five Detective Mitch Lawson after I let him slide

right into second base on his couch without even *trying* to
tag him with the ball.

"Okay," I agreed.

*     *     *

# Mitch

Ten minutes later, Mitch watched Mara fall asleep.

Carefully he rolled, set the alarm, turned out the light,
rolled back and pulled both beautiful females into his arms.

Then he fell asleep.

*     *     *

# Billy

Billy lay staring at the dark ceiling after tiptoeing back to
bed.

He'd gotten up because he'd heard Billie getting sick. It
didn't happen often, but when his sister got sick, he had to
take care of her.

Then he'd hid and watched (when he could) and listened
the whole time Auntie Mara and Mitch took care of her.

That was why he heard what Auntie Mara said.

She didn't have the money to keep them and she was
scared.

She could change her mind.

She could *change her mind*.

And he couldn't let her change her mind.

He'd also heard what Mitch said.

Mitch was on Billy and Billie's side and was trying to
make sure Auntie Mara didn't get too scared.

This meant two things for Billy.

It meant he had to do everything he could to keep Mitch around so Mitch could keep Auntie Mara from being scared and leaving them.

It also meant he and Billie had to be real, extra good so they didn't make Auntie Mara want to go away for other reasons.

He could be good, especially for Auntie Mara, and he could be certain Billie was good.

As for keeping Mitch around, he didn't figure he had to work too hard to do that. Mitch liked Auntie Mara, like, *a lot.* Guys didn't look at girls like Mitch looked at Auntie Mara if they didn't like them and like them *a lot.* And guys didn't touch girls and get close to them all the time like Mitch did with Auntie Mara if they didn't like them and like them *a lot.*

Still, he'd have to do his part to keep Mitch around.

He didn't mind that, he liked Mitch. Mitch was an okay guy and bought Billie a pink teddy bear (twice, he knew, though Billie didn't, and Billy wasn't going to tell her).

And anyway, Auntie Mara looked at Mitch (when he wasn't watching) like Mitch looked at Auntie Mara (and he didn't care if she was watching), so Billy figured she'd want him to stick around too.

*       *       *

## Mitch

Four hours later, Mitch's alarm sounded.

He was on his back and, just like last night, there was one beautiful child female and one beautiful adult female pressed into his side, both their arms thrown over his gut.

Billie's head was at his ribs, Mara's on his shoulder, but this time, Mara's leg was tangled with one of his.

He carefully but quickly threw out an arm, turned off the alarm then put his hand on Billie's forehead.

Cool and clammy, her hair slightly wet, the fever had broken. It came on fast and broke just as fast. Thank Christ.

He turned his head and stretched his hand out again, reset the alarm for morning then cautiously slid out of bed, taking care to replace his body with a pillow under Mara and Billie, but neither female moved even to twitch.

He didn't think for a second of moving to the couch. Instead he walked out of his bedroom, went into the living room, locked the door, turned out the lights, moved through the apartment and back to his room.

He slid back in bed, settled on his back, moving the pillow and replacing it with his body and both beautiful child and adult females snuggled back into him.

He stared at the dark ceiling thinking about hearing Mara call him "my Mitch." He also thought of how she went wild with just the brush of his thumb on her hard nipple.

He grinned at the dark ceiling.

Then he fell asleep.

# CHAPTER EIGHTEEN

## Dream Come True

MY EYES SLOWLY opened and, just like yesterday, upon waking, I was profoundly confused.

And, just like yesterday, this was because my vision was filled with a criminally attractive, smooth-skinned, hard-muscled wall of chest, along with the top of Billie's head pressed to the sculpted ridges of some ribs. Billie's and my arms slung over a flat, carved stomach.

I blinked and, just like yesterday, the chest was still there and Billie was still there, but this time I also felt my bare leg tangled with the soft-cotton-covered hardness of Mitch's.

Oh boy.

Drowsily, I asked myself again how this all happened and how it happened so fast.

Even if I wasn't just awake, *again*, with a bare-chested Mitch (and Billie) and was fully cogitating, I wouldn't have been able to come up with an answer.

Just because my life sucked (mostly, except the part about gentle, sweet, good guy Mitch, Billy and Billie being in it), I decided to give myself a gift and tipped my head back. As I did, I saw a familiar corded throat and a familiar strong, dark-stubbled jaw. And then I was again close-up, staring at Ten Point Five Detective Mitch Lawson's profile in sleep.

I also saw his lips, which now I knew could do amazing things not only when they were pressed against mine, but they could also do amazing things when they were wrapped round my nipple.

And thinking these thoughts while looking at his male beauty and remembering last night (before Billie hurled), I couldn't breathe.

Then the part about Billie hurling came back to me. All thoughts of being in bed again with beautiful Mitch and the maybe more disturbing (but definitely not unpleasant in the least) thoughts of being on Mitch's couch with Mitch flew out of my head. Only thoughts of Billie invaded.

I looked to the clock, and it was six minutes before the alarm was meant to sound. Clearly, Mitch didn't wake me to check on Billie.

Carefully, I extricated my arm from his stomach and touched Billie's forehead.

Cool.

Thank God.

I listened to the room. I could faintly hear both of them breathing, but Billie wasn't breathing heavily. She was breathing deeply, steadily and, from what I could tell, healthily.

I closed my eyes and sighed in relief.

No emergency room visit and the bill that went with it.

Mental note: Talk to Mr. Pierson about getting them both on my insurance.

Mental note part two: Do not think about how much that insurance would cost. I already had enough in my life to freak me out. I didn't need to make any additions.

Then I cautiously moved away, slid out of bed and pulled

the covers back over Billie. As I straightened, Mitch moved and I froze. I watched with bated breath as he rolled to his side, his arm curling around Billie, but neither woke. Both of their eyes stayed closed and Billie pressed her cheek to the area under his pectorals.

I stared because Mitch was beautiful in his sleep. But he was indescribably beautiful being a good, kind man who was sleeping wrapped protectively around a sleeping six-year-old girl. A girl who had a sunny disposition (when she wasn't barfing or in a shitty mood as a precursor to said barfing) but who also had a shitheel of a dad whose criminal activities and weaknesses made her unsafe and could have gotten her hurt.

My beautiful, Teflon-coated cousin had never had this and would never have it with Bill in her life. Not when she had a nightmare and needed to feel safe. Not when she was sick and needed comfort.

Not ever.

Now she had it.

What met my eyes was the stuff posters were made of, but knowing the two beings filling my vision, I knew that what met my eyes were what dreams were made of.

How, on God's green earth, did my life shift so this vision could meet my eyes?

I had no answer for that, and I had no time to come up with an answer. I decided instantly Billie was not going to school that day, which meant it was good it was my day off. But Billy had to get to school, and I had to get him there.

Silently I moved around the bed, went to the chair and grabbed Mitch's flannel shirt that I'd tossed there yesterday morning.

I shrugged it on and left the room. Closing the door quietly behind me, I hustled down the hall to the kitchen at the same time I re-secured the ponytail that I'd slept in. Once I hit the kitchen, I searched the cupboards and started a pot of coffee, then went back down the hall to the bedroom where Billy was sleeping. I walked in and approached the air mattress on the floor where Billy was.

I did a knees-closed squat and gently shook his shoulder. He opened his eyes and looked at me groggily.

"Time for your shower, buddy," I whispered.

"'Kay, Auntie Mara," he whispered back without hesitation, got out of bed wearing one of the new pairs of PJs I bought him, loose shorts and a loose tee and he shuffled out of the room to the bathroom.

I decided to get a cup of coffee while he had a shower. I'd go to Mitch's room and get my stuff to do my business in the hall bathroom after Billy was done. This way I could have a shower prior to taking Billy to school, and Mitch could use his to get ready for his day.

I was standing in front of the coffeepot pouring coffee into a mug with a splash of milk at the bottom. I shoved the coffeepot back into the coffeemaker and set the mug down in order to grab a spoon when it happened.

Two strong arms closed around me, one at my ribs, one at my chest. My body went statue-still, but my head tipped down and I saw strong, bare forearms just as I felt lips at my neck.

"Mornin', baby," Mitch whispered there, and a trill raced up my spine as I experienced a dream come true.

Mitch wrapping his arms around me and whispering a really good "mornin'" to me.

I liked that.

No, I loved that.

And I wanted it every morning for forever.

"Mitch," I whispered back, unable to say anything else.

His arms gave me a squeeze and his lips didn't move from the skin at my neck when he asked, "You sleep okay?"

"Uh…" I answered, my vision blurry, my body still solid, my mind awhirl.

Apparently that was answer enough for Mitch because his lips moved from my neck to my ear, where he murmured, "I slept fuckin' great."

"Um…" I muttered.

"You feel good, curled into me, warm and soft."

Oh God.

"Uh…"

His arms squeezed. "Though, you'd probably feel better, there wasn't a six-year-old between us."

Oh God!

"Um…"

"Billie's fever broke," he informed me.

"Um…yeah," I mumbled. "I checked before I got up."

"Mm," he murmured in my ear causing another, stronger trill to go up my spine. So strong, my body trembled with it. I got another arm squeeze, then Mitch's arms went away, but not a second later his hands were at my hips. I felt his heat leave my back, but only so he could turn me, then his heat was at my front and his arms wrapped around me again, one low at my back, one high at my shoulder blades.

I looked into the depths of his soulful eyes and instantly got lost.

"You should have woken me," he whispered, his face so close I felt his words on my lips.

"Why?" I whispered back, still lost in his eyes (and his heat and his strong arms wrapped around me).

"Because you left me in bed with a six-year-old,"

he replied, this was said softly, gently and not with any accusation.

"So?"

"Baby, she isn't my kid."

"She likes you."

"She still isn't my kid. You there, it's cool. Me alone in bed with Billie, not so much."

Crap.

Okay, there it was. I was a dork thinking they looked like a poster. I'd screwed up, as usual, and made Mitch feel uncomfortable.

"Sorry," I whispered.

His arms tightened, the one at my shoulder blades shifted up, and his fingers sifted into my ponytail.

"It's okay," he whispered back. and I was sliding back into getting lost in his eyes even though his lids were lowering at the same time his head was lowering, and his lips were a breath away from mine.

"Mitch," I called, but my lips moved against his lips. Then my lips couldn't move at all because his lips were on mine. His hand was cupping the back of my head to tilt it to one side, his slanted the other way, and his tongue traced the crease of my lips until those lips opened and his tongue swept inside.

Oh God.

There it was again.

Oh *God!*

He tasted good, he felt good and he kissed *great*.

My hands slid up his back, and my fingers dug in at his lats as he kissed me, and he tasted so good, I kissed him right back.

Finally, Mitch's lips left mine, trailed down my cheek to my ear, where he growled, just as his arms squeezed, "Christ, I love your mouth."

There I was again, pressed tight to Mitch, breathing hard, wrapped in his arms.

How did this keep happening?

"Mitch—" I started.

His head came up, his eyes locked on mine and he interrupted me, "When's your next day off?"

I blinked. "What?"

His arm low at my hips tightened further. "Your next day off, sweetheart."

"Um . . . today," I answered.

He grinned, then said softly, "I know, honey. When's your *next* day off?"

"Uh . . . Friday."

"Thursday night, we're gettin' a babysitter."

I blinked at his intimate words, words said by a dad to a mom, a husband to a wife, more words I liked, and repeated, "What?"

"A babysitter."

"Why?"

"'Cause Thursday night I'm takin' you out. I'm feedin' you. I'm gettin' you intoxicated. Then I'm bringin' you home and I'm doin' other things to you. Things I'm gonna keep doin' that'll take me deep into Friday, and I don't want the kids interrupting me while I do them."

My toes curled, my knees wobbled and my nipples started tingling.

Oh boy.

I struggled to find my way back to Mara World, which was safer and far more sane, and started, "I don't—"

I stopped speaking when I heard the door to the hall bathroom open. Billy was out of the shower.

Mitch's head went back another two inches and turned slightly before he murmured, "Kids interrupting."

My hands moved so they were pressed against his chest, not a good thing to do, as all my fingers encountered on their journey was warm, hard, sleek skin.

I powered through this and started, "Mitch—"

At that moment there was a knock on the door.

Mitch's head turned the other way, my gaze followed his and we both stared at the front door.

"Who could that be?" I whispered.

"No clue," Mitch replied, not in a whisper. He let me go, and my hands flew back so my palms could press against the counter to hold myself up, and I watched Mitch move to the door.

He looked through the peephole and then I watched him drop his head, shake it, his neck twisted and his eyes hit me. I saw they were amused at the same time a little annoyed. Then he turned back to the door, pulled off the chain, twisted the lock and opened it.

"You couldn't help yourself, could you?" he asked whoever was outside the door, and his voice was the same mixture of amused and a little annoyed.

"My brother doesn't call me at nine o'clock at night to discuss the care of a fevered child...as in *never*...so you're right. I couldn't help myself," a female's voice came at me. Then I saw Mitch move back as I saw a woman with Mitch's dark hair cut in an attractive style that brushed her shoulders, natural waves flowing through it. She was tall, like Mitch, though not as tall as Mitch. And she was built, not like Mitch. She was all tits and ass and obvious attitude.

She was followed by an older version of her who could be no one but Mitch's mother.

And I was right. She wore twinsets.

With scarves.

Attractive ones.

Oh...dear...*God!*

"Hi there, you must be Mara," Mrs. Lawson called when she saw me. "I'm Mitch's mom, Sue Ellen."

My brain took that unfortunate moment to remind me I was wearing a nightie and Mitch's shirt, and Mitch was wearing nothing but a pair of drawstring pajama bottoms. This collided with the thought that I was at Mitch's house early in the morning wearing nothing but a nightie, panties and Mitch's shirt, and Mitch was in nothing but pajama bottoms and what Mitch's mom and sister would think of this.

"Hey," I replied before I could start hyperventilating.

Mitch's sister started walking toward the bar, and her smiling eyes moved to me. "I'm Penny, Mitch's sister," she introduced herself casually, like it was perfectly okay to perpetrate an early morning surprise attack on your hot brother's neighbor. Even if that neighbor was staying with your hot brother while she was having one in a long line of crises into which she'd sucked your hot brother.

Which, by the way, it was *not*.

"Uh...hey," I returned. "I'm Mara, um..." I had no further information to give because they obviously already knew who I was, and I wasn't certain what I was to Mitch. Except last night he'd called me his Mara, and just thinking about him doing that made goose flesh rise on my skin.

I hoped they couldn't see it.

Penny ignored me trailing off stupidly and asked, "How's Billie?"

"Fever broke," Mitch answered. Having closed the door, he was moving too. Toward me. And I noted he seemed laid-back about this new and unusual turn of events, like his mother and sister frequently happened by unannounced, and maybe they did. "It came on fast and she was cool before the second dose, so it left just as fast."

"That's good," Mrs. Lawson murmured, coming to stand by Penny at the bar.

"Would you guys like some, um…coffee?" I asked, pulling up my hostessing skills and wondering if I should because it wasn't my house, also because I probably should excuse myself to go put on some clothes.

Mitch was already getting mugs as Mrs. Lawson replied, "That'd be great."

"Love a cup," Penny added.

Although I asked to be polite, I didn't know how to feel about their response considering their response meant they were staying awhile. And weirdly they didn't seem surprised I was playing hostess in Mitch's kitchen while wearing a nightie and his flannel.

Mitch set the mugs down, and I grabbed the coffeepot and filled them. No one said anything so I latched onto something Mitch said, and when he returned to me with the gallon jug of milk, I asked, "What do you mean, Billie was cool before the second dose?"

He splashed milk into two mugs and then set the jug aside, answering, "Set the alarm like I said I'd do. It woke me up, I checked her and she was good."

At his words, forgetting my audience, I stared at his handsome profile as he grabbed a spoon from the drawer and reached out to the sugar bowl.

Then I asked, "Why didn't you wake me?"

"No need, she was cool," Mitch answered, spooning sugar into the milky mugs.

"But why didn't you wake me?" I repeated, Mitch's head turned and his eyes caught mine.

"There was no need, sweetheart," he repeated with variation. "She was cool, you were both out, so I just went back to sleep."

I felt my brows knit. "You just went back to sleep?"

"Well, yes and no. I got up, turned out the lights, locked the front door and then I came back to bed and went to sleep."

I stared at him, lips parted.

He woke up to check Billie, found she was okay, got out of his bed *not* to go sleep on the couch, but instead he turned out the lights, locked the front door and came back to his bed, a bed I was in with Billie.

Why would he do that? Why?

He turned and handed coffees to his mother and sister, and they, I noticed vaguely, watched us closely. Then he turned back and grabbed his, which he took black. He lifted it to his lips. I opened my mouth to speak.

"Hey," I heard Billy mumble, and my eyes jerked to my little cousin, who was walking out dressed for school in a pair of new jeans and one of the new tees I bought him. His hair was combed and he was looking like the perfect child.

"Hey there, you must be Billy," Mrs. Lawson grinned at him. "I'm Mitch's mom, Sue Ellen, and this is my daughter, Mitch's sister Penny."

"Hey," Penny smiled.

"Hey," Billy smiled back then climbed up on a stool and looked at Mitch. "Can you do oatmeal again, Mitch?" he asked.

"Sure, Bud," Mitch muttered, put his coffee mug down and went to a cupboard to get a glass.

"Cool, thanks," Billy muttered back.

Okay, this was weird. This was insane. This was nuts. But I couldn't cope with any of that now. My life was on its head, as it would be, considering I was now in charge of two kids, my cousin was in jail and the Russian mob, amongst others, wanted him dead. And my apartment was a crime scene. And my mother and aunt were in town. *And* me *and* my two new kids were essentially living with my hot guy neighbor I'd secretly been in love with for years. I needed to focus and not on Mitch, Mitch's apparently nosy sister and equally nosy mom.

I grabbed my coffee mug, took a fortifying sip of caffeine and walked to stand across the counter from Billy.

"Billy, honey, Billie got sick last night so she's going to stay home with me today," I told him.

"She did?" Billy asked, his face suddenly awash with concern, but he looked strangely like he was hiding something.

I couldn't ask or pay too close attention because Mitch took all of it when he stated firmly, "She is not."

I turned to him in surprise to see his words weren't the only thing that was firm. His face was firm too, and this made me even more surprised.

"Yes, she is," I told him.

"She's fine," he replied, coming to my side and putting a glass of milk in front of Billy. "Fever broke. She's good."

"She puked her guts out last night, Mitch," I reminded him.

"She did?" Billy asked and I looked at him.

"Yes, buddy, she did. She's okay now," I assured him. "But I want her to rest today."

"She's good, Mara," Mitch butted in. "And she's missed enough school, something I learned yesterday when I talked to her teacher. Apparently, her dad didn't make her go. But now she's fine and she's going to school."

My head turned to Mitch. "Maybe she's fine, but she might have a relapse, and I don't want her at school when she has a relapse. I want her at home and I want to be around if she does."

"She has a relapse, the school will call and you or I'll go get her," Mitch returned.

"That would be a waste of time," I replied. "What *wouldn't* be a waste of time would be if she had a relapse and she was already home."

"She's goin' to school, Mara," Mitch declared, and I felt my blood pressure ratcheting higher.

"She's not, Mitch," I declared right back, then I thought of something and I looked at Billy. "Maybe you shouldn't go to school either."

I watched my cousin's eyes light with delight at the thought of missing school, but I heard Mitch speak.

"Why the hell not?" he asked, and I looked back at him.

"What if he has her bug?" I asked back. "It came on fast, Mitch. She was fine one minute, though she was grumpy and didn't want to go to bed. Two hours later she was throwing up on the living room carpet and had a temperature of one hundred and three. That could happen to Billy, and if it does, I want him right here."

"Bud gets sick, the school calls and you or I go get *him*," Mitch fired back.

Yes, my blood pressure was definitely ratcheting higher and that was why I put my hands on my hips, leaned into him and snapped, "That would be a waste of time too."

"Baby, they're both going to school," Mitch announced.

"Honey, they are *not*," I decreed.

Mitch glared at me. I glared back.

Then he said, "Just for the record, sweetheart, I've decided I like the Mara who lives in her own world and ums and uhs and doesn't hand me attitude. Let's go back to her."

After that, I replied, "Just for the record, honey lumpkin, I know why you like the Mara who lives in her own world because that Mara lets you have your way. But when I'm worried about my kids, and you disagree with me, we're *not* going back to her. And, by the way, I'll remind you, yesterday you promised we'd be a team and *talk* about decisions regarding the kids."

"Uh...baby," he looked around, and my glare heated when I noted he was looking around sarcastically, then his eyes hit mine and he stated, "That's what we're doin'. We're talkin'."

Luckily, before I exploded, at this point Penny butted in and she did this by saying, "Can I just say, I freaking love this."

"Not as much as me, sweetie," Mrs. Lawson added, and my eyes snapped to them to see they were both smiling huge.

Before I could freak out that I had forgotten my audience, Mitch spoke.

"Maybe one of you can make yourself useful and go wake up Billie so she can shower and get ready for school," he suggested toward his mother and sister in a way that it was no suggestion at all.

"Please don't," I put in quickly. "She needs her rest, and, not to be rude, she doesn't know either of you and I don't want her to be alarmed."

Mitch's eyes sliced back to me and he growled, "Mara."

I couldn't growl, but I tried my best and returned, "Mitch."

"How about I make myself useful by being the voice of experience and saying, sorry, Mara, but Mitch's right, she'll probably be okay," Penny stated. I bit my lip, and her eyes went to her brother. "But I'm more sorry, Mitch, because Mara's more right. She'll probably be okay, but if it was one of my kids and they were puking their guts out and had a fever, no way they'd be in school the next day." Then her eyes turned to Billy and her face gentled. "And even sorrier for you, honey, because, if you were my kid, I'd make you go and come get you if you got sick."

"That's what I'd do too," Mrs. Lawson agreed.

"I'm good with going to school," Billy chimed in. My gaze went to him because his eyes not five minutes ago lit with delight at the thought of missing school, and anyway, what kid was good with going to school?

"That settles it," Mitch decided, and I looked back to him. "Sorted," he finished, turned to the cupboard and pulled out the box of oatmeal while I watched. And as I processed what was happening in my head, I realized I was also seething.

Then I asked Mitch's back, "Did our discussion yesterday about teamwork penetrate..." I hesitated for emphasis before finishing, *"at all*?"

He put the oatmeal box down and turned to me. I glared into his dancing, beautiful, fathomless, dark-brown eyes then suddenly found myself crushed to his long, hard body, his strong arms caging me in.

In my ear, he muttered his answer. "Yes, but also kind of no."

"I didn't think so," I returned acidly, my hands at his waist pushing back.

His head lifted up, he smiled down at me and asked, "You want oatmeal?"

I glared up at him and I really wanted to say no, and there were a lot of other things I really wanted to say. But I couldn't, because, firstly, his mother and sister were there, and, secondly, I'd had his oatmeal yesterday; he squirted maple syrup in it mid-nuke and it was really good.

"Yes," I snapped.

His smile got bigger, he gave me a squeeze, let me go and turned to the oatmeal. I turned to my coffee mug, which was sitting in front of Billy. That was when I saw Mrs. Lawson and Penny, still smiling huge, and Billy, his eyes going from me to Mitch and back again, his expression again fifty years older than he was.

I decided to ignore all of this and concentrate on caffeine.

It was the best decision I'd made all morning.

# CHAPTER NINETEEN

## Harsh, Bright Light of Mara World

I STARED AT myself in Mitch's bathroom mirror.

Seeing all that was me, I realized I'd made a huge mistake. *Huge.* Enormous.

My eyes moved over my made-up face. Then they moved over the hair I'd curled into big, soft curls and let fall around my shoulders. They took in the silky, sapphire-colored, blousy top I had on, which came up in gathers to my neck and wrapped around with a wide sash that tied at the back of my neck, totally exposing my shoulders, arms and back. And, last, they took in the nice jeans and awesome silver belt I was wearing.

And I knew.

I knew I couldn't do this. I had to rectify my mistake.

I heard the front door open.

Mitch was back from taking the kids to Penny's. We were going out to dinner.

So that meant I had to rectify my mistake *now.*

\*   \*   \*

I was clueless at the best of times, but apparently when my life was in turmoil, something that hadn't happened since

I'd moved away from my crazy, mean mom; it hadn't happened because I guarded against it every second of every day, I was even more clueless.

But two days before, I'd woken up in a dream come true after a night that included spending time with Mitch on the couch, which was (almost) a different kind of dream come true. I fought it but not hard enough. It lulled me, sneaking up on me, taking over my safe cocoon and wrapping me in one that felt safer, snugger, warmer and much, much better.

\*     \*     \*

The morning Mitch's mom and sister came over, Mitch made oatmeal while decreeing he was taking Billy to school. He did this again without discussing it with me. Then again, he was going out, and I had Billie to look after, so I didn't argue since his bossy edict made sense.

He had a shower while I talked to his (surprisingly) easy to gab with mom and sister, who were both really nice. Penny was very forthright and equally very funny, and his mom let Penny mostly carry the show while smiling sweetly a lot.

Mitch took off to take Billy to school and himself to work. But not before he grabbed my hand, led me to the door where we stood with our audience watching (including Billy standing *right there*) and said good-bye like an old married couple. That was to say he curved an arm around my waist, pulled my body into contact with his, brushed his lips against mine, then muttered there, causing a belly whoosh, "See you tonight, honey."

Then he and Billy were gone. I was in a daze that took a while to shake off, and Mrs. Lawson (who insisted I call her Sue Ellen) and Penny hung around and gabbed with me until Billie got up. They stayed long enough to meet Billie and for Billie to charm them, then they left.

Mitch called me late morning to ask about Billie, and I slid deeper into my dream world listening to his deep voice on my cell phone. In this dream world, I told him she was fine, up, her appetite was normal and all seemed well in Billie world.

Then he asked me about my day, and I told him I was doing laundry, going to the grocery store and picking up Billy. I asked if I could go to my place to do the laundry, and he told me to use his washer and dryer. I decided not to argue because there was no purpose, but I would add laundry detergent to my grocery list so we didn't use all of his.

Still in the dream world, I shared that I'd called my insurance agent the day before, and asked Mitch if I could get into my apartment the next day because the agent was coming over to inspect the damage and make a report. To this, Mitch told me he didn't want me over there alone. He asked when the agent was coming and informed me he'd meet him instead. I argued about this because the agent was coming at eleven and Mitch would have to leave work. Mitch told me the station was just a ten-minute drive, and Pierson's was not, and it wasn't a big deal. Then I told Mitch he was doing too much, and he said something in his gentle voice that ended with "baby," and I immediately agreed with a breathy, "Kay."

Argument over.

I asked him if he wanted pizza for dinner. He said that would be great and informed me his sister and mother liked me. I let the happy whoosh that created flow through me before I informed him I liked them.

The conversation went on with him telling me we had reservations at North for Thursday night. I informed him I liked North because I did and I also spoke so I wouldn't hyperventilate at the thought of an actual, bona fide, official date with Ten Point Five Detective Mitch Lawson. Then he told me Billie and Billy were spending that night at Penny's house. I didn't argue about this either because I figured at this point I was turning insane and also thinking about why Billy and Billie were spending the night with Penny would *definitely* make me hyperventilate.

We hung up after what was a surprisingly lengthy, easy, informative but chatty, warm, familiar and intimate conversation.

So, with Mitch off the phone, I allowed myself to hyperventilate.

I loaded Billie up in my car, got the stuff for my barbeque chicken pizza, came home and immediately put the chicken to marinade. I did laundry and cleaned the house from top to bottom as a small thank-you to Mitch for being so cool and letting us stay there. Then I went to go get Billy. When we were home I helped him with his homework. Then, because it was warm and summer was coming, we all walked to the playground down the greenbelt and Billy horsed around while Billie sat in my lap and we swung in a swing.

We came back and I made the pizza; I had to do the crust by hand because my breadmaker was at my house.

Then Mitch came home.

"Mitch!" Billie shouted, launching herself off the couch, hurtling the short expanse to the door that he'd taken one step through and wrapping her arms around his hips. She gave him a tight hug and leaned her head way back to look up his long length. "We're havin' Auntie Mara's chicken pizza!"

Mitch's hand cupped the back of her head as he grinned down at her and muttered, "I know, gorgeous." He leaned down, picked her up, stepped out of the door with her in his arms and closed it while asking, "You doin' better, honey?"

She nodded enthusiastically.

"Good," he murmured, and I actually *saw* his arms give her a squeeze, which made another sweet whoosh swoop through my belly. Then his eyes went to Billy and he called, "Hey, Bud."

"Hey, Mitch. My homework's all done," Billy announced swiftly, and the swift way he announced it was not in a braggy kid way or the precursor to asking for something after pointing out he'd been good. It was something else, something that didn't sit right with me. I studied him trying to figure it out, but stopped when Mitch plonked Billie over the back of the couch so she was seated beside me, then his lips were at my neck.

"Hey, sweetheart," he whispered there then kissed me.

My chest warmed, and I turned and tipped back my head as he slightly lifted his.

"Hey," I whispered, immediately lost in his eyes.

"Finally," he murmured, those eyes now smiling, "I get your pizza."

At that I frowned.

And at that, Mitch burst out laughing. I felt his fingers wrap around my ponytail, he gently tugged my head back farther and touched his laughing mouth to mine.

Obviously, I quit frowning.

He let me go and walked toward his bedroom, shrugging off his jacket.

I watched him go, unable to shrug off the safer, snugger, warmer, better cocoon that was fitting itself around me, and this was mostly because I didn't try.

We ate pizza, and we did it at the dining room table because Mitch decreed we would. And as we ate pizza at his dining room table, I slid deeper into my dream world because I'd never had this, never, not in my life. Sitting around a cool table. Eating great pizza (if I did say so myself). Listening to kids jabber and a beautiful man's deep, attractive voice interject. Watching people I cared about smile and share their days, their lives, their thoughts.

And I knew Billy and Billie hadn't had that either, and I knew they liked it as much as me.

Maybe more.

Watching Billie's animation, which, if it could be believed, had ratcheted up three notches while her own personal safe, snug, warm cocoon fit around her. And watching Billy watch Mitch and emulate the way he used his utensils and sat in his chair, finally having a good, decent man as role model...

Definitely more.

My safer, snugger, warmer and much, much better cocoon only felt slightly funny when Billy announced, what appeared to be desperately, that he was going to do the dishes. Then he also apparently desperately went about doing that quickly, so neither Mitch nor I could talk him out of it or help. He didn't even let us clear the table.

I watched this, feeling troubled, then I felt something else. That something was coming from Mitch. So my eyes moved to him and saw that he, too, was watching Billy working diligently in the kitchen, and his eyes were also troubled.

He must have felt my gaze on him, his came to me, I tipped my head to the side, and he whispered, "Later, sweetheart," so I nodded.

Mitch was stretched out on the couch watching a baseball game after I'd gotten the kids to bed. I rounded the couch, his eyes came to me, and my eyes went to him.

"Come here, baby."

My gaze drifted over him, and he looked so good lying on his couch, his eyes on me as gentle as his voice had been, my mind settled deeply in my dream world and my body automatically drifted to him. When I was within arm's reach, he did an ab curl, his fingers gripped my hips, and then I was tucked with the couch at my back, his side at my front and my cheek was to his chest.

"Finish the game with me, and then I'll let you go to bed," he muttered.

" 'Kay," I muttered back.

His arm curled around my back, and his fingers trailed random patterns over the material of my jeans at my hip. I sighed and wrapped my arm around his stomach.

See? Totally insane.

I heard his voice rumble even as I felt it when he murmured, "Your pizza isn't good."

I blinked, but I was so deep in my dream world, snuggled on the couch with Mitch, that was all I had the capacity to do before I murmured back, "It isn't?"

His fingers dug into my hip when he replied, "No, honey. It's fuckin' great."

I didn't know I could relax more into him, but at his words, I did and I added a squeeze of my arm around his stomach.

His arm around my back reciprocated the squeeze.

Then he muttered, "Thanks for cleaning the house."

He noticed.

God, he was *so* nice.

"You're welcome. Thanks for letting us stay," I muttered back on another squeeze of his abs.

"You're welcome," he whispered.

Another whoosh swept through my belly, then his fingers

went back to trailing, and I stared vacantly at the game. Mitch stared at it too, and I figured his wasn't vacant, but with all that was happening and another full day, I didn't have the energy to lift my head to look. All I had the energy to do was feel his warm, hard body at my front, the relaxing movements of his fingers at my hip, the steadiness of his chest rising and falling with his breathing.

My lids were getting heavy when the TV suddenly went off, and just as suddenly I was on my feet and one of his arms was around me, the other hand at my jaw tipping my head back. Then his mouth was on mine, mine was open, his tongue slid in for a sweet, delicious touch to the tip of mine, and then his lips were gone.

"Go to bed, sweetheart," he murmured.

"'Kay," I murmured back.

His arm gave me a squeeze, his lips gave me a grin and he turned me, gave me a gentle shove, and my feet took me to his bedroom.

I didn't know if he had his pajamas, and I didn't know if he had a blanket or pillow. In record time I was in my nightie in his bed fast asleep. So I didn't know he came in, got his pajamas, changed in his bathroom and nabbed a pillow I wasn't using after sliding my hair off my neck then gliding a finger along my jaw before leaving the room, closing the door and bedding down on the couch.

\*     \*     \*

The next morning my eyes opened, and I heard Mitch, Billy and Billie in the kitchen.

I closed my eyes.

Then I smiled into the pillow.

I rolled out of bed, did my bathroom business, tugged on Mitch's flannel and headed to the kitchen for coffee,

Mitch's oatmeal and to help Mitch get the kids ready for school.

*       *       *

When I got back to Mitch's place after work, I saw a note on the kitchen counter.

It said:

Sweetheart,
The kids are with me on the greenbelt. They've had a snack. We're going out to dinner when you get home. Come find us.

                                                        M

He wrote, *when you get home.*
Home.
Oh boy. I liked that.
I went to Mitch's room, changed into jeans and a tee, making a mental note to ask Mitch when I could get back to my apartment for cleanup (and to move back in), but also so I could get more stuff. I slipped on some flip-flops and went to go find them.

As I walked down the back steps to the green space behind our unit, I saw LaTanya and Brent sitting at a picnic table with a woman I didn't know. They were watching Mitch, Derek and Billy playing catch with another extremely hot guy and two mini–hot guys (also who I didn't know) at the same time watching Billie race around chasing what looked like nothing, but I was assuming in her imagination was something.

I got greetings, Billie's was how she greeted Mitch, which was to say a body collision followed by a hip hug, then she went back to chasing imaginary butterflies (or whatever). Mitch's was distant (as in physically, since he didn't quit playing catch), but not distant emotionally, because his eyes warmed, his face got soft and his beautiful mouth smiled when he saw me. I also got an introduction and a handshake from the woman I didn't know, who was Tess O'Hara (of Tessa's Bakery!). She was the woman of Brock Lucas (the extremely hot guy), who was Mitch's partner (Oh my God! His partner! Cop partners were like family!), who gave me a chin lift, and the two boys were Joel and Rex, Brock's sons (Oh my God *again!*), and we were going out to dinner with them (Oh my God, God, *God!*) after catch.

After I managed the herculean task of not hyperventilating and/or fainting, I joined Tess, LaTanya and Brent on the picnic table and watched Mitch, Derek, Brock, Joel, Rex and Billy playing catch.

And that was when I started fretting.

Not because of my crazy life living in a dream world. Not because I'd found out that day my new charges' insurance was going to suck a huge amount out of my paycheck every two weeks. Not because my day was ending with Mitch playing catch with Billy and us going out to (another) family dinner, this being extended *cop* family, including his partner and *his* family. Not because I hadn't heard from Mom and Aunt Lulamae in a while and I knew this meant they'd retreated in order to plot, and that did not bode good things.

No, I was fretting because Billy was not really good with a baseball mitt or throwing a ball. This was likely because he'd never tossed a ball with his father. But that wasn't it either. It was the fact that it was clear he *wanted* to be good not because he actually wanted to be good but because, I was guessing from his behavior which was openly anxious, he didn't want to annoy or disappoint Mitch.

And he seemed not to cotton onto the fact that Mitch, nor Brock nor Derek, for that matter, were anywhere near annoyed or disappointed. All the men were patient and encouraging, not in an overbearing way, in a natural, calm way that was not penetrating Billy at all. The more they tossed the ball, the more anxious Billy became whenever he missed a catch or threw wild, which was nearly every time.

"This isn't good," I muttered, as I watched Billy miss another catch that Mitch tossed what would have been straight into his mitt if he hadn't screwed up his concentration, tried too hard and moved his mitt at the last minute.

"He'll relax, babe," LaTanya muttered back. "Remember this is as new to him as it is to you and Mitch."

"He's freaking out," I whispered.

"Totally," Brent whispered back, and I looked at him to see he was concentrating on Billy too. "He's *all* wound up."

"It's because he thinks Mitch, Brock and Derek are cool, but that's only because Mitch, Brock and Derek *are* cool and he doesn't want to be not cool," Tess explained. Then she bumped me softly with her shoulder and whispered, "He'll calm down, Mara. It'll be okay."

"That's not it," I told her.

"That's totally it," LaTanya butted in.

I shook my head, thinking about the last day or two and replied, "He's like a kid robot. It's not just playing catch. I think he's wound up all the time."

"That's weird," Brent observed. "You'd think he'd relax, being away from his dad and someplace safe."

I silently agreed as I watched Billy throw the ball to Derek. It went way high, and Derek leaped and just tagged it before it flew over the tip of his mitt. Billy watched Derek land, and his face screwed up so tight, it was hard to watch.

Too hard.

And that was when I was done.

I prepared to make a move to go to him, but then I heard Mitch call, "A minute, guys."

He had his gloved hand pointed to Derek, palm down. Derek tossed the ball to Mitch and Mitch caught it in his glove like it was second nature as he walked toward Billy. When he got to Billy, he crouched low.

Billy took a step back. Mitch's hand lifted, curled around Billy's shoulder and he carefully guided the little boy between his opened, bent legs. Mitch spoke to him and Billy's head tipped down, staring at the grass, concentrating. Billy bit his lips. Then Billy's head jerked and his eyes caught Mitch's.

I held my breath.

Mitch grinned at Billy. Billy grinned back. Mitch's hand still at Billy's shoulder gave him a gentle-rough shake, he straightened and walked away.

Billy licked his lips and took two steps back. Mitch turned and tossed the ball to him, and Billy stood still, watched it fall into his glove and he curled the glove around it.

The minute it did, I jumped up, threw my arms straight in the air and shouted, "Whoop! Whoop! Go Billy!"

Billy's eyes shot to me, shock in them as Brent, Tess and LaTanya jumped up next to me and shouted too. His face cracked into a hesitant smile and his eyes cut to Mitch.

"Right here, Winchell," Mitch called, slapping the inside of his mitt. "Focus, Bud, keep your eyes on my mitt, don't think about anything and let go."

Billy nodded, wound up and let go. The ball flew high and to Mitch's right, but not nearly as far as it had been. Mitch caught it easily, and Billy's face lit into a huge smile as Mitch threw a smile back at him.

"Awesome!" Derek yelled.

"Go Billy! Go Billy! Go Billy!" Brent started chanting. LaTanya, Tess and I joined in, and Billie ran up to us, adding her voice to the cheer as she wrapped her arms around my hips. A blush crawled up Billy's face, and he bit his lip again, but he did it through a smile.

Mitch tossed to Derek and Derek tossed to Brock and Brock tossed to Billy quickly, not giving Billy a chance to think about it, and Billy caught it again. We cheered again. Billy's blush got redder, and he immediately threw the ball at Mitch again and it nearly landed right in his mitt. Mitch only had to adjust a few inches.

Another cheer from the peanut gallery, louder and crazier this time.

Derek started laughing. Brock threw a grin at his woman (which, seriously, was hot). Mitch smiled at the turf, shaking his head before he lifted it again and fired a shot at Derek. Derek caught it and instantly fired the ball at Billy, who had to reach for it, but he caught it again. Another crazy, loud, wild cheer.

And so it went, Mitch, Brock, Derek and even (very patient, I might add) Joel and Rex didn't give Billy the chance to screw up by concentrating too hard or thinking about his nervousness. They even switched it up, with Mitch catching Billy's pass and then passing straight back to Billy, and Billy fell into that game too.

The peanut gallery settled in at the picnic table as the boys settled into their game of catch. Billy missed some, but they were few and far between, and his tosses weren't dead-on accurate but they were much better, and finally he even gained enough confidence to put some oomph behind them.

Billie climbed up on the top of the picnic table, got on

her knees behind me, pulled my hair out of its ponytail and started to play with it as Brent, LaTanya, Tess and I started talking about everything under the sun. Through this I watched Billy relax and start to enjoy himself, and the guys started to chat about whatever guys chatted about when they played catch.

Eventually my eyes strayed to Mitch and then they strayed over Mitch's perfect body moving athletically as he chatted to our friend, his partner, his partner's boys and my beloved cousin.

And I was lulled deeper into my insane dream world that shouldn't be mine, but I couldn't let it go.

And I couldn't let it go because the sun was shining. It was May in Colorado. It was warm. I was with a bunch of people I loved, new people who were cool, and although everything was very, very wrong in Mara World, in this world, in that gleaming, perfect moment, everything was very, very *right*.

\*     \*     \*

After catch we went out with Tess, Brock and Brock's boys.

We had a great dinner that was pandemonium (mostly because of Billie, who clearly couldn't decide if she had a bigger crush on Joel or Rex, so she lavished attention on both of them in addition to Mitch, who was definitely now her third most favorite person in the world, behind Billy and me, and she wanted him to know it). And the entire time we were out I didn't feel like I was in an insane dream world that wasn't mine.

I didn't feel that at all.

Not even when dinner was over and Mitch scooted his chair close, wrapped his arm around the back of mine and idly played with a lock of my hair while he talked to Brock.

Not even then.

I felt like this was real, it was mine and I liked it.

It felt freaking *great*.

So I stayed there.

* * *

The next morning started like the last and, except for Mitch letting me into my apartment to get my stuff to dress for our date, was mostly the same.

But it wasn't going to end the same.

And it wasn't until I was dressed, made up, ready for our date and staring at myself in Mitch's mirror that I realized my mistake.

And this was when the silken cocoon that was crafted snug, safe and warm around me, made from Mitch's warmth and kindness, completely shredded.

And when it did, the harsh, bright light of Mara World glared in, reminding me who I was, who he was and how this was all likely to end.

I blinked at myself in the mirror as I heard Mitch come through the front door.

And it was then I knew, for the kids' sakes, my sake, Mitch's sake and mostly the sake of all of our hearts, I had to yank all of us back into the glaring light of Mara World before it was too late.

# CHAPTER TWENTY

## Before It's Too Late

"Mara, sweetheart, you ready?" Mitch called from his living room-slash-kitchen-slash-dining area.

It was on unsteady legs in silver, strappy, stiletto-heeled sandals that I walked out, finally determined to explain to Mitch about Mara World and his place in it.

In other words, he didn't *have* a place.

My dedication to this task took an instant and direct hit when I cleared the mouth of the hall and saw Mitch standing at the edge of his bar wearing an espresso-colored tailored shirt that looked hot on him, a matching espresso-colored sports jacket over it that also looked hot on him, a fabulous, dark-brown belt and somewhat faded jeans that definitely looked hot on him. His head was tipped back and he was taking a slug from a bottle of beer while I lamented the fact that I was in his bathroom getting ready while he was in his bedroom changing clothes. Therefore, I'd missed seeing his gorgeousness (and thus would have been prepared to see his returned gorgeousness) before he'd left to take the kids to his sister's.

Instead, I was thunderstruck by just how beautiful he was from top-to-toe.

His eyes slid around the beer, his chin tipped down, and I absorbed my second direct hit right after my first when his beer hand dropped and his dark brown eyes went from warm to scorching in a nanosecond.

"Jesus," he muttered.

I stopped four feet away, pulled myself together and announced, "Mitch, we have to talk."

It was like I didn't even speak. He set the beer aside as his burning gaze traveled me top-to-toe and back again, slowing on occasion, but roaming me randomly, lazily. It made me feel a kind of funny I'd never felt before. A beautiful kind of funny. A kind of funny I'd not even felt when I was in his arms, so, obviously, it was a seriously beautiful kind of funny.

"Jesus," he murmured again.

"Mitch, did you hear me?" I asked, powering past that beautiful funny feeling.

His eyes finally moved to mine.

"Come here, baby," he ordered in his gentle voice, but this one had an additional rumble that felt like a physical thing. A warm, sweet, infinitely sexy physical thing.

Another direct hit.

"Mitch, I asked if you heard me."

"Come here," he repeated.

"We need to talk," I said quietly.

"You need to talk, we'll talk at dinner," he returned. "Right now *I* need you to come here."

"Mitch—" I started and he moved.

He lunged, reached out a hand, his fingers wrapping around my wrist. He lunged back and I went flying forward, colliding with his body and his arms clamped around me.

"Fuck," he muttered, and I tipped my head back to look at him as I caught my breath at suddenly finding myself in his arms, which was definitely not, in any way, where I wanted to be when I said what I needed to say. "I knew your hair looked good down but, Christ, not that good."

Wow. That was supernice.

No, no. I needed focus. Fo . . . cus!

"Mitch, I need you to pay attention to me," I told him.

His hand slid up into my hair as his eyes roamed my head and he murmured, "Oh, I'm payin' attention, sweetheart."

"Mitch!" I snapped, my hands, which had landed on his chest, curled into the lapels of his jacket, and his eyes cut to mine.

"Don't," he said suddenly and I blinked.

"Pardon?" I asked.

"Mara, I see you're screwing yourself up to say somethin' that's likely gonna piss me off and ruin my plans for tonight, so, I'm askin' you, don't."

I blinked again. Then I informed him, "We need to talk."

"Do you think we need to talk about how nice it felt, lyin' together watchin' baseball?" he asked.

I stared up at him and felt my brows draw together. "I didn't watch baseball."

"Okay, do you think we need to talk about how nice it felt, lyin' together, me watchin' baseball and you zoned out?"

I sucked in an annoyed breath because he was ruining my plans by talking at all, *and* his talking meant he was reminding me how good that did, indeed, feel, and I snapped, "No."

"All right, then do you think we need to talk about how great every kiss was that we've shared from the first to the last?"

My body grew tight and I bit out, "Absolutely not."

"You're sure you don't want to know how good I think you taste?" he asked.

Oh boy. Mitch saying that felt like a warm, sweet, infinitely sexy physical thing too.

Crap.

"No," I repeated.

"And how fuckin' great you feel when you press into me and hold on tight."

He was totally ruining my plans!

"No!" My voice was getting louder.

"And you don't want to tell me how much you like it, just as much as me."

"Mitch—"

"Best kiss I ever had," he went on. "Every single one."

God, *God*.

That was nice.

I closed my eyes, opened them and whispered, "Stop it."

He didn't stop it. "Best kisses you've ever had too. You told me, baby. That first one you told me straight out, and I know the rest felt the same." His head bent nearer to mine and his voice got lower when he said softly, "Especially when I had you on your back in my couch."

He'd done a lot of things with his mouth when I was on my back in his couch, and he was right, all of it was the best I ever had. All of it.

"Please, I need to say something," I begged softly.

His arms gave me a squeeze, his fingers twisted in my hair, his face dipped super close to mine and he said, "No you don't, Mara. Unless it's to tell me you want, just as bad as me, to find out where all we've shared could lead. Anything else outta your mouth, right now, I do not want to hear."

"It's important," I told him quietly.

"It's gonna be fucked up."

I stared at him and returned, "No, it's not."

"I been gone for half an hour and so have the kids. In that time, you've been alone and thinkin' about tonight. This means you've had time with nothing to distract you to start to panic about tonight. And *this* means you've had time to insert your head right back up your ass, and I'm tellin' you, Mara, I been waitin' four years for tonight, so I'm not lettin' you fuck this shit up."

Another direct hit, right on target. Bull's-eye. All my battle stations were crumbling to dust.

"You've been waiting four years for tonight?" I asked in a voice that was foreign to my own ears, and I knew why. It stupid, stupid, stupidly held hope.

"Baby, I told you that the other night," he reminded me.

"But—" I started, but he cut me off.

"I moved in, you had a man," he told me a fact I knew, and I knew he knew, and went on. "He was an asshole, and I knew this then because most of the time I saw you goin' to him and not him comin' to you. A man's got a woman like you, he doesn't make her come to him. He goes to her. I knew this after he was gone because the asshole *was* gone, and only an asshole lets go of a good thing."

Ohmigod! Another direct hit.

He had to stop talking. I had to *make* him stop talking.

"Mitch—"

"Oh no, Mara, you wanna talk, we're talkin'. We're gettin' this shit outta the way and we're doin' it fast so we don't lose our reservation."

I stared up at him and then glared up at him. "Yes, *I* want to talk, but *you're* the one who's doing all the talking."

"That's because I can see from your face I don't give a shit what you have to say."

My glare heated up and I asked, "Did you just say that?"

"Yep," he replied without hesitation.

"What I have to say is just as important as what you have to say," I informed him.

"No, what you have to say will be fucked up and twisted, and I'm not gonna stand here listenin' to you fuck up and twist what has been a really good fuckin' week, Billie freaking out and hurling notwithstanding. And I'm not gonna stand here listening to it, *because* we've had a really good week because somehow I managed to pull your head outta your ass so we could have that good week, and because right now you look fucking unbelievable. I'm hungry and I wanna eat. And I wanna do it sittin' across a table from you looking like you do right now. Then I wanna bring you home, figure out how to get you out of that sexy-as-hell top and see if I can get you to let yourself go enough so you'll let me fuck you in those even-sexier fuckin' shoes."

I glared at him even though his words seared through me like wildfire.

Then I declared, "This is insane."

"I'd ask why you think that, except I don't care," he shot back.

"I think that because it's insane!" I snapped.

"Jesus, Mara," he gritted.

I got down to it. "People like you don't spend time with, go out with or have sex with people like me."

As the words came out of my mouth, his face went hard.

When I was done, he sucked in breath and his head tipped back so all I could see was the column of his throat and the underside of his strong jaw before he muttered to the ceiling, "Jesus, fuck, she's back there again." Before I could say a word, his chin dipped down, his glittering, dark eyes came to mine, and his arms gave me a firm squeeze when he replied, "Baby, I'd probably find whatever twisted, fucked-up reason you spewed that shit interesting if I was gonna listen to whatever twisted, fucked-up reason you spewed that shit, which I'm not gonna do. And I'm not gonna do it because I've *already* listened to you spewing that twisted, fucked-up shit. I didn't agree with you then. I don't agree with you now. But now, I got the last week to prove that I'm right and you are fuckin' *wrong*."

"Mitch!" I yelled. "This is not going to work."

"It's been workin' for a week," he pointed out.

"That's because I've been living in a dream world," I returned, and his brows shot together.

"What the fuck?" he whispered.

"This isn't the real world, Mitch," I informed him.

"It *is*, Mara," he informed me.

"It isn't going to work!" I cried, getting desperate.

His eyes moved over my face and he studied me a moment before he noted softly, "I see, you've wrapped yourself in your cocoon and you're not lettin' go."

"No," I totally lied. "I just know it isn't going to work."

"How can you know that when you haven't let go long enough to try and make it work for longer than a fuckin' week?"

"I already told you how. People like you don't spend time with people like me!" I fired back.

"Yeah, Mara, and *I* already explained this shit to you. I don't care that your cousin is an assclown, your mom and aunt are nightmares and don't mind lettin' everyone know it and you've got a juvie record," Mitch returned, and my body turned to stone.

Ohmigod.

*Ohmigod.*

"What?" I whispered.

I vaguely watched Mitch's angry, frustrated features turn alert, and his arms tightened around me.

"Mara—" he started.

"You know about my juvenile file?" I was still whispering.

Mitch's arms got even tighter as his face got more alert.

Then he answered quietly, "I got a friend who's got a friend who did him a favor, unsealed your record, and I know you and your cousin Bill used to be partners in crime."

My stomach plunged, and I tried to pull out of his arms but they got even tighter.

Mitch kept talking. "Mara, the operative words in that are 'used to be.' You've been clean for fourteen years."

"You had someone unseal my record?" Yes, I was *still* whispering.

"Yeah, I did. You were so closed off, in your own world, for two years after that guy left; you gave me no in, nothin', not one thing, sealed up tight. I wanted to know what your gig was, so I looked into you. Great credit. No debt. Decent savings. Some investments, all safe, no risk. No parking tickets. No traffic violations. Only two jobs and three apartments in thirteen years. But when you were a kid, you got hauled in for public intoxication four times before you were sixteen, once for possession of marijuana and once for drunk and disorderly. Kid shit that all kids do, except you were with an assclown who was older than you but wasn't smart enough to keep you safe and not get you caught."

He said a lot of words and not a single one registered on me.

"You had someone unseal my record?" I repeated.

His arms gave me a slight shake. "Yeah, Mara, I did. I did it a while ago, baby, and when I say a while ago, I mean before I even fixed your washer, and I'm tellin' you," he leaned even closer to me, *"I don't care."*

This time, my hearing was selective.

"I was young," I whispered.

"I know that."

"Home life wasn't good," I continued to whisper, and Mitch's face changed again. Gone were the hints of angry and frustrated, now he was just alert. *Hyper*alert.

"How not good?" he asked softly.

Again I didn't hear him.

"I was young. Bill was young. We were close then."

"Mara—"

I turned my head away and closed my eyes, whispering, "You looked into me."

It was then I felt my heart beating, and it was doing this hard.

He knew about Bill. He'd seen Bill in his element and that was not good. He'd met my mom and Aunt Lulamae and he knew about them and that was not good either.

All of that was bad.

But this was worse.

I was already a Two Point Five, but him knowing about my juvie record, me being stupid, me doing stupid things, me doing more stupid things because I was stupid enough to do them with Bill yanked me down to a Two. Him *ever* knowing about my home life would put me around a One. Maybe a Point Seven Five. No one wanted to be with a Point Seven Five. *No one.* Except maybe other Point Seven Fives or lower, and I'd already had a lifetime of being around those and I wasn't going back to that.

I'd worked hard to get away from that. I'd worked hard to put it behind me. I'd worked hard to have a savings. A decent apartment. Nice furniture. Nice clothes. Good friends.

I'd worked hard.

"Mara," he called.

"Let me go," I whispered and pushed feebly at his chest.

His arms got tight and he muttered, "Shit, Jesus, Mara, sweetheart, look at me."

Then it hit me. How angry Mitch got when he walked into Bill's house. How furious he was with Bill. How he'd lost it.

And at the same time this hit me, it hit me that if Mitch could find this out, Child Protection Services could too.

My head snapped around and my eyes opened. "I'm not like him. Not like what you saw. I'm not like Bill. I left that behind. I left that at home."

"Jesus, Mara," Mitch said quietly, watching me closely.

"Bill didn't leave it behind. I left it behind. Swear to God, I left it behind," I told him fervently.

"I know, baby."

"I'll never let that touch Billy and Billie." My hands clenched his lapels again, and I got up on my toes to get in his face. "I promise, Mitch. *Never.*"

His eyes bored into mine and he whispered, "Fucking hell, honey, wherever you are now, get the fuck outta there and come back to me."

I shook my head and kept on target. "You can tell them, anyone, you tell them I promised you and I'll make certain of it. I'd die before I let that touch those kids, Mitch. I swear to God. I knew he was a drunk and I knew he got high, but I never knew it got that bad. I never knew they saw. I never knew they saw what he did. I never knew it until I saw it when you saw it. I knew it was bad, but I didn't know it was that bad. I wouldn't have left them there if I knew it. Swear to God. *Swear* to *God.*" My hands clenched harder into his lapels. "They're out now and they're never going back. I promise, no matter how hard it gets, what it costs, they're never going back." I pulled his lapels out slightly then pushed them in and whispered, "I swear to God, they're never going back."

His hand slid from my hair to curl around the side of my head, and his face got within an inch of mine. "Mara, baby, come back to me."

I didn't go back to him.

I went back to my earlier, far, far more important theme.

"We'll never work," I whispered.

"Mara, stop it and come back to me."

"The likes of you aren't for the likes of me," I told him softly.

"Jesus, baby," he said softly back, his thumb sweeping my cheekbone, his eyes roaming my face.

"I need to go."

"You're not gonna go."

"I need to go," I stated urgently.

"Sweetheart, I'm not gonna let you go. You were right, we need to talk."

"I need to go," I warned, "before it's too late."

He opened his mouth to speak, but it was too late.

There was a loud knock in the breezeway. Not at Mitch's door. Distant.

I knew it was at mine when I heard my mother shout, "Marabelle Jolene Hanover! We're done fuckin' with you! Open this goddamned, *fuckin'* door!"

Not again!

I froze in Mitch's arms, my head jerking toward his door, and I felt his arms get tight.

Then I tipped my head back to see he'd pressed his lips together like he was fighting against a smile, and my eyes narrowed on his mouth, not finding one thing funny. Then something came to me, and my eyes shot to his.

"My name is Marabelle Jolene Hanover," I told him in a whisper.

"What?" he whispered back, but that one word trembled, and I knew it was with suppressed laughter.

"If that isn't a trailer trash name...for trailer trash," I added, "then nothing is."

His lips twitched and he muttered, "Baby."

"It is, admit it," I pushed.

"Actually, I think it's pretty."

He was so full of it.

"It's trailer trash," I returned.

He shook his head, his lips twitching.

Twitching!

Then he said, "It's pretty. It's even kinda sweet. And it's both these things because it's yours."

My name wasn't sweet.

But he was.

Argh!

I changed tactics.

"What's your name?" I asked.

"You know my name," he answered.

"Your full name," I pressed.

"Mitchell James Lawson," he told me.

"Right," I mumbled, and his arms gave me another squeeze.

"And?" he asked.

"Your name is the name of a hot cop, a hot baseball player or the third cousin of a king."

His body started shaking as he turned his head in an unsuccessful attempt to hide his smile.

*"Marabelle!"* I heard Mom screech. "We're sortin' this shit right...*fuckin'*...*now*!"

I closed my eyes.

"They'll go away in a minute, and I'll call North to tell them we're gonna be late," Mitch said calmly, and I opened my eyes to stare at him, *not* calmly. In fact, I was pretty certain my eyes were bugging out of my head.

"Mitch!" I hissed.

"It's gonna be all right," Mitch soothed, his hands traveling up and down my back, most of which was bare, so this felt really good. "I'm giving them this one. I don't have time to deal with their bullshit and get you to dinner. They'll give up and go away then we can go eat, and we'll talk while we eat."

Jeez, he was stubborn.

Of course I was too, but I decided not to think about my stubbornness. Only his.

"We're not going to work," I whispered, again returning to my earlier theme (see? Stubborn).

His full attention focused on me and did it in a way I braced as one of his hands slid up my neck and into my hair.

Then his head dropped, his mouth captured mine and he kissed me, hard, wet, deep, thorough and *long*.

Very long.

And very, *very* well.

So long and so well, when he was done, he lifted his head and gazed down at me, the haze he created took its time to clear, and I heard it.

Nothing.

"I think they're gone," I whispered.

He cocked his head and listened. Then he let me go, grabbed my hand and dragged me toward the door saying, "Thank Christ, let's go eat. I'm fuckin' starved."

Yep, that's what he said.

Not like we had a drama.

Not like he heard a word I said.

Not like the Trailer Trash Twins had again come calling.

No, like we often went out to dinner and all that had gone before was like a last-minute phone call that was a minor diversion before we could get out the door.

Yes, Detective Mitchell James Lawson was *stubborn*.

More stubborn than me.

Damn.

# CHAPTER TWENTY-ONE

## Drug of Choice

MY EYES OPENED slowly and they instantly took in everything.

I was in Mitch's big bed. Down the bed I could see his club chair, and draped over the club chair was my silky, sapphire top and jeans. These were tangled with a man's espresso-colored, tailored shirt, matching sports jacket and another pair of jeans with a brown belt threaded through its loops. My shoes were on the floor as were a pair of men's boots.

There was heat behind me, and I knew what this heat was. It was Mitch. There was weight on my waist, and I knew what this weight was. It was Mitch's arm.

I felt warm and safe and I knew why this was. I was in Mitch's bed, in Mitch's apartment with Mitch.

And no Billie.

Billie *and* Billy were in another house, not here.

Oh boy.

\*　　\*　　\*

North was an Italian restaurant in Cherry Creek. I'd been there twice before. The food was fabulous, the décor gorgeous—dark wood, cream leather seats with hints of lime green and bright orange. It was awesome.

Nearly the minute we arrived, Mitch being a detective, stubborn and clearly, I was belatedly realizing, having an insane desire to wheedle himself into the life of a Two Point Five, took advantage of my highly emotional state.

He barely had his beer, me my passion fruit frizzante, and our waitress had just turned away from our table after getting our food order when the interrogation began.

"I wanted you to do this in your time, at your pace, but after watchin' you go wherever the fuck you went in my apartment I'm seein' I can't let you do this in your time and at your pace. So, right now, you're gonna tell me about your mom," he ordered.

I looked anywhere but at him, took a sip of my refreshing, delicious drink and tried to get my wits about me after experiencing the drama with Mitch, which included a side order of my mom. At the same time I was trying to figure out a way to do *anything* but tell him about my mom.

Unfortunately, I did this with my left hand resting on the table. Therefore, I found my left hand stretched halfway across the table and my fingers laced with Mitch's.

Mitch's fingers laced with mine felt nice. And not a little nice.

A lot.

Damn.

I put my glass down and looked at our hands. Then I looked at Mitch.

"I don't think—"

His fingers squeezed mine. "Tell me." His voice was very firm.

I decided first to try bitchy. "It's really none of your business."

He shook his head. "I know you're filtering this information so you don't have to deal with it, so I'll keep tellin' you until it sinks in. Mara, you're gonna be in my bed and my life, and when you get a new one, I'm gonna be in your bed and your life. And, cluein' you in, you might take a good look at things and notice you're *already* in my bed and my life. So, since I intend for that to keep goin', I'm gonna have to know about your life. Not what you've built for the now, but what you survived to get to the now. So," his fingers gave mine another gentle squeeze, "tell me about your mom."

I glared at him then informed him, "You're filtering information too, such as me explaining about boundaries and then me telling you that you have to move on."

"I'm not filtering, sweetheart. I'm ignoring that shit because it's whacked. Now, tell me about your mom."

"It's not whacked," I replied.

"It is," he returned then pushed, "Tell me about your mom."

"It is not."

Yet another finger squeeze and then, "Mara, baby, tell...me...about...your...mom."

My head tipped to the side and my eyes narrowed. "You're very stubborn."

"Tell me about your mom."

"And annoying."

"Tell me about your mom."

"And bossy."

"Mara, your mom."

"And you can be a jerk."

"Mara—"

I rolled my eyes and said to the ceiling, "Jeez, all right, I'll tell you about my mom."

This was not me giving in. This was my new strategy.

I decided that maybe he *should* know about my mom. Maybe, even though it was clear he was always alert, very insightful, often figured me out and already knew a lot about me, maybe he was somehow blind to my Two Point Five-edness.

So I decided to let him in on it.

I took another sip of my frizzante, put the glass on the table and launched in, not looking into his eyes—finding anywhere to look but at him—as I recolored the Mara he thought me to be.

"My mom's a drunk. So's Aunt Lulamae. Functioning alcoholics. They smoke, cigarettes and pot. They carouse. They party. They're both in their fifties now and even though I haven't spoken to or seen either one of them in over a decade, except our loving reunion at the store, I suspect this behavior hasn't changed."

"It's not good your mom and aunt are functioning alcoholics, Mara, but none of that is really that bad," Mitch pointed out.

My eyes went to his beautiful ones. So brown, so warm, so deep. Fathomless. I wanted to drown in them, get pulled under, swim in his gaze for the rest of my life.

Instead, I pulled in a soft breath, steeled myself and I gave to him all he needed to understand why he was not for the likes of me.

"My first living memory is watching my mother having sex on the couch in our trailer with a hairy truck driver."

Mitch's gaze grew intense.

"She knew I was there," I added.

Mitch's fingers spasmed in mine.

"She didn't stop even after she saw me," I continued.

"Jesus, sweetheart," Mitch murmured.

"I walked out when she was giving him a blowjob, and

I finally wandered back to my room when he started doing her doggie-style."

Mitch's jaw got hard.

"I remember every second," I whispered. "It's burned into my brain."

Mitch sucked in breath through his nose.

"I was four," I finished.

He closed his eyes. I thought I knew what this meant so I ignored the brutal clutch that suddenly had hold of my heart, squeezing the life out of me. I looked away and took another sip of my drink.

Keeping my eyes on anything but him, I went on, "I don't know who my father is because my mother doesn't know who my father is. I grew up in a small town. Everyone in that town knew about Mom and Aunt Lulamae, so everyone in that town thought certain things about me. Parents, kids, teachers, everyone. Parents and teachers thought I was trash and they treated me like trash. Not even when I was young did they treat me any differently. I was tarred with her brush from the minute I entered this world, and I knew nothing different every breath I took in it. Parents didn't let their daughters come over to my house or me go over to their daughters'. Teachers barely even looked at me. When I got older, boys assumed I was easy. This was not fun, because it was difficult to convince boys who thought you were easy that you were not easy. Therefore after a few *very* not fun dates, I stopped dating. I had two friends, my cousin Bill and a girl named Lynette, whose parents were the only parents in town who were nice to me."

When I took in a breath, Mitch urged on another finger squeeze, "Look at me."

I didn't look at him, because I was certain what I would see. And I didn't want to see it.

But I did keep talking.

"Aunt Lulamae had been married to Bill's dad, but they got divorced and he stuck around town. Their divorce was bitter and it was ugly. And before they split up, it was loud and their dysfunction and hatred played out for everyone in town to see, in their trailer, outside their trailer, in *Mom's* trailer, in bars, on sidewalks. And after they split up, it went on just the same. Bill's sister has another father, but he didn't even stick around to see her born. Bill had the same reputation as me, and, when I was young, I felt it was the two of us against the world, so I latched on because I needed somebody. As he got older, he responded differently than me to all that was happening. He was a couple of years older than me, and I got caught in that because I was young and stupid. I didn't realize that what I was doing was solidifying in everyone's mind that I was just like Melbamae and Lulamae Hanover. But it was more. Being with Bill meant *not* being around them, and I hated to be around them so I escaped any way I could."

I took another sip of my drink, and Mitch gave my hand another squeeze and a gentle tug.

"Mara, sweetheart, look at me," he called softly.

I still didn't look at him as I set my glass down and continued my story.

"It was Lynette who saved me, her and her parents. All through senior year she told me I had to get away, but I knew in my heart I'd never get away. I knew I was destined to have some crappy job making just above minimum wage and living in a trailer, just like my mom, just like Aunt Lulamae. And I'd live in that town knowing everyone looked down on me. But for graduation, Lynette's parents gave me an old car, but it was one that worked really well because Lynette's uncle was a mechanic, and they also gave me a thousand dollars."

My eyes slid across his face so fast I couldn't register his expression and I kept on going but in a whisper.

"It was a nice thing to do. No one had ever been that nice to me, that generous. The tank was filled up, they had a cooler in it filled with pop, sandwiches in Ziploc bags and candy bars, and Lynette, her dad and mom told me to get in that car and go. So I packed up everything I owned, some clothes, my music—that was everything I owned—and I drove. I got on I-80 and headed west. The minute I hit Denver, the second I saw the Front Range, I knew this was the place for me. The city was huge, no one here knew me, and the mountains were beautiful and I wanted to see that beauty every day. I didn't have much beauty in my life, so it seemed a good idea to be somewhere that I could see beauty every day. So I stayed." I sucked in a deep breath and ended my story with, "And, since you looked into me, you know the rest."

"Did any of those boys who thought you were easy hurt you?" Mitch asked gently, and I chanced a glance at him to see he looked his usual alert but otherwise his face was studiously blank.

"Not in the way you're thinking, no. But it got physical, and that physical was unpleasant, but mostly it was what they said to me, the way they looked at me and the way they talked about me afterwards that was not nice. The girls did it too, and girls can be way nastier than boys could ever hope to be."

"Did your mom look out for you at all?"

I shrugged. "It would have been better if she thought of me as just an annoying drain on her meager resources, but she didn't. She thought I thought I was too big for my britches and told me so, repeatedly. She thought I was uppity and told me that too. I got good grades, but she didn't think that was something to be proud of. She made fun of me. She had a lot of boyfriends who were really just fuck buddies, and she made fun of me in front of them too. When I got older and her special friends realized I was no longer a girl but *a girl*, they got ideas. Sometimes they acted on them. This ticked her off, and then she started to see me as competition. She didn't protect me from them. She shouted at me, called me a slut, then she'd call me a tease. I couldn't win either way." I shrugged again and looked away when Mitch's eyes darkened, and not in a sexy way, in an angry way. "I used to slip out at night, especially if she had someone over or she had a lot of someones over and she was partying. I'd go to Bill's trailer, sleep on the floor by his bed or go to Lynette's. She had a double bed. I thought her bed was huge." I pulled in a short breath, let it out on a soft sigh and whispered, "I loved her bed." Then I blinked, pulled myself together and kept talking, "I used to climb in her window. Her parents knew I was doing it, but they never said a thing."

"Let's go back to the men in your mother's life trying it on with you," Mitch demanded in a careful way, and I looked back at him.

"It wasn't that, Mitch. I wasn't violated, or not completely," I told him without a hint of emotion. "They'd come in my room, be handsy, but they were usually drunk or high, so I'd get away. Then I learned to get away earlier so they didn't even get to take a shot. Some of them were even nice. Some of them, I think, knew what it was like being Melbamae's daughter. A couple of them tried to be like dads to me." I shook my head and looked away, muttering, "Melbamae hated that most of all."

I grabbed my drink and took the last sip, setting the glass down and staring at the floor beside our table. Through this, Mitch didn't speak. Through all of it, Mitch kept hold of my hand. When it hit me he wasn't talking, just sitting there holding my hand, my eyes drifted to his.

The instant they did, he asked, "You do know she isn't you?"

"I know," I whispered.

"And you know that isn't your life and it really never was."

I pressed my lips together and shrugged again. My eyes started to slide away, but Mitch's fingers tensed in mine to the point where it almost hurt. It definitely caught my attention. At the same time his hand gave mine a rough jerk, pulling it toward him, which meant I had no choice but to lean in, and my eyes flew back to his.

"I don't understand how your mind works, baby," he said softly, also leaning into me, "how you twist shit around. But that was not your life then and it isn't your life now. Instead of you sitting there looking at anything but me, thinkin' I'm gonna judge you for shit that was never in your control, you should be sitting there proud in the knowledge that you got the fuck out and made somethin' of yourself, made somethin' of your life."

"I—"

He shook his head, his fingers tensed even deeper in mine, and I clamped my mouth shut.

"I've told you this before and I'll say it again. In my job I see a lotta shit, a lot, and it is rare, Mara, unbelievably, fuckin' rare that any kid is born to a life like yours and has the strength to get the fuck out and make something of themselves."

"I sell beds, Mitch," I reminded him. "I'm not the president of the free world. I don't even have a college education."

"Who cares?" he asked back, quick as a flash.

"I don't own a house."

"Neither do I," he pointed out.

Hmm. This was true.

"Do you know who your father is?" I asked and his eyes flared.

"Yeah, and you're gonna know him too because you're gonna meet him."

I shook my head. "Don't you see, Mitch? I don't even know who my father is."

"Again, honey, that says nothin' about *you*. Again, you were born to that. You didn't take that away from yourself. Your mother took it away from you."

I tried a different strategy. "Do you have a college education?" I asked.

"Yeah," he answered, and my eyes started sliding away again.

That got my hand another jerk.

"Eyes back to me," he growled in a way my eyes went back to him. "Me havin' a college degree means I live in a different zone than you?"

"And your mother wears twinsets," I reminded him.

He blinked. Then he stared at me.

He shook his head and his lips twitched before he said, "Sweetheart, do you not see that shit's whacked?"

"No," I pointed out the obvious.

"Well, it's whacked," he returned.

I leaned deeper toward him and looked him straight in his fathomless, beautiful eyes.

"Two weeks ago, you walked through a window into my world and you lost your mind, Mitch. You took one look at Bill and the state of Billy and Billie's lives and you lost your mind. That is my family. That is my life. And you don't understand this because it isn't your life, but there is no way to escape it. There is no way. Because it haunts you. It's your cousin in jail and facing prison if he survives to his trial. It's his kids in your house, one worried about her daddy when he's done nothing to deserve it, the other worried about everything when he should be worried about getting to the next level on some video game. It knocks on your door and shouts the unit down so your neighbor has to confront it in the breezeway. It's a beautiful, kind man looking into you and finding you have a juvie file. It never goes away. It's always there. It isn't history. It's in my blood. It's *me*."

"No, Mara, two weeks ago, I walked into *your cousin's house*. I did this after I had dinner with a beautiful woman and two really good kids, and I lost my mind because that assclown didn't give a fuck that his kids ran away and hadn't had anything to eat all day. His house was a disaster and he was drunk and stoned and he didn't even flinch when his kids saw him that way. I lost my mind because their clothes didn't fit and their shoes were comin' apart, and he had vodka and smack and smokes. And I lost my mind because he didn't apologize to you that you had to drop everything and look out for his kids. And you did it in a way that I knew you were a practiced hand, and I knew you were a practiced hand because he's an assclown."

I stared at him as he lifted our hands, unlaced our fingers but kept hold of my hand, tight, palm to palm, fingers wrapped around, and his eyes locked with mine.

"But it was three and a half weeks ago I walked into *your* world. A clean apartment, nice furniture, flowers on your bedspread, and I found out you only own a hammer. I found out you have no clue that men buy mattresses and beds from you because you wear tight skirts that show off your great ass. Because you got legs that go on forever. Because you pin up your hair and all this makes them stand by beds and mattresses and they buy them from you because all they're thinkin' is that they want you with your hair down, their hands on your ass and those legs wrapped around them *in* that bed *with them*. That bed could be made of nails and they wouldn't give a fuck. They're all about buyin' a fantasy, and you rake in your commission but have no fucking clue."

Ohmigod. Did he seriously think that was true?

"Mitch—"

"And I found out you have great taste in music, and the reason you'd barely look at me for four years is that you're pathologically shy."

"Mitch—"

"And it's cute."

"Please, Mitch—"

"And this was great fuckin' news because you bein' shy meant you were into me, which meant I finally was open to make a play."

"Stop it," I whispered.

"But it was seein' those two kids respond to you and how you responded to them that made me understand it was worth the effort to take on what I knew would be the frustrating task of extracting your head outta your ass."

"Stop it." This time I said those two words on a hiss.

"I already knew you looked great in shorts, great in a bikini, you were a great cook, worked hard and your friends love to spend time with you."

All thoughts flew from my head, and I blinked at him, mortified. "You've seen me in a bikini?"

He ignored me. "So I made my play."

"When have you seen me in a bikini?"

"And now we're gonna make a deal."

I blinked again and stiffened. "What deal?"

"We're gonna go back to the place I got you this last week. You're gonna loosen up, come out of your cocoon, for good this time, and give me a shot. And I'm gonna take that shot and use it to convince you that you are not what you think you are, but instead what everyone else knows you to be."

I yanked at my hand in his, but he only held on stronger.

"Let my hand go," I requested on a demand.

"No," he denied. "Agree to the deal."

I stared at him then reminded him, "You do know that you taking that shot comes with two kids, a fucked-up cousin who has the Russian mob after him and whatever Mom and Lulamae dream up. They might be functional alcoholics, and over the years they may have killed an alarming number of brain cells through a variety of mood-altering methods, but when they're on a tear, it can get ugly," I paused, "or, *uglier.*"

"Mara, baby, open your eyes for long enough to remember I've been livin' this alongside you the last week. I'm totally clued in, sweetheart, it's *you* who isn't."

That was when it hit me.

He had been. Mitch had been living this with me the last week.

No, that wasn't exactly true. He hadn't only been living it with me; he'd been taking care of things for me and for the kids. I'd been too busy, too tired and too freaked out to realize the fullness of his assistance. For over a week, without Mitch, I would never have made it. I'd had a very short taste of going it alone, and it exhausted me in a way I knew would seep into my bones. I'd have had to take time off. I would have had to load up a sick Billie and wake up her brother so I could go to the drugstore to get her Tylenol. In fact, I wouldn't have even known to *get* her some Tylenol.

Though, I probably would have called Roberta and learned that.

Still, it would have been harder without him.

A lot harder.

Exhausting.

I stared at Mitch. He'd done all that without complaint, without looking tired, without getting pissed, without me asking. And through all that, he also took care of me, snuggling with me on the couch when I needed to zone out. Making me chili. Making me breakfast right along with the kids. Turning off my alarm so I could sleep in.

What sane man in the whole of the United States of America takes on a pathologically shy, Two Point Five woman who only owns a hammer? A woman who doesn't know there's a valve to switch off the water? A woman who runs away on what was, apparently, your first date and stands him up on your second? Then suddenly she finds herself the guardian of two children and has a family that was sent to earth straight from hell because even the devil himself didn't want to spend time with them?

"You're a very unusual man, Detective Mitch Lawson, and I think maybe this is because you aren't totally sane," I blurted because the words bubbled up inside of me and forced their way out before I could hold them back.

When they did, Mitch blinked then he threw his head back and laughed.

I watched him laugh thinking that was proof he *was* insane, at the same time thinking the same thing I always thought when he laughed. And that was that he looked unbelievably good when he laughed.

When he stopped laughing, he leaned toward me and lifted our hands toward his mouth.

"Are you sayin' we have a deal?"

"No." I shook my head, and the humor fled from his face, so I hastily explained, "I play this game with you, Mitch, it's not only me playing it. Two other people are involved."

"Remember, Mara, I know that."

"This doesn't work, then they—"

"I ever give you cause to think I'd fuck you over *or* them?"

"No, but—"

"What I have with you and what I want to have with you is exclusive to what I have with each of those kids. What they have from me is what they'll always have from me, if they want it, whether I still have something with you or not."

I felt my throat close and wet hit my eyes.

God, he was really a great guy.

"You like them," I whispered.

"They're good kids," he replied.

"They like you," I told him.

"I know."

I pressed my lips together, swallowed and then pulled in a deep breath to control my tears before they spilled over and ruined my makeup.

Mitch watched this without a word.

Then he asked, "Do we have a deal?"

"You and me are against all the laws in the universe," I explained.

"No, you and me are against all the laws in twisted, fucked-up Mara World, but I'm gonna straighten out Mara World, so, answer me, do we have a deal?"

I bit my lip. I considered this deal. And I knew it would be me who was insane if I made it.

Then, because I *was* insane, I whispered, "We do, if you promise me one thing."

His hand tensed and his eyes stayed locked to mine. "What?"

I kept whispering when I said, "When you figure it out and move onto a beautiful life, don't regret the time you wasted on me."

He stared at me a second then closed his eyes, turned his head and brought our hands to his lips. He just rested them there, and he did this for what seemed like a long time.

He slid my knuckles across his lips, opened his eyes and faced me.

Then he whispered back, "I promise I'll never regret being with you, Mara."

I nodded. "Then we have a deal."

That was when our antipasti arrived.

*       *       *

We shared a three-course meal. Mitch had another beer, and I had two glasses of wine.

During our meal Mitch didn't let me descend into a freak-out about making a stupid deal that would lead to heartbreak and, likely, me spending the rest of my days reading the works of Sylvia Plath (and the like).

Instead, I learned that Mitch had been born in Pennsylvania, and his father had moved them to Colorado when he was five. I also learned Penny was his older sister and he had a younger sister named Judy who was a physical therapist at a rehabilitation center in Vail.

He further shared the scary news that he'd been engaged to his high school sweetheart, who stayed his sweetheart through college. He went on to share the crazy news that he broke it off with her when he became the cop he wanted to be and he didn't go to work for her daddy at his bank like she wanted him to do, and she started to get bitchy.

He also shared the infinitely *scarier* news that he moved into our complex because it had a gym and a running trail, but he expected only to be there a couple of years while he saved to put down on a house. This news was infinitely scarier because he stayed there because he liked the gym, the running trail and seeing me in shorts or catching a glimpse of me next to the pool wearing a bikini in the summer.

As this knowledge threatened to break the hold he had on my freak-out, Mitch deftly steered the conversation to music and movies. However, he lost his hold upon finding out I was an action movie freak. Then he promptly declared I was the perfect woman because I had a great ass, long legs, "fantastic fuckin' hair, which looks even better when it's down," liked baseball, "though...the Cubs...uh, baby" (this muttered on a teasing grin), and I also liked to watch things blow up.

At that, I started fidgeting in my seat, biting my lip, looking anywhere but at him and trying not to hyperventilate, at the same time wondering if he'd seen *The A-Team*. Mitch paid the bill and led me to the sidewalk.

He stopped us there, and I tipped my head up to look at him.

"Can you walk more than a block on those heels?" he asked.

"Why?" I answered with a question.

"Can you walk more than a block on those heels?" he repeated.

"Yes," I answered because I was getting to know Detective Mitch Lawson, fast, and I might be able to walk more than a block on my heels, but my feet would start to hurt if I had to stand there and beat him at stubborn, which might take an eternity.

His arm slid along my shoulders, and he turned me

into the boutique section of Cherry Creek. I slid my arm along his waist, liking the feel of it there with his hip and thigh sometimes brushing against mine as we walked. Two blocks up and one block in, he stopped us in front of a shop.

"That's Penny's," he said, tipping his head to Design Fusion, the shop I already knew was his sister's. A shop I'd been in once and left because the stuff in it was awesome, but the price tags were more than a little scary.

I stared at the shop, all its cool furniture and even cooler accessories, then I looked up at Mitch.

"That's a great shop," I whispered.

"You know she furnished my apartment," Mitch stated, I nodded and he went on. "You're pathologically shy, and Penny's a pathological decorator. She's redecorated each of her kids' rooms about five times. She has three, and the oldest one is seven. And that's just her kids' rooms. She's redecorated other rooms in her house so many times, I've lost count. Her husband, Evan, has declared citizen's divorce twice. I was there both times. It wasn't pretty."

"Yikes," I muttered, looking into the windows at the expensive but gorgeous wares on display and thinking if her kids' rooms had that stuff in them, five times over, the unknown Evan must be a bazillionaire or he should be nominated for sainthood.

"He's an excavator," Mitch continued, giving me the information that Evan was far from a bazillionaire and therefore sainthood was forthcoming. "They have a sofa in their house that cost nearly ten thousand dollars." I gasped, and my eyes shot to his. "She's a nut. She's a pain in the ass. She's got champagne tastes, and Evan's never gonna be able to afford anything other than a beer budget. So he talked her into opening this shop so she could get champagne wholesale."

"Smart move," I noted.

"Yeah, now she can talk other people into spending *their* money. But it's still her drug, sweetheart, and he's made it so she can get her fix every day."

I studied him because I was realizing this wasn't just his latest conversational gambit to take my mind off freaking out, but that he was trying to tell me something.

Mitch kept talking. "Penny's the type of woman you don't ignore because Penny's the type of woman who not only doesn't like to be ignored, but won't allow it. But, during the NCAA basketball playoffs, Evan disappears. You do not disturb Evan during *any* basketball game, but to the outside world he ceases to exist during the playoffs."

I waited for it. Mitch gave it to me.

"She gets this about him and ties herself in knots making sure nothing stops Evan getting his drug of choice. Not kids. Not phone calls. Not the need to get up and get another beer. Nothing."

"So they enable each other," I remarked, Mitch smiled and turned me so we were front to front and both his arms were around me.

"No," he said softly. "They love each other. They know what the other likes, they know what the other needs to feed whatever is hungry in their soul and they give it to them. At least Penny does but Evan does too with only a minimal amount of bitching."

I put my hands on his chest and asked, "What's your drug of choice?"

"I've no idea," he answered. "It's not up to me to figure it out. But whoever I decide to share my life with needs to be a woman who ties herself in knots to give it to me."

Oh boy. There it was.

"Mitch—"

"But only because I know I'm a man who'll figure hers out and give it to her in return."

And he was. I knew this to be true right down deep to the very heart of me.

"This is very heavy for a first date," I decided to point out, considering Mitch had switched from doing anything to make me *not* freak out, to saying a bunch of stuff that could do nothing *but* freak me out.

"I've shared more breakfasts with you than any woman I've dated in the last year and a half," Mitch returned. "I know what you look like in the morning. I know what you act like when you come home tired after work. I know that you pick the least expensive thing on the menu, either to be nice or to be annoying in order to put me off. But I think it's to be nice because you *are* nice and also both times you thought you'd be spending time with just me, you dressed in a way that would not, in any way, put me off. I know you cuddle when you're sleeping. I know you take only milk in your coffee and you make coffee strong. I know you're really good with kids. And I know that you use music and scents to regulate your mood. So I'm thinking this is not a first date. This is more like us hittin' the six month mark. And the six month mark is when you stop talkin' about shit that really doesn't matter and start talkin' about shit that means everything."

Okay. I'd hit it. I was freaking out. And I decided Mitch needed to know that.

Therefore, I told him, "You're freaking me out."

Then he freaked me out more by saying, "Good. My first strategy is working."

I blinked. Then I stared. Then I asked, "Pardon?"

His head dipped closer to me. "I don't know what's

gonna work with you, sweetheart, so I'm tryin' this first and we'll see. I need to switch things up..." he trailed off and I kept staring.

It was then I decided to share, "I like calm and to have peace of mind."

"Kiss that good-bye," Mitch advised.

Not a good answer.

"Um..." I mumbled, trying to pull away and failing. In fact, Mitch's arms brought me closer and his face dipped even nearer.

"Now, before I take you home, I need you to explain something."

"And I need another glass of wine," I retorted with the God's honest truth.

"I'll get you one at home. Now you need to explain something."

"No, I really think I need a glass of wine, like, ten minutes ago."

Mitch was not to be denied. "Why did you leave me in bed with Billie?"

This threw me. It also, for some reason, scared me. And it scared me because that was a couple of days ago. He'd made it relatively clear he wasn't happy I'd done it then, but him asking about it again made it clear he *really* wasn't happy I'd done it.

My voice was quiet and even small when I reminded him, "I already apologized for that."

"I know you did, and I told you it was okay. Now I want to know why you did it."

Confusion edged into my fear, and my head tipped to the side. "Why?"

"Why do I want to know?"

"Yeah."

"I just do."

I bit my lip and realized that suddenly everything that was me needed to be certain that I answered his question in the way he needed it to be answered. And that made me even more scared.

Then I decided to tell him, "I didn't think it was the wrong thing to do."

"Why?"

"Why?"

"Yes, why?"

"I . . . because I didn't think it was wrong."

"She's six. I'm a grown man. I've known her less than a month. You don't leave a grown man alone in bed wrapped around a six-year-old."

Oh God. I'd not only done something wrong, the way he explained it made it sound like I'd *really* done something wrong. In fact, I'd done something revolting.

"You got her Tylenol," I blurted my defense on a whisper.

Mitch's brows drew together. "What?"

"You got her Tylenol," I repeated.

One of his hands slid up the skin of my back to sift into my hair as he murmured, "Mara—"

"We were," I hurried on, "making out. On the couch. We'd been talking. Before that, you asked me if she was down, like, I don't know, you were her dad or something. Then she came out and threw up. And it was . . . I was scared. I didn't know what to do and parents . . ."

I shook my head, feeling stupid, feeling exposed and looked away then looked back to him because I couldn't give up. I had to explain because it was important.

"Parents when they're starting out, they don't know what to do. And you found out what to do and did it. You went to the drugstore, like any dad would do. Not like Bill would do. If Billie was puking, Billy would probably take care of her. Bill would...Bill might not even be there, but he probably wouldn't even wake up. But you went to the drugstore. Then you stayed with us. And she was shivering so hard and she didn't want you to go. She wanted you there. And it was just...we were just...I forgot who we were, and I thought, I thought..." I shook my head again, closed my eyes tight, pressed my lips together, opened my eyes and whispered, "I thought she'd never had a good dad, and I've never even had a dad, but I thought...if you had a dad and you got sick, the best place to be was pressed close to your dad, and he'd make you feel better." I pulled in a breath, dropped my eyes from the intensity of his and looked at his throat. "I didn't leave her in bed with Mitch. I left her in bed with the man who took care of her when she was sick. I didn't think it was wrong. I never considered it was wrong. I actually thought," I pulled in another breath, and my voice dropped lower when I admitted, "I actually thought it was beautiful."

His hand cupped the back of my head and he pressed my face into his throat. Tears filled my eyes and my fingers clenched into his shirt.

God, I wasn't only a Two Point Five, I was an idiot. Why did he even want that deal he made me agree to at dinner? Why? It didn't make sense.

"I'm sorry I made you uncomfortable. I didn't even think," I told his throat.

"Quiet," he replied softly.

"I'm sorry," I repeated.

Lips to my hair, Mitch said gently, "Mara, honey, I needed to know why you did that because it occurred to me after you told your story that there's a reason you're pathologically shy around men you're attracted to. And that reason might not be healthy. And I gotta know what I got on my hands with you." I tried to tilt my head back, but he kept it in his throat and kept speaking. "But what you just told me is not unhealthy. What you just told me tells me that I've already broken through that cocoon."

"You really haven't," I blurted in all honesty.

"Baby, you just told me you think of me as Billie's new dad to your new mom. Soon, those kids are gonna be yours officially, and any guy lucky enough to get you is gonna have to be a guy lucky enough that you think he'll make a decent dad to those kids. And, obviously, you think that of me. So if that isn't a big, freaking tear in the shit you got wound tight around you, nothin' is."

My head jerked back, taking his hand with it, and I looked at him.

"I don't think of you as Billie's new dad."

"Baby, you do. You just said it."

Shit! I did!

"It may have sounded that way, but I don't think of you as Billie's new dad." Though, thinking on it, that was a kind of lie because, truthfully, I kind of did.

"At the time, you didn't blink before you asked, 'are you doin' the drugstore run or am I?' It was a given to you I'd be there through whatever we had on our hands with Billie. You didn't ask me if I minded goin' to the store. You assumed one or the other of us would make the run to get Billie what she needed."

"I wasn't thinking clearly then, because I was scared and she was sick. But I don't think of you as her new dad. That's crazy!"

Another kind of but definitely desperate lie.

"Okay, then when you were layin' it out for me about

how *we* make decisions as a *team* about those kids, something which you not only laid out but you also reminded me about, you did not lay it out and say what you say goes because you're their guardian. You said we're a team and we discuss decisions and make them together. And that was even before Billie got sick."

Shit. I did that too.

I didn't respond. I just glared at him.

"Right now, take a second, go back and think about what you just said to me, fuck, *all* that you've said to me when it comes to Bud and Billie," he ordered firmly.

I glared at him. Then I took a second to go back and think about what I just said to him and *all* I'd said to him, but I didn't need to because, essentially, I did say that. All of it.

"I didn't actually mean it that way." This time I semi-lied.

"No, you don't actually mean it that way *now*, now that you're not freaking out and being honest. Now, you're freaking out a different way and lyin' through your teeth."

God, I hated it when he figured me out.

Mitch wasn't done talking, but when he spoke again he pulled me closer as he leaned his face to within an inch of mine and his voice was low, gentle and sweet when he rocked my world.

"That's another thing that doesn't turn me off, sweetheart, knowin' that you come with those kids, and you need to know that. You also need to know I want kids of my own, two of them. But I don't care, if this works out between me and you, that the kids we have will have an older brother and sister that don't have my blood, just my heart."

I blinked up at him knowing my lips were parted but my

body had melted into his, at the same time I felt the tears sting my nose. I was about to cry because Mitch had obviously already let Billy and Billie into his heart. And I was about to cry just thinking about making kids with Mitch, which wouldn't be a dream come true. It would be something better. More beautiful. Beyond a dream and I didn't know what that was. All I knew was that I wanted it like I wanted a lifetime of his good mornings and him looking at me the way he did when I walked into his living room that night and coming home to me and kissing my neck then my lips when he was laughing.

"Did you hear me?" he asked when I said not a word.

"Yes," I whispered.

"So you don't have to lie about thinkin' that about me and Billie, because I don't mind."

I decided to change the subject immediately. Mostly because I was about to burst into tears and I didn't want to do that on my first date with Detective Mitch Lawson. The date had already been harrowing enough.

"Well, you can forget about the whole me being shy around men unhealthy thing because I'm all right with men. It's just *you* I'm not all right with."

"Why?" he asked.

"Because you're you," I answered.

"Why?" he persisted.

"Because you're annoying, stubborn and tell me I have my head up my ass."

He grinned and his fingers started sliding through my hair as he muttered, "Jesus, you're full of shit.

I totally was.

"Am not."

"Mara, you had a problem with me for four years, and in those four years you had no idea I was annoying and stubborn, and I hadn't told you you had your head up your ass."

"You're absolutely right. I had a problem with you for four years because you're hot and I knew you were out of my league. *Now* I have a problem with you because you're annoying, stubborn, told me I had my head up my ass *and*, I forgot to mention, you can be a jerk."

His grin became a smile and his voice was soft and teasing when he said, "Glad we got that straightened out, baby."

"Will you take me home now?" I asked tartly, which was kind of a stupid thing to ask considering "home" was *his* home, and I could definitely get in more trouble there, and I knew I was already in some serious trouble.

His eyes grew dark and his arm tightened around me when he muttered, "Absolutely."

He so totally got how much trouble I could get into at "home," mostly because he was going to get me into that trouble, and, obviously, he was looking forward to it.

Damn.

Then he let me go but started to guide me back toward North with his arm around my shoulders and my arm around his waist, as I shared honestly, "You do know because you've just freaked me way the heck out that you're taking me home and then sleeping on the couch. I'm lighting candles in your room, listening to my iPod and reevaluating my decision to make a deal with you."

"No, what I know is I'm taking you home, and when we get there I'm gonna put a fair amount of effort into tearing that cocoon open wide." His arm gave me a squeeze as he finished, "I'm not done with you tonight."

"We're done tonight."

"We're not."

"We *so* are."

I said this as his cell rang, so he didn't reply, instead he reached into his inside jacket pocket and took it out. He sighed when he looked at the display, hit a button and put it to his ear, all the while still walking with his arm around my shoulders.

"Lawson," he answered, then listened. "No, now is not a good time. I can't do it," he said, listened more and then, "You don't get it. I *really* can't do it. Mara and I have plans tonight." He stopped talking, listened more, then said, "Call Chavez." More listening, then, "Then call Nightingale." He stopped us and stared down at his boots while he listened. Then he said, "This doesn't make me happy." More listening, then, "Right. I'll do it, but you owe me, and when I say that, I mean huge. Get me?" He listened again, sighed then lifted his head and his eyes hit mine. "I gotta drop Mara off at my place and I'll be there. Don't do something maverick and get your ass filled with holes before I get there. I don't wanna be in the ER half the night and fillin' out paperwork the other half." Another pause then, "Later."

He ended the call and curled me into his front.

"New deal," he said.

Oh boy. I was already tense from the "ass filled with holes" and "ER half the night" comments. I didn't need the added pressure of a new deal with Mitch.

"Mitch—"

"I take you home, you hang out, watch TV, drink wine, light your candles, listen to music, whatever. But whatever you do, you do it *not* reevaluating your decision, but doing what you promised and sticking with me. I gotta go out and I'll be out for a while. When you're tired, you go to sleep in my bed."

"Mitch—"

"Baby, I won't be in it with you, which sucks for me, but I got a friend who needs backup tonight, and none of the other guys are free. He needs someone to work this with him but even if he doesn't get someone, he'll work it anyway so I gotta take his back."

"You won't be in it with me?" I asked.

"This is gonna take a while."

I stared at him. Then I whispered, "Is it safe?"

"It will be if I'm there. It won't be if he goes in alone."

"You're sure it's safe," I pushed.

This time he stared at me, and his voice was gentle when he answered, "My job is not safe. Day to day, my job could mean anything."

Oh *God!*

"But," he continued, "what we're doin' in the grand scheme of things is safe . . . *ish*."

"That's not a good answer, Mitch," I whispered.

"It's an honest one, Mara," he returned quietly. "Now, baby, will you do me a favor and, even without me close, stay with me in the real world and crawl into my bed tonight so I know I got somethin' good to come home to when I'm done with this shit?"

"Yes," my mouth said before my head caught up.

He grinned at me. Then his hand came to my jaw, tipped my head back and he touched his mouth to mine.

When he lifted his head half an inch, he muttered, "Brilliant. Now I know I can pull the dangerous-job card to get you to be sweet." My eyes narrowed. "Finally," he whispered against my lips as both his arms closed around me, "I've found a good use for it."

Then he touched his mouth to mine again, this time longer; his mouth wasn't closed, neither was mine and there was liberal tongue action.

Now *that* was brilliant.

When he broke the kiss and walked me back to North, I didn't share with him that he didn't have to use his job or freak me out enough to get what he wanted. All he had to do was kiss me and I'd be putty in his hands.

Not even that, all he had to do was call me "baby."

*       *       *

Mitch took me home and kissed me at his door, not long and lingeringly, which I had to admit sucked. Then he told me not to worry if I woke up in the morning and he still wasn't there. Whatever this was, it was going to take time, apparently.

Then he disappeared.

I washed my face and moisturized and got into my nightie and his flannel. Then I lit his candles and I put one of my Chill-Out playlists on his stereo.

Then I did something I hadn't had time to do with any attention.

I inspected his house.

You could learn a lot just from music, and if his music was garbage that would be an instant deal breaker.

It was then I snooped without hesitation. He pushed this deal, so I was going to find out what I got myself into.

I already knew his sister had good taste, and his apartment looked like a show home but comfier and more lived in. I'd learned the day I cleaned it, but also living there for a few days, that Mitch wasn't exactly tidy, but he wasn't a slob. Opened and unopened mail on a variety of surfaces (this I had organized). Sports jackets thrown over his very cool dining room chairs (these I had hung up). Sports magazines here and there, many of which should long since have been thrown away (these I'd stacked).

It was then I found he had great taste in music, excellent actually, more eclectic than mine and he invested heavily in CDs, which was almost unheard of these days, but it was something I liked. He also had great taste in movies, as evidenced by his DVD collection, heavy on the action with a good intermingling of thrillers. We were a half and half with the same taste in books. He read thrillers, as did I, but he also read true crime, which I did not.

I moved to the kitchen and noted what I'd previously noted. He drank American beer in bottles. I also noted he clearly cooked, and when he did, he cooked more than chili. It wasn't like he had a larder readily stocked just in case he was in the mood to whip up a cake. But he had spices that would indicate his culinary arsenal included more than chili and staples that evidenced that arsenal was a lot more than chili.

His medicine cabinet in the bathroom confirmed what I knew, that he didn't use product in his hair. It also gave me the added and weirdly interesting fact that he was an ibuprofen person, just like me. No aspirin or acetaminophen to be found, again, just like me (if you didn't count the recent addition of children's Tylenol).

I stopped snooping, started listening to music, stopped listening to music and then, yet again, I crawled into Mitch's bed.

His bed was awesome, but he really needed a mattress from Pierson's. His mattress didn't suck, but it was nowhere near a Spring Deluxe. It wasn't even in the same range as a Slumber Excelsior.

I decided to focus on advising Mitch on back health and the importance of having the proper mattress rather than the fact that I was again in Detective Mitch Lawson's very cool apartment. I was again going to sleep by climbing into Detective Mitch Lawson's very cool bed. But this time after the scary but undeniable fact that we'd had our first official date, during which I had a feeling I agreed to be his girlfriend.

And throughout all this, I did not once slip out of the real world where Mitch lived and back into Mara World, and mostly this was because I was concentrating on trying to keep at bay worried thoughts of Mitch out there providing backup on something that was safe...*ish*.

Then I fell asleep.

*        *        *

And now it was now. I was alone, as in no kids, in Mitch's apartment, in Mitch's bed *with* Mitch, as, apparently, sometime during the night he'd come home (safe and sound, thank God) and gotten in bed with me.

Oh boy.

I decided, since he had worked late, he needed his beauty rest so I was going to slip out quietly and let him have it.

Carefully, I started to move and got nary an inch before his arm around my belly got tight. I went back two inches, hit his warm, solid body, and I felt his face burrow in my hair.

"Where you goin'?" he mumbled sleepily.

"I thought I'd get up but let you rest," I offered thoughtfully.

"Uh-uh," he growled decisively.

Oh *boy!*

# CHAPTER TWENTY-TWO

## Oatmeal for Lunch

"BACK HEALTH IS very important."

Yes, this was what came out of my mouth after Mitch denied my exit from his bed.

His arm got tighter and he murmured, "What?"

"Lumbar support in mattresses, your mattress is very comfortable, but you need more lumbar support. You have an active lifestyle, but everyone needs to take care of their back."

Mitch was silent. Then I felt his body start shaking and I felt my body moving, and that was because Mitch was turning it to face him. Then I was facing him, feeling his arms around me and his hands moving on me over my nightie, but I was too busy staring at his handsome face, his smiling lips and his somewhat sleepy and way more than somewhat hot eyes to pay attention to his hands.

"You gonna set me up with a good mattress, baby?" he asked, his voice still slightly growly with sleep and way hot. So hot I felt it seven places, and those would be my scalp tingling, my breasts swelling, my chest getting warm, between my legs getting wet and all my toes on both feet curling.

"Uh…" I mumbled, he grinned and rolled so he was mostly on top of me. That was when I whispered, "Mitch."

And that was when his lips hit mine, his eyes held mine and he whispered, "Let's see if I can tear that cocoon wide open and let my Mara fly."

Then his head slanted and he kissed me.

His kiss was not sleepy. It was sweet, warm, gentle and wet. Then it got sweeter, warmer and wetter but not gentler. I realized my hands were on his sleek, warm skin and his sleek, warm skin felt really freaking good and my hands wanted to explore. So I let them. Then I realized his hands over my nightie were exploring too, and I liked it, a lot. About this time his kiss got even sweeter, even warmer, a whole lot wetter and *way* deeper, and I liked that even better. So much, I kissed him back the same way.

His hand glided up my side, in and over my breast and, immediately, his thumb swept hard against my tight nipple, and I liked that most of all. So much, my body arched and I planted a foot in the bed, rolling Mitch and going with him. Once I had him on his back with his long, powerful body under mine, I suddenly found I needed to discover to its fullest extent his sleek skin and hard muscle. And to do this, my discovery needed to be multisensory.

So my hands moved over his chest, his ribs, his belly and his sides as my lips moved to his stubble-rough jaw, his neck, his throat, across his collarbone and down. Then my lips, tongue and hands moved everywhere, touching, sweeping, tasting. I added teeth and there was nipping, and it was not only *hot*, it was *beautiful*. Everywhere I touched, tasted, nipped, how his muscles would jump. The way his arm around my shoulders would tighten. The short growl that would surge up his throat. The way the fingers of his other hand glided into the hair at one side of my head to cup it at the back. I loved it, all if it, every inch, every reaction, *everything*.

Then I went down, tracing the contours of his abs with my tongue as the fingers of one hand slid up his side, the other one went to the drawstring of his pajama bottoms.

I tugged.

He growled again, his fingers flexing against my head, and that gorgeous sound shot straight between my legs. My lips swept to the side then down, and I trailed my tongue along the line of muscle that curved inward from his hip down to his groin. Suddenly his hand in my hair was gone, both of his hands were in my armpits, and he was hauling me up his body.

Then he was kissing me, his arm tight around me, his other hand fisted in my hair. He knifed to sitting without our mouths disengaging, our tongues tangled and my knees were forced to slide up so I was straddling him. When I settled, I felt his cock hard beneath me and in that instant, I knew I needed it. *Needed it*.

I needed Mitch.

My mouth broke from his as my arm around him squeezed tight, I ground my hips down, rubbing myself against him, and my neck arched back.

Mitch's hands went into my nightie, up, *swoosh*, and it was gone. He tossed it aside and didn't delay with wrapping one arm tight around my waist, the other hand going to my breast, lifting it. My head tipped down, and I watched him guide it to his mouth. His lips closed around my nipple and he sucked hard.

My hips bucked in his lap and he growled against my nipple, which felt so good, God, so damned good, I whimpered. Both my hands slid into his hair, and I watched Mitch work my nipple, my hips rolling. Yes, God, yes, watching the beauty that was his face, feeling what his mouth was doing, I *needed him.*

"Honey," I called, my voice trembling, but he didn't respond.

His hand left my breast, and that arm wrapped around my waist as his other hand went to my other breast, and he repeated what he did to the first while I again watched.

My hips bucked again as the suction came, then they bucked again with an added low, desperate moan, which tore from my throat as his tongue circled.

"Mitch," I tried again, my voice throaty. "Honey," I called, my fingers fisting in his hair and his head tipped back, his eyes searing me with the fire burning in them. And my mouth went instantly to his, not to kiss him, but to whisper, "I need you, honey."

I watched up close as his eyes flashed in a seriously, *seriously* hot way, and both his arms wrapped tight around me.

"You sayin' you're ready, baby?" he whispered against my lips, his voice gruff and so, so beautiful.

"Yes," I breathed.

"Sure?"

God, *God*, he was *such* a good guy.

My arms circled his shoulders tight, and my hips rolled again in his lap, and my breathy, "Yes," was sharper, impatient, more demanding.

And obviously convincing.

He heard it. I knew it because I was suddenly on my back, and Mitch's torso was heavy on mine, his long arm stretched out to the nightstand.

I slid my leg out from between his hips, his head jerked down to look at me, but I just lifted my knees as I hooked my thumbs in my panties and tugged them up my thighs.

That was when his head jerked down to my legs then it went back to the nightstand. I freed my panties from my ankles, tossed them aside and barely let them loose before Mitch moved fully over me, at the same time rolling his hips as a demand for me to open my legs.

I did and his hips fell through.

Okay, God, *God*.

Damn but he felt good there.

My eyes went to his face to see him tearing a condom packet with his even, white teeth (which was hot too!), and his eyes were on me. The packet disappeared, and I felt his hand working between us as his eyes held mine captive. My breath escalated so I was near panting with anticipation.

This was happening. This was *going to happen*.

And I could *not* wait.

"You on the pill, sweetheart?" he asked quietly.

"No," I answered impatiently, lifting my hips a smidgeon to make my point and his lips twitched.

"Doctor's appointment, priority," he ordered.

"'Kay," I agreed.

Then I felt him and my lips parted. It was just the tip of him, the promise of him, but already it was *perfect*.

His hands moved to my hips, gliding down my thighs, hooking behind my knees, he pulled my legs up and then swung them in so they circled him. One of his arms lifted, he planted his forearm in the bed by my shoulder, his fingers in my hair while the other hand stayed at my leg, gliding down, oh so slowly, down, down, as his beautiful, fathomless, soulful, burning, dark brown eyes held mine, his handsome face close and his cock slowly, oh so slowly, glided inside.

His fingers at my leg moved in and down and curled around the cheek of my behind just as he seated himself full inside me.

Mitch was inside me, connected to me, holding my eyes, his breath mingled with mine, and I was wrapped around him in every way I could wrap myself around him.

I hadn't had a lot of beauty in my life, but I knew, in that moment, feeling him filling me, his long fingers in my hair, his eyes staring into mine, gentle, warm, beautiful, telling me without words he really liked where he was and that was with me, that even if I had a life filled with beauty, no moment would be more beautiful than that.

And that was why my arms pulled him even closer, my legs tightened around him and tears filled my eyes.

He saw them and when he did, he groaned, his head dipped, his nose slid along mine and his lips whispered against mine, "My Mara, so fuckin' sweet."

Then he started moving.

And that was even more beautiful.

He did it like he kissed me on the couch, gentle, sweet, unhurried, kissing me tender but deep sometimes, his mouth and tongue working my neck other times. I knew he paid attention, he listened, he fclt, and he went faster, harder, but only when I was ready. I was holding him close, tight, my hand in his hair, his tongue in my mouth, his cock driving deep, when it started to come over me. Shock pierced my system as it occurred to me I was about to have an orgasm just with a man moving inside me.

Then it happened, my head shot back, my limbs convulsed and my lips whispered, "Mitch, baby," and I had an orgasm just with a man moving inside me, and that man being Mitch, it was the best, sweetest, longest orgasm *in my life*.

Oh God.

God.

*Perfect.*

My neck righted, and I felt him still moving inside me, fast, hard, deep, God, gorgeous, as my eyes opened and I saw his on me. His face was dark, his eyes intense, his breath labored. His forearm moved up an inch so his fingers drove into my hair then fisted, pushing up, so my head went up and his mouth crushed down on mine just as his hand at my ass pulled up hard. He drove deeper, harder, faster, and I whimpered into his mouth as his tongue worked mine, and his cock worked me.

He stopped kissing me and growled against my lips, "If it's too much, baby, you gotta—"

"Don't stop," I begged because my limbs were tensing, my sex was spasming. "Don't stop, Mitch, baby, please."

He didn't stop, his mouth crushed down on mine again, his hand at my ass hauled me up further to take him even deeper. It was then that I had the second best, sweetest, far more intense (but not as long) orgasm *in my life*. It was beyond perfect because, as I cried out into Mitch's mouth, he groaned into mine as he buried himself to the root and stayed planted.

It took some time to come down because I didn't push it. I did it savoring his weight, his fingers in my hair, his lips moving tenderly on mine, his hand at my ass gliding up and becoming an arm wrapped possessively around the top of my hips.

His lips slid across my cheek and to my ear, and his arm around my hips gave me a squeeze when he asked in a whisper, "How's the real world feel this mornin', baby?"

My arms and legs tensed, his head came up, and I saw his unbelievably sexy, satisfied face and his eyes warmer and gentler and more beautiful than I'd ever seen them (and that was saying something).

Seeing that, I answered, I did it openly, honestly, exposing everything, and I did it by grinning.

He grinned back.

He dipped his head, touched his mouth to mine in a light kiss then said against it, "Don't move."

After that, he carefully slid out, rolled off me and out of bed, flicking the covers over me, and I blinked at the ceiling as I closed my legs. I turned to my side, pulling my knees up, tucking my hands under my cheek on the pillow. I caught just a glimpse of his contoured back and his beautiful behind in his pajama bottoms before he disappeared into the bathroom.

Unlike what everyone thought of me in Iowa, I left that small town a virgin. It wasn't until I was twenty and had been dating a guy in Denver for three months that I gave it up.

This did not go well, mostly because sex was messed up in my head due to my mother's antics, her fuck buddies trying it on with me, and the boys in high school being jerks.

Unfortunately, my boyfriend at the time was also young. He was very good-looking (definite Ten material, looks-wise, I would find out after giving him my virginity that he was more like a One Point Five otherwise). He'd also invested three months in his score, and to say he was disappointed and insensitive would have been an understatement. He was pissed, he said some not very nice things while still in my bed, he left and I never heard from him again.

Needless to say, after that, I wasn't fired up to jump in the sack again, and it wasn't until Destry that I gave it another go.

Destry was, at first, very patient, and this was one of the reasons I stayed with him even though, most other times, he was a jerk. He was older than my first boyfriend and seemed to enjoy coaxing a response from me. Considering my first experience was shit, it took him even longer to get me into his bed (four-and-a-half months). Once there, he again was patient, seemingly understanding, and seemingly enjoyed being my teacher which was another reason why I stayed with him. I was hesitant to the point of shy, but that didn't mean I didn't learn from Destry or enjoy what we did. I did. I just didn't learn fast enough.

Therefore, he lost patience with being my teacher when my responses didn't satisfy him or I wasn't up for trying new things that made me uncomfortable.

He broke up with me before he broke through.

After that, I never thought about it much. It wasn't that sex freaked me out, it was just that I didn't have anyone in my life, so I didn't need to think about it.

It was now I knew why my responses to Destry weren't satisfactory.

Because Destry was not only not a good teacher, he was shit in bed.

And I knew this because Mitch was not shit in bed. Mitch was gentle and intuitive. Mitch didn't put effort into sex, he just naturally guided the flow, and where he guided it was freaking sensational.

Which meant he didn't even have to try to teach me. I didn't have to think. I didn't have to try. With Mitch guiding me it came effortlessly, and I knew this because I came effortlessly.

Twice.

*Twice!*

All this meant what we just shared was *amazing*. It was *beautiful*. And it was *perfect*.

It was so amazing, beautiful and perfect, for the first time in my life, I got stuck in the real world, stuck in Mitch World. I liked it there a whole lot, so I closed my eyes and grinned.

Then my eyes flew open and my grin faded.

My first boyfriend, I made him wait three months. Destry, four and a half.

Mitch...

I counted it down.

Oh God!

We'd only had our first bona fide, official date the night before.

And I'd given it up the next day!

Ohmigod!

Despair surged through me, washing out my after-great-sex-with-Mitch glow. I heard the toilet flush as I rolled, reached and tagged my nightie off the floor. I was sitting up and struggling with pulling it on when I felt the bed move because Mitch was climbing in it.

Oh God.

I had my back to him and was pulling my nightie down to my waist when his arm hooked around that waist and I was going backward.

I collided with the hard wall of his chest, his mouth went to my ear and he fell to the side, taking me with him while saying, "Waste of time, sweetheart. I got the day off, Penny's takin' the kids to school. We have until we pick them up to have fun, and we're gonna take that time to have fun. And, as cute as that nightie is, it no longer factors." We'd hit the mattress and pillows, and his other arm curved around me, his teeth nipped my shoulder gently before his face went back into my neck and he finished, "Though, I'll let you have oatmeal to keep up your stamina, but if you have to eat it wearin' somethin', you wear my shirt."

Belly whoosh.

"Mitch—"

"Also, you gotta know, we're eatin' it in bed."

Belly whoosh part two!

Shit.

"Mitch!"

He slid away, rolled me to my back and then slid right back in, smiling down at me.

God, he was beautiful.

"What?" he asked.

"I'm not easy," I declared, his smile faded a little and he blinked.

Then he repeated, "What?"

"I'm not easy," I also repeated. "I know it seems that way since we had our first date last night and we, uh... *did it* just now, but I'm not easy. I've had two lovers. The first, we dated for three months before, um... you know... And with Destry, since the other guy was kind of, um... a jerk, we dated for four and a half. I don't know what happened with us, but you need to know, I'm not easy."

Mitch was up on a forearm and his other arm was across me, hand resting on the bed, and he didn't move, nor did he take his eyes from me even after I stopped talking.

So I kept talking, and to show I was sincere, I lifted a hand, placed it on his chest and got up on the other elbow before I whispered, "I need you to know that."

He said nothing and still didn't move.

"It's important you know that," I kept going.

Not a move, not a noise. His eyes were on me, and he looked like he was thinking. About what, I had no clue since he was doing it without speaking, but whatever it was, it was important.

But what I was saying was important too, so my hand slid up to his neck and my fingers curled around and, still whispering, I semirepeated, "It's important."

Finally, he spoke, and when he did it was to say, "Sweetheart, shut up."

I blinked.

Then I asked, "What?"

"Shut up."

"Shut up?"

"Yeah."

I felt my brows draw together. "I'm telling you something important to me and you're telling me to shut up?"

"Yeah."

I opened my mouth, but nothing came out because Mitch finally moved. And how he moved was both his arms locked around me, he rolled to his back, me going with him then sat up so I was again forced to straddle him. His arms unlocked only for one to clamp low on my hips and the other one to glide up so his fingers were wrapped around the back of my neck with three of them up in my hair, and he tilted my face down to his.

Then he spoke.

"Okay, I gotta get this right so it penetrates without you twisting it like somehow you managed to twist it in your head that I'd think for one fuckin' second you're easy, so here we go."

Uh-oh.

Now I knew what he was thinking that looked so important.

Before I could commit to my burgeoning freak-out, Mitch kept talking.

"Not counting the time I watched you with that moron but still wanted you, we're talkin' two years, Mara, two... *fuckin'*... years it took me to get you naked on your back in my bed. Sweetheart, I think you can rest assured that's pretty much the definition of 'not easy.' "

I stared at him thinking this was true.

Kind of.

"But, we—"

He shook his head and his arm squeezed as did his fingers, so I stopped talking.

"You ran away from me on our first date. You stood me up our second. You gave me attitude the first time your ass was in my truck. You gave me my marching orders in the breezeway before I even got close to getting in there. Billie interrupted me the first time I got to second base. I slept in my bed with you and a six-year-old twice before I even got you out on a date. And I had to promise my sister she could decorate your apartment when you got your insurance check to get her to babysit so I could actually finally fuckin' take you out on that date," he recounted, then finished with, "Honey, trust me, that is *not* easy."

I blinked.

Then I asked, "You promised Penny she could decorate my apartment?"

"Yeah, and don't fight her. She'll listen to you and she's good, but mostly she's determined. Do yourself *and* me a favor and just let her do it."

"But, Mitch, her stuff costs—"

He pulled my face even closer and grinned before he said, "Baby, the markup is outrageous. Wholesale, her stuff costs the same as normal furniture."

Wow.

That meant I could afford Design Fusion stuff in my apartment.

That was cool!

"Mara," Mitch called into my thoughts, which were right then centered on how I wanted the sofa I saw in Penny's shop window in my living room. I focused on him to see he was no longer grinning but looked very serious.

Therefore, I braced.

This was good because the second I did, in a low voice heavy with meaning and his fingers at my neck tensing to drive his point home, he stated firmly, "You are *not* Melbamae Hanover. You are *not* a skank. You are *not* easy. You are so far from trailer trash it isn't funny. You are not what those kids and parents and your mother's fuck buddies took you to be. You're Mara, you're sweet, you're beautiful, and I will not forget until the day I die how beautiful it felt to slide inside you, with you wrapped around me, see your eyes get wet and know straight in my gut that you felt how beautiful it was too."

My eyes got wet right then listening to his words. My arms slid around his shoulders as those words seeped into me, *deep* into me, straight and true in a way even I, who had a special talent for doing it, could not twist them even if I tried.

But I wasn't going to try.

"Mitch," I whispered, then said no more. I couldn't say anything since my throat was closing, but also because I didn't know what to say.

He wasn't done, and I knew this when he pulled me close, dropped back and rolled so he was on top of me, his hips between my legs.

His face was close when he whispered, "Your hair was softer than I expected it to be, more beautiful when it's down than I expected it to be. You're sweeter than I expected you to be, funnier, more loyal. And I expected all that to be phenomenal so, I gotta tell you, baby, it pleases me no fuckin' end to learn the reality is off the charts. Better than that, when you get pissed, I gotta fight against goin' hard. When you smile, I gotta fight against goin' hard. And when you look deep into my eyes and see whatever the fuck you see, and I know how much you like it because it's written all over your face, I gotta fight against goin' hard. But even with the promise of that, finally havin' you is another reality that's off the charts. My guess?" he asked, then didn't wait for me to answer. "Your mother hated you because she knew you were better than her, and every day you were a reminder that you would be exactly what you are. So she tried to undermine it. Bring you down by bein' a serious, fuckin' bitch and, honest to God, I've seen a lot, heard even more, but she's in contention for the worst fuckin' mom in history. And still, you beat her because you are all that is you. And, sweetheart, there is a lot that is you, and it isn't only me who sees that all of it is good. It's just now only me who gets *all* of it and, after waitin' years for you, to say that, too, pleases me no fuckin' end is one serious fuckin' understatement."

"You have to stop talking," I whispered back, my heart swelling so big it felt like it would explode out of my chest. A chest that was so warm it was burning, hot and fierce.

"I'm not gonna stop talkin' until I know you get what I'm sayin' to you and don't sweep it aside, determined to believe what that bitch wanted you to believe."

"You have to stop talking," I repeated in a whisper.

"Mara, I'm not—"

My hand went from his shoulder to press my fingers against his lips.

Then I told him quietly, "I'm not sweeping it aside." I slid my fingers from his lips across his cheek and back into his hair as I lifted up and replaced my fingers with my mouth and whispered, "I get what you're saying to me." I brushed my lips against his and kept whispering when I said, "Now, you have to make me oatmeal. Because my estimate is we have eight hours for you to convince me I'm the Mara of your world before everything crashes back in on us, I get scared and/or freak out and/or panic and/or another calamity happens I'm certain I won't survive. Until I survive it with, obviously, your help and all you said to me is less easy to believe."

I stopped talking (finally) and bearing my soul (finally) and held my breath as Mitch's fathomless eyes stared deep into mine.

Then he asked, "Eight hours?"

"Until we pick up the kids," I answered.

His neck twisted, his eyes going to his alarm clock, then they came back to me, and when they did I liked the teasing light in them because it was mixed with something *way* sexy.

"That's gonna take a lot of work," he whispered.

God, I hoped so.

I smiled at him, lifted up again and brushed my lips against his before I said softly, "That's why we need oatmeal."

His weight hit me, and my head hit the pillows when he muttered against my mouth, "I'll get it in a minute."

"I need stamina," I muttered back.

His hands glided up my sides, taking my nightie with them, as he kept muttering, "I'll get it for you in a minute, baby."

"But—" He rolled his hips, which were between my legs, and I felt why he needed a minute, which meant, suddenly, *I* needed a minute, so I gave in, "'Kay, we'll get it in a minute."

He smiled against my mouth. I smiled against his.

Then he kissed me.

Then he did a lot of other things to me while I did things to him.

In the end, we had oatmeal for lunch.

# CHAPTER TWENTY-THREE

## Mornin'

*Six weeks later...*

I CAME HARD, so hard my back arched and my hands flew behind me to grip Mitch's thighs as I gasped for breath. I rolled my hips at the same time I ground down on his rock-hard cock.

I was still coming when his thumb left my sweet spot and his hand moved to my hip, his other hand already at my other hip. They slid up and curled around my rib cage, pulling me down to him. His lips captured mine, his tongue drove inside my mouth, his arms wrapped around me and he rolled us then started thrusting, hard and deep. I lifted my knees and hips to give him more, my arms circling his shoulders.

Holding him close, my fingers gliding into his thick, soft hair, I took the thrusts of his tongue in my mouth and his cock between my legs. I took his grunts in my mouth, then I finally took his deep, hard drives between my legs as his ragged groan tore down my throat.

Coming down, his lips slid to my neck, where he nuzzled me as his cock moved gently inside me. The fingers of one of my hands glided through his hair as the other one drifted across the warm skin of his back.

My soul sighed, but my heart took flight.

His head came up, his sated, sexy eyes caught mine, and he muttered, "Mornin'."

I stared at him a second, pressed my head in the pillow, my thighs to his sides, my arms tightened around him, and I burst out laughing.

This was because he'd woken me with his hands then his mouth and, until he'd said that word, neither of us had spoken any others.

When I quit laughing, tipped my chin down and opened my eyes to look at him, he'd stopped moving inside me, was planted deep but his hand was up. The tips of his fingers were moving along my temple and hairline, and he was smiling at me.

"Morning," I whispered and felt the humor slide from my features as a memory came to me.

Mitch saw it, I knew it because his smile died, his face softened with curiosity and his fabulous lips whispered, "What?"

"Remember that night when Billie got sick?" I asked quietly.

His fingers drifted down my hairline to curl around my neck, and his thumb came out to stroke my jaw when he answered, "Yeah."

"Remember the next morning when you came into the kitchen and wrapped your arms around me?" I asked, and his thumb stalled as his eyes grew intense.

"Yeah," he whispered.

"You said, 'mornin'' then, against my neck, with your arms around me, and I thought then that I wanted you to say that to me like that every morning for forever."

His fingers tensed on my neck, his face got closer, his eyes got more intense, and his voice was gruff when he murmured, "Mara."

I grinned at him then informed him, "This one was *way* better."

His body started shaking. His hand left my neck so both arms could wrap around me, and he gave me an open-mouthed kiss (while laughing, by the way, which made it *fabulous*). He rolled us, unfortunately disengaging our bodies, but fortunately taking me with him while kissing me and settling on his back with me on top.

When he ended the kiss, my head came up, and I looked down at my man, who had his arms around me, laughter still in his eyes, and again my soul sighed.

He started talking.

"Right, baby, this mornin' the play is, I get the bathroom first, then I get Bud up and in the shower while you shower, and I make coffee and breakfast. You get outta the shower, get Billie up, we have breakfast, you get Billie in the shower and do your thing and help her do her thing while I shower then we go. You with me?"

"Yeah," I replied.

"Ready?" he asked.

"Yeah," I said on a grin, used to this, liking this; we did it every morning.

"Break," he whispered, lifted his head, kissed me quickly then rolled me off him and rolled the other way while flicking up the covers.

I watched as he walked into my bathroom.

My soul sighed again, and it was a good one.

Mitch closed the door, and I rolled to my back, pulling the covers up to my chest.

It was June, and summer had hit the Rockies with

surprising vigor. Usually, you could expect anything through May and into June, even blizzards, but it had been warm and sunny, afternoon thundershowers nearly every day for weeks taking the heat off and leaving the nights cool and crisp.

The six weeks since Mitch hauled me into the real world were the six best weeks of my life, bar none. Not a single day I'd lived in Mara World even came close.

*      *      *

First, I sorted out birth control. Mitch said it was a priority, and I agreed.

I wanted nothing between Mitch and me, so, without delay, I made that so and went on the pill.

*      *      *

Second, Mom and Aunt Lulamae had totally disappeared from Colorado. A call to Lynette and her subsequent recon mission told me they were back home. This was likely because they'd run out of funds to use to make my life hell and didn't have their usual cadre of drunks and assholes whose wallets they could steal money from after they'd passed out.

Incidentally, I had shared everything with Lynette in a marathon phone call while my ass was planted in a lounge chair by the pool. It was hard to concentrate on all the important stuff I was telling her because Mitch showed halfway through our conversation, sweaty from a workout at the gym, and he looked hot sweaty.

It became harder to concentrate when my sunglassed eyes got a look at his face as he was walking toward me, and I knew he seriously liked my bikini.

It was even harder to concentrate (for obvious reasons) when, right in the middle of me listening to Lynette, he kissed me, hard but closed-mouthed.

And it continued to be hard to concentrate when Billy and Billie noticed him, and he spent the next ten minutes standing at the pool's edge picking them up and throwing them in the water. They'd get out, and he'd do it again and again.

And lastly, it was hard to concentrate seeing as his hotness increased beyond measure because he was sweaty, smiling and laughing a lot while making Billy smile and laugh a lot and Billie smile and squeal a lot. I wasn't the only one to notice, and I had to tear my sunglassed gaze away from my man and my kids when my possessive-woman radar pinged, and I'd need to glare down bikini-clad women who were drooling and giving him come-hither looks.

But I managed it.

Lynette was beside herself with glee, informing me (repeatedly) "she told me so" as to the fact I was *so* a Ten Point Five.

"You might even be an Eleven!" she'd shrieked.

I couldn't say I believed her (definitely not about the Eleven part). But that didn't mean Mitch tearing my cocoon wide open and helping me fly didn't mean I wasn't (mostly) convinced I was at least a firm Eight.

But it wasn't Lynette who convinced me of that, it was Mitch.

She was planning a trip out to meet Mitch, Billy and Billie in August, and her parents were considering coming with her. I hadn't seen her in three years, since her last trip out, and I hadn't seen her folks in thirteen.

I couldn't wait.

\*     \*     \*

Third, Bill was broke, incarcerated and had obviously played his trump card first. He was awaiting trial with a public defender preparing his defense, something Mitch told me would not go well. Firstly because he was guilty, secondly because he already had two strikes and thirdly because he was stupidly refusing to plea bargain.

I never heard from him, and the kids never heard from him. But I had visited him once, and only once, and I did this with Mitch standing at my back (Mitch's decree), so the visit didn't go well. Still, it probably wouldn't have gone well even if Mitch wasn't there. It lasted long enough for me to pick up my phone and Bill to pick up his, while his angry eyes stayed glued through the glass to Mitch, then they dropped to me, and he said into his phone, "Fuck you, Mara. Fuck *you*." Then he hung up the phone, got up and walked to the guard.

I walked out trembling and trying not to cry while Mitch held me close with an arm around my shoulders. When I got out, I was still trembling and trying not to shout, when it hit me that I was looking after his kids, kids I intended to raise until they were old enough to build their own lives. My apartment had been ransacked because of him. He'd set Mom and Aunt Lulamae on me, and he had absolutely nothing to be pissed about. But I had a lot to be pissed about.

I shared all I was pissed about with Mitch in his SUV. I did this in detail and at length, and I included family history that went way, *way* back, something I never shared with *anyone*, but I was on a roll. I only stopped when we got to his apartment, he handed me a glass of wine, kissed me hard to shut me up, lifted his head, and I focused on him (finally) to see his eyes were dancing.

Then he muttered, "Gotta go to Bray and Brent's to get the kids. You gonna tear my place apart in the two minutes it'll take me to do that, or are you gonna light a fuckin' candle, take a sip of wine and get your shit together?"

I glared at him.

Then I mumbled, "Door number two."

"Right," he mumbled back, kissed me again, this time not hard but a lot longer. Then he went to go get the kids.

In the two minutes he was away, I did what I promised him I would do, but I also took that time to freak out that during my rant I'd shared family history with Mitch. Ugly, revealing family history, and he might take that two minutes to realize I was a Two Point Five.

He didn't. He came back with Billie over his shoulder in a fireman's hold, and she was squealing with delight. Billy was following, grinning up at them. And Mitch declared he was going to teach Billy how to man a grill.

Then he'd made hamburgers while Billie and I sorted the fixin's. Billie and I fried French fries and made salad (well, I did, she watched, sitting on the counter and babbling) while Mitch was out on his balcony showing Billy how to grill.

I cancelled my freak-out, sipped my wine, ate dinner with my family and got the kids to bed. I forced Mitch to watch a Cubs game on TV with me (Cubs win!) before I gave him his reward for being a really nice guy, and I did this when we were in his bed.

*     *     *

When the police freed my apartment for cleanup, I was dreading the job not only because it was going to be a big one, but also I didn't want to get elbow deep in the proof that all that I'd worked so hard to build had been destroyed.

Mitch, being Mitch, dealt with this too.

When I had a day off, he sorted his mother getting the kids from school, then he sorted it so LaTanya, Tess, Penny and the women of two other buddies he had on the force, Jet and Roxie, came over.

I was kind of in awe of Jet and Roxie, seeing as their stories had hit the paper then they'd had books written about their love affairs with their current husbands. But they were really cool and a little crazy. And with the five of us working, it didn't take very long at all, regardless of the fact that, upon getting into it, it was worse than I thought, and there was very little that could be salvaged.

But those five being the five they were actually made it kind of fun. Especially considering Penny had brought along brochures and catalogues and spent a liberal amount of time explaining her "vision," which was a vision I liked a whole lot. Therefore, Penny ordered needed furniture and a variety of other trimmings the next day. She, Sue Ellen and I went shopping twice (once with LaTanya) to sort out the rest (dishes, sheets, etc.), and Mitch (once with Derek) watched the kids while we were out so Billie wouldn't be let in on what had happened. Then Mitch took Billy to do what I decreed was the "man stuff," in other words, they bought my new TV, DVD player, PlayStation and stereo while Billie and I stayed home, which meant she got her nails polished and I got to watch *Finding Nemo*.

We had stored the purchases at my place but stayed at Mitch's until Penny's order fully arrived a week and a half ago. Mr. Pierson scheduled the delivery of the new mattresses the same day. While I was at work, Penny (with Sue Ellen's help) personally "styled" my apartment, arranging furniture, lamps, pictures on the walls. They'd even put the sheets on the beds, the dishes in the cupboards and Billie's teddy bear on her made-up bed.

In the end, it looked *awesome*.

That night after school, the kids and I moved back in.

Billie had totally bought the story that we were with Mitch because my apartment was getting redecorated. Billy knew better but, as usual, to protect his sister, he kept her in the dark.

*       *       *

When we moved back to my place, so did Mitch (kind of). Without asking (but I was not going to argue), he put a toothbrush in my (new) toothbrush holder, shave cream, razors and deodorant in my medicine cabinet and a variety of sports jackets, shirts and jeans in my closet, shoving my stuff aside to put underwear, tees, pajamas and socks in my drawers.

After he did this, I rearranged my drawers so he had two of his own. I did this while fighting back tears. Not tears caused by Mitch being invasive, but tears caused by Mitch making a statement I liked and that was, he was in my life, my kids' lives and he intended to stay there even if there was now a breezeway separating us.

Mitch walked into the bedroom with me mid-rearrange and mid-sniffle.

And this was when Mitch finally tore away the last hints of my cocoon at the same time he managed the heretofore impossible task of convincing me I was at least an Eight.

He unwittingly started on this mission when he heard the sniffle, walked to me, straightened me away from a drawer, wrapped his arms around me and pulled me close.

Then he dipped his head and locked his eyes with my brimming with wet ones.

He studied the wet then he spoke quietly.

"Kids need stability. The stability necessity pushed us to is them having two homes that are across a breezeway. So our play is, the stability Bud and Billie are gonna keep havin' is home is here *and* my place. Circumstances mean you're in my bed, they're in theirs in the second bedroom, and I'll deal with decent beds for them soon as I have a chance. Most of the time, though, I'm in your bed so they're in theirs here. I moved some of my shit in here. I want you to double up on what you and the kids need and move some of your shit to my place. Wherever they are and *you* are, home will just be home, not runnin' back and forth to get shampoo and clean T-shirts."

His arms gave me a squeeze, his face dipped closer and his voice dipped lower.

"My thinkin' is, they should ride this right along with us, baby; they're used to an us that's together, and I don't think we should shake that up now seein' as there's a physical reason to be apart. They're comfortable both places, and we'll go all out to keep them that way. Bud is clued into what's goin' on with you and me, and Billie doesn't care as long as the people she loves are happy. It's all good." His eyes held mine, his arms tightened and he asked gently, "You with me?"

"Yeah," I whispered.

"Baby," his arms gave me another squeeze, "this is a big decision to make for those kids. You sayin' 'yeah' means you're expecting to stay in my life so I'll be stayin' in theirs. You can suggest another play, and, this soon with what we got, I swear, I'll be cool with that. I'm tellin' you what I think but askin' you if you're with me, and I'm not expecting a quick 'yeah.' "

"Mitch, honey," I gave him a squeeze back, "the answer is ... *yeah*."

"Sweetheart—"

I pressed closer, he stopped talking, I slid my hand to curl around the side of his neck and I whispered, "Kids need stability, sure, but it's not the *where* that needs to be stable it's the *who*. I know that. I lived in the same trailer all my life and it wasn't a healthy place to be. They lived in the same place with Bill all their lives and that wasn't a healthy place to be either. I don't think they care where they sleep as long as you and I are there, and since you and I will be there then the answer to the play you're suggesting is *yeah*."

He held my eyes then slowly closed his, drew in a deep breath, let it out and opened them again. It was then I realized my answer was both important and the one Mitch wanted to hear. The former, I knew, and the latter meant everything to me.

And, incidentally, that was the first time I felt my soul sigh and it felt freaking *great*.

As I was experiencing just how great that felt, Mitch went on, "Right, then, you're cool with that, we'll talk about the rest."

Oh boy.

I was pretty happy right then, happier than I'd been my whole life. I wasn't sure about "the rest."

Then Mitch gave me the rest.

"I talked to the office and they got two three-bedroom units opening up. One in August, one in September. My lease is up in November. They told me yours is up next January. They also told me if we move into a unit in this complex and give them plenty of advance notice, they'll waive the penalty for jumping one of our leases."

*We* move?

*We move?*

I was nowhere near coping with that when Mitch kept talking.

"I'm not thinking that's our play."

I didn't know if that was a relief or a disappointment.

I didn't get the time to decide; Mitch wasn't done.

"It's a buyer's market," he announced. I sucked in breath at these words, and he kept speaking, "I've been considering finding a place. The time has come for me to quit pissin' away my money on rent, and I've had enough for a down payment for a while. The kids already need to move to a different school, it'd be good if they made a move, *any* move, those moves are permanent ones. I'm thinkin' about buyin' a place and I'll want your input 'cause, come January, all stays this good, you, Bud and Billie will be movin' in it with me. We find someplace, we get them in a school close to it."

My chest was moving rapidly and this was because I was near to hyperventilating.

Mitch continued, "Not big on Bud and Billie sharin' a room for another six months, but they're used to it and they're both still kids. One way or another, on the horizon they'll have their own space."

I was hearing him but I was stuck on what he said earlier.

"You want us to move in with you?"

"Yeah."

"You want us to move in with you." I repeated, but not in question form this time.

His brows drew together and he repeated too, "Yeah."

"But...uh...Mitch," I started. "We've been together just over a month."

"I look like a man who doesn't know what he wants?" Mitch asked, and I blinked.

No, he not only didn't look like that kind of man, he

didn't act like that kind of man, and this was because he wasn't that kind of man.

"No," I whispered.

"Okay, then do I look like a man who wouldn't recognize he's got what he wants when he finds it?"

Ohmigod!

My chest started burning and I forced out another, "No."

Mitch held my eyes and drew in a short breath.

Then he said, "I'm not talkin' about tomorrow. I'm talkin' about January. I was already thinkin', come November, it was time for me to make a move. That wasn't about you, but now you and those kids are in my life, it's become about you so you'll need to be in on this. Shit goes down between us that's not good, which, baby," he gave me another squeeze, "is not gonna happen, then you all still have your place. But if it doesn't, six months from now or before, if we're ready, you either jump your lease or give it up, and we keep on keepin' on but in a house we own where we got privacy and those kids do too."

I stared at him.

Mitch allowed this for two seconds then prompted, "You with me?"

"You think I'm a Ten Point Five," I blurted on a whisper.

His brows drew together again and he asked, "What?"

"Or, at the very least, an Eight," I blathered on.

"Uh, baby . . . *what*?"

I stared at him some more.

I felt his arms around me while we were standing in my bedroom. A bedroom his sister helped me decorate. A bedroom where his kickass sports jackets and shirts were in my closet, his boxers and socks in my drawers and our conversation was about moving in together even though we'd semi-kinda-already moved in together.

So I let it all hang out.

"You're a Ten Point Five," I informed him.

"Baby...*what*?" he asked, slightly confused, slightly impatient, slightly annoyed because, I figured, he knew what I was saying.

"Mara's World has zones, Ones to Threes, Fours to Sixes and Sevens to Tens," I told him quietly, his face registered less confusion and more annoyance, but I powered on. "You're a Ten Point Five."

"Mara—"

"Mom convinced me I was a Two Point Five."

Mitch fell silent, but he did this while his face darkened ominously.

I studied his face before I felt tears stinging my nose again and I whispered, "I'm not a Two Point Five, am I?"

"No," he stated, firmly and immediately.

My eyes went unfocused as my mouth breathed, "I'm not a Two Point Five."

I felt his hand glide up my neck into my hair, and I refocused to see his face super close.

"First, honey, people are people, and every single one of them is different. You wanna classify them, okay, but in the real world people do what they do, each one making their own decisions that define their lives. Some are good, some are bad, some are a combination of both, but every single one is different and they're subject to change. So, second, the decisions you've made in your life define you, and if you can't look inside and see who you've created, then you need to open your eyes, baby, and look around at the people who care about you and see through them who you've created. If I need to make my point by talking about this bullshit classification you've come up with then, no, you are absolutely not a Two Point Five. You are nowhere near a Two Point Five, and to say it pisses me off even *more* that your bitch of a mom and those assholes in that town you grew up in twisted your head to make you think your whole life you are is putting it mildly."

He was right. Lynette said it. Mr. Pierson acted it. Roberta did too. LaTanya, Derek, Bradon, Brent...even Billy and Billie loved me, trusted me, liked being with me and weren't afraid to show it.

And neither was Mitch. In fact, from the minute he walked into my house to look at my faucet, he gave no indication whatsoever he thought I was a Two Point Five, just that he not only didn't mind being there, but he wanted to come back for pizza.

Oh God! I was *such* a dork!

Therefore, I replied, "I'm a dork."

Mitch shook his head while looking at the ceiling, his arms going way tight. Then he looked at me and stated irritably, "Jesus, Mara, you are not a Two Point Five and you are also *not* a fuckin' dork. Somethin' else, it does *not* make me happy to hear you talk about yourself that way. And, last, you gotta look out for two kids and they gotta learn to have confidence in themselves to make the right decisions in order to define their lives the right way. And the person who needs to teach them that is *you*. You can't do that, baby, if you don't see who you are and how beautiful that woman is."

"You're annoyed with me," I pointed out the obvious.

"Uh...yeah," he confirmed the obvious. "But I've also had more than my fair share of experience with people and with women..."

Hmm. He could say that again, especially the latter.

Mitch kept talking.

"And I'm clued into the fact that no matter how hard I can make you come, no really good orgasm is gonna erase your perceptions of yourself and replace them with how I see you. I know what I got on my hands. I also know that most women who look like you have their heads up their asses in a different, far more annoying way. So the bright side is, what happened to you, even though you're as beautiful as you are, you'll never think your shit doesn't stink. And I gotta say, sweetheart, I get your sweet, I get your attitude, I get your mouth and I get all that without conceit and you thinkin' you can lead me around by my dick, so this is not a bad thing *at all*."

"Well, it's good you can look on the bright side," I muttered, my eyes sliding to his shoulder and then they flew back to his face when he burst out laughing, his arms closing around me so tight the breath went out of me.

Then he quit laughing, his arms loosened (slightly) and his face got in mine. "Been seein' a lot of the bright side for a little over a month now," he whispered, and I got a belly whoosh.

"Mitch—" I whispered back.

He cut me off saying, "We got kids to feed. So, gettin' back to the matter at hand, me buyin' a house, you and the kids in on that, are you with me?"

I stared into his gentle, soulful eyes, eyes I'd woken up to every morning for over a month, eyes I wanted to wake up to every day for the rest of my life, and I knew I was with him. I was with him then, I'd been with him since the first time I told him I was weeks ago, and if I could manage it, I would be with him until I took my last breath on that earth.

"Baby, are you with me?" he prompted.

"Yeah," I agreed softly.

"Good," he whispered, I smiled, and then he asked, "Ready?"

"Yeah," I repeated.

"Break," he murmured, touched his mouth to mine then let me go and walked into the bathroom.

I turned and finished rearranging my drawers, but I didn't do it crying.

I did it smiling.

\*     \*     \*

Although things had settled down and…well, just plain *settled* in huge and significant ways, there was one cloud over our literal and figurative sunny days, and this was Billy.

Mitch was right. Billie didn't care where she was or what she was doing just as long as the people she loved around her were happy. She didn't need to blossom, her Teflon-coated delight in the world was invincible.

But something was up with Billy.

He stuck to one, the other or both of us like glue. He was often asking Mitch to toss a ball with him (and Mitch did). He asked Mitch or me to help him with his home-work every night. He asked me to teach him how to do the laundry. He did the dishes. He helped make dinner. He kept his room tidy. He dragged out the vacuum and vacuumed the entire house. He inventoried the cupboards and wrote stuff on the grocery list. If you were at the store, he'd dash through the aisles to grab stuff so you wouldn't have to push the cart down each one. If Billie started to get tired and irritable, he fawned over her. If I was tired, he offered to read her to sleep.

If he was with me, and Mitch wasn't around, he asked about Mitch all the time. Where was he? What was he doing? When was he coming home? Didn't I think Mitch's hamburgers were the best? Wasn't it cool how Mitch could do multiplication questions in his head without writing anything down?

After our first date, four times in one day he asked when he and Billie could go back to Penny's house to spend the night. Then, two weeks later, when Mitch and I had another night on our own with Sue Ellen looking after the kids, when he got home the next afternoon he asked twice when they were again going to Sue Ellen's.

Then, three days ago, Mitch and I were having an inconsequential tiff in his SUV, about what, I didn't even remember. The kids were with us, and I felt something rolling through the truck that made me feel weird. I turned to look into the backseat, and I saw Billy staring out the side window, his profile hard, his teeth clenched, his hands in fists, his shoulders bunched, but his lip was trembling. He looked terrified and near tears.

It alarmed me, and I immediately quit having terse words with Mitch, gave him a look and jerked my head toward the back. Mitch's eyes went to the rearview mirror then they went to the road, and his jaw got so tight, a muscle jumped there.

Later, in bed, Mitch pulled me on top of him and stated, "You get pissed, I get pissed, we have our words private, not in front of the kids."

"You saw it then," I whispered.

"Yeah, I saw it."

I told him something I guessed he already knew, considering he was a cop and very insightful, "He's not right, Mitch, something is wrong with him."

"You live bad, sweetheart, and you taste good, you'd do anything to keep it. You know that."

I really did.

I nodded.

Mitch continued, saying softly, "He's terrified."

I bit my lip. "Yeah," I agreed, then asked, "Should we talk to him about it?"

Mitch studied me, but he did this thinking.

Then he said, "Don't know. He thinks we cottoned on, might cause more anxiety. We play it cool and give him day-to-day good and steady, he might relax."

"I'm going to talk to Bobbie at work about it," I told him, and it was his turn to nod.

"I mentioned it to Slim," he informed me, surprising me. "Slim caught on when we played catch, though it was hard to miss."

Slim was Brock, Mitch's partner's nickname.

Brock was good. Brock had two boys. Brock probably had a wealth of experience.

"And what does he say?"

"He says if he thinks we cottoned on, it might cause more anxiety. If we play it cool and give him steady, he might relax," Mitch said on a grin.

"Great," I muttered, and Mitch's arm gave me a squeeze.

"Our play, we give him two weeks. He doesn't settle in, we talk again and decide who talks to him. You with me?"

I smiled and whispered, "Yeah. But if you 'ready, break' me, I'm going to protest the play."

His head tilted on the pillow and his lips twitched. "Why's that?"

I pressed my body into his and told him, "Because I'm comfy."

"Sweetheart, you can't sleep on me," he pointed out.

"Who's talking about sleeping?" I asked, and his eyes flashed.

Then his hands moved. Then my hands moved.

Then our mouths and tongues moved. Then other parts of us did the moving.

By the time we broke, I was way more comfy; in fact, I was nearly catatonic. But, even so, I got up and cleaned up, put my nightie and panties back on, and Mitch tugged on his pajama bottoms. We got naked, obviously, but we didn't sleep naked. It wouldn't do for Billie to come in and puke, and us to be in our birthday suits.

This concerned me. I'd been scheduled for my foster care classes, and CPS had not been around again, although Mitch had informed them of the situation with my apartment and told me I could probably expect another visit when we returned to it.

But I didn't know how they'd feel about me sleeping with my boyfriend every night with the kids in the same house. Even if that boyfriend was nice guy, good guy Detective Mitchell James Lawson. I didn't need them to have any reason to shake up the good and steady we were giving the kids.

So, curled into Mitch, I sleepily shared this concern.

To which Mitch, not sleepy at all, replied, "Anyone tries to take those kids from you, Mara, they deal with me."

I blinked at his shadowed chest then lifted my head to look at his shadowed face.

"Pardon?"

"You got enough to worry about, don't worry about CPS. I don't know where they stand on shit like this, but they hear you got a sleepover boyfriend and try to place those kids somewhere else, I'll create a shitstorm like they've never seen. So don't worry about it."

"How will you do that?"

"Don't worry about it."

"Mitch—"

I stopped talking when he rolled into me so he was on me, totally on me. All his weight and his hands were at either side of my head, fingers in my hair, his shadowy face close to mine. Even though I couldn't see him, I could definitely feel his intensity.

"You didn't learn this from the one you had, but I learned it from mine. Parents do anything to protect their kids. *Anything.* Whatever they have to do. They exhaust themselves. They bleed themselves dry. They run themselves ragged. They do whatever they have to do. My mom and dad are good now, but growin' up we didn't have a lot, and I never felt it. I didn't even fuckin' *realize* it until I was out on my own and looked back at my life. I didn't need for anything, I rarely wanted for anything. They did that for me and worked themselves to the bone to do it. They taught me life lessons and they let me take my share of falls, but the real shit of life, they cushioned me from. Bud and Billie have already taken their share of falls. That's done for them, Mara, and if it has to be me who sees to it, I'll see to it."

I was breathing heavy because *he* was heavy on me, but it was more. A lot more.

"I . . . I don't know what to say," I wheezed. He heard the wheeze and took one hand out of my hair to plant his forearm in bed beside me and take some of his weight off me.

"Nothin' to say," he told me. "I just laid out the way it is."

"Mitch—"

He stopped me talking by touching his mouth to mine then whispering, "Go to sleep, baby."

"I think—"

"Don't think," he growled, his intensity returning. "Hear this. Four years I watched you be cute and I enjoyed watchin' your ass move in your tight skirts. But in five minutes at a fuckin' Stop 'n' Go my world was rocked seein' you with those two kids. Not two hours later, a woman came up to us and told us we had a beautiful family. I didn't get it because we didn't have it then, but I get it now. She was right. But I also learned I have somethin' else on my hands. I gotta protect those kids from any more falls and I gotta protect my woman from takin' any more too, and I'll exhaust myself, bleed myself dry and run myself ragged to see to doin' that."

I stared up at him, silent and completely motionless.

Then I burst into tears.

Mitch rolled with me in his arms, and I cried in them too.

When I quit crying, Mitch's hand came to my face and his thumb swept across my wet cheek while he whispered, "Never believed in this shit, but now I'm thinkin' I fell in love with the promise of you the first time I saw you."

My body bucked as my breath hitched and the tears came back.

"Mitch—"

"And Bud and Billie mean more to me because they were the catalyst that got me in and gave me you. Just lucky they came with."

Another hitch, another buck, another broken, "Mitch—"

"I love you, sweetheart," he whispered.

I shoved my face in his neck and burst into tears again. These lasted longer.

When they faded, silently, he turned me and curled into my body, holding me close, his face in the back of my hair.

And when the tightness in his arm around me relaxed, I whispered, "You're my dream man."

"I know."

I blinked at my shadowed pillow. "Pardon?"

"Mara, baby, I never believed this shit either, but now I know you were made for me. So, seein' as that's true, it goes the other way too."

Oh my God.

"I was...I was...*made for you*?"

"I'm a cop for a reason, honey."

"So you were made to save me," I guessed, not sure I liked that.

"No, I was made to protect you, and you were made in a way that it would always be worth the effort."

Okay, that was good. I was definitely sure I liked *that*.

Too much.

"Oh shit," I whispered, lips trembling, "I think I'm going to cry again."

His body shook, but his arm got tight as his face burrowed deeper into my hair, and I listened to him chuckle.

Which kinda pissed me off.

"Mitch! You don't laugh during a heart to heart."

"You do during one that involves Marabelle Jolene Hanover."

I found myself glaring at my dark pillow. Then I realized I was exhausted from an orgasm, two crying jags and a heart to heart with Detective Mitch Lawson.

So I muttered, "Whatever," which got me another chuckle.

And...*whatever*.

I snuggled backward into Mitch, and his arm got tighter. His breath went steady and it got looser.

But I didn't fall asleep. I stared at the obscure folds of my pillow and played his words in my mind.

Then I played them again.

And repeat.

And each time, my soul sighed.

Then I went to sleep.

*          *          *

That was three days ago.

Now the kids were out of school, it was Saturday, Mitch and I were both off, and we were taking the kids to Elitch Gardens. Billy and Billie were beside themselves with excitement seeing as they'd never been to an amusement park in their lives.

I was too, seeing as I hadn't either.

Mitch was too (in his hot guy, macho cop way), seeing as he got to give that to all of us.

Mitch came out of the bathroom, walked to his pajama bottoms on the floor, tagged them and pulled them up, all while I watched. Then I started to get up, pushing up to a hand, but instead of Mitch heading out to go wake up Billy, he came to the bed and sat on the side.

He lifted his hand, pushed my hair over my shoulder, his fingers curled around my neck and he drew me near him as he leaned into me.

Then, his eyes holding mine, he whispered, "Best good morning I ever had was the first time you wrapped that mouth of yours around my cock."

I sucked in breath as my nipples started tingling, but he wasn't done.

"Fuck, baby, knew I loved that mouth of yours, but after that, loved it more. Just like everything about you, the reality is better than expected. Off the fuckin' charts."

"Mitch," I whispered back, my hand lifting to curl tight around his wrist.

I watched his eyes smile as he finished, "Gonna have to work hard to top that."

I knew my eyes were smiling too because my mouth was doing it when I promised, "I'll see what I can do."

Then he changed the subject. "Just to let you know, you're right about the Spring Deluxe. Your mattress is the shit, baby."

"Told you," I reminded him.

He grinned.

Then he whispered, "But I'd sleep on a bed of nails, I was sleeping next to you."

I blinked. Then tears filled my eyes.

Mitch watched this, his thumb sweeping my cheek, then he leaned in, touched his lips to mine, got up and walked out to wake up Billy.

I watched, then, when the door closed behind his beautiful back and great ass, I flopped back on the bed and stared at the ceiling, deep breathing.

Then I heard Billie screech, *"Elitch Gardens!"*

Well, I guessed that meant I didn't have to wake her up.

I heard her little feet beating on the floor, I heard a bang on the bedroom door and then I heard Mitch's deep voice saying on a lie, since I was not in the shower, I was in the bed and naked, "She's in the shower, gorgeous."

At this information, Billie switched targets immediately.

"Can we have donuts?"

"We'll swing by on the way to the park," Mitch answered.

*"Yippee!"* Billie squealed.

That was when I smiled at the ceiling.

Let me just say, I liked the real world.

The real world was *awesome*.

And I was going to stay there a while.

Hopefully forever.

*     *     *

"T-minus two freaking seconds before we're out the door, baby," Mitch called impatiently from the front door. Billy and Billie were standing with him, Billie bouncing on her toes and even Billy was fidgeting with excitement.

I was rushing around.

"I need to get sunblock," I told him.

"You can buy that stuff at the park," Mitch called to me because I was running down the hall.

"Bud, did you get a hat?" I yelled from the bathroom, ignoring Mitch and grabbing the kids' sunblock from their medicine cabinet.

"Yeah, Auntie Mara," Billy yelled back.

"Billie, honey, did you—?"

*"I have a hat!"* Billie screamed. "Let's go, let's go, *let's go*!"

I shoved the sunblock in my big purse while rushing down the hall.

I got to the door.

Then I took them all in and muttered, "Right, let's go."

*"Yippee!"* Billie screeched.

Mitch opened the door, and she raced out of it, Billy raced after her and I tipped my eyes up to his smiling ones.

"Yippee," I said softly, smiling huge.

Mitch's eyes dropped to my mouth, then his arm hooked me at the waist, he pulled me to him, his mouth came down on mine and he gave me a short, hot, wet kiss.

Finally he let my mouth go but not my waist, guided me out the door and held me close as we stood outside together while he checked to make sure it was locked.

And there I was doing what I never thought in a million years two months ago I would be doing ever in my life. I was standing in the breezeway pressed close to Ten Point Five Detective Mitch Lawson waiting for him to check to see if my door was locked.

I was thirty-one years old and my man took me on my first family visit to an amusement park.

I was wrong.

I didn't like the real world.

I loved it.

Because it felt like a dream.

# CHAPTER TWENTY-FOUR

## Our Kids

I JUMPED DOWN from Mitch's SUV, slammed the door and watched with a small, tired smile as a zombie Billy jumped down from the backseat.

The park was a hit. The kids had a freaking blast and I had one too.

But, best of all, all day Mitch's eyes were lit with a light that was new to me, but it was a light that I liked. It was not his normal sense of humor, which was usually easy to trip for Billy, Billie and me. And it was not because it was a sunny day, we had the day off and we were at an amusement park.

It was something else.

I loved him, this I knew. He was my dream man. He thought we were made for each other, and I loved that he thought that. As the days and weeks went by and we clicked naturally into each other's lives, the kids clicking with us, I was even coming to believe he was right.

But that day he gave us all something more.

Yes, with all that he'd given us, he'd given us something more.

We had a blast. The kids were tuckered out because they'd been on the go all day filled with excitement, wonder, adrenalin and a lot of crappy food. Billy, Billie and I, we loved it. Every second of it.

But that light that shone in Mitch's eyes told me he loved it more. Not because he liked roller coasters and crappy food.

No, because he liked to see us happy, he liked to make us that way and he didn't mind us knowing it.

From the beginning, he'd demonstrated generosity, selflessness and protectiveness, but there was something beautiful about sensing his contentment grow as the hours passed and he got more out of giving something to us than we got out of having it.

I knew before that Mitch would make a great dad.

But I knew right then that he'd build a beautiful family.

I knew this because he was already doing it.

And knowing that, I loved him more.

Billy slammed his door, taking my mind off my happy thoughts. Then, surprisingly, he drifted to me, his body careening into mine. He slid an arm around my waist, leaning heavily into me, and I took his weight, thinking that was beautiful too.

I slid an arm around his shoulders and looked through the SUV windows to see Mitch bent into the backseat. He'd unbuckled a dead-to-the-world Billie and was pulling her out of her booster seat. I watched as he secured her, her little legs around his waist, her head on his shoulder, her arms dangling heavily, Mitch's arm under her booty. He slammed the door, and his other arm wrapped around her back to hold her close to his torso.

Incidentally, that was beautiful too.

I moved Billy toward the sidewalk as Billie and Mitch moved that way and Mitch bleeped the locks.

"The stuff," I called quietly to Mitch, referring to the

variety of souvenirs and spoils of victories Mitch and Billy
had won playing games at the park, which were in the back
of Mitch's truck.

"Put her down," Mitch replied just as quietly. "Then I'll
come back and get it."

I nodded and Billy and I met Mitch and Billie on the
sidewalk. I watched Mitch take me and Billy in, again his
face registering contentment, that light in his eyes I could
see in the evening dark, his lips tipping up. Mine tipped up
back at him and my soul sighed.

Maybe that was what he was feeling. His soul sighing.

And, I had to admit, mine sighed again just thinking we
gave him that, especially with all he was giving us.

We walked up the steps side by side, and I gave Billy's
shoulders a squeeze.

"Did you have a good day, Bud?" I asked softly.

"Best ever," he muttered.

*Best ever.*

He was right. It was the best ever. For all of us. Maybe
even Mitch.

I looked back at Mitch to see his still-curved lips brushing the top of Billie's hair.

Yes. It was the best ever. Even for Mitch.

Yeah, oh yeah, I loved Detective Mitchell James Lawson. I loved the family we were building. And I loved that
he loved it too.

I looked down to my feet, concentrating on executing
the last few steps. My body was pleasantly exhausted, and I
didn't want to do a face plant on the stairs to end a great day.
Billy's body remained heavy against mine as we climbed,
and I kept my gaze at my feet as we made it to the breezeway, my mind winding down, my thoughts happy.

Therefore when I heard Mitch whisper a clipped, "No,"

which was shortly followed by a soft, intensely angry, "*Hell* no," it so surprised me in the mood I sensed we were all in I lifted my head and twisted my neck to look at him.

His face was carved in stone.

What on earth?

He stopped and I automatically stopped with him, Billy stopping with me. Then I looked where Mitch was looking, and I felt my body turn to stone just like Mitch's face. And I knew when Billy saw them because his body did the same against mine.

Mom and Aunt Lulamae were standing outside my door. Their eyes were on us. Their hair was amped out to maximum volume. Their makeup was a tribute to raccoons. Their cleavage was bared. Their arms were crossed on their chests, pushing them up and baring more.

And their faces were smirking.

I knew why.

Standing with them was Jez.

*Jez!*

Billie's mother.

My heart had stopped when my body turned to stone, but taking in Jez, it started stuttering madly. No rhythm, it tripped unsteadily as my pleasure after the best day ever oozed out and fear settled in.

I hadn't seen her in six years. She took off within months of Billie being born. She was bad news then, and she looked like bad news now.

Worse.

She looked strung out, too thin and her clothing matched the skank level of my mom and aunt's. It was clear she didn't pay much mind to her toilette except to cake on more makeup than even Mom and Aunt Lulamae wore. I didn't even think this was possible, but there it was in the lit breezeway. Proof.

Bill.

Bill had activated Mom and Aunt Lulamae to find her and bring her here to fuck with me.

And fucking with me meant fucking with Mitch, Billy and Billie.

Oh God.

I felt Billy's body start shaking against me. Not little shakes, *quakes*. It rocked his frame and shook me out of my terrified surprise.

He knew Jez, of course; it had been a long time ago, but he remembered her. Even though he was very young, he avoided her even then with instincts honed from living in that world. And considering he was nine going on ninety, he knew why she was there now.

And also, he'd never, not once, laid eyes on Melbamae and Lulamae Hanover. But he knew who they were, and he knew why they were there now.

I shuffled Billy and myself closer to Mitch and whispered urgently, "That's Jez. Billie's birth mother. Not Bud's, *Billie's*."

"Right," Mitch clipped, his tone even angrier, his mood rolling dangerously through the breezeway, his body still rock solid.

"Late night for two little kids," Mom called, still smirking, and Mitch moved.

Not to my door. Not to his door.

To Derek and LaTanya's door.

I was surprised by this, but I followed, pulling a still-shaking Billy with me and keeping my eyes on the Trailer Trash Trio.

Mitch spoke not a word, but lifted a fist and pounded on the door. I didn't know what he was doing and I didn't ask. He was clearly going to lead and I was definitely going to follow.

Aunt Lulamae made a move toward us, arms coming uncrossed, torso bent slightly, eyes on Billy. When she did, I shifted closer to Mitch, my arm tightening around Billy, I positioned so I was between her and my cousin, Billy between Mitch and me.

"Hello, Billy, I'm your grand-momma," she cooed, and Billy shoved his body closer to me in a way it seemed he wanted me to absorb it.

I held him tighter.

"Far's I can see, she grew up kinda pretty." I heard Jez mutter, and my gaze cut to her to see her eyes on Billie, mild curiosity in them and not much else.

I found this surprising too, not to mention a little alarming. Furthermore, I found her assessment of Billie as "kinda pretty" insane. Even asleep and mostly hidden from view by Mitch, anyone could see Billie was gorgeous.

She was Billie's mother and hadn't seen her daughter in six years.

Mild curiosity and an inane comment?

What was that all about?

I didn't ask, not that I would have, but I didn't have the time. This was because Mitch spoke.

"Not one step closer," he growled in a way that made even Aunt Lulamae stop and look at him.

"I—" she started.

"Not another word either," Mitch went on, his voice low and vibrating, so furious it felt physical. "We'll deal with you in a minute."

Aunt Lulamae's torso straightened with a snap and her eyes narrowed.

"Those're my grandbabies," she hissed.

Before Mitch could respond, the door opened and Derek was there.

Then we weren't.

This was because Mitch rounded me and Billy, herding us, forcing us with his movements through the door, around Derek. And once we were inside, he slammed the door behind us.

I saw immediately that there was a mini–cocktail extravaganza in progress. There were martini glasses in hands and decimated platters of food. On the coffee table were two silver cocktail shakers, a bucket of ice and bottles of booze and mixers. I had seen this all many times before. Once she settled in, LaTanya wasn't one to waste time sashaying into the kitchen to mix cocktails. She set up where it was comfortable and stayed there.

Bray and Brent were on the couch.

So was LaTanya's cousin Elvira.

Elvira.

I wasn't certain what Mitch's plan was. What I was certain of was that in any plan, Elvira was a wildcard.

I knew Elvira, seeing as she was a staple at LaTanya's cocktail extravaganzas. Elvira had great style, a sister and brother who worked her last nerves and she didn't mind telling everyone about it so she did (at length). She also had an interesting job herding the cats that were a bunch of men whose business was a little hazy but my sense was they were private investigators (or the like) and, once you got to know her, she could be hilarious.

But if LaTanya Delight deserved a capital "D," her cousin Elvira's Attitude deserved a capital "A." Pretty much anything could come out of Elvira's mouth, and she was scary nosy. She didn't have a filter. She said what she thought, she said it straight, and she had a lot of opinions.

I liked her, but I had to admit, she always scared me a little. During another mini–cocktail extravaganza of

LaTanya's, that one *sans* Elvira, LaTanya shared that she felt the same way about her cousin.

Now Elvira, Bray, Brent, LaTanya and Derek were all staring at us with various expressions of surprise on their faces, and I didn't blame them. We'd barged right in and there we were.

"Is everything—?" Derek started, but just then we heard a pounding knock on the door.

All eyes (including mine) went to it, but Mitch started talking.

"The Trailer Trash Twins are in the breezeway," he explained quietly, striding straight to Derek and LaTanya's second bedroom, which they used as a half-office/half-man cave. When I saw him on the move, I trailed, taking Billy with me. So did Derek. So did LaTanya. And Bray, Brent and Elvira all got up and followed us.

Mitch kept talking as he moved, carrying the still sleeping (thankfully) Billie.

"They brought reinforcements. Billie's mom," he stated as he walked into the room. Billy and I followed, so did Derek and LaTanya. Bray, Brent and Elvira huddled at the door.

I heard several sucked-in breaths, and I was guessing they came from LaTanya, Brent and Bray. For his part, Derek's face got tight.

Mitch bent and I watched by the light coming through the opened door as he carefully deposited Billie on Derek's man cave couch, arranged her comfortably and then reached out an arm to grab a throw from the back of it. He tossed it over her, twitching it so it covered her.

When she was down, we all heard another pound come at the door.

Everyone's heads twisted in that direction except

Mitch's. He moved swiftly, his movements controlled, fluid but economical, like he was holding himself in check. He also didn't hesitate, and Bray, Brent and Elvira had to jump out of his way as his long legs took him out the door.

My arm still around a trembling Billy, I hurried after him, guiding Billy with me and giving him a firm squeeze.

"It's going to be okay, honey," I whispered as we moved, and his head tipped back woodenly, his terrified eyes hit mine and my heart clenched. "Promise, Bud." I kept whispering. "Everything's going to be okay." I gave him another squeeze. "Promise."

We made it to the living room, but Billy didn't even nod, and the terror didn't leave his face. I stopped us and looked to the door when I heard Mitch speak.

He had it open, but his body was blocking it, and I saw Aunt Lulamae was standing on the other side.

"Five minutes," he bit out.

"Fuck five minutes," Aunt Lulamae returned. "We been waitin' an hour."

"Then you'll wait another five minutes or you'll find your ass in the back of a cruiser and you'll be facing harassment charges," Mitch fired back, and I just got the chance to see her head jerk and her eyes narrow before he shut the door in her face.

He turned, walked directly to Billy and crouched in front of him.

One of his hands came up, curled around the side of Billy's neck and he pulled him roughly yet tenderly away from my body and to within an inch of his face.

"I got this, Bud," he said in a low, deeper than normal voice, his eyes locked with Billy's.

Billy didn't respond.

Mitch gave him a gentle shake with his hand at his neck.

"I promise you, I got this. You believe me?"

Billy didn't move, nor did he speak.

"Bud?" Mitch prompted on another gentle shake, and finally Billy nodded.

My heart skipped when Mitch pulled Billy to him and rested his forehead against my cousin's for half a second before he let him go and straightened.

Then he looked at LaTanya.

"Door closed to Billie. Shit goes down, I don't want her hearin' it. You gotta move her back to your room, I need you to do that. Yeah?" he asked, and LaTanya nodded then rushed to the man cave.

Mitch looked to Derek.

"I don't want those women around the kids, and I don't want them knowin' I live across the breezeway. That's why we're here. In a minute, Mara and me are goin' out there, we're takin' them into Mara's apartment and we're dealin' with 'em. You hear shit you don't like, like those bitches gettin' loud and threatening, you call Slim. He knows what's goin' on and he'll know what to do. You don't like what you hear, you call. No hesitation. Right?"

Derek nodded.

Mitch looked at Bray and Brent.

"Keep Bud company. He's freaked."

Bray and Brent nodded, and Brent detached from Bray and moved toward Billy.

Mitch's eyes came to me, and they moved over my face. I knew he didn't like what he saw, but he powered through it and said quietly, "Let's go, sweetheart."

It was my turn to nod.

"I'm goin' with," Elvira announced right as I started to move toward Mitch, and both Mitch and my eyes went to her.

Oh boy. Here we go. Elvira was butting into Mitch's plans.

"No," he denied.

"Uh ... *yeah*, hot guy, macho man, decorated, squeaky-clean po-lice detective," she shot back, and there it was. The Attitude. "I spend my time around hot guy, macho men, almost *all* my time, but even if I didn't, it wouldn't take a psychologist to read you are one seriously pissed off hot guy, macho man, po-lice detective. And I'll repeat, you're decorated and squeaky clean. You need to keep your shit and stay that way, and, my read, you got about a half a millimeter left on your hold on your control."

I figured her read was right.

She kept talking.

"You both also need a witness to whatever goes down over there. I'm not either of ya'll's neighbor or best friend," she lifted a hand, finger pointed down, her well-formed nail, I distractedly noticed, painted an awesome midnight violet color. She circled her finger between Mitch and me then she dropped her hand. "So that witness is gonna be me."

Well, one thing I now knew: LaTanya had shared with her cousin about Mitch, me, Billy and Billie.

The other thing I knew was that Elvira didn't just have Attitude, she was wise.

Mitch came to the same conclusion because it was then he nodded and muttered, "Let's go."

Mitch spoke, and Elvira and I moved, following him out the door and into the breezeway.

"Where's my grandbabies?" Aunt Lulamae asked before Derek and LaTanya's door even closed.

"We'll talk at Mara's place," Mitch replied, moving directly to my door, key at the ready.

"I wanna see my grandbabies!" Aunt Lulamae was getting loud.

Mitch stopped, pivoted on his boot, stalked to Aunt Lulamae, and even Aunt Lulamae, who had never been the brightest bulb in the box, was smart enough to see she'd pushed him too far. She flinched and cowered when he got in her space and leaned into her face.

I held my breath.

"We've been at an amusement park all day. Your grand-daughter is exhausted and sleeping. Your grandson does not know you, but with all your bullshit, he's scared shit-less of you. Right now, he's in that apartment," Mitch's arm went up and he pointed at Derek and LaTanya's door, "shiv-erin', he's so fuckin' scared. Now, you wanna convince anyone you give one shit about those kids, you'll keep your fuckin' voice down and you'll wait the thirty fuckin' sec-onds it takes to get into Mara's place so we can talk. Your other choice is to have it out out here, which means in about ten minutes your ass will be in a fuckin' cruiser. You got a second to nod you agree or let loose. Your choice. That second starts now."

She immediately nodded.

I let out my breath.

Mitch stalked to my door, opened it but didn't walk through. He stopped in the doorway and his eyes sliced to me as his hand reached out.

I walked directly to him, Elvira at my back, and when I got to him, my hand came up. His fingers closed around it and we walked in, Elvira following, the Trailer Trash Trio bringing up the rear.

Mitch's hand gave mine a squeeze, and he ordered gen-tly, "Hit some lights, honey, then right back at my side."

I looked up at him, nodded and wandered the room quickly, turning on the lamps on either side of the couch. Mitch positioned himself six feet into the apartment, hands to his hips. Elvira went to sit on a stool at my bar, back to the counter, body facing the showdown. It was then I noticed that her clingy, wraparound dress was pretty spectacular, and if I survived this without having a mental collapse, I needed to ask where she got it. Mom, Aunt Lulamae and Jez were all standing just inside my door, looking around my apartment with astonished expressions on their faces.

I understood this. Seriously, Penny did a great job. My apartment was awesome.

Jez's expression melted to indifference as her eyes drifted to Mitch. It was all the same to her, and, vaguely, I wondered what she was even doing there. She didn't seem a participant so much as an observer.

Mom's and Aunt Lulamae's gazes came to me as I made it to Mitch's side, and their expressions shifted to scorn.

"Who's she?" Jez asked, her head tipping to Elvira, but Mom spoke over her, and what Mom said took precedence, at least according to Mitch.

"Knew it, always knew it." She threw her hand out, indicating my apartment. "Slutty little tease always had your nose in the air, thinkin' you're better than everybody, thinkin' you're somethin' you are *not*."

Obviously, she said this to me.

And, very obviously, considering the already suffocating air in the room went thick as paste, Mitch, seriously pissed, got more pissed.

*A lot* more.

"For this discussion, you direct any communication to me. You do not talk to Mara," he clipped out this order, and Mom looked at him.

"And why would I do that?" she snapped.

"Because you're standin' there thinkin' you got the upper hand when you don't. And if you don't smarten up fast and play this right, I'm gonna unleash a world of hurt on you, your sister and your sister's son. And part of playing this right is not disrespecting my woman to her face or mine," Mitch replied, one of his hands staying at his hip, the other one sliding around my waist and pulling me close.

"That a threat?" Aunt Lulamae asked.

"Nope," Mitch answered.

"High and mighty cop, you think you got the system on your side," Mom stated, her lip curled. "But we got ourselves a lawyer, Lulamae, Jez and me. And he says the system likes to place kids with blood relatives, the closer the better. Not some second cousin, but a momma or a grandma. And Jez here, now she's all set to move into a trailer close to me and Lulamae so those kids got *all sorts* of family close by to take care 'a them and see they got what they need."

After she said this, her face changed, and I knew that change. I knew it because I'd seen it often in my life. And I knew it heralded her doing something that was not just her normal ugly, but her vastly more hideously nasty.

And I was right because she went on to say, "And, Jez here bein' Billie's mom and all, we're happy just to have the girl. You can have the boy."

My heart clenched so hard I feared it would rupture, and Mitch's arm spasmed tight around my waist.

They had a lawyer.

And they were happy to break up the kids.

They had *a lawyer* and they were *happy to break up the kids*.

"I see you're not just not all that smart. You're plain stupid," Mitch returned quietly, his eyes locked on Mom.

"Got a lawyer who don't think the same way," Aunt Lulamae fired back.

"No," Mitch replied, his gaze slicing to Lulamae. "You

got a lawyer who's happy to take your money on a case he knows he has no hope of winning."

Mom shook her head. "See *you're* not too smart. Don't you see? We're offerin' you a deal. We take the girl. You want him, you can have the boy. Everyone's happy."

*The girl.*

*The boy.*

Why did her calling Billy and Billie that hurt so much?

I started having trouble breathing.

"You're not taking Billie," Mitch declared.

"Jez is her momma," Aunt Lulamae stated. "And my boy gets to pick who he wants to raise his kids, and he picks Jez, Melba and me."

"Bill doesn't get to decide shit," Mitch shot back.

That was when Aunt Lulamae's expression went from ugly to nasty.

She had something, I could tell by the look in her eyes. She was saving her ace and was about to play it.

I braced and she played it.

"He didn't when he was facin' all them charges. He does now, seein' as he's talkin' with the DA to make a deal to provide testimony in return for immunity," Aunt Lulamae returned fire, I stopped breathing altogether and felt Mitch's body get tight.

Mom smiled in a way that made me clutch Mitch's shirt at the back.

"He's got good stuff. So good, they're willin' to give into all his demands. And one a' those demands is he gets to say where his kids're gonna be. Now, *you're* smart, *you* deal. We're willin' to give you the boy, but we take the girl," she said.

I knew Mitch was preparing to speak, but he didn't get the chance.

This was because, in a flash that lasted a nanosecond, it all came to me.

Jez didn't care about Billie. Whether she was moving into a trailer close to them or not, she was there because she was getting something out of it. What, I had no clue. But whatever she was getting, it wasn't her daughter that she wanted.

And I had no idea how Mom and Aunt Lulamae were paying for an attorney. They had no money and neither did Bill. Whatever fee they agreed to was probably taken out in trade, and I knew whatever they were giving some sleaze-bag lawyer to get him to take their case would lose its luster and lose it quickly.

And there was no judge in the land who would take two children from a woman who gave them a stable home, food, clothes and good people in their lives and plant them in a trailer two states away to live with women of proven bad character.

And Bill knew this.

But he didn't care.

He just wanted to fuck with me. Probably with Mitch too. But definitely with me.

And he was using his children to do it.

But that flash I had wasn't just understanding what was happening right then in my apartment. It was understanding what Mitch had been telling me, what people who knew and cared about me had been saying and showing all my life.

I was not a Two Point Five. Behaving the way they behaved, speaking the way they spoke, making the threats they were making would not occur to me. I would never, not in a million years, do any of that.

Because that was not me.

And it never had been.

So when the reply came, it was me who gave it.

"Get out of my house," I said quietly, and all eyes turned to me.

"What?" Mom asked.

"Get out of my house. Now," I repeated, with an added directive.

Mom's eyes narrowed. "Marabelle Jolene, have you been listenin'?"

"I have," I told her. "And I'm not listening anymore. I'm not breathing your air anymore. I'm done. You laid it out, now I will. This is the last conversation we'll have not through attorneys. Unless I *have* to see you, I will never see you again. Do your worst. Right now, we're done."

"You don't get this," Aunt Lulamae butted in, "but my Bill's got good shit on someone. They're kissin' his ass to get it. You don't take this deal, Marabelle, you could lose *both* those kids."

"And you don't get this," I retorted. "I do not *care*. If you think for one second I'm allowing you ... or *her*," I jerked my head at Jez, "anywhere near my kids, think again. It's not going to happen."

"You're wrong," Aunt Lulamae returned.

"We'll see," I replied instantly. "Now, get out."

Mom leaned a bit toward me and said with soft menace, "You need to think about this deal, girl."

My voice was clear and strong when I shot back, "No, I don't. And you know I don't. And you know *why* I don't. But I'll point it out. You both have records. I don't. Neither of you have ever had steady employment in your lives. I have. Neither of you have seen those children until ten minutes ago. You haven't sent birthday cards or Christmas presents. They've lived their whole lives in Denver; they've never been out of state and definitely not to Iowa. Their father is a drunk, drug addict dealer with two strikes. That woman," I jerked my head at Jez, "left her infant daughter and didn't see her again until whatever reason brought her here. And if you think we won't figure out what you bribed her with to get her here, seeing as my man's a freaking *decorated* police detective, you're even *more* stupid than I thought, and I had a lifetime of evidence suggesting you're flat-out dumb."

My eyes pinpointed Mom and Aunt Lulamae in turn, and my voice dipped quieter.

"And I have a really good memory. A *really* good one. You push this, you take this to court, I'll be calling up all sorts of stuff on both of you," my eyes shifted and narrowed on Jez, "*all* of you. There is no way in hell you're taking either of my kids from me. And yes," I looked to Aunt Lulamae, "I said they're *my* kids because they are *my kids*. And seeing as they're mine, I love them and they love me, I will exhaust myself, I will run myself ragged, I will bleed myself dry, and I will do this to make sure they're safe, protected and stay *with me*. You're here simply because Bill is stupid, he's petty, he blames me for his mistakes and he wants to fuck with me. He knows he has no prayer in the world. He's smart enough to know that. He's using you, but *you're* not smart enough to know that. Now, you can take this further and endure me wiping the floor with the lot of you in a courtroom or you can crawl away and stay away. Because you are not welcome here, you are not welcome in my home, my life or my kids' lives and you never, *ever* will be."

When I finished, I held their eyes and I was calm, in control and breathing steadily. And although Mitch's arm around my waist giving me a strong squeeze felt great, I didn't need it.

I didn't need it.

Because I wasn't a Two Point Five. I wasn't an Eight. I wasn't a Ten.

Mitch was right. My classification system was bullshit.

Bottom line, what I was is a decent person.

And I always had been.

"Fuck me," Jez muttered, studying, me, "didn't buy into this shit."

"Shush," Aunt Lulamae hissed to Jez, "we got this."

My body jolted in surprise when I heard a burst of laughter. I looked toward my kitchen to see Elvira had an arm thrown out to hold onto the edge of the counter, and her entire, petite, rounded body was visibly shaking with hilarity. Her head was thrown back, and her other hand was beating, palm flat, at her well-endowed chest.

She continued to laugh for a while then she sobered, still chuckling and wiping under her eye as she noted the obvious, "Hilarious. You got this. Ohmigod, that's funny."

"You think they got more sway than the district attorney?" Mom asked, sweeping an arm out to Mitch and me.

Elvira totally sobered and focused sharp eyes on my mother.

And when she spoke, her voice was quiet.

"Yeah. Let me explain somethin', not to save you trouble, but to save them the pain in the ass all you all got written all over you," on the "them" she jerked her head toward Mitch and me. "Detective Mitch Lawson is well-known in these parts for bein' a good cop, and when I say well-known, I mean he's made the papers. He decides he and his girlfriend are gonna take in a coupla kids that don't have it too good and give them good, and the DA decides to give them to the likes of you just so he can get some info from a dirtbag, the papers get hold of that, he's not gonna look too

good. The DA likes lookin' good. And, in case you haven't
clued in, I think Mara and Mitch here are willin' to throw
just about anything at you and won't mind wadin' in with
the media to keep those kids safe."

She turned her head to Mitch and me.

Then she said, "Sorry, gotta lay this shit out."

Before either of us could respond, she turned her head
back to the Trailer Trash Trio, and when she spoke again,
her voice was even quieter.

"Now, I know all about Bill Winchell. And I know who
he's got dirt on. And I know that person gets whiff that he's
talkin', the number of breaths Bill Winchell's got left to
breathe on this earth just lowered significantly. Police protective custody or not, he's dead man walkin'. If he's too stupid to know that, he's your boy, you go talk to him and you
educate him. Right now he's facin' a not very happy future
that includes a limited wardrobe selection. But at least he's
got a future. He talks, he won't have that. You get me?"

I looked from Elvira to the Trailer Trash Trio to see
Jez still looked indifferent. Mom was studying Elvira
closely. But, surprising me, Aunt Lulamae looked pale and
uncertain.

Elvira spoke again, and when I looked back at her, I saw
her eyes were on Mitch.

"I know the boys are fired up to take that guy down, but
that stupid cracker's makin' this play just to fuck with you;
he needs a wakeup call." Her eyes honed in on Mitch and
she finished, "And you know it."

"We'll tell him to add the witness protection program to
the deal," Mom said, and everyone looked at her.

"You can tell him that, but Winchell won't get it," Elvira
replied. "He might have info, but not enough to buy him
that kinda deal."

"You can't know that," Mom returned.

"Woman, you don't know me, but what I do, I know everything that's goin' down in Denver. I know that. I know a lot more. And I know your boy don't shut up, next time you see him, he'll be in a coffin," Elvira retorted.

Everyone was silent. Aunt Lulamae shifted. Mom glared at Elvira. Jez looked like if she had a watch (which she didn't), she'd check it.

Mitch finally spoke.

"I think you've been invited to leave."

Mom transferred her glare to Mitch. Jez took a half step toward the door.

Aunt Lulamae looked at Mitch too and asked on a jerk of her head toward Elvira, "What she said, is it true?"

"Yes," Mitch said flatly.

Aunt Lulamae looked at Mom. Mom continued to glare at Mitch.

And that was when I knew Mom was the mastermind (as it were) of all of this. This was not about Bill, Billy and Billie.

This was about her and me.

This was about her taking me down a notch.

Mitch was right again.

All my life I had been in a competition with my mother. She wanted to take me down, hold me down, best me. She made nothing of her life, and she wanted to make sure I didn't make anything of mine, because if I did, it would make her feel worse about the fact she'd thrown hers away.

And there I stood next to a good man, a handsome man, a solid, respectable man in a fabulously decorated apartment. And across the breezeway were two children who adored me and a cadre of friends who had my back.

And she couldn't stand it.

"Move on," I whispered, and I felt Mitch's arm tighten and saw Mom's eyes come to me.

"What?" she snapped.

"You don't exist for me, not anymore. Not after this, not even before this, but definitely not after. We're done. I've moved on. Now you need to move on too," I advised.

"Marabelle Hanover, don't you stand there and tell your momma what to do," she kept snapping.

"Okay then, don't move on. Your choice. But take your bitterness and regret for throwing away your life somewhere else. Don't you see?" I lifted a hand and kept it up. "You can't beat me."

I dropped my hand and held her eyes.

Mom glared into mine and then hers went to Mitch.

"You're a fool," she stated, and my body got tight and so did Mitch's. "See she's conned you with her fancy-ass clothes and her fancy-ass apartment into thinkin' that she's somethin' she isn't. You go home, ask anyone. They'll tell you exactly who Marabelle Jolene Hanover is."

"No," Mitch replied, "they'll tell me who Melbamae Hanover is, and, one look at you, I know the woman you are and I know Mara is not that woman."

"You go to Iowa, they'll tell you," Mom pushed.

"I already responded to that, not gonna do it again," Mitch muttered, then said straight out, "Now, I'll remind you, you've been invited to leave."

Mom gave up on Mitch and looked back at me.

"You can't run away from who you are."

"Wrong, Mom," I replied. "I was never who you thought I was, so I never had anything to run away from. But I did run away, not from who you thought I was but from *you*. I did it thirteen years ago. It's done. I'm gone. I've been gone a long time. Move on."

"He'll see who you are, he'll figure it out and he'll leave you," she told me.

"Jeez!" I cried. "I didn't pick Mitch up at a truck stop, Mom, take him home and get him drunk on cheap whiskey. I'm not you, and Mitch knew that before I did. You have no idea what you're talking about. Now, for God's sake, it's late, I'm tired, my kids are tired and Bud's freaked. I need to get them home, Bud calmed down and my family to sleep. So can you please *just leave*?"

"I—" Mom started but Mitch cut her off.

"Mara asked you to leave."

Mom's narrowed eyes went to Mitch.

"I'm gonna say what I—" she began again, but Mitch cut her off again.

"Mara asked you to leave."

Mom leaned in and her voice rose when she started, "I *will say* what—"

Mitch let me go and moved.

Luckily, Elvira moved before him. Hopping off the barstool onto her strappy, high-heeled sandals, she moved to the Trailer Trash Trio and she did it bossy.

"Right, conversation over. You chose wrong, now's the time for attorneys," she said, herding the Trailer Trash Trio closer to the door.

"We're not done," Mom snapped.

"You're done," Mitch replied, still advancing but doing it slowly.

"We're not done!" Mom shouted, and Elvira leaned around Jez and opened the door.

Jez exited immediately. She didn't buy into this scene. Whatever they offered her wasn't much, definitely not worth the headaches she had to know I was ready to create. I fancied the minute I lost sight of her she went up in a poof of smoke.

Aunt Lulamae grabbed Mom's arm, but Mom stood firm in the door, nose to nose with Elvira, and Mitch was now at Elvira's back.

Mom opened her mouth to be nasty, but Elvira beat her to it.

"Okay, woman, see you don't get this, but the legal occupant of a residence asks you to leave, you do not get a choice with that. They do it repeatedly, you do not comply with their request, things can get ugly. You've been repeatedly asked to leave by the tenant of this apartment *and* her partner, who happens to be a police detective, and you've been asked in front of a witness. You diggin' in," she shook her head, "not good. Now, you can walk out that door, make a stupid decision and call your lawyer, or you can be led out that door in cuffs. I'm feelin' hot-guy, macho-man, pissed-off vibes at my back, so my guess is you got about five seconds. Think fast."

Mom glared at Elvira.

Aunt Lulamae tugged at her arm.

Mom stood firm and moved her glare to Mitch.

All I could see was Mitch's back, but he stood firm too.

Aunt Lulamae tugged at her arm again.

Mom transferred her glare to me.

Then she sneered.

Then she whispered, "What was I thinkin'? You were never worth the trouble. *Never.*"

I saw Mitch's body get tight out of the corner of my eyes, but I held my mother's glare. I didn't bother myself to reply because I knew she was wrong and, seriously, she wasn't worth any additional effort.

Mom waited.

Elvira and Mitch stood firm.

Aunt Lulamae again tugged Mom's arm.

"Bitch," Mom hissed, turned on her platform stripper shoe and stomped out.

And that was it. The last thing my mother likely would say to me.

Figured.

Aunt Lulamae avoided all eyes and followed.

Elvira shut and locked the door.

I sighed.

Mitch turned on his boot and stalked toward me.

My relief evaporated at the look on his face and the intensity of his gait. I had a second to brace before he was right in my space. Then I was in his arms and he was kissing me, hard, deep and wet. The kiss was a surprise, but it was also a kiss from Mitch, which was to say a really good one, so I melted in his arms and mine circled his shoulders.

Finally, he tore his mouth from mine, my eyes fluttered open and I saw his eyes burning into mine.

"That was...fucking...*phenomenal*," he whispered fiercely.

Oh. Now I understood the intensity and the kiss.

I grinned and pressed closer.

Then I whispered back, "Thanks."

Mitch grinned too, and his arms gave me a squeeze.

"Mm-hmm, that one's good," we heard Elvira mutter, and we looked her way to see she had her phone up and pointed at us. I heard what sounded like a camera phone shutter click then, "Nope," she went on, "that one's better."

"Uh...what are you doing?" I asked, and Elvira looked from her phone to me.

"I get that it's bad timin', hon, but my girls are chompin' at the bit about you. Me and Tess been givin' them the lowdown, but neither of us have pictorial verification that

Mitch got himself a sweet little hottie. Gwen, Cam and Beanpole have been all over Tess and me, and even though Tess said things are intense with you two, they're gettin' impatient. Cam and Beanpole, I can handle. But Gwen is Hawk's woman, Hawk's my boss and Hawk pretty much gives her anything she wants. And when I say that, I mean he buys her twelve-hundred-dollar shoes."

She looked back to her phone and started hitting buttons as I blinked at the idea of a man buying a woman twelve-hundred-dollar shoes at the same time blinking at the fact that there *were* twelve-hundred-dollar shoes. I mean, in some vague recess of my mind, I knew such entities existed, but only in some vague recess of my mind.

As I struggled with this information as well as recovery from the aftermath of a Trailer Trash Trio trauma and Mitch's "I'm proud of you" kiss, Elvira continued.

"So, Gwen recruited Hawk to put the pressure on. He pretty much don't care who Mitch is givin' the business. He *does* care about Gwen, givin' her what she wants and, probably more importantly, gettin' her to shut up about it. And Hawk's kinda scary. Even to me. So I'll just text them this photo. Give them somethin' to go on." She kept hitting buttons and kept talking. "We'll schedule a sit-down so they can give you the third degree over cosmos. I'm thinkin' Club 'cause they got them kickass glasses. Or the Cruise Room. I'll set it up."

I looked from Elvira, who was still punching buttons, to Mitch, who was staring at Elvira like he didn't know whether to laugh or kick her ass out.

Then I looked back to Elvira, who was *still* punching buttons.

"Are you saying that you're texting photos of Mitch and me to women I don't know?"

She looked from her phone to me. "Yep, kind of. Actually, I'm texting them photos of you in Mitch's arms."

Those arms tightened as I asked, "But why?"

"Because they know Mitch," she answered instantly. "They also like Mitch, and they wanna be certain Mitch is with a woman they approve of. Now, you just had a drama, and before that spent the day with Mitch and two kids at Elitch's, and you still look hot. I included this intel with my picture texts. This'll go over good. Not a lotta women look good after a day with two kids in an amusement park. I tell them about the exhaust-yourself, run-yourself-ragged, bleed-yourself-dry speech you laid out about two kids that aren't even yours, that'll go over good too. But you gotta do cosmos in a little black dress to *really* win them over, and that's on you."

"I don't own a little black dress," I told her.

Her attention went back to her phone. "That's okay, we'll go shoppin'."

"Uh...I need to hire an attorney, not shop for a little black dress," I reminded her.

She pressed a button and muttered, "There." Then she looked at me. "Right, so, quick, I mentioned Hawk. He's a scary-ass, motherfucking commando. When I say that, I do not lie. So I'll repeat, he's a scary-ass, motherfucking *commando.* So, when your mind conjures up a vision of a commando, that's Hawk. And Hawk likes kids. But he don't like kids bein' scared and bein' used for bullshit family dramas. I tell him this, which, by the way, I'm totally tellin' him this, even though he don't know those kids, like, at all, he's gonna go psycho badass, motherfucking commando. And the Trailer Trash Twins won't know what hit 'em."

Holy cow.

"Elvira—" Mitch started, his voice low, one of his arms

dropping, his body turning toward Elvira, but she wasn't to be denied.

"Sorry, Mitch. Good as done."

"Do not get Hawk involved in this," Mitch ordered.

"Right, so, quick *for you*," she stated. "Your woman is hot, she's got curves, she's got ass, she's got legs, my guess is you've noticed that. Now, she might drink cosmos with us girls, but she'll come home *drunk*, to *you*, in a *little black dress*. You want that and not her money goin' to attorneys to deal once and for all with those skanky hos, you look the other way, and I let loose Hawk and his band of not-so-merry men. That way, not only do you get your woman home drunk in a little black dress, you get to turn your attention to those two kids, one of 'em who is across the way right now, scared outta his little-kid brain."

I wasn't certain I knew what unleashing a psycho badass, motherfucking commando entailed.

I was certain we needed to see to Billy.

So I turned into Mitch, put my hand on his chest and whispered, "Honey, we really do need to see to Bud."

Mitch scowled at Elvira a second, then his arm around me gave me a squeeze, he looked down at me and murmured, "Right."

I leaned further into him and murmured back, "Right."

"We done here?" Elvira asked, and Mitch and I looked at her.

"We're done," Mitch answered, moving both of us toward her at the door.

"Thanks, Elvira," I said as she opened it.

"No skin off my nose. Ain't me gonna make those hos run for their lives on their stripper shoes. It's Hawk," she muttered, sticking her head out the door but doing it performing a side-to-side scan like she, too, was a commando checking that the coast was clear. Then she looked back at me, "Though, wouldn't mind bein' in on that operation."

I grinned.

Elvira grinned back then forged across the breezeway.

Obviously, the coast was clear.

"Baby," Mitch called softly as he guided us into the breezeway.

I looked up at him to see he was looking down at me.

"The time to talk with Billy is now. He's tired, but I don't want him in bed stewin' on this shit. I want him in bed breathin' easy."

I nodded my agreement.

Mitch wasn't done.

"I'm gonna lead the discussion. You trust me with that?"

Like he had to ask.

"Of course," I answered.

"Good," he muttered, his eyes leaving me and going straight as we neared Derek and LaTanya's door.

"Mitch," I called, slowing, and in doing so, he slowed too.

"Yeah?" he asked, looking back down at me.

My arm around him gave him a squeeze.

"Best day ever, baby," I whispered.

I watched the preoccupation shift from his eyes as they lit with that light I'd been seeing all day.

Then he repeated, not in a question, "Yeah."

And he guided us into Derek and LaTanya's apartment so we could get our kids.

# CHAPTER TWENTY-FIVE

## Men Don't Have Moments

WE GOT THE kids home, leaving Elvira behind to give the scoop to Derek, LaTanya, Bray and Brent. I struggled with Billie's loose limbs and dead-weight body to get her out of her clothes, into her PJs and tucked into bed with her pink teddy, while Mitch got Billy into the bathroom to change and brush his teeth.

Mitch was pouring me a glass of wine while I lit candles when we heard Billy come out of the bathroom.

My eyes went to Mitch to see his on me, then, his eyes not leaving me, he called, "Bud, come into the livin' room for a minute, yeah?"

I finished with the candle as Mitch moved out of the kitchen with my glass and a bottle of beer for himself. Billy appeared in his loose shorts and tee at the mouth to the hall.

Mitch stopped on his way to my new, super-awesome couch. (And yes, I got the one from Penny's window. I asked for it, and she felt it agreed with her "vision," so there it was, in my living room).

"I know you're tired, Bud, but we gotta talk about something before you hit the sack. You cool with that?"

Billy, his head tipped back, his eyes on Mitch, again looking fifty, hesitated a moment before he nodded.

"Couch," Mitch ordered softly.

Billy nodded again, and both he and Mitch moved.

I went to the couch. Mitch arrived first and handed me my glass. Then he tilted his head to the couch and I sat. Mitch took a tug off his beer, put it on the coffee table, then sat next to me, but he left a couple of feet of space between us. Billy came around the couch while I took a sip of my wine and he stopped, appearing uncertain.

Mitch wasn't.

"Sit here, Bud, between Mara and me."

Billy's shoulders shifted strangely then he walked to us and sat in the small space between Mitch and me. Instantly, I turned my body into his, crossed my legs and took his hand.

Billy's head dropped and he looked at our hands. I gave his a squeeze, and his eyes lifted to mine. That was when I gave him a small smile.

He didn't return it. He was worried, my sweet Billy.

Mitch lifted both his legs and deposited his boots on my coffee table but he did this at a slight angle, effectively boxing Billy in.

No.

*Cocooning* him in a physical nest of care and family.

God. Seriously. I loved Mitch Lawson. I loved him anyway but I loved him enough that when he was cocooning Billy with me in a nest of safety, I wasn't going to give him stick for putting his boots on my new coffee table.

Billy's eyes went to Mitch's legs.

He didn't miss it either. Then again, Billy rarely missed anything.

"Right, look at me, Bud," Mitch ordered gently. Billy's

head came up and his neck twisted so he could give Mitch his eyes. Mitch didn't delay. "There's some things you need to know. The most important of those things is that I've fallen in love with Mara."

My lips parted, and I was pretty sure my eyes bugged out.

Well, this wasn't where I expected him to go. I didn't mind it. I just didn't expect it.

At all.

Mitch kept talking.

"She feels the same for me."

I blinked then looked down to see Billy's head had swung toward me. I closed my mouth so I could use it to smile and squeezed his hand again.

Mitch kept going, and Billy looked back at him.

"The man who gets Mara gets you and Billie. I'm that man. What you gotta get is, while fallin' in love with Mara, I fell in love with you and your sister. Straight up, Bud, no lie. The feelings I feel for Mara are hers, the feelings I feel for Billie are hers, and the feelings I feel for you are yours. You all have my love, not collectively, individually. Do you understand me?"

"I..." Billy whispered, then finished softly, "no."

Mitch nodded. "Right. What I mean is, I didn't fall in love with you all as a whole. I fell in love with each of you because of who you are. I don't care about you because you come with Mara. I care about you because you're a good kid. You're smart. You're loyal. And you love and look out for your sister and Mara. I know grown men who do not have a character as fine as yours. Those are the reasons I love you. There are different reasons I love Billie. And there are different reasons I love Mara. Today, what we had together was good. But the feelings I feel for you aren't feelings I have to have in order to have Mara. They're feelings you earned. Now, you with me?"

"I think so," Billy replied quietly, and I gave his hand another squeeze.

Mitch continued.

"Okay, you're with me on that, I'll explain this. You've got my love, so do Billie and Mara. Billie loves all of us. Mara loves all of us and, my guess is, you do too. We have that so that makes us a family."

I felt tears sting my eyes as I watched Billy swallow and wet shimmer in his.

Mitch wasn't done.

"Life goes like I hope, you'll be dancin' with Mara at your wedding, and your sister will be dancing with me at hers."

Oh my God!

My hand spasmed in Billy's, and his curled tight around mine.

Mitch kept talking.

"Between then and now, not every day is going to be like today, where we're happy, doin' fun stuff and laughin'. We're gonna have bad times. But those will be ours and we'll work through them. My job, Mara's job from now until you become a man is to make sure no one outside this family gives you or your sister a bad time. Mara took on that role and let me be a part of that team. We both take that seriously. Those women you saw, Bud, we've dealt with them. That's done. Nothing will harm you. Not again. Not like that. Nothing. Mara will see to it. I'll see to it."

Mitch leaned in close and his voice dropped.

"You been the man of the family a while, Bud, but it's your time to stop worrying. I told you earlier I got this. I had it. So did Mara. It's done. Whatever you got in your head, you let it go. It is not you and Billie against the world anymore. You've got people at your back. You need to let that weight go, buddy. In a family, we all look out for each other. It is not up to you alone to take care of everybody. You need to let that weight go, give some to me, give some to Mara and just be Bud."

Billy studied Mitch for a long moment, then he asked in a small voice, "Is that woman gonna take Billie away?"

"No," Mitch and I both answered instantly, and Billy looked between both of us.

Then he looked at me. "Are you gonna get custody of us, like, permanent?"

"Yes," I again answered instantly.

"Tomorrow, Mara and I'll be talkin' to a lawyer," Mitch put in, this was news to me, good news, and Billy and I looked at him. "We'll be working at making Mara your legal, permanent guardian, and when the time comes, we'll add me."

I pressed my lips together.

Billy wasn't ready to believe.

"Stuff happens, Mitch, bad stuff. And Billie—"

Mitch cut him off, "You don't worry about it. You let Mara and me worry about it."

"But, what if you two break up?"

I held my breath.

Mitch leaned deeper into Billy and whispered, "Look at me."

"I am lookin' at you, Mitch," Billy whispered back.

"No, Bud, really look at me," Mitch ordered on another whisper.

I let out my breath and took in another one.

Billy concentrated hard on Mitch's face.

Mitch spoke.

"All my life, since I could remember, I wanted to be a

cop. That's all I ever wanted to be. Watched the shows on TV, all the movies. I wanted that to be me. So I made that me. I love my job. I'm proud of what I do. And ever since I knew about girls and knew I'd someday have one of my own, I knew the kind I wanted. Just like knowin' I wanted to be a cop, I knew the kind of woman I wanted for me. So I found that woman and she's sittin' on this couch."

My heart skipped, I let out my breath and closed my eyes.

God, that felt good.

No, that felt *great*.

I opened my eyes as Mitch kept going.

"And I grew up in a close family, and I always knew I wanted one of those too. So, I cannot promise you life is gonna run perfect. I cannot tell the future. What I can say is, what we have when you and me are tossin' a ball or mannin' the grill or sittin' at the table doin' your homework, that means something to me. It's important to me. And when something's important, you take care of it. I have times like that with your sister and Mara. Those times mean something to me. They're important, and I'll promise you this right now, I'll do everything in my power to take care of it, all of it, all of you. I can't tell the future, but I can promise you that. Now, do you trust me?"

Billy's hand clenched mine as he whispered, "I trust you, Mitch," and I felt a tear slide down my cheek.

Mitch didn't miss a beat. "Good," he muttered. "So, Mara appreciates it when you run the vacuum, and we'll expect you to do your chores and get good grades, but you gotta stop knockin' yourself out to make life smooth for everybody. From now on, you just be Bud. Let life be what it's gonna be and trust in the fact that we'll face whatever's comin' as a family. Can you do that for Mara and me?"

"Yes," Billy whispered as his hand held mine harder and another tear fell down my cheek.

"Good," Mitch muttered again, then he lifted a hand, curled it around Billy's neck and he pulled him even closer to his face. And when he got him close, his face changed in a way I understood immediately, and I prayed Billy, who didn't miss anything, understood it too.

But he didn't have to.

Because Mitch laid it out.

"I love you, Bud," he whispered to Billy, and two more tears escaped.

"I love you too, Mitch," Billy whispered back, my breath hitched and both males' eyes came to me.

I waved my wineglass at them and murmured, "Don't mind me. Have your moment."

Mitch leaned back, letting Billy go and grinning at me. "Men don't have moments."

"You do," I returned. "I'm witnessing one."

"This isn't a moment, honey, it's a meeting of the minds," Mitch contradicted me.

"It's a moment, Mitch," I contradicted him.

Mitch transferred his grin to Billy and asked, "Are we having a moment?"

Billy stared up at Mitch then he looked at me.

Then he answered, "Nope."

Billy didn't even know what a moment was. He was just agreeing with Mitch because Mitch was a guy and I was a girl who was crying.

I rolled my eyes, gave his hand another squeeze, let it go and swiped at the wet on my face, muttering, "Whatever."

When I quit swiping, I looked back at my boys to see them sharing a smile.

Witnessing that, it took some effort, but only one more

tear escaped rather than me bursting into thousands of them. I succeeded in this endeavor by doing what any girl would do to succeed in this endeavor. I sucked back more wine.

"Right. That's done, bedtime," Mitch decreed, lifting his legs off the coffee table so Billy could get through.

Billy jumped up and rounded the couch while Mitch and I watched him go.

He stopped halfway to the mouth of the hall and turned back to Mitch.

"Thanks for today, Mitch, it was fun."

"We'll do it again, Bud," Mitch replied. "Now hit the sack. Yeah?"

Billy nodded. "Yeah. 'Night, Mitch," he muttered, looked at me and called, "'Night, Auntie Mara."

"Goodnight, honey," I called back.

Billy resumed moving to his room. I looked at Mitch mostly because he'd leaned into me and shoved an arm between me and the couch. He was pulling me into him, and I was concentrating on not spilling any wine as he executed this maneuver.

I succeeded and was settling into my man to relax with him, wine and candles when we heard, "Auntie Mara?"

Mitch and I both twisted our necks to look over the back of the couch. When we did, we saw Billy standing just outside the shadows at the mouth of the hall.

"Yeah, honey?" I called back.

Billy held my eyes.

Then he announced, "Billie looks like you."

I didn't know where he was going with this, but I answered with the truth. "Yes, she does, Bud."

"Do you think I look like Mitch?" Billy asked.

Oh God.

Oh *God*.

"Yes," I answered softly.

"That woman at that restaurant, she said we had a beautiful family," Billy reminded me, and Mitch's arm around me grew tight.

"She did," I told him. "And we didn't get it then, but she was right."

Billy kept hold of my eyes then his shifted to Mitch before they moved to the floor and he asked, "Mitch, you marry Auntie Mara, can Billie and me have your name?"

Oh God!

God, God, *God!*

"You want it, then absolutely," Mitch replied.

I started deep breathing.

Billy's eyes came back to me.

And, even though he whispered it, I heard him when he said, "You should know, I love you too, Auntie Mara."

Then he disappeared in the shadows.

My breath hitched again, and this time I didn't succeed in holding back the thousands of tears. Luckily, I did succeed in not bursting into loud ones, just lots of silent ones.

Mitch divested me of my wineglass, I burrowed into him, and when he'd put my glass by his beer on the coffee table, he pulled me into both of his arms.

It took some time, but I pulled myself together.

Then I whispered into his neck, "I love you Detective Mitchell James Lawson."

Mitch's arms gave me a squeeze. "I know, baby. I love you too."

"That was done well, honey." I shifted to kiss his throat, then tilted my head back to look at him to find he'd tipped his down to look at me. "Thank you."

"Anytime and every time, sweetheart," Mitch replied.

I liked that.

Anytime and every time, now and throughout our lives with our family.

Again, my soul sighed, but my mouth smiled.

"Proud as hell of you, what you did earlier with your mother and aunt," Mitch told me.

My smile got bigger, and I informed him, "Just so you know, your kiss communicated that."

Mitch smiled back at me. "Right."

"Something else you should know," I whispered. "I was able to do that because of you."

"Mara—" he started, but I shook my head and pressed deeper into him.

"No, it was in me to say it, but it was you who opened my eyes to who I am. I've always been a decent person, and even if you weren't standing there, I'd do everything I could to make certain I kept those kids safe. But it felt good standing there with you. It felt good realizing that was who I am and who I always was. And it felt good to move beyond what I believed myself to be. And you guided me there. So..." I grinned and pressed even closer, "thank you."

Mitch dipped his head, and against my lips whispered, "You're welcome, baby."

Against his, my grin became a smile.

Mitch brushed his mouth against my smile, pulled back half an inch and noted, "I'm done with heavy. Time to zone out in front of a game."

Zoning out on the couch with Mitch, wine, candles and baseball.

The perfect end to an (almost) perfect day.

"Right," I whispered. Mitch grinned, then in thirty seconds the TV was on, Mitch's boots were off. He had me tucked between his reclined body and the couch, my wineglass in one hand, my cheek on his chest. His arm was around my back, hand curved around my hip, his beer in his other hand.

I sipped wine and zoned out.

Mitch sipped beer and watched the game.

Yes.

The perfect end to an (almost) perfect day.

Me, Mitch, wine, beer, baseball and, sleeping in the next room, Billy and Billie.

# CHAPTER TWENTY-SIX

## The Rain Always Stops

*Two days later...*

I WAS DRESSED for work because I was going to work after.

Tight, light-beige pencil skirt. Cute, light-peach blouse. High-heeled, tan slingback pumps. My hair pulled back in a twisted bun at the nape of my neck.

Mitch liked the way I dressed for work. He told me he thought it was sexy, though he didn't like me selling mattresses to men dressed that way. But seeing as Mitch and I had four mouths to feed, he understood.

I was sitting at the little desk. Mitch, like last time, was standing behind me.

I was not nervous. I was not worried. I had no idea where the money would come from to pay for the meeting with the lawyer we had yesterday and the work he would do in the coming months. And I had no idea what reaction I was imminently going to get.

I also didn't care.

I'd find the money, and the man who was about to get bad news didn't deserve my nerves or worry.

The buzzer sounded, and I felt Mitch's tension at my back as my head turned toward the door.

Mitch, unlike me, was concerned. But his concern was about me. I told him I was okay, but he didn't believe me.

He would see he had nothing to worry about.

I watched Bill in his orange jumpsuit and white T-shirt move through the door.

He looked thinner, but he had better coloring and a decent haircut. Apparently, they had barbers in jail. And they were probably free, so Bill availed himself since he didn't have to make the taxing decision of whether to use his money on a haircut or filth to inject in his system.

Bill's face screwed up when he saw me, but he came to the chair at the little desk beyond the glass opposite me. He sat, his eyes on me, then they went to Mitch.

I grabbed the phone.

Bill's eyes dropped to me.

He didn't move.

I held the phone to my ear and waited.

He still didn't move.

It was Mitch who lost patience, leaned in and rapped on the glass with his knuckles. Then he jerked two fingers toward the phone.

Bill scowled at him then snatched up the phone.

The instant he had it at his ear, I spoke.

"Don't be nasty, hang up and walk away," I said swiftly. "What I have to say is important, and you need to hear it."

"Not sure anything you have to say is important, Mara, not anymore," Bill replied, his eyes filled with hate, his mouth and nose creased into a sneer.

"It's about Billy and Billie, so if you think that's true that means what I've decided to do is definitely what needs to be done," I returned, then went on, "Though, I knew that anyway."

Bill glared at me then his eyes flicked up to Mitch before coming back to me.

"Say what you gotta say so I can get you outta my face. I'd rather be in lockdown with a bunch of psycho slime-balls than sittin' here with you, so I think you get where I'm comin' from when it comes to you," Bill retorted.

"Oh," I whispered, "I got that when you sent my mom and your mom after me. And if I didn't get it then, I got it when you set them to finding Jez in order to use her to threaten me, Billy and Billie."

Bill's face didn't change. He kept up the glare and the sneer. He felt no remorse, not even knowing how his doing that would affect me and not even thinking that it might also affect his children.

I kept talking.

"When Billy saw Jez, he remembered her and he freaked out, Bill."

Bill just continued glaring at me.

"So bad, he was shaking."

Bill uttered not a word.

"Just in case you care, Billie was asleep and didn't see her."

Nothing from Bill.

I sighed, thinking I shouldn't be surprised considering he was an assclown.

I got down to the matter at hand.

"Mitch and I met with an attorney yesterday and we hired him. We're moving forward with getting permanent custody of the children."

"And I care about this because...?" Bill asked, and I blinked.

Then I asked back, "Pardon?"

"I got a lotta shit to worry about, Mara. I don't need more. Because of you, I got a 24/7 job of watchin' my back. Don't need to spend my time thinkin' 'bout whatever the fuck you're up to. You're all fired up to show your pig boyfriend you're a good person by takin' my kids, have at it. I end this gig breathin' then I'll worry about you."

"And Billy and Billie," I put in.

"What?" he clipped.

"You end this breathing, you'll worry about me *and* Billy and Billie," I stated.

"Whatever," he muttered.

God, my cousin was an assclown.

"Not whatever, Bill. Your son thinks you're a piece of shit, and your daughter has shed tears worrying about you. So it's not whatever. Those are your children and—"

Bill cut me off, "Not for long, if you and your cop get what you want, so what do you care?"

He had a point.

Time to move onto the hard part.

"You could make this easier if you cooperated," I told him, and he grinned, but it was not a nice grin.

"Right," he whispered through his ugly grin, "that's not gonna happen."

Total assclown.

"You don't get this, Bill. I'm not asking for me. I'm asking for Billy and Billie."

"Not gonna happen," he repeated.

I stared at him.

Then I pulled in a deep breath.

Then I said softly, "All those nights, I escaped Mom, her men, her parties, I went to you. All those nights, we talked in the dark about what we were going to do, where we were going to go, who we were going to be. All those nights, all we talked about was that wherever we went, whatever we became, it had to be a place where we could be who we wanted to be, not what people thought we were. I never gave up that dream, Bill, and I don't know when you did. I also don't care. I'm not responsible for what's happening to you. *You* are. But you want to pin that on me? Fine. Do it. I don't care about that either. What I care about, the *only* thing I care about, is making certain that Billy and Billie do not lead the life you and I led through no fault of our own. Now they have nice beds. They have nice clothes. They have new shoes. Billy's getting really good at playing catch, and Mitch is teaching him how to bat and he's getting good at that too. Billie sleeps every night with a pink teddy bear that she loves. They're clean. They go to school. They eat three meals a day. They laugh a lot. They're around people who care about them and that they get their homework done and to bed on time. All of that is simple, but you and me, Bill, we know that the simple stuff is everything. I'm giving them that. So is Mitch. You didn't. I'm asking you to do me a favor, and that favor is to let Mitch and me keep giving them that. You have to sign a piece of paper. That's it. You do your time, sort yourself out, you get out, we can talk about you having a place in their lives. But only if you sort yourself out and only if you never, ever lay claim to them again. They have a family now. They're content. They're happy. Do me a favor and let me keep giving them that. And doing me that favor is *you* giving them that."

Bill leaned into me, eyes narrowed, and said slowly, "Not . . . gonna . . . *happen*."

I nodded. I knew it.

Still, I had to give it a shot.

Then I said, "Fine. But it *is* going to happen, Bill. It's just going to take longer. And after it's done, you get to live the rest of your life knowing your son hates you. And coming to the understanding that as time passes, you'll become just a hazy memory to your daughter after you squandered the love she gave to you. And you can twist that in your head to try to pin that on me too, but I know, deep down somewhere inside you, you'll know that's not true. You'll know I gave them what you and I always wanted. And you'll know when Billy finds someone he loves and wants to spend the rest of his life with, he'll be dancing with me at his wedding. And you'll also know when Billie finds someone to give her heart to, she'll be dancing with Mitch. And you know that'll be on you too."

His face twisted and he hissed, "Fuck you, Mara."

But I shook my head.

"You're saying fuck me, but what you're doing, you're fucking Billy and Billie. What you do to me affects your children. So, Bill Winchell, you just proved you *are* what everyone back home thought you were. You're an assclown with shit for brains who doesn't care about anyone but himself. And you have to live with that too."

He opened his mouth to speak, but I didn't hear what he had to say.

I put the phone back in its cradle, pushed my chair back and didn't look at him as I turned to Mitch. I caught his hand, his long, strong fingers curled tight and warm around mine, and I didn't look back as we walked out.

We were out of the room and walking down the hall when Mitch muttered, "I'll call the attorney."

"Okay," I whispered.

His fingers squeezed mine. "You all right?"

"Yes," I answered.

His fingers squeezed mine again, but his hand also tugged as he brought us to a stop.

I looked up at him.

"Sure?" he asked softly.

"The only thing I have to worry about is paying the attorney. I spent a lot of years saving for a rainy day." I gave him a small smile. "So, it's raining. Whatever. The rain always stops."

Mitch's eyes moved over my face. Then he smiled back. He lifted his other hand, curled it around the side of my neck and pulled me in and up.

He kissed me, fast, hard but closed-mouthed.

Then he whispered against my lips, "Get to work, sweetheart."

I grinned against his.

Then I moved away, Mitch walked me to my car and I got to work.

# CHAPTER TWENTY-SEVEN

## Operation Drunk Sex Later

*Two weeks, two days later...*

"I'M BACK, BABY!" Mitch called from my living room-
slash-kitchen-slash-dining room.

He'd taken the kids to spend the night at Penny's. Not so
we could have a night out, so I could go out with the girls
and he could go to work. He had something happening
with a case he was working on, and he was doing overtime.
I had a new little black dress and new sexy, strappy, high-
heeled black sandals, and I was meeting the girls ("the
girls" being Roberta, LaTanya, Elvira, Tess and Elvira's
friends Gwen, Cam and Tracy) for drinks at Club.

The little black dress and sexy new shoes I was currently wearing were purchased because we were in the
throes of Pierson's Mattress and Bed's annual summer
madness sale, and apparently half of Denver needed a mattress and/or bed. I was run off my feet, but my commissions were killer.

Of course, I wanted to bank them to pay the attorney's
fees, but, with Mitch's overtime on this big case and seeing as he clearly absorbed Elvira's lesson about little black

dresses, he encouraged me to go shopping with her (which I did) and spoil myself (which meant spoiling him).

So now I was wearing my first-ever LBD. It was sleeveless. It was black jersey. It was shorter than any dress I'd ever worn. It had no back (at all). It was clingy in a lot of places and tight in all the others.

And the shoes even turned *me* on they were so hot.

I'd added heavy makeup (something I never did, but it looked pretty good, even if I did say so myself). I'd also added lots of hair (something else I never did, but ditto with it looking good).

And now I was good to go.

And good to go meant Mitch driving me to Club. I had to work that day, but the girls had met for dinner at Club and I was meeting them there. I had eaten a quick turkey sandwich when I got home while Mitch took the kids to Penny's. I was going to text him when it was time to come home, and if he could get me (and LaTanya), he would. If he couldn't, Elvira promised that Hawk, who was showing to get Gwen and Elvira and anyone else who needed a ride, would give me a ride.

My night was all planned and effortless for me. All I had to do was get glamorous, show up and suck back cocktails.

After a day of selling mattresses, that was all I had in me.

Incidentally, I was not worried about meeting three women who were curious about me. Yes, this was how far beyond my classification system I was. Three months ago, sitting down with three women who would be judging if I was good enough for Detective Mitch Lawson would have sent me over the edge.

Now?

Whatever.

If they didn't like me, I didn't have it in me to care.

Mitch liked me. That was all that mattered.

I turned from the mirror in the bathroom, hit the light and called back to Mitch, "I'm ready to go if you are!"

I went to my bed, grabbed my little black purse, turned out the lamp I had on by the bed and sashayed on my four-inch heels out the door. I moved down the hall and saw Mitch at my bar, eyes down, and he was flipping through a file on the bar, but as I moved out of the mouth of the hall, his eyes came to me.

"Do you want to leave now?" I asked, continuing toward him. "LaTanya texted me. They're there already, so…"

I trailed off because the look on his face finally registered in me.

Yes.

*In* me.

In fact, it registered in me, through me, on me and *all over me*.

I stopped dead.

When I did, Mitch immediately moved toward me, his eyes on my dress.

"Mitch—" I started.

"I don't wanna leave now."

Oh boy.

"Mitch," I whispered and started moving back because he was nearly on me and he wasn't stopping.

When I started moving back, he kept moving forward, so I kept walking backward.

"Jesus, baby, knew your legs were long but…*fuck*." His eyes were now on my legs and his voice was hot, low, growly and intense. I felt hot just listening to it.

Oh boy!

"Mitch, you have to catch bad guys," I reminded him as

I moved backward through the shadows of the hall and he kept after me.

He shifted swiftly in a way that gave me no choice but to shift with him, and this meant we moved through the door to my bedroom.

"Mitch!" I cried, putting my hands to his chest. "Bad guys?" I reminded him.

His hands curled around my hips. "They'll still be bad guys after I fuck you."

*Oh boy!*

"Mitch." I was back to whispering.

Mitch's fingers curled into my tight, stretchy skirt and yanked it up to my waist.

Admittedly, that skirt was so short, it didn't have far to go.

Still, this was hot.

I dropped my bag, and my fingers curled into his shirt to hold on seeing as my legs had gone weak.

Mitch shifted again, I felt bed behind my legs then he moved, and the lamp by my bed was back on.

I stood there, legs trembling as he leaned back several inches, and his hot eyes traveled down my fevered body, stopping at my hips, where he could see my little, lacy, black panties. Then his hot eyes moved to mine as his body moved into me, and his hands moved back, both of them diving into my panties to cup my ass.

I did a full-body tremble.

"Not waitin' 'til you're home and drunk to fuck you. Doin' it now *and* doin' it then."

Oh...

*Boy.*

"Honey—" I whispered, then I said no more because his mouth was on mine.

Then his tongue was in my mouth.

Then mine was in his.

His hands moved down, yanking my panties down with them. I felt them slither down my legs and land softly at my feet.

I did another full-body tremble and held onto Mitch.

"Step outta them," he ordered on another growl, this one thicker. I did as I was told, my sandaled feet barely free of them before Mitch's fingers clenched into my thighs right under my ass. He lifted me up, fingers digging into my flesh to spread my legs. I helped and then I found my back to the bed, Mitch on me, his mouth again on mine.

There was a lot of kissing, a lot of groping and his fingers were toying between my legs. My hand was palming his hard crotch, my whimpers drifting into his mouth when his lips disengaged from mine and slid across my cheek to my ear.

He pressed his cock into my hand as he slid two fingers into my wetness and he whispered in my ear, "Gonna fuck you hard, baby."

Oh God.

I liked that.

Mitch was a gentle lover, intuitive, thoughtful, only taking me hard when he knew I was ready for it.

And he knew I was ready for it.

He wasn't done talking.

"Want you sittin' there, drinkin' with your girls but still throbbing because of me."

Oh God.

I wanted that too. So much, my hips bucked against his hand.

His thumb put pressure on my sweet spot and they bucked again.

I turned my head and whispered, "Okay," in his ear.

"Free me," he ordered, and, my hands shaking, I unbuckled his belt, unbuttoned his jeans then pushed them down his hips.

His head came up, his eyes captured mine and my calves wrapped around his thighs. I got a little thrill at feeling his jeans rub against my skin. Then his fingers and thumb disappeared, and I got a much bigger thrill when his cock drove inside.

My lips parted, my eyes closed and my neck arched.

He kept thrusting, fast, hard, deep, and his mouth went to my neck, his voice gruff, he asked in a whisper, "How many ways you gonna take it?"

I righted my head and slid the fingers of both my hands into his hair. His head came up and he kept driving fast and hard as I whispered back, "How many ways you wanna give it?"

He didn't answer verbally.

No, he pulled out, rolled off, then I found myself on my belly, then I found myself up on my knees, then I had his hands at my hips yanking me back as he took me on my knees. My back arched, pressing my chest into the bed. His hands slid up to my ribs, the pads of his fingers digging deep as he kept pulling me back and thrusting into me.

"Yes," I whispered into the comforter.

"You like that?" Mitch growled.

He knew the answer to that. We'd done this before; I liked it before.

It had never been this hard, this fierce, this hot.

Still.

"Yes," I repeated.

Then he was gone but not for long. I was flipped over, yanked up with one of his arms wrapped around my waist, both my legs wrapped around his hips. He shifted us, and my back slammed against the headboard and wall, and his cock slammed up inside me.

"Oh God," I breathed.

Mitch's arm slanted, one of his hands curling around the cheek of my ass, tilting my hips to take more of him. His other hand captured mine and held it to the wall by my head, his eyes locked on mine, his searing into me, hotter than I'd ever seen them.

This was beautiful. This was fantastic. This was *hot*.

"Baby," I whispered.

"Fingers between your legs, sweetheart, I wanna feel you make yourself come while I fuck you."

"Okay," I agreed instantly, then moved to do as I was told.

Oh God.

Yes.

That was more beautiful. Beyond fantastic. Sizzling.

Our lips touching, our breath mingling, our eyes locked, Mitch's hand tightened in mine when I whimpered, and he knew what that meant.

"Give that to me," he growled.

"Yes, honey," I whispered.

"Now, baby, give it to me."

My lips parted, my eyes closed, my hand clenched his as my legs clasped his hips. I felt Mitch's tongue slide between my lips as his cock kept driving inside me, and the orgasm scored through me.

Three minutes later, my arms tight around him, one of my hands in his hair, my legs clutching his bucking hips, his face in my neck, he rammed deep, stayed planted, groaned into my neck and gave it back.

I bent my neck and kissed his skin right where his soft, dark hair curled around his ear.

Then I whispered there, "I love your hair."

I felt his smile against my skin then I felt and heard his strange response of, "Sucks."

"Pardon?"

His head came up, and his hand still at my ass gave me a squeeze, just as his arm that was now around my back gave me one too.

"Sucks," he repeated, looking down at me. His face was sated, his eyes still hot, but in a languid, satisfied way (that made them hotter, by the way), both made him even more handsome than he was normally.

Which was to say, right then, my man was downright beautiful.

"What sucks?" I whispered, feeling languid and satisfied too, not only because I just had fantastic, multiposition sex with my gorgeous boyfriend. Also because he had it with me, he liked having it with me, and he didn't mind me knowing it.

"Want you to have fifteen of those dresses so I can fuck you in all fifteen. But that would mean more overtime, which would mean I wouldn't have the time to fuck you in them. And that sucks."

I felt my lips tip up, and I said softly, "One is good enough for me."

I watched his lips tip up too, and he replied softly, "Yeah, one is definitely good enough."

My man thought I was hot. My man thought I was sexy. My man took one look at me in my LBD and couldn't keep his hands off me.

My soul sighed again.

His eyes moved over my face and hair before they came back to mine, and he murmured, "Your hair looked great before, baby, but now it looks fucking fantastic."

"Sex hair," I muttered, wondering if the girls would notice I had sex hair and thinking Roberta and LaTanya wouldn't miss it. It was highly likely Elvira wouldn't either.

Mitch chuckled, pulled out but dropped to his back, taking me with him. Then he righted his jeans even as I straddled him.

I lifted my head, looked down at him and whispered, "I need to go clean up."

His hands, finished with his jeans, both went to cup the cheeks of my ass as he whispered back, "I know."

He didn't move. Or, more to the point, his hands didn't leave my ass.

"Are you going to let me go so I can do that?" I asked.

"I am but I don't wanna," he answered, and I stared down at him in my bed, my body relaxed but still tingling from the orgasm he gave me, my sex still throbbing from his cock driving inside me, and it hit me again this was my life. This man was mine.

And I remembered when he fixed my washer. I watched him walk through my house to get to the bathroom and how I wanted that to be commonplace.

Now it was.

He slept in my bed. He showered in my shower. We were a team taking care of our kids. And he'd just fucked me hard, I was off to do my thing, he was off to do his thing, and he didn't want to let me go.

"What?" I heard Mitch ask gently, and I realized my eyes were on him but I wasn't seeing him, even though my thoughts were also on him. His hands slid from my bottom to become arms wrapped around me, and before I could answer, he asked, "Baby, what're you thinkin'?"

"You know how you said you were into me since you saw me four years ago?" I asked back.

"Yeah," he answered.

"Well, I was into you too," I told him and he grinned.

"I know."

I shook my head. "No, what I mean is, I was so into you, I convinced myself I was in love with you. So, when you first came in here to change my washer and I was such a dork, it was a form of torture because I was such a dork. And at the same time I wanted nothing more than to see you move through my house like you moved through my house every day and now...well...you do. Uh..." I hesitated, "move through my house every day that is."

"You weren't a dork," Mitch said softly.

"I totally was," I replied just as softly, and he grinned again.

"Okay, you were, but you were a cute one."

I rolled my eyes.

Mitch's arms gave me a squeeze, and when I rolled my eyes back to him I saw he wasn't grinning anymore.

"Best thing that ever happened to me, that shredded washer," he whispered.

"Too bad I didn't know what a washer was, or I would have shredded it myself," I whispered back, and he burst out laughing.

Then he rolled, shifted, moved and we were both on our feet with Mitch yanking down my skirt.

"Clean up, honey," he muttered. "And I'll take you to your girls." He dipped his head and touched my lips with his before he turned and walked out of the room.

I nabbed my panties and walked into the bathroom to clean up, and, while there, I ascertained I did, in fact, have sex hair. I left it like it was. So Roberta, LaTanya and Elvira cottoned on and gave me stick.

Whatever.

I had a hot-guy, police detective who couldn't keep his hands off me. I could go to drinks with the girls with sex hair. I could go anywhere with sex hair. I should be shouting it from the rooftops, *Look at me! I have sex hair given to me by Detective Mitch Lawson!*

I grinned to myself as I did my business, retraced my steps, grabbed my forgotten bag and walked to Mitch, who was back at his file at the bar. I made it to him, my eyes going down to the file and my eyebrows snapping together at what I saw right before his arm slid along my waist and he shut the folder.

"Right," he muttered, his arm tensing to move us, "let's hit the road."

My body locked and I looked up at him.

"Why do you have a sketch of Otis?"

His head tilted slightly to the side and he asked, "What?"

"In that folder," I tipped my head to the folder. "Why do you have a sketch of Mr. Pierson's cousin Otis?"

It was then Mitch's brows knitted, and he studied me closely. He looked down at the folder, flipped it open and flipped through papers until he reached the sketch of Otis.

"Are you talking about that?" he asked, tapping the sketch with his finger, but his words were strange, cautious.

"Yeah," I answered, looking at the sketch, then I looked at Mitch. "That's Otis Pierson. Mr. Pierson's cousin. He works at the store."

Mitch stared at me, his arm suddenly very tight, but he didn't say a word.

Crap!

I knew what that meant, seeing as he was a police detective and that was a folder probably from work, and in it was a sketch of Otis.

It was me who was talking cautiously when I asked, "Is Otis in trouble?"

"Mara—" Mitch started, but I kept talking.

"I mean, I wouldn't be surprised. Otis is kind of like Mr. Pierson's Bill, except, I thought, without the felonious aspects."

"Mara—" Mitch began again, but I kept right on talking.

"Still, that would stink, you investigating a member of Mr. Pierson's family."

"Mara, baby," his arm gave me a squeeze, his voice coming at me carefully, gently, "that sketch is the sketch the artist drew from the description Bud gave him of the man that came to their house."

My body locked.

Then I whispered, "What?"

"Fuck," Mitch whispered back, and his eyes drifted over my head.

"Mitch," I called, putting my hand on his chest and pushing in lightly. "Are you serious? That's the bad man Billie was talking about?"

"Fuck, fuck, *fuck*!" Mitch clipped then lifted a hand, tore his fingers through his hair and looked down at the sketch.

"Mitch!" I cried, beginning to get freaked. "Talk to me!"

He looked at me and declared strangely, "The mattresses."

I shook my head. "Honey, you aren't making sense."

His head dipped closer to mine, and his other arm curled around me. "You say that man works for Bob Pierson?"

I nodded my head. "Yes. In the warehouse. He does a lot of the ordering, or he did until he kept messing it up."

"Jesus, shit," Mitch muttered, looking over my head again.

"Mitch!" I exclaimed, pressing into his chest again, and his eyes came back to me.

"Sweetheart, when your place was tossed, it was *tossed*. But there was special attention paid to the mattresses. They were decimated, all the beds were."

Oh God.

He was right. They were.

"Has this Otis guy been in your space at work? Giving you extra attention? Giving you any attention *at all*?" Mitch asked, and I shook my head.

"No," I added my negative answer verbally. "He doesn't come to the showroom. Mr. Pierson doesn't let him. He turns off the customers because he's creepy."

And he was.

Totally creepy.

Probably even creepier to two little kids.

God, how was this happening?

Mitch told me.

"He's into something. He hid something in the mattresses. Made a mistake, lost it, whatever it was. Yours got delivered, he thought it was in them and he came looking for it. It either was or it wasn't. My guess is it wasn't, seeing as he started with the mattresses, thought you found it and moved through the house to try to find where you hid it. If he hasn't been in your space, he's probably since found it. Would he have access to your home address, either in employee databases or delivery records?"

"Yes," I answered. "Not employee databases, but he's responsible for getting the product onto the trucks for delivery. He has access to all information pertaining to deliveries."

"Shit, Jesus, fuck, I shoulda showed you that sketch," Mitch muttered, looking back at the sketch.

I pressed my hand into his chest again and got his eyes back. "You couldn't know. I didn't know anything that was going down with Bill. How could you know this had any connection with where I worked? That's crazy."

"I should have shown it to you," he kind of repeated.

"Mitch, I told you I didn't know anything about Bill and his life, but even if I didn't tell you, you knew when you walked in his house with Bud, Billie and me. I was freaked and you notice everything. You couldn't know I'd know who was visiting. It's a one in a million connection."

"Mara, honey, you dot all the i's, you cross all the t's. It's basic police work. I should...have...*shown you*."

His voice was growly, and not in a good way, so I decided to reply quietly, "Okay."

"His last name is Pierson?" Mitch asked instantly, and I nodded. "How long's he been workin' there?"

"Not as long as me. Three years. He moved to Denver from Kansas City, I think. Mr. Pierson helped him out, gave him a job. I don't know why he moved. I just know that he didn't have any marketable skills, so Mr. Pierson took the hit of taking him on for the family."

"Outside of him being creepy, you feel any bad vibes from this guy, see any bad guys hangin' around him, see him actin' strange, cagey, wrong?"

"No about the bad guys, but he's creepy because he's always acting strange and cagey. I didn't get bad vibes other than the sense that he's clearly the fuckup of the family, but I thought he was just kind of an idiot. Saying that, though, a while ago, he overordered a bunch of Spring Deluxes. Like, *a bunch*. Mr. Pierson was not pleased. They're our highest-end model. We don't move a lot of them, so it was

more stupid than normal, him overordering Spring Deluxe.
I could see him overordering the Dream Weaver, even the
Slumber Excelsior, we move loads of those. The Spring
Deluxe . . . ?" I trailed off and shook my head.

Mitch gave me a half-smile and noted, "You know, that
doesn't mean shit to me."

"What I'm saying is, we *never* sell a lot of Spring
Deluxe, so that's a huge fuckup. Even on sale, they're hard
to move. The others, on sale, they're awesome bargains
and affordable for a lot of people. So if you're going to
overorder something, it would never be the Spring Deluxe."
Mitch stared at me, and I finished on a mutter, "Just trust
me. You know mattresses, you know what I'm talking
about."

"Right, baby, how 'bout I just trust you. I'll also
look into this Otis Pierson. I'll also be sendin' someone
in to have a closer look at him and keep an eye on him.
And I'll also be makin' certain my woman does not
get within ten feet of him. You have reason to go to the
warehouse?"

I shook my head.

Mitch nodded his once. "Good. Don't change that.
He gets near you, you get away from him. You are *never*
around him in a place that's not public, and that includes
the break room. You see him in the parking lot, you get in
the car, lock the doors, get your car in motion and call me
as soon as you can. I'll talk to Bill."

Oh great.

That wasn't going to work, and Mitch knew it. We knew
this because Mitch already tried it after Billie had her bad
night. Bill didn't give up anything.

Still, I reminded him of this fact.

"I'm not sure that's going to work, honey."

"It doesn't then Slim will talk to him. He doesn't talk to Slim, Eddie'll talk to him. Eddie doesn't work, Hank will. Hank doesn't work, I'll call Tack."

I blinked at a name I didn't know.

Then I asked, "Tack?"

He nodded. "Tack, that's his club name. He was born Kane Allen. He's the president of the Chaos Motorcycle Club, and I know he's got a boy in lockdown right now. Tack gets a word to his boy, his boy corners Bill in lockdown, I get the info I need."

I stared at him.

Then I whispered, "You know the president of a biker gang?"

His arms gave me a squeeze. "Baby, I'm a cop. I know a lotta people, and a lot of the lotta people I know aren't one hundred percent solid citizens."

"Um..." I started hesitantly, "does this president of a biker gang perhaps owe you a favor?"

"No," Mitch answered, which meant if he did this, he'd owe the president of a biker gang a favor.

"Is that a good idea?" I asked quietly.

"No, owin' Tack is not good. But I also got a woman and two kids who sleep on three almost-brand-new Spring Deluxes. Since she got them delivered, my ass, most nights, has been in her bed, and the kids have been off school, so my mom's been here watchin' 'em if you and me aren't. The windows for another break-in have been short, and he probably knows your boyfriend is a cop, so if he's lookin' for a chance, he's probably bein' cautious. I can't know if he's found what he was lookin' for, and I'm not takin' any chances. Even if he has, I wanna know why he destroyed everything you owned, how he's connected to your cousin, and I want to ascertain you, Bud and Billie are under no threat. And I'll do what I gotta do to ascertain that. Even owe a favor to the president of a biker gang."

Well, one could say he had a point there.

"Okay," I whispered.

"Okay," Mitch replied.

"I have to say," I started to inform him, "this has kind of freaked *and* bummed me out and put me off a night of cosmos and women I don't know giving me the third degree to make sure I'm good enough for you."

Mitch smiled.

Then his arms got tight around me and he returned, "And I have to say pretty much nothing puts me off a night that's gonna end with you drunk on cosmos and still in that dress and those shoes. And considering the sex was seriously fuckin' hot when you *weren't* drunk, I'm lookin' forward to how much hotter it could get when you *are*."

Suddenly, I was back in the mood for a night of cosmos and women I didn't know giving me the third degree to make sure I was good enough for Mitch.

"Right," I said firmly, "off we go. Time for me to commence Operation Drunk Sex Later."

Mitch burst out laughing.

I smiled as he did it.

When he was done, still grinning, he assured me, "I'm gonna make it okay."

And, still smiling, I assured him instantly, "I know."

He stopped grinning, and I knew he liked that I trusted him, just how deeply and just how immediately when he whispered, "Fuck, Mara, I love you."

I didn't stop smiling when I whispered back, "I know."

But whispering that made Mitch grin again.

Then he kissed me.

He let me go, moved through the house to turn out the lights as I moved to the door and waited for him.

He took me to Club, where I commenced Operation Drunk Sex Later, but only after he walked me in, greeted the already at least one-sheet-to-the-wind girl gang and laid a hot, wet, heavy one on me.

I sat down, got introduced, ordered my cosmo and heard the gorgeous, blond Gwen say to the equally gorgeous, African American Camille, "Sex hair. Mitch got the business before going to work. She'll do."

Third degree over.

I passed.

It was time to get drunk.

# CHAPTER TWENTY-EIGHT

## Chestnut

I WAS THREE sips away from the end of cosmo number four. Kenny had already picked up Roberta. A handsome black man introduced as Leo had picked up Cam and Tracy. Brock had come to get Tess. Mitch had texted that things were going to go later than he expected, so I should catch a ride with Hawk, he would get home as soon as he could and I was not to take off my dress or shoes (it was a long text and a bossy one, a *sexy* bossy one). And Elvira, Gwen, LaTanya and I were waiting for Hawk to show to take us home.

I was also giggling myself sick, the kind of giggles that are silent, but your whole body shakes and your stomach muscles hurt. Although I was giggling myself sick, I didn't exactly know why. And I didn't know why because Gwen was relating the story of the aftermath of her man, Cabe "Hawk" Delgado, getting kidnapped, and her story was kind of scary. If that happened to Mitch, I would be beside myself.

But the way she was telling it was hysterical. Because Hawk got kidnapped, he pretty much rescued himself then, after they were reunited and everything was okay, he lectured Gwen on how to be a commando's woman. And although his rules were as scary as the story, I couldn't help it, they were also scary funny.

"Then," Gwen kept going, wiping under her eye, "he said, 'Confirm you get me, babe.'"

Elvira, LaTanya and I burst into gales of laughter. Why? Again, I didn't know. Possibly because I was three sips away from the end of cosmo number four and therefore significantly beyond tipsy.

Then Gwen affected a superdeep man's voice and said, "Confirm...you...*get*...me."

Hearing her talk like that, the hilarity was too much. I found I couldn't hold my head up anymore, so it crashed down onto my hand on the table and I left it there as my shoulders shook with my laughter.

I was close to pulling myself together when I heard a man's immensely attractive, deep voice say, "Jesus, babe. How drunk are you?"

My torso shot to straight, my head tipped back and my mouth dropped right open.

Holy cow.

"Hey, baby," Gwen said to the tall, built, gorgeous man looming over our table, but I couldn't tear my eyes from him. He was just so...damn...*hot*, I didn't have it in me even to close my mouth.

Wow.

*Wow.*

Detective Mitchell James Lawson was the most beautiful man I'd seen, the perfect male specimen from top to toe, and now I knew, inside as well as out.

This man who Gwen called "baby" (ohmigod!) was the second most beautiful man I'd seen, but in ways entirely different from Mitch. He was tall, black haired and had an unbelievably great body. Mitch had all this too, of course, though he had dark brown hair that you could run your fingers through, not black and cropped short. But where you knew Mitch was good to the core, gentle, kind, all this just from a look, this guy was not that.

He was dangerous.

The good kind.

"Hi," I breathed, and his eyes went from Gwen to me.

My breasts swelled.

"You Mara Hanover?" he asked.

"Yes," I said, still breathy.

"You Lawson's?" he asked.

"Absolutely," I answered.

His mouth twitched. Then his eyes went back to his woman.

"So, you're all shitfaced," he observed, then finished, "or at least Mara is."

"Nope, we all are," Gwen replied airily, if a little slurred.

"Fantastic," Hawk muttered, eyeing the intoxicated remnants of the girl gang and not hiding the fact he was not a big fan of dragging our drunk asses home. He then asked the table at large, "Can any of you walk, or do I have to carry you?"

I loved Mitch. I wanted to spend the rest of my life with Mitch. I wanted to make babies with Mitch. I wanted to grow old with Mitch.

But I also wanted this man called Hawk to carry me. I didn't even care where he carried me. I just wanted him to do it.

And I was drunk enough to share this.

"I vote for being carried," I announced, and Gwen, Elvira and LaTanya burst into more gales of laughter.

Hawk's eyes came back to me and my heart fluttered. They moved over me and my legs started tingling.

Then they came back to my face. "Lawson see you in that dress?"

I nodded.

"Gave her the business before they came out," Elvira volunteered. Hawk looked at her while she spoke, then he looked back at me.

When he did, I leaned in and up and whispered, "It was *hot*."

His lips twitched again.

That was hot too.

*Hot!*

"Right," he stated. "Seein' as you're hammered, this might not penetrate, but I'll say it anyway. You lookin' like you do, wearin' that dress and bein' Lawson's woman, he is not gonna want my hands on you. Unless, say, you were lookin' like you do and filled with bullets. So, to keep your man happy, my advice is you should attempt to ambulate. You start to go down, I'll catch you. Deal?"

Gwen bumped me when she leaned in to me, and I tore my eyes away from the hot guy to look at her.

"I think this is good advice," she slurred. "Mitch is sweet, and trust me, Hawk can be sweet too. But even if I was wearing sweats and had ratty-assed hair, he would lose his mind if any man touched me. Mitch may be sweet, but he's got that in him. I can tell."

I nodded to Gwen thinking that what she said was true. Mitch felt pretty intensely about me, in this dress and out of it. I didn't think he'd take the news that a hot guy had carried me to his car very well.

I turned to Hawk. "I'll attempt to ambulate."

"Good call," he muttered, his eyes going to Gwen and his lips twitching again.

Totally...

Hot!

Then I heard him ask softly, "Sweet Pea, tab?"

"We haven't paid, baby," she answered softly.

Ohmigod!

He called Gwen "Sweet Pea."

He *could* be sweet.

Hawk headed to the bar, and I turned back to Gwen and declared, "He's the second love of my life."

Elvira and LaTanya both burst out laughing again, but Gwen's slightly hazy eyes grew more than slightly dreamy and she whispered, "He's the only love of mine."

I liked that for her. She was gorgeous, definitely. But she was also very funny and really sweet. If I was still classifying, she'd be a firm eleven. She deserved a dangerous hot guy. Totally.

"I like that for you," I whispered back, she focused on me (kind of) and smiled.

"Think Hawk's in the mood to move, so you got 'em, suck 'em back," Elvira ordered then did as she told us to do and slammed back half a cosmo. She put her glass down and declared, "He gets back, Hawk on the move, we gotta be ready to roll."

I took her direction, quickly sucking back the rest of my cosmo. Hawk was a commando, and although gorgeous, definitely scary. If he was in the mood to move, I wasn't going to give him any lip.

He came back while we were all getting up and snatching our purses. Being awesome and becoming even more awesome, he pulled both Gwen and my chairs out as we pushed up.

A gentleman.

Totally the second love of my life.

Once I gained my feet and ascertained my legs were going to support me, I looked up at Hawk. "How much do I owe you for the tab?"

"On me," he replied.

"No, really, I had four cosmos. How much—?"

His black eyes focused on me and I shut up.

"On me," he repeated firmly.

"Okeydokey," I muttered.

He grinned.

My nipples started tingling.

Then he kept talking. "You get to the truck, got a folder for you."

I blinked up at him.

Then I asked, "Pardon?"

"Melbamae and Lulamae Hanover?"

I felt my lips part but I didn't reply.

I didn't need to reply, he read my face.

"Sent a man, he had a word. Did some diggin', created a file. They give you shit, which would surprise the fuck outta me if they do, my man reported he was thorough, then you turn that file over to your attorney and you're golden. Yeah?"

I pressed my lips together so I wouldn't burst into drunken tears.

He *was* sweet.

"Mara?" he called, then prompted, "Yeah?"

"I'll make you one of my barbeque chicken pizzas," I blurted, and that was when I got his smile.

And it was a nice smile.

A *really* nice one.

He had two dimples.

*Two!*

Holy *cow.*

Gwen, who was standing beside him, her arm tucked through his, leaned around him and told me, "Cabe's body is his temple. You want to give payback, buy him a big vat of protein powder or a coupon for a lifetime supply of cottage cheese." She grinned. "But I'll take the pizza."

"You're on," I whispered, then I looked up at Hawk. "Thank you."

"You're welcome," Hawk's deep, attractive voice replied quietly.

Yep. So totally the second love of my life.

"Yo!" Elvira called. "We goin' or can I order another cocktail?"

Hawk's gaze sliced to her, and I bit my lip.

Elvira raised her brows. Hawk shook his head.

Then he started walking.

Without a word, the girl gang teetered behind him and Gwen.

We were ten feet from the door when my purse rang. In my inebriated state, I slowed and clumsily pulled my phone out of my purse. I slowed more when I saw on the display it said, "Mitch calling."

I took the call and put my phone to my ear.

"Hey, honey," I answered.

"Hey, sweetheart," he replied, and I got a heart flutter, breasts swelling, legs tingling and nipples hardening all at once. "Done here. I'll swing by Club and get you."

I shook my head and put my hand to the door that had swung closed behind LaTanya.

"Hawk just showed. I'm walking out the door now." I pushed it opened, stopping and looking out into the parking lot to locate the others. I saw they were well ahead of me, so I hastened my step as I walked out the door and went on, "And I'm walking to his truck all by myself."

Mitch's voice was trembling with laughter when he asked, "You're what?"

"I'm walking…"

I trailed off and stopped walking when I heard the screeching of tires close. My head turned to see a car coming into the parking lot at high speed. This shocked me, but it also alarmed me because it appeared it was coming right at me. Vaguely, I heard the roar of motorcycles, not one, but several. But this didn't register, because seeing that car racing toward me, I didn't think of anything but getting out of the way.

So I got out of the way, drunk and running on high heels, which, by the way, was *not* easy.

The car came to a screeching halt while curving and cutting me off so I had to stop too as I heard Hawk's voice shout, "Mara! This way. Run!"

One of the doors to the car opened, a man came out, he was big and scarier than Hawk, but not in a good way, and I pivoted on my foot and started running toward Hawk.

Another car was coming in at high speed from the other direction. It cut me off from Hawk, who was running toward me, and I awkwardly had to take last-minute evasive maneuvers. My ankle turned, I wobbled and I threw both my arms out to stop myself from going down. My heart was racing, my adrenalin pumping and my mind was blank of anything but surprise and fear.

Then, suddenly, from out of nowhere there were motor-cycles everywhere.

*Everywhere.*

Shooting through the two cars, all through the parking lot and, as I continued to stagger, one shot right toward me.

Before I could avoid it, I was hooked at the waist by

something strong and solid, and I couldn't hold back my, *"Oof!"*

Then my ass was planted *in front* of the rider.

"Hold on," a gravelly voice ordered.

"I—"

*"Hold the fuck on!"* the gravelly voice barked.

Even as we kept cruising, I turned to face him, my arms sliding around his middle. His arm around me went back to the bike handle, and he must have given it some gas because we shot out of the parking lot.

Oh God.

*What was happening?*

"What's happening?" I asked.

"Keep quiet and stay calm. You're safe," he answered as, from my vantage point of looking over his shoulder behind us I saw the rest of the motorcycles line up behind ours.

"Safe? Safe from what? Who are you?" I asked, and tipped my head back to see a strong jaw, a partial view of a goatee and longish, dark hair curling around a muscled neck and his ear.

"I'm Tack."

Oh boy.

"President of a biker gang Tack?"

His chin tipped down slightly, but not enough for me to get a good look at him before his eyes went back to the road, and he muttered, "See Lawson's told you about me."

"Uh—" I started.

He cut me off. "Motorcycle club."

"What?" I asked.

"Chaos isn't a gang. It's a club."

From the firm tone of his gravelly voice sounding over the roar of the motorcycle I noted that, clearly, this was an important distinction.

Right.

"Um . . . sorry," I murmured.

"Just keep quiet and hold on," he ordered, and I thought this was good advice seeing as I'd never been on a motorcycle. I also didn't know you could ride on a motorcycle like this. It didn't feel very safe, though he seemed in command.

Still, probably better if he had nothing to concentrate on but the road and making sure we didn't crash and die, since neither of us were wearing helmets.

We roared onto Speer Boulevard, then we turned and roared up University Boulevard, then another turn and down we roared on Alameda, then another turn and more roaring down Broadway, and then we turned into the enormous forecourt of a mechanic's garage.

He parked in front of a long rectangular building, and all the bikes roared in beside us like they practiced this formation often and they were the motorcycle equivalent of the Air Force Thunderbirds.

It was then that I realized somewhere along the way I'd lost my phone and purse.

And I'd been talking to Mitch when it all happened.

"Oh no," I whispered, staring at Tack's neck.

"Hop off, chestnut."

I blinked and looked up at him to see his shadowed face looking down at me.

"What?"

"Can't get off until you let me go and get off, so hop off, chestnut."

"Chestnut?"

"Your hair," he grunted. "Now hop . . . *off.*"

And it was then I noticed that I still had my arms tight around him. Considering his tone was becoming impatient, I felt it prudent at that juncture to let him go and hop off.

So I did that and stood unsteadily beside his bike while his brethren closed ranks.

He threw his leg off, grabbed my hand and started walking with wide strides toward the rectangular building taking me with him.

"Um . . . Mr., uh . . . Tack—"

"Just Tack," he interrupted, not breaking stride and dragging me toward the door to the building.

"Right, uh . . . Tack. I lost my phone. I was on a call to my boyfriend, um—"

He pushed open the door at the same time he twisted his neck and ordered, "Dog, call Lawson. Tell him we got his woman at the compound and she's safe."

He knew who I was?

"You know who I am?" I asked as he dragged me into what looked kind of like the rec room of a house except a lot bigger and decorated in shades of seedy bar.

"Make it my business to know everything worth knowin' in Denver," he muttered, stopped and stopped me with a tug on my hand.

And since the lights were on I saw him.

Wow.

I'd had a lifetime of rough, gruff men like him visiting my mom's trailer and even some of them coming in to visit me in my room. Therefore, I was not big on rough, gruff men who required haircuts and needed to carve out some time to trim their facial hair.

But he was different.

He had some silver in his unruly black hair. He also had visible tattoos, and lots of them. Further, he had fabulous bone structure, a dominant brow, a strong jaw. His goatee was long at the chin, but for some reason I liked it and I figured this reason was because he wore it well. He had lines radiating from the sides of his eyes and they were extremely attractive.

And he had very, *very* blue eyes.

"You're dangerous hot too, but a different kind," I blurted, unfortunately still drunk, regardless of the drama I found myself involved in.

His eyes narrowed on me, his head tilted to the side, then his goatee moved as both ends of his mouth tipped up slightly.

Oh yes. Dangerous hot.

He turned his head to the boys who followed us in and ordered, "Lockdown Ride. Eyes on the perimeter. No one gets in except Delgado and Lawson."

On that, he started walking while dragging me behind him again. He took me around a bar to a hallway that had lots of doors off of it.

"Do you know what's going on?" I asked as he dragged me.

"You know Grigori Lescheva?" he asked back.

Russian mob.

I felt my stomach clench.

Oh boy.

This could not be good.

"I know *of* him," I answered as he pushed open a door.

Then he turned on a light and I saw it was a bedroom, a very untidy one.

He pulled me in, stopped us and looked down at me. "Well, he knows you."

Fantastic.

Tack wasn't done.

"He also knows your cousin was talkin' with the DA."

Damn.

Tack kept going.

"And he also knows you recently had a sit-down with him."

Shit.

"Uh..." I mumbled, unable to wrap my head around this.

"And last, he knows you got a connection with that shit-for-brains Otis Pierson."

Shit!

"I barely know Otis," I told Tack. "I just kind of work with him. And I think he's creepy."

"Might be so, but Lescheva's got a problem, he's comprehensive about solvin' it."

That *really* didn't sound good.

"Are you saying that he thinks I'm part of his problem?" I asked.

"I'm sayin' that you got a connection with two people who are bein' serious pains in his ass. He's made note 'a that, and when he sweeps up a mess, he's thorough."

I stared up at him and whispered, "That's insane."

"Chestnut, this guy's Russian mob. Not one of them is right in the head."

This was probably true.

"How are you involved in this?" I asked.

"Your cousin and Pierson are bein' a pain in Lescheva's ass, he's a pain in mine," Tack answered, but didn't elucidate further.

I left it at that as my drunken, stunned brain chugged through this information, and when it did, my body locked. All except my hand, which shot out to Tack, my fingers curling tight into his black tee.

"My kids," I whispered.

His head was tipped down to stare at my fist in his tee. I was unfortunately familiar with biker guys, so I knew they weren't big on your touching them unless this was invited, but I didn't remove my hand. Instead, I pulled his shirt out and then pushed it back in, taking a step toward him, and his eyes came to me.

"My kids. Bud and Billie. They're Bill's kids, but they're mine. If this guy is comprehensive, will he—?"

"Fuck," he clipped, cutting me off then he roared, *"Brick!"*

Oh God.

*Oh God!*

I pushed in closer, my heart tripping over itself, I added my other fist in his shirt and whispered, "Tack."

"We're on it," he muttered. The door opened, and a big biker with a small beer gut and a lot of russet-brown hair held back in a man-bun swung in with the door. "Winchell's kids," Tack said to the big guy

The big guy's face went hard and he muttered, "Fuck."

"They're at Mitch's sister's house. Her name is Penny," I told them, adding her address, then a thought occurred to me and my fists tightened in his tee. "Oh God, Tack. She has kids too!"

"Call Lawson," Tack ordered the guy in the door. "Get on that."

The big guy nodded then he was gone.

"Oh God," I whispered.

"We're on it," Tack repeated.

"Oh God!" I cried.

His hands came to my shoulders and squeezed.

"Babe, we're . . . *on it.*"

I stared up into his very, *very* blue eyes.

"Trust me," he said softly.

I just kept staring up into his very, *very* blue eyes.

I didn't trust bikers. Again unfortunately, I'd known a lot of them, and the ones I knew were not trustworthy.

But staring into his eyes, standing there still drunk, totally alive, with bikers going out to take care of my kids, a call being made to my man and *not* being in a car whisked to the unknown—but definitely unsafe—with the Russian mob, I trusted him.

So I nodded.

He squeezed my shoulders.

Then he said quietly, "I'll be back. Stay here."

I nodded again.

Then he was gone and I was staring at a closed door.

# CHAPTER TWENTY-NINE

## They Come Outta This Alive,
## They're Mine

WHAT WAS PROBABLY fifteen minutes later but felt like fifteen days, the door opened and I turned to see another rough, gruff biker, this one younger, standing in the doorway, hand to the doorknob, eyes on me.

"You come with me," he ordered, then he was no longer in the doorway.

I hurried out of the room after him then hustled down the hall. He turned and I turned with him to see Gwen and LaTanya standing at the bar in the biker rec room. I also distractedly noted my purse was sitting on the bar.

LaTanya immediately broke away from Gwen and came to me, her face awash with relief at seeing me alive and unharmed. This was quickly followed by concern when she got a good look at my face.

"Honey, are you okay?" she asked, arriving at me and grabbing my upper arms.

"No," I whispered.

"What's happening?" she asked.

"Bill," I answered, still whispering.

Her face scrunched, indicating she got me and was still worried, but now also pissed off.

"We got your purse," she told me softly, her hands giving my arms a squeeze. "But the bad news is, about seven motorcycles rode over your phone. It's dust."

Fabulous.

"Yo!" we heard and we both jumped. LaTanya let me go and we turned toward the bar to see Elvira had popped up from behind it. She had her gaze trained on the young biker who was with us. "You got any vodka?" she asked him.

I stared.

Only Elvira would make herself at home in a motorcycle club's rec room.

"You don't find it back there, we don't got it," young biker replied.

"You good to do a liquor store run?" Elvira asked and I blinked. "While you're out, we'll need Cointreau, cranberry juice and limes too."

Young biker stared at her like she'd been beamed behind his brothers' bar straight from Venus.

"Uh . . . negative," he eventually replied.

"I don't do bourbon or tequila," she informed him.

"I don't care," he informed her, and she planted a hand on her hip.

Oh boy.

The Attitude.

"We're in crisis mode *and* little black dresses. Crisis plus LBDs equals alcohol consumption. Strike that, any crisis *at all* equals alcohol consumption. I gotta keep my girls steady in the face of the unknown, and we're your guests," she educated him.

"Work with what you got," he returned, and she glared.

Then she muttered, "Tequila shots it is," and turned to the shelves behind the bar, which held a variety of glasses.

I looked at young biker and stated, "I don't need tequila. I need to know what's going on."

"Boys get back, you'll get briefed," he replied.

"Do you have any preliminary intel?" Gwen asked, and from her words I figured she'd had ongoing commando's woman lessons.

"Boys get back, you'll get briefed," he repeated.

I gave up on him and looked to Gwen. "Where's Hawk?"

She looked at me and answered, "He dropped us off and then he took off."

"Does he know what's going on?" I asked.

"Well, he knows Tack, and he knew who those guys were in the cars that were after you, so I'm thinking… yeah," she answered. "Though he didn't share," she finished quietly.

Damn.

I moved to her, and LaTanya trailed me. "Can you call him?"

"Uh…no, honey, sorry," she said softly. "When I say he took off, I mean he took off to wade into whatever is going on. And when he's involved in an operation, I leave him be and let him concentrate."

This was probably smart.

Still, even knowing hot-guy commando Hawk was in play didn't stop me from shaking, which I belatedly realized I'd started doing.

"Elvira, tequila," LaTanya muttered, and I knew she saw me shaking.

Then she grabbed my hand, and I looked at her.

"It's the Russian mob cleaning up Bill's mess. Tack told me. And I'm not involved, like, *at all*, and they came after me. They'll go after Bud and Billie."

"You can't know that," she said gently.

"When I told Tack about Bud and Billie, he got some-one on it right away. So, yes, I can know that," I replied.

She pressed her lips together and looked at Gwen.

Gwen looked at me. "I know Tack, Mara. He's a good guy. A really good guy. If he's got someone on it, they won't mess around."

This didn't make me feel better either, though I was get-ting a suspicion president of a motorcycle club Tack was not like any of the bikers I'd met in my mother's trailer.

"Tequila, hon, now," Elvira ordered softly, and my eyes went to her.

"I'm already drunk, I don't need more. I need my wits about me," I explained.

"Tequila, Mara, now," Elvira kind of repeated.

"But—" I started.

"Don't know how long it's gonna last, but you're on a bumpy ride. You got your girls, but you need more. Listen to Elvira. Smooth the edges. Tequila. Now," she demanded.

I swallowed. Then I nodded. The girl gang bellied up to the bar. I took my shot glass from Elvira. The other girls each grabbed one, and in unison we belted them back.

I put my shot glass on the bar while wincing.

LaTanya, who hadn't let go of my hand, squeezed it.

We heard a door open just then and we also heard a man's angry voice barking, "You got this fucked up shit, you tell the fuckin' cops about it."

I knew that voice.

Brock.

I pulled my hand from LaTanya's and raced around the bar to see Brock striding in using an angry gait, and he was just behind Tack.

"We don't roll that way, man, and you know it," Tack growled.

I stopped, eyes on Brock, and asked, "What's going on?"

His eyes cut to me, and his face changed.

It was not a good change.

It was the worst change of all.

My legs trembled.

Oh God, no.

"No," I whispered, my gaze darting to Tack, who was wearing the same expression. "No," I repeated, and I felt an arm slide around my waist but didn't tear my gaze from the two men.

Brock moved swiftly to me, stopped in front of me and ordered gently, "Need you to sit down, Mara."

"Tell me," I returned quietly.

"Mara, honey, I need you to—"

I knew it, I could read it on his face and I couldn't hold it back.

Therefore I lost it.

*"Tell me!"* I shrieked.

"They got the kids," he replied quickly, and I stared at him, my lungs hollowing out, but other than that, nothing, just numbness invading every inch of me.

"Penny and Evan?" I forced between my lips.

"Evan's roughed up, but he's okay. They didn't touch their kids," Brock answered.

Evan tried to step in.

Mitch's brother-in-law tried to step in with the Russian mob.

He was roughed up but okay.

He could have been killed.

And my cousin put him in that position.

I continued to stare at Brock.

"Let's get you to a couch," he said softly, moving toward

me, but I took a step back, detaching from the arm I saw now was Gwen's. I also lifted my hand, palm up, to Brock, who stopped when I moved.

"Tell me what's happening to get them back," I demanded.

Brock didn't delay with his answer. "Tack's mobilized his boys, Delgado his and Mitch is mobilizing the DPD. The call is also out to the Nightingale men."

"And this means?" I pressed.

"This means Tack needs to brief me, he needs to get on his bike, I need to get to Mitch and we need to get them back," Brock replied.

"Then do that," I ordered. "Now."

He jerked up his chin, then Brock and Tack moved. Tack stared into my eyes as he passed me. Brock grabbed my hand and gave it a quick squeeze when he did. They walked swiftly through the biker rec room and disappeared behind a door.

I stared at the door.

"Breathe, honey," Gwen whispered at my side.

"They've got my kids," I whispered back.

"Honey—" she started, but I interrupted her.

"The Russian mob has my kids."

Her arm slid around my waist again then went tight. LaTanya took my hand again, and hers went tight.

I stood still and staring at the doors Brock and Tack disappeared behind.

Bill.

Fucking with me, he fucked his kids. Fucking up his life, he fucked up his kids'.

Bill.

*Bill!*

I tried to protect them.

And I failed.

The Russian mob had my kids.

I tugged my hand free from LaTanya's and lifted both. Sliding my fingers into my hair, I pressed my palms to my forehead.

"They hurt them, I'll kill them," I whispered to the floor.

"Let's sit down." I heard Elvira suggest.

"They hurt them, I'll kill them then I'll kill Bill."

"Move her to a couch." Again from Elvira, but not a suggestion this time.

"They've got my kids," I whispered, and on the second word, my voice broke.

I felt pressure on my waist, then my body was moving, then I found myself sitting on a couch.

Two seconds later, the door Brock and Tack had disappeared behind opened, and both men came out and both came directly to me.

Brock crouched down in front of me and captured my eyes.

"Hang tight, Mara, we'll get them," he said quietly. "Now I gotta get to Mitch. He's not calling because he's busy, but he wants you to know he's on it."

I nodded.

Mitch was on it.

Finally, I felt a little better. Mitch would never, *never* let anything happen to our kids.

Brock nodded back, reached out a hand, squeezed my knee, straightened then prowled out.

Tack filled my vision.

I held my breath at the look in his eyes.

Yes, *very* dangerous hot guy.

"I underestimated the situation. This is my fuckup.

We'll get them, chestnut, then *we'll get them*," his gravelly voice promised.

I held his eyes, and my voice vibrated when I whispered, "Yes. Please. *Get them*."

I understood him.

He understood me.

He nodded.

Then he was gone.

\*      \*      \*

## Mitch

"Man, let me talk to him. You know this is not a good idea," Hank Nightingale said from his side.

"I'm on this," Mitch growled.

Hank looked behind him at Eddie Chavez, who was following.

Eddie shook his head.

Hank muttered, "Fuck."

Mitch ignored him and Chavez, walked direct to the interrogation room, opened the door and saw Bill Winchell sitting at the table in his orange jumpsuit. At their entry, Winchell's head came up, his eyes narrowed on Mitch and his face twisted with hate.

Two seconds later, Bill Winchell was against the wall with Mitch's hand wrapped around his throat.

Hank at one side, Eddie at the other, Hank murmured, "Stand down."

"Lescheva's got the kids," Mitch growled in Winchell's face and watched it pale. "He went after Mara. Pure luck he doesn't have her too."

He felt Winchell force a swallow under his hand.

"You talk to me now. No DA. No deal. You get nothin' except the hope what you give us keeps those kids alive. What were you into with him, and what was Pierson's part of the play?" Mitch demanded to know.

"Mitch, man, stand down," Hank kept at it.

Mitch pressed Winchell deeper into the wall using his hand and body to do it.

"Talk to me *now*," Mitch clipped.

"He's..." Winchell forced another swallow, "he's... Lescheva's got my little girl?"

"And Bud," Mitch confirmed. "Now fuckin' *talk!*" he barked.

"My boy," Winchell whispered.

He didn't have time for this.

His kids were...

They were...

Fuck, he didn't have any fucking *time*.

Mitch got nose to nose with him and roared, *"Talk!"*

"I'll talk, dude, I'll talk," Winchell forced out.

Mitch released his throat and stepped back. Eddie and Hank relaxed at his sides, and Winchell put a hand to his throat and began to move forward.

Mitch put a hand to Winchell's chest and pushed him against the wall. "We're not gettin' comfortable, havin' a beer and chattin' about football. When I say talk now, I mean talk...*now*."

Winchell's eyes came to his.

Then he said, "The mattresses."

"Got that," Mitch clipped. "What about them?"

"They don't sell," Winchell explained.

"Got that too," Mitch bit out. "Tell me somethin' I don't got."

Winchell nodded.

"Mara, she told me about them. She said they don't sell. Said they always have a supply, but they sit in the warehouse for a while. When she talked about it, I thought it was the perfect place to hide stash. Pierson is a good guy, family man, family business, single store, not a chain. Gives to charity. Looks out for his employees. No one would ever think he had a boatload of illegal shit stashed in his warehouse. I owed Lescheva, he was gettin' impatient. I knew he had problems with storage, so I told him my idea. He liked it, did the recon, found Otis was a weak link. He recruited him, stayed distant, left the operation to Otis and me."

"And what's the stash?" Mitch asked, and Winchell shook his head but answered.

"Anything he needed. H. Blow. Stolen passports. Jewels. Whatever."

"And the overorder?" Mitch pushed.

"Lescheva got greedy," Winchell told him. "It was working. They move a load of product in that store but not that brand of mattress. Lescheva wanted to store more stuff there, Otis ordered a shitload of mattresses to hold it. He knows his cousin thinks he's a fuckup so he'd never cotton on. And he didn't."

"You remember they tossed Mara's place?" Mitch asked, and Winchell nodded. "Was it because of the mattresses?" Mitch pressed.

Winchell nodded again. "Pierson thinks Otis is a fuckup because he is. Heard word in lockdown he lost track of some shit he was holdin' for Lescheva, mattresses went out, so did some shit. He had to find it," Winchell answered.

"He find it?" Mitch asked.

"Is he alive?" Winchell asked back.

"Don't know," Mitch replied. "We can't find him."

"Then no," Winchell answered.

"Fuck," Eddie muttered.

Mitch kept going.

"You know what he lost?"

Winchell shook his head. "Could be anything."

Mitch stared at him.

Then he whispered, "You put her out there."

Winchell held his eyes, but his face remained pale and, even being the definition of an assclown, he couldn't hide the remorse.

"You put her out there, using her place of work, using her boss, then you kept putting her out there after she took on those kids," Mitch continued.

Winchell said nothing.

"And you put your kids out there," Mitch kept at it.

"Kept them fed," Winchell whispered his weak excuse.

"No, it kept you in smack and booze and smokes, you piece of shit," Mitch shot back. "You put them out there. All of them. You fuckin' put them out there, and now that psycho asshole has got," he leaned in, "*my kids*."

Winchell's eyes narrowed. "They're mine, Lawson."

"Wrong," Mitch bit out, then he shared, "Bud asked to take my name." At that, Winchell's face blanched further. "I'm marrying your cousin, and we're adopting them and both of them are taking my name. They stopped being yours at a Stop 'n' Go on Zuni months ago. You need to get this, Winchell, this needs to sink in, so listen to me closely. They come outta this alive, they're *mine*."

Winchell opened his mouth to speak, but Mitch was done.

So done, Winchell didn't get a word out before Detective Mitch Lawson was out the door.

# CHAPTER THIRTY

## You Came

### Mitch

MITCH ANGLED OUT of his truck, seeing Tack among the huddle and taking a deep breath.

The huddle included Slim, Tack, Delgado and a local private investigator, Hank Nightingale's brother, Lee Nightingale and Lee's second in command, Luke Stark.

Heavy hitters. Denver's elite.

At least that was something.

Slim detached from the group and walked quickly to Mitch. He stopped right in front of him, and Mitch allowed Slim to cut him off.

"Your shit together?" Slim asked quietly.

"No," Mitch answered honestly.

"Right. This fuckwad had Tess, Joey, Rex, I'd be where you are right now. And you'd be right where I am, and that is standin' here tellin' you to get your shit together."

Mitch stared at his partner.

Slim kept talking.

"Mara's good. She's holdin' it together. She's got her girls around her. She's keepin' her shit."

That was his Mara.

A survivor.

Slim wasn't done.

"You know Chaos has issues and you know they do not team up with the local PD to sort that shit out."

"He shoulda talked," Mitch said low. "Women and children are involved."

"Brother, listen to me," Slim got close. "Been talkin' to those guys, and not only are you and me surprised as shit Lescheva made a play on a cop's woman and the kids he's lookin' after, Tack, Hawk *and* Lee had no fuckin' clue Mara was even on radar. Tack got word and mobilized. That's why she's sittin' in Chaos's compound with her girls and a guard of Chaos and not wherever Bud and Billie are. The word he heard was about Mara, not those kids. He moved the minute he heard she was in danger. He's in this mess because he's tryin' to get his boys clean. This is not on him even though he's feelin' this shit and he's feelin' it deep. It isn't on him. This is on Lescheva."

Mitch continued to stare at his partner. Then he jerked his chin up.

He got his shit together while walking around Slim to the huddle.

"You and Lucas are not here," Delgado stated quietly the minute they arrived.

"We're not wastin' time with that shit," Mitch replied. "We're here. Now we discuss the play."

Luke Stark shifted, and Mitch gave him his eyes.

"Lawson, this shit's about to get dirty," Stark warned.

"Is this necessary information for me to have to discuss the play?" Mitch returned.

"It's necessary information for you to have, this goes

south, you and Lucas are involved, you both lose your jobs and got no way to feed your kids," Nightingale put in.

"We're wasting time," Mitch growled.

"You're clean," Tack reminded him. "You wanna stay that way, you get in your truck, you go to Ride and you look after your woman."

Mitch took in a deep breath.

Then he looked Tack in the eyes.

"He has my kids," Mitch said slowly. "He tried to get my woman," he kept speaking slowly. "Now, let's . . . discuss . . . *the play*."

Tack stared at him.

Then he muttered, "Respect."

Respect from Kane Allen.

Jesus.

Mitch let out his breath.

"Right," Delgado spoke, and Mitch looked at him. "The play . . ."

\*       \*       \*

The men moved through the parking lot, rounding the building and walking down the alley behind the restaurant and they did it knowing they were not moving outside radar.

Therefore it was no surprise when the door opened before they arrived.

The men inside knew the players, therefore the two soldiers at the door didn't even bother to attempt pat downs.

The surprise came after they moved through the deserted kitchen to the back room. And this surprise was two of Nightingale's men, Kai Mason and Vance Crowe, and two of Delgado's men, Jorge Alvarado and Brett Day, emerging from the shadows of the restaurant and outflanking Lescheva's men, who were bringing up the rear.

The maneuver, once instigated, made the thick air thicker.

"Grigori will not like this," one of Lescheva's men warned Tack, but Tack ignored him and pushed open the door.

They walked into a room decorated in reds, a large circular table in the middle. Lescheva and his four closest lieutenants were sitting around it and, even though it was nearing two in the morning, they were eating dinner and drinking vodka.

Busy night. Late dinner.

Seeing Lescheva, Mitch locked it down and held his shit. It took effort, but he did it.

Lescheva's men barely glanced at them when their guests arrived, continuing to eat. Gnats entered the room. Unworthy of their notice.

Stupid.

When Hawk Delgado, Lee Nightingale, Luke Stark and Kane Allen entered a room, you took notice. You didn't, they'd note that disrespect. They were all major players in Denver. And they had good memories.

But Lescheva wasn't so dumb. He sat back, eyes on Tack, and he smiled.

"Strange bedfellows," he remarked to Tack.

They were. Mitch knew it. Tack and Chaos Motorcycle Club skidded the edges of the real world and the criminal underworld. Tack had a knack for it, but the balancing act was precarious, and it was touch and go whether he'd continue to succeed, considering there were members of his club who absolutely did *not* have a knack for it. Delgado and Nightingale were versions of the same, but their morals were less dubious, though not by much. It wasn't that they participated in criminal activity. It was that their activities could be construed as criminal. They all knew about each other, but until Hawk's woman, Gwen, found trouble a while ago, they had always carefully kept their business separate.

Mitch Lawson and Brock "Slim" Lucas had no business being there. Lescheva was under federal investigation. They screwed this pooch, they'd lose their jobs.

Lescheva knew this.

"Where are the kids?" Tack replied, and that was pure Tack. Everyone knew it. Kane "Tack" Allen didn't fuck around.

Lescheva's brows went up. "Kids?"

"We talk deal," Tack returned, and Mitch got tense.

The only deal Grigori Lescheva wanted from Kane Allen and his motorcycle club was for Tack to backtrack from the maneuvers that took his club out of the criminal underworld they inhabited to skidding the edges of it. Chaos used to transport Lescheva's shit and warehouse it. They'd had a knack for that too. For reasons Mitch did not know but shocked the shit out of everyone on the grid, Tack's hostile takeover of Chaos meant under his leadership they'd broken a number of alliances. Lescheva was hiding illegal shit in mattresses because Chaos no longer provided safe shipment and storage. It was not a secret Lescheva was not happy with Chaos, and primarily Tack.

Slim said Tack was feeling this deep, thought it was his fuckup. That said, they had not discussed his making a deal with Lescheva as part of their play. Kane Allen, however, had a code he lived by, a way of doing things, and his moves were often unexpected. If Tack felt this deep enough, the code he lived by, to get Bud and Billie safe, Tack could decide to take his boys back into the game.

And Denver didn't need that.

This was why Lescheva's eyes skidded through Mitch and Slim before going back to Tack. Tack intimating he'd talk deal with two cops at his back was also pure Tack.

Unexpected.

"I know nothing of..." Lescheva spoke then hesitated before finishing, "kids."

This was the wrong answer, and Lescheva and his men knew it when two minutes later, three of them were on their backs on the floor, one was against a wall, five of them were disarmed, and all of them had guns trained on them.

Except Lescheva, who sat opposite Tack at the table, his eyes flaring, pissed.

"That was not smart," he whispered.

It wasn't. Delgado, Nightingale, their men and Chaos just bought a shitload of trouble.

That said, those men lived trouble, fed off it.

They didn't care.

"Where are the kids?" Tack repeated.

Lescheva didn't respond.

Tack waited.

Lescheva held his eyes.

Mitch's finger on the trigger of his gun aimed at one of Lescheva's lieutenants who was on his back on the floor got itchy.

"Sacrifice them," Tack said low. "Make a call. Bring someone in play. They get word to us. We go in. You're removed. No blowback on you."

Lescheva didn't move.

"Sacrifice your men," Tack ordered.

"I make some calls, I find these kids for you, what do you have for me?" Lescheva returned.

"What do you want?" Tack asked, and Lescheva's eyes flicked to Mitch before going back to Tack.

"Access," he answered.

"I'm thinkin' you don't get this, but you got a man in this room with a gun in his hand aimed at one of your boys, and you know where his kids are. He's got a badge, but, I'll repeat, you know where his kids are. Quit fuckin' around and *talk*," Tack barked the last word and Lescheva smiled.

Then he looked at Mitch.

Then he stated, "Access to lockdown."

He wanted Bill Winchell.

"Your call, Lawson, make it," Tack stated.

"Find somethin' else you want," Mitch, eyes on Lescheva, responded, and Lescheva's smile got bigger.

"Your woman, she's very beautiful," he said softly, and the tense room got suffocating.

"Make another offer," Mitch replied through clenched teeth, ignoring the comment, making the play, drawing him out.

Lescheva studied him. Then he said softly, "I have a thorn in my side."

"I do too, and tonight I learned I got more than one. But I'm not gonna do what you want done. It isn't in you to understand this, but I got two kids to raise and I become that man, I'm not fit for that job. Now make another offer."

Lescheva nodded.

Then he started, "There are police right now searching Pierson's Mattress and Bed warehouse. There are things in that warehouse that—"

"You know who I am," Mitch cut him off. "You know this is wasting time. I am not interfering with an investigation. You fucked up, tied your shit to two assclowns.

You take that hit. Now make another offer and think smart before making it."

"These children, do you think they're safe?" Lescheva asked.

Jesus, fuck, he wanted to lay hands on this fucking guy.

"I think they better be," Mitch answered.

"If you care about them, as it would appear you do, I believe it is *you* who should," he paused then finished, "think smart."

"Is that a threat?" Mitch asked, and Lescheva's chin gave the barest jerk.

He studied Mitch for long moments.

Then he whispered, "Wire."

Mitch allowed himself to smile. And he did this even though Mitch nor any of the men were wearing wires.

They just wanted Lescheva to think they were.

"Interesting," Lescheva muttered, holding Mitch's eyes.

"Got another offer?" Mitch asked.

"This is unorthodox," Lescheva remarked.

Jesus, this guy liked to talk.

"Do you have another offer?" Mitch pushed.

"Inadmissible," Lescheva noted.

"It comes to that, we'll see," Mitch lied. "Now, you're not making an offer, I'll make you one. You make a call, I get my kids, and you assure me that my woman and our children cease to exist for you and your men. You are then free to do what you have to do, Chaos does what they have to do, and the feds do what they have to do. This is forgotten. Something happens to my woman or my kids, ever, memories become sharp. Lescheva, my advice, you need to chalk this up as a fail and regroup. You got problems, and the men in this room, I know you get it, they will add to those problems. I'm aware you can multitask, but the men in this room feel like playing with you, even you aren't that good. Make the call."

Lescheva's brows went up. "Forgotten?"

"Forgotten," Mitch answered.

"Do you speak for everyone?" Lescheva asked.

"Everyone in this room," Mitch answered.

"There is one other small matter," Lescheva remarked.

"Otis Pierson," Mitch guessed correctly.

Lescheva dipped his head to the side.

Mitch held his eyes.

Then, forcing it past the acid in his mouth, he stated, "I ask no questions, you tell no lies."

There was his give.

Now it was up to Lescheva to let him take.

Lescheva studied Mitch then he looked at Tack.

"We are not done, you and me," he said quietly.

"No, man, we are not," Tack agreed, and Lescheva again smiled.

"You often surprise me," Lescheva remarked to Tack.

"That's me," Tack replied. "Full of surprises. Now, you gonna give Lawson his assurances and make your call, or are we gonna get out our knitting needles and chat while we make scarves?"

"A worthy adversary is full of surprises," Lescheva muttered.

"Man, seriously? We are not in a Bond movie. Make the fuckin' call," Tack clipped, and at his loss of patience, everyone in the room shifted.

Lescheva looked to Mitch. "It would be a shame if any harm were to come to the beautiful Mara Hanover."

He'd been watching her.

And he liked watching her.

Fuck.

Mitch drew in breath, and the men in the room shifted again.

"I will see that doesn't happen," Lescheva said quietly.

"My kids," Mitch prompted.

Lescheva's brows went up. "You claim them?"

"They're mine," Mitch stated.

Lescheva studied him.

Then he whispered, "This, I did not know."

He'd been watching, but he didn't understand what he saw. Mitch got this. Lescheva thought Mitch's moves were about Mara, and they were. But it wasn't only about her.

It was the closest he'd get to an apology.

And it didn't mean smack, because he also went after Mara even knowing she was Mitch's.

Mitch didn't reply.

Lescheva lifted his chin.

Assent.

"The call," Mitch pushed.

"I'll find these children for you," Lescheva stated gregariously.

"You do that, as in, now," Delgado entered the conversation, and Lescheva looked to him then he looked to Tack.

Then he muttered, "Strange bedfellows," and he did this while reaching into his inside suit coat pocket.

The room went wired, and two guns moved to him.

Lescheva smiled calmly, and his hand came out with his phone.

\*     \*     \*

"Clear!"

"Clear!"

"Clear!"

Mitch heard the men's calls as he moved through the house, his gun up, his flashlight up under it.

He moved up the stairs, Slim at his back. At the top landing, two ways to go. He turned, flicking two fingers right to Slim. Slim jerked up his chin, took the last two stairs and moved right.

Mitch moved left.

"Clear!" he heard from downstairs.

The right play was Lescheva ordered his men to move out, leaving the kids.

Leaving the kids.

Mitch hoped to Christ they'd moved out and left the kids.

Standing beside the first closed door on the upstairs landing, he threw it open then moved into the doorway, gun up, flashlight up.

In the corner there was a twin bed.

In the corner of the bed, back to the wall, there was Bud.

Asleep with her head on his thigh was Billie.

"Got them!" Mitch called. His eyes scanned the otherwise empty room, he dropped his gun and moved swiftly to the bed. "Here now, Bud. Safe. Yeah?"

Mitch kept his light low but shining on the children. Both kids were healthy, clean, in their pajamas. Bud had pulled a blanket over Billie. No blood, no visible injuries.

Thank Christ.

Thank *Christ*.

Mitch holstered his gun and arrived at the bed realizing Bud hadn't spoken, and Mitch's eyes stopped scanning for injuries and focused on the boy.

"You came," Bud whispered.

"Of course, buddy," Mitch whispered back.

"You came," Bud repeated so soft Mitch almost didn't hear him.

Then Mitch watched the tear fall from his eye and slide down his cheek.

A burn hit his chest and Mitch found it hard to breathe.

He locked it down.

No blood. No visible injuries. They were safe.

Safe.

Now it was time to go home.

"Let's get you home," Mitch whispered, reached out and carefully lifted a dead-to-the-world Billie to cradle her in his arms as he felt Slim enter the room behind him.

He straightened, and Bud scrambled off the bed.

"Hey, Bud, you good?" Slim asked.

Mitch looked down at him and watched him nod.

"Wanna take my hand?" Slim asked, extending his own.

Bud looked at it.

Then he lifted his hand closest to Mitch, and Mitch felt Bud's fingers curl into the belt on his jeans.

"I'm good," Bud whispered to Slim.

"Right," Slim replied quietly, reached out his extended hand and tousled Bud's hair.

"Let's go get Mara," Mitch muttered and moved out of the room, Billie in his arms held close to his chest, Bud moving close to his side, his hand still latched onto Mitch's belt.

*     *     *

Mitch's cell phone rang.

It didn't wake him. He had not been sleeping, not even to doze.

He opened his eyes.

Upon opening his eyes, over the shining, dark hair of Billie's head, he saw Mara's head on her pillow, her eyes open and alert on him.

She hadn't slept either.

He already knew that.

He rolled away from Billie, who was sleeping cradled between them, and on his roll he saw Bud pop up on the other side of Mara.

She'd made them sleep all together in her bed. When they arrived at the Chaos compound, he saw she'd been holding it together. She continued to hold it together as she checked over the kids and Mitch. She lost it when they got home, and demanded they all sleep together.

Billie was still out, and Bud and Mitch both saw the wisdom of giving into her demand. She needed that, they gave it to her.

It was good she had a king-size bed.

Mitch twisted, grabbed his phone from the night-stand, looked at his display, hit the button and put it to his ear.

He then threw back the covers and said, "Yeah," into the phone as he turned back, shaking his head at Mara and Bud.

Then he walked out of the room as Eddie Chavez spoke into his ear.

"Someone wants a word. Thinkin' you'll wanna give it to him."

Mitch closed the door behind him and walked into Mara's living room. Weak light was coming from around her blinds. It was just after dawn.

"Right," he said into the phone.

"Hang on," Chavez muttered.

Mitch went to the back of Mara's new couch. Then he leaned into it, his eyes to the hall.

And there she was in another one of her sweet nighties. She'd followed him.

"Lawson?" he heard in his ear.

Bill.

"Yeah," he answered, as he watched Mara move to him.

Fuck, that nightie was sweet.

But the look on her face was not.

He felt the burn in his chest as he stretched his arm toward her and he battled to lock it down.

They were home. Safe. No injuries.

Safe.

Home.

She moved directly into his space, and he curled his arm around her, bringing her even closer.

She settled her weight into him.

Bill spoke.

"Detective Chavez says they're good."

"They are," Mitch confirmed.

No reply.

Mitch was tired and he had his woman and children to think about. Today was most definitely a fucking donut day. He needed to make a donut run. He didn't need to waste time on an assclown.

"We done?" he prompted.

"Tell her to send me the papers."

Mitch's body tightened, and he felt Mara's tighten against his as her hand settled on his tee-covered chest.

"What?"

"Mara," Bill stated. "Tell her to send me the papers to give her permanent custody of the kids. I'll sign 'em."

"You'll relinquish all claim?" Mitch asked, then heard and felt Mara's indrawn breath.

There was a pause then a quiet, "Yeah."

"Now and forever, Winchell," Mitch declared.

Another pause then quieter, "Yeah."

"Say it," Mitch ordered.

Another pause then a whispered, "Now and forever, Lawson."

"Right," Mitch clipped. "Now we're done."

"Lawson?" Bill called quickly.

"What?"

Another pause then, "Give 'em a good life."

"Already am," Mitch replied.

"Mara too."

Mitch made no reply and closed his eyes.

"Promise me that, for them, for Mara, give them a good life."

Mitch opened his eyes and looked down at his woman, felt her soft body against his, her hand light on his chest, trust, love and hope shining in her eyes.

Jesus, she was beautiful. Never, not in his life, had he seen anything as beautiful as she was right then.

"I promise," he replied.

"Thanks, dude," Bill whispered.

Mitch ended the call.

"Bill?" Mara asked instantly.

"He wants us to send the papers."

She closed her eyes and did a face-plant in his tee as her arms wound around his middle.

Mitch tossed his phone on the couch and curled his arms around her.

He again felt her pull in a soft breath.

Then she moved her head so her cheek was against his chest.

"We need to go see Penny and Evan," she said quietly.

"She's fine, Evan's fine. Told you that already, baby. They're good. They're more worried about you and the kids than you are about them."

"We need to go see them," Mara semirepeated.

"All right, sweetheart, after donuts," Mitch relented.

She fell silent.

Then she asked softly, "Is it over?"

"It's over."

"You're sure?"

"It's over, honey."

Mara fell silent again.

She was mulling it over. He knew she'd do that and then trust him.

And he loved that about her.

She turned her head so her forehead was pressed to his chest, her arms went tight around him, and she whispered, "I love you, Detective Mitchell James Lawson."

There it was. She'd mulled it over and trusted him.

Mitch dropped his head and, lips to her fucking fantastic-smelling hair, he whispered, "I love you too, Marabelle Jolene Hanover."

Mara held onto Mitch and Mitch held onto Mara.

There was a flurry of rapid movement, Mitch tensed and looked up to see Billie flying toward them, arms in the air, hands waving. Bud was standing, leaning against the wall at the mouth of the hall.

Billie's little body collided with both of theirs and she threw her arms around their hips, tipping her head way back, she screeched, *"Donuts!"*

Someone had been eavesdropping.

Mitch looked at Bud.

Bud was smiling a crooked smile.

Mitch grinned at his boy.

Then he looked down at his girl.

"Donuts," he confirmed.

Billie jumped up and down, shaking Mitch with Mara

as she did, then she disengaged and ran back from where she came, hands again waving in the air, mouth again screeching, *"Donuts!"*

"Teflon." He heard Mara murmur and felt her body shaking against his.

Mitch moved his eyes from a still crookedly smiling Bud to look down at Mara, who now had her head tipped back, and she was smiling too.

He'd lied to her the first time her ass was in his truck.

Her smile was totally wonky.

Just like Billie's.

And just like Billie's, it lit up the room.

Beautiful.

So beautiful he had no choice.

He bent his head, put his mouth to hers and kissed it from her lips.

*        *        *

*Two days later...*

When Mitch walked into Pierson's Mattress and Bed, he saw Mara, Roberta and two other sales associates with customers, and there were a number more customers milling about the store.

Roberta's customer was a woman.

Mara's was a man.

Mitch sighed, gave his woman a chin lift, took her return smile, and gave her friend a low wave. Then his eyes went to the window at the back of the store.

Bob was standing at the window looking out at him.

Mitch wound his way through the displays, and by the time he hit the door to the back hall, Bob was standing in it.

"You got a minute?" Mitch asked quietly.

Bob nodded and threw an arm out behind him, indicating Mitch should precede him.

Mitch did so and Bob followed.

Bob had given Mara the day off after the drama, but she'd gone in the next two days, although Bob told her she didn't have to.

She explained this by saying, "Honey, I have four mouths to feed. It's paid time off, but my pay is nothing to my commissions."

"Four?" Mitch had asked.

"Bud, Billie, you and me," she stated.

"You got help with that," he reminded her.

"I know." She smiled then reminded him, "We're a team, and I can't let down the side. Anyway, commissions and a future without attorney's fees means more little black dresses."

At that, he let it go.

She didn't need the commissions. She needed normalcy.

Mitch gave it to her.

Further, he was looking forward to a future that included a selection of little black dresses.

And the truth of the matter was, Bob needed Mara. It was still the summer madness sale, not to mention news coverage about what happened at Pierson's had been extensive. Though, luckily, considering the operation to find Bud and Billie had been unofficial, the media had not stumbled onto that information, and Mara and the kids did not factor into the story.

Although Bob's warehouse was blocked by yellow police tape, the police were still sifting through it, and his stock would likely not be released for a while, this did not keep the customers away. In fact, Mara told Mitch it was a madhouse, and the customers were happy to wait for the release of stock in order to have their mattress from the now infamous Pierson's Mattress and Bed.

Considering his business, Mitch never understood the allure of crime to the average citizen, but he couldn't deny it was there. And this was further proof.

He and Bob made it into Bob's office, and Bob closed the door behind them. Mitch stood, waiting for Bob to call the scene. He'd sit opposite Bob at his desk if Bob needed to play it that way. He'd stand if Bob needed to keep his feet.

Bob needed to keep his feet.

Mitch faced him and crossed his arms on his chest.

Then he said gently, "I don't have good news."

Bob Pierson had done nothing but give a shot to a member of his family who didn't deserve it and couldn't find one elsewhere. For this kindness, he'd been informed that, stitched expertly in his mattresses and stashed in hiding places throughout the warehouse, the police had found a variety of narcotics, small stolen goods and forged passports. He also had to contact all buyers of the Spring Deluxe to recall their mattresses and replace them with new stock, which Bob had to purchase at a loss.

He'd taken a hit to his business and reputation that, due to his personality, he'd recover from. But it still had hit him hard, and the effects were visible in the deeper lines of his face, the light that was no longer in his eyes and the way he held his frame. This was not just being betrayed by a man whom he'd shown kindness, but the fact that his cousin's proclivities had affected a woman he knew well and cared about deeply in addition to the two children she claimed as her own.

That was the kind of man Bob Pierson was. He didn't

blame Mara for Bill's part in it. He blamed himself for Otis's.

"Otis?" Bob asked quietly.

Mitch nodded. "I'm sorry, Bob. I wanted to tell you in person. Two hours ago, we found his body."

Bob pulled in an audible breath through his nose. Then he nodded.

Mitch went on.

"Lescheva was careful. There's nothing tying him to what was found in your warehouse. The only trail we have leads to Otis and Bill. They not only stashed it, they distributed it to dealers, and Bill himself sold. Bill has confessed, and he isn't pointing a finger at Lescheva or any of his crew. According to him, the entire operation was him and Otis. This is frustrating for us, but a smart move for Bill. A confession will lighten his sentence. His taking the fall without naming names means he won't breathe free for a while, but at least he'll keep breathing."

"I suppose this is understandable," Bob muttered, and Mitch couldn't read him. It could be the Russian mob didn't concern him and he was looking forward and planning to recover to a point where his life would be free of these ties, even if he wasn't the one who made them in the first place. It could be he wanted retribution, but knew he was powerless to get it.

Mitch didn't press. Bob didn't wish to share, his call.

Mitch was quiet a moment, then he said softly, "I'm sorry, Bob."

Bob held his eyes and replied softly, "I should have known. He was always a troublemaker."

Mitch shook his head. "Don't. Don't take on that guilt. You did right by your family. He did wrong. It's that simple. Keep it that simple."

Bob continued to hold his eyes. Then he nodded.

Mitch decided to move on and allow Bob to do the same.

"I'll talk to Mara. She'll make her barbeque chicken pizza. You and your wife can come over. Yeah?"

Bob smiled. It was small but genuine.

"I've heard about Mara's pizza."

"It's the shit," Mitch informed him, and Bob's smile got bigger.

Then it faded.

"She never had one, and I think of my staff as family, so I hope you don't find this strange, but I feel like a father figure to her. And feeling that, I want you to take this as it's meant. I'm pleased when she finally chose, she chose well, Mitch. I approve."

That was when Mitch smiled.

"Thanks," he muttered.

"No," Bob muttered back, "thank you."

Mitch gave him a chin lift. Bob returned it then led him out.

On the showroom floor, they shook hands. Then Mitch's eyes located his woman and his body moved her way.

She was still with her male customer.

The man's gaze came to Mitch as did Mara's.

"Sorry to interrupt, this'll just take a second then I gotta go," Mitch told the man, then he wrapped his arm around Mara, hauled her stiff with surprise body against his and kissed her, short, hard but very wet.

When he lifted his head, her body was no longer stiff and she was blinking.

"See you when you get home tonight, baby," he whispered, looked to the now visibly disappointed man, jerked up his chin, looked back at his woman, gave her a grin and let her go.

His work was done.

He walked out seeing Roberta's huge, bright smile.

He had Roberta's approval too.

He gave her another low wave.

She returned it, but hers wasn't low.

He looked to the floor, shook his head and, grinning, Mitch walked out.

*     *     *

# Mara

*Five days later…*

"We're leaving, three minutes!" I called, grinning at Roberta, who was standing opposite me at the bar, her kids in their swimsuits barely containing themselves in the living room.

We both had the day off and we were taking our kids to the pool. They were going to horse around while we worked on our tans. Then we were going to come back, shower and go to Casa Bonita.

A celebration.

Mitch was at the station with the papers from our attorney.

Bill was relinquishing custody.

Yes, a celebration. And nothing said celebration like dinner with your friends at a crazy family restaurant that served Mexican food and had strolling musicians and cliff divers.

"Auntie Mara!" Billie shouted, and I could tell by her voice she was behind closed doors in the bathroom. "My suit's all messed up! I can't fix it!"

"I'll go," Bobbie muttered, and moved toward the hall as my new cell phone sitting on the counter rang.

I looked down to see the display said, "Unknown caller."

My brows knit, and I wondered if Mitch was calling from an extension at the station. I picked it up, took the call and put it to my ear.

"Hello," I greeted.

"Chestnut." I heard a gravelly voice say.

Holy cow.

"Tack," I whispered.

"Yo, babe," he replied, like he called me to gab every day.

How weird.

What did I do now? Outside an intense drama, I'd never had a conversation with a biker that I liked before, and I hadn't heard from him since it all went down.

I decided to ask, "Uh...how are you?"

"Wonderin' how I keep missin' my shot at the good ones," he replied, even more weirdly.

"Pardon?" I asked.

"Nothin', darlin'," he muttered, then went on, "just wanted to say, I made you a promise."

My breath caught.

Tack wasn't done.

"Haven't forgotten it."

"Okay," I whispered.

"And I won't."

"Uh...okay," I repeated.

"My world, shit like that goes down, someone pays."

Oh boy.

Maybe I should let him off the hook about his promise.

"Tack—"

"Stay beautiful," he ordered, then he was gone.

I stared at my phone.

"Who was that?" I heard Bobbie ask, and I looked up to see her and Billie in her cute, little, hot-pink bathing suit with the baby-pink ruffles on her booty, and they were walking into the living room-slash-kitchen-slash-dining room.

"My angel of vengeance," I answered, and she blinked.

Then she smiled and asked, "What?"

"Nothing," I murmured.

*"Pool!"* Billie shrieked.

I smiled at my girl.

I tossed my cell in my beach bag, grabbed the handles, moved around the counter in my flip-flops and replied, "Pool." Then I shouted, "Bud! Light a fire under it!"

Bud ran into the room in his trunks and a tee.

Bobbie corralled her kids.

We walked out of my apartment and headed to the pool.

Once I was lounging, I called Mitch to tell him about my phone call from Tack. He made no comment (though he did give me heavy silence for a moment) and then he shared that he was at the attorney's office handing off the papers Bill signed.

I looked at the kids horsing around in the pool.

"They're yours, sweetheart," Mitch said softly in my ear.

They were.

My soul sighed.

"Hurry home tonight," I said softly back. "Casa Bonita. Bray and Brent confirmed, though they did it under protest and informed me they'll be wearing disguises because if any of their gay posse sees them in Casa Bonita they'll get kicked out of the club. Tess called and told me she, Brock and the kids are meeting us there. So are Kenny and his kids. LaTanya and Derek are following us."

"Got it."

"We'll be ready when you get home."

"Got it."

"We still on for those viewings with the real estate agent on Saturday?" I asked.

"Yep," he answered, then threw out his own question. "You sittin' by the pool right now in a bikini?"

"Yep," I answered.

"Fuck," he muttered.

I grinned.

My man thought I was hot.

"I'm also covered in suntan oil," I shared.

I heard that sound I knew and loved come from deep in his chest, Mitch's immensely attractive chuckle.

Then he said, his voice deep and vibrating with his laughter, "Mara."

I closed my eyes.

That was mine.

Mine.

A life ahead of me with a beautiful, good man who said my name often with his deep voice vibrating with laughter.

And again, my soul sighed.

"Auntie Mara!" Billie yelled. "Come dunk me!"

I opened my eyes.

"The princess speaks," Mitch muttered again, a smile in his voice.

"You know it," I replied, my smile in mine.

"And love it."

My soul sighed yet again.

That was mine too.

All mine.

"Right," I whispered. "Love you, baby."

"Love you too, honey."

"Ready?" I asked.

"Ready," he replied, a smile again in his voice.

"Break," I whispered, my smile also in mine.

Then he was gone.

# EPILOGUE

## Hometown Bud Lawson

## Mitch

*Thirteen years later...*

"THAT SHIRT BURNIN' your skin?"

Mitch was looking down at his wife, who was wearing a Colorado Rockies jersey.

The number on the back: 9.

"Absolutely not," she replied, and he grinned.

"Any Cubs fans see you in that, they're gonna throw you out of the Die-Hard Club," Mitch warned.

"I'll take my chances," Mara muttered.

Mitch grinned.

"We're late, we're late! Sorry, we're late." They both heard, and Mara's head turned as Mitch's eyes went down the row to see Billie and her latest boyfriend scooting along the row, her dark hair shining in the bright Colorado sun, way too fucking much of her long, tanned legs exposed by her short-shorts.

It was early April. It should be cold. At least chilly.

Not in Colorado. It was eighty-six degrees and had been for two weeks.

Tomorrow the forecast was snow.

But today, Billie was in short-shorts, and she had been for two weeks. Mitch knew this from the evidence of her legs being tan.

"For the record," Mitch muttered, his eyes having moved to Billie's most recent, "I do not like that guy."

He felt Mara's gaze and he looked down at her to see her lips pressed together but her eyes dancing.

Then she unpressed her lips and whispered, "You never do."

"I like this guy less," Mitch informed her.

Mara's shoulders started shaking as her eyes continued dancing and she pressed her lips together again.

"And also, you need to have a word with her about those fuckin' shorts," Mitch went on.

Mara's entire body started shaking.

"I'm not jokin'," he whispered.

"You never are," she whispered back.

No, he never was. When Billie hit fifteen, what Mara called the Battle of Skin commenced. Mitch thought Billie exposed too much. Billie disagreed. Mara waded in, explaining to Mitch that he was overprotective. Mitch explained to Mara that was his job. Mara told Mitch to relax. Mitch told Mara it wasn't his job to relax. It was his job not to let his girl leave the house exposing too much skin, seeing as he was a guy and he knew what guys had in their heads. Especially at fifteen. And sixteen. And, like Billie's most recent, twenty-one.

Mitch lost a lot. Women, he found, since his fucking house was full of them, ganged up on you. They also had staying power. It was worth the effort, but it wasn't worth the headache you got in the long run. So he always gave the effort, but he usually gave in.

Billie was nineteen, he got that. But his girl would be forty, and he'd always give a shit.

About everything.

"We're here!" Billie cried, then sat her ass down in the empty seat beside Mara while whatever-the-fuck-his-name-was (Mitch didn't trouble himself with remembering them, he'd learned that early) sat next to her. His girl's eyes came right to him. "And, Mitch, it wasn't Ridge's fault we were late. It was mine."

Ridge.

Right. The kid's name was Ridge.

Fuck.

Who named their kid Ridge?

"Dad! Mom! Shift! I wanna sit by Billie!"

Mitch turned to his daughter, who was sitting next to him.

His ten-year-old Faith was Billie cloned. Lots of energy. Lots of smiles. Lots of laughter. Lots of love. In five years, Mitch would hit a new level of hell when Faith realized she was beautiful, had a fantastic figure and the power to toy with men at her whim.

"Good, I wanna sit by Daddy," he heard this said softly, and his eyes moved from the dark-haired, blue-eyed Faith to the seat next to her, where his eight-year-old, dark-haired, brown-eyed Marcie sat.

Marcie looked like her father but she acted like her mother. Sweet. Shy. Smart. Quiet. Loyal. Unconsciously funny. And clueless to just how beautiful she was and how much love she provoked.

He loved his Faith, but Faith grew up two years ago.

Marcie was his little girl and always would be.

They shifted, and Faith got her spot by her adored

Billie. They immediately commenced conniving, heads close, and Mitch figured Billie was sharing how to break men's hearts. A skill, incidentally, she'd been honing also since she was fifteen.

The only hope Mitch had was that Ridge's days were numbered.

They always were.

Mitch sighed and put his arm around Marcie.

Her eyes were on the field.

"It's gonna start soon," she whispered.

Her excitement was in her long legs, which were swinging. It was also in her voice.

Faith was Billie's.

Marcie was Bud's.

The sun rose and set for Marcie through her brother. This was also true about her father. Marcie adored the men in her life beyond reason.

Again, just like her mom.

"Yeah, baby, it's gonna start soon," Mitch murmured.

She tipped her brown eyes to his and grinned a wonky grin.

Fuck, but he loved seeing his wife's grin on his daughter's face.

Mitch grinned back.

Then he felt Mara's fingers on his hand moving to lace through his. They curled tight, and his returned the gesture as his eyes went to his wife.

Her eyes were on the field.

Mitch followed her gaze.

Warm ups.

Bud was smiling.

Mitch smiled too.

* * *

*Forty-five minutes later…*

They were standing, all of them. Everyone. The entirety of Coors Field. The vast space was filled with applause and the roar of the crowd as the announcer excitedly announced, "His first at bat for the Rockies, hometown Bud Lawson hits a two-run homerun! What a welcome home!"

Mitch watched Bud jog the bases, and he felt Mara's weight pressed into his side.

He heard the hitch of her breath over the ovation their boy was getting.

She was crying.

Mitch stopped clapping and wrapped an arm around her shoulders, but he didn't take his eyes from Bud.

He jogged down the third baseline to home, his cleat hitting home plate, the crowd still wild.

He accepted the high fives, low fives and fist bumps from his teammates as he walked to the dugout.

Five feet from the steps, he stopped dead, looked over the roof of the dugout and right at his family.

Then he lifted his arm, pointed at them and grinned.

That was when he heard four females' loud hitched breaths.

They weren't far away, and Bud saw it. He dropped his arm, caught Mitch's eyes and shook his head.

He, too, until recently, lived his life in a houseful of women. He knew Mitch's pain.

Then his grin faded. He held Mitch's eyes and thumped his fist to his chest over his heart.

Mitch lifted his chin to his boy.

Mara's body bucked with her sob against his side. Mitch's arm tightened around her as she shifted so her front was pressed to his side and both her arms were around his middle.

Then Bud jogged to the dugout and disappeared.

"Daddy," Marcie called, her fingers in his tee yanking, and he looked down at her. "Bud got a homerun his first time at bat!" she cried excitedly.

His Marcie always got excited when Bud got a homerun even though she'd seen it often. They'd flown to Tucson as much as they could to watch Bud play for the Wildcats at the University of Arizona.

"I know, baby," Mitch replied. "I saw."

"And he pointed at us!" Faith cried from their other side, and Mitch looked to her to see her head tipped back and her arm pointed up. "Look! We're on the big screen!"

Mitch didn't look. This was because he caught sight of Billie and saw her eyes on him. They were bright.

Mara's eyes, filled with love and trust.

He grinned at her.

Her grin was wonky when she grinned back.

Seeing that, not for the first time in thirteen years and probably not the last, Mitch wondered about Bill Winchell. The first time he saw that grin in a Stop 'n' Go he knew it was worth fighting and dying for. Exhausting yourself. Running yourself ragged. Bleeding yourself dry.

The last time the kids saw Bill was when he was drunk and high after they'd spent the day running away from him. He'd been true to his word. He'd relinquished all claim then and forever. He was alive, Mitch knew, out of prison and living with his mom in her trailer in Iowa. Mara's mom died of heart disease two years ago. Her friend Lynette shared the news, and they did not attend her funeral. Lulamae lived on. Neither of them nor Bill had darkened Mitch and Mara's door again.

So Bill had kept his promise.

So had Mitch.

And, Mitch figured, that was the best thing Bill Winchell had to give to his kids. Mitch's promise to give them a good life and unfettered access to Mara's love.

Therefore, in the end, not entirely an assclown.

Mitch's mind moved from these thoughts as his gaze dropped.

Jesus, Billie's man-boy had his arm low around her waist, his fingers close to her hip.

He took in the hand then he looked to Ridge.

Ridge caught his look, his head jerked and his hand shifted up to the acceptable zone of her waist.

His work done, looking away, Mitch caught Billie rolling her eyes at Mara. He'd seen this a lot and it didn't faze him. Never did. Billie perfected the eye roll at age seven.

They sat with the rest of the crowd as the next batter took the box.

Mara dropped her head to his shoulder.

It was after the batter fouled out that Mara's head shifted and her lips came to his ear.

"I knew it," she whispered.

Mitch turned his head and, up close, looked into his wife's unusual but beautiful blue eyes.

"Knew what?" he asked.

"That you'd build a beautiful family."

Mitch felt that in his gut and it felt good, like it always did when Mara hit him with her sweetness.

He lifted his hand and cupped her jaw. "Sweetheart—"

"Thank you, honey," she kept whispering.

"For what?"

"A good life and a beautiful family."

"You had a hand in that," he reminded her.

"I know. We're a team. Thank you for giving me that too."

Fuck, he loved his wife.

He couldn't think of a response so he decided to smile.

Mara smiled back, Billie's wonky smile, the smile his wife had given their daughter, and he couldn't help it.

He bent his head and kissed it off her lips.

And he kept doing it even as he heard Faith announce with practiced exasperation, undoubtedly to Ridge, "They do this a lot."

And he kept doing it through Billie's softer, much sweeter and not exasperated at all, "And they always have. As long as I can remember."

Please see the next page for

an excerpt from

# MOTORCYCLE MAN.

# CHAPTER ONE

## I'll Make You Coffee

IT WAS TEN to eight when I held my breath and turned off Broadway into the wide, cement-covered drive that took me around the big warehouse auto supply store that was part of Ride's operation. I made it to the forecourt of the three bay garage that was the other part of Ride's operation.

I studied the mammoth garage as I approached.

Ride Custom Cars and Bikes, my new place of employment, was world famous. Movie stars and Saudi Arabian sheiks bought cars and bikes from them. Their cars and bikes had been in magazines and they were commissioned for movies. Everyone in Denver knew about them. Hell, everyone in Colorado knew about them and I was pretty sure most everyone in the United States too. I was pretty sure of this because I knew not that first thing about custom cars and bikes. In fact, I knew nothing about non-custom cars and bikes, but I still knew about Ride.

I also knew the Chaos Motorcycle Club owned the garage and four auto supply stores, this one in Denver, one in Boulder, another in Colorado Springs and the last one that just opened in Fort Collins. I knew the Chaos Motorcycle Club too. They were famous because of Ride and because many of their rough and ready looking members had been photographed with their custom bikes and cars.

I also knew them because I'd partied with them.

And that day I was starting as the new office manager of the garage.

And that day was only one, single day after I'd been laid by Tack, the president of Chaos Motorcycle Club and, essentially, my boss.

And lastly, that day was only one single day and one single night after Tack had slam, bam, thank you ma'am'ed me.

"God," I whispered to my windshield as I parked in front and just beside the steps that led up to the door next to the triple bays of the garage, a door with a sign over it that said, "Office", "I'm *such* a stupid, stupid, *idiot*."

But I wasn't an idiot. No, I was a slut.

I didn't know how to cope with being a slut. I'd never been one before. I did not jump into bed with men I barely knew. I did not have flights of fancy where I thought they were beautiful, perfect, motorcycle man daydreams come to life and therefore did tequila shots with them and then had hours of wild, crazy, delicious, *fantastic* sex with them.

That was not me at all.

I was not the kind of person who lived life like Tack did. I was thirty-five and I had lived a careful, quiet, risk-free life. I weighed decisions. I measured pros versus cons. I wrote lists. I made plans. I organized. I thought ahead. I never took one step where I wasn't absolutely certain where my foot would land. And if I found myself in a situation that was unsure, I exited said situation, pronto.

Until two months ago when I looked at my life and the toxic people in it and I knew I had to get out.

So I got out. I didn't plan it. I didn't measure the pros and cons. I didn't organize my exit strategy. I didn't think ahead. When I'd had the epiphany and realized where I was, how dangerous it was, how unhealthy it was, I had no idea where I'd land when I jumped off the ride that was my life. I just straightened from my desk chair at work, grabbed my personal belongings, shoved them in a box and walked out. I didn't even tell my boss I was going. I just went.

And I didn't go back.

For the next two months I bought the paper every Wednesday and opened it to the want ads section. On each page of the want ads, I closed my eyes and pointed. If I was qualified for the job my finger touched, I applied for it.

That was the extent of my plan.

My best friend Lanie thought I was nuts. I couldn't say she was wrong. I had no idea what I was doing, why I was doing it, where I was going and what would happen once I got there.

All I knew was that I had to do it.

So I was.

Now I was here and here was where I decided I needed to be. I'd spent all day the day before trying to figure out if I should show for my new job or not. I'd screwed everything up, literally, and I hadn't even started the job yet. I didn't want to see Tack. I never wanted to see him again. The very thought was so humiliating, I felt my skin burning and I had that very thought nearly constantly since I slid out of his bed, dressed and, mortified, slithered out of his room.

But I had been out of work for two months. I had a nest egg but I also had a mortgage. I had to find employment. I had to start my life again. Whatever I was supposed to be doing, I had to do it. Whatever I needed to find, I had to find it.

There was no going back now. I'd jumped out of the roller coaster at the top of the crest, just before it took the plunge and I was falling.

I had to land sometime and it was here that I was going to land.

So I'd been a slut. There were lots of sluts out there, hundreds of thousands of them. Maybe millions. They went to work every day and some of them surely went to a workplace where there were people with whom they'd had sex. They probably didn't blink. Their skin probably didn't burn with mortification. They probably didn't care. They probably just found a new workmate or random guy that made their heart beat faster and their skin tingle with excitement and then they slept with him. They probably liked it. No, they probably loved it.

That was part of life, wasn't it? That was part of living, right? You did stupid stuff because it felt good and if you screwed up, you moved on. Everyone did that. Everyone.

Now, even me.

And damn it, I'd been on a scary, freaky roller coaster for a long freaking time. That whole time, I had my eyes closed and ignored the scary, freaky stuff that was happening around me. I was too scared to open my eyes and take a risk on life.

No more of that.

So I slept with my boss. Who cared?

I sucked in a deep breath, hitched my purse on my shoulder, threw the door to my car open and got out. Then I looked around the space. It was early and clearly bikers didn't do early. There was no one there. There was a line of bikes, five of them parked in front of the compound, which was a long, rectangular building to the side of the forecourt separating the garage from the auto supply store. There was a beat up pickup truck parked behind the auto supply store. Nothing else. No movement. No sound.

Eloise was supposed to meet me at eight to show me

the ropes. I figured I was early but I walked up the steps and tried the door anyway. It was locked. I turned to face the forecourt and looked at my watch. Seven minutes to eight.

I'd wait.

I took my purse off my shoulder, dug my cell out, flipped it open, slid my purse straps back over my shoulder and texted Lanie.

*I'm here.*

Approximately five seconds later, Lanie texted back.

*OMG! Why? Are you nuts?*

I'd told my best friend about the motorcycle club party I'd attended and I'd told her about my new boss's slam, bam, thank you ma'am. I did this in an attempt to stop my skin from burning when I thought of it because every girl knew, a problem shared with her best friend was a problem lost. Though, I'd learned a new life lesson and this was that those problems mostly were discussions of what to wear on first dates or whether or not you should invest in that fabulous wrought iron wine rack from Pottery Barn and not the fact that you'd had a one night stand with your new boss. I learned this because even after sharing with Lanie, it didn't help.

Lanie was of a mind that I shouldn't show at my new job and what I should do was my want ad finger pointing thing for another two months, or twelve, just as long as I never entered Tack's breathing space again. Then again, Lanie had a really good job as an advertising executive and was living with her fiancé, Elliott. She didn't have to worry about her nest egg depleting not only because she was talented, in great demand and therefore made a more than decent salary but also because Elliott was a genius computer programmer and made big bucks. Huge. She was spending ten thousand dollars on flowers alone for her wedding. Their catering budget sent my heart into spasm. And her dress cost more than my car.

My thumb went across the number pad and I texted back, *Not nuts. I need a paycheck.*

Five seconds later, Lanie texted, *What if you see him?*

I was prepared for that and I'd spent a lot of time preparing for seeing Tack again. Indeed, I'd spent all night doing it considering I had all of two hours of sleep.

*If I see him, I see him,* I texted back. *I'm embracing my inner slut.*

To this, I received, *You don't have an inner slut!!! You're Tyra Masters. Tyra Masters is NOT a slut!!!*

*She is now,* I replied, adding, *or she was Saturday night.*

*No more flying solo,* Lanie texted in return then right on its heels came, *Any and all future social events you attend, I'm your wingman.*

I smiled at my phone, heard a door slam and my head came up. Then my lungs seized.

Shit! There was Tack standing outside the door to the Club's Compound. He was wearing faded jeans, motorcycle boots and a skintight white t-shirt. Even from a distance I could see his hair was a sexy, messy bedhead. And I knew why since he was currently making out with a tall, thin, dark-haired woman and when I say making out, I mean *making out.* They were going at it, her hands at his fantastic ass, his hands at hers.

God, I'd been in his bed Saturday night and he had a new woman in his bed last night, Sunday. And he hadn't walked me to the door and made out with me to say goodbye. Hell, he hadn't even said good-bye.

Damn.

I closed my eyes tight and swallowed and when I did, it hurt...a lot.

Okay, maybe I couldn't do this.

I opened my eyes and pinned them to the phone, my thumb flying over the number pad.

*He just walked out of the Compound,* I told Lanie.

Two seconds later, I received, *OMG!!!!*

*He's making out with a brunette,* I informed her.

*OMG!! OMG!!! OMG!!!! Get out of there!* Lanie texted back.

I heard an engine cough to life and lifted my head to see the brunette in the beat up pickup. My eyes slid to Tack to see his on me. My gaze shot back to the truck to see the brunette was waving at Tack but he was done with her. I knew this because she was waving at him but when I looked back to him he was not paying a bit of attention to her and was walking my way.

I looked back down at my phone and typed in, *She's taking off. He's coming to me.*

I sent my message and stared at the phone, not lifting my head and trying hard not to bite my lip or, say, have an embarrassment-induced seizure.

"Red," I heard when my phone beeped in my hand and luckily I didn't have to lift my head immediately because I was reading Lanie's latest message.

*Escape, Tyra, go, go, go!!!!*

"Red," I heard from closer and I finally lifted my head to see that Tack was three of the eight steps up and climbing toward me.

He looked good. Everything about him looked good. The way his clothes fit. The way his hair looked like he'd just got out of bed and run his fingers through it. The way those lines radiated out the sides of his eyes. The way his body moved.

Nope, I couldn't be a slut. I should have listened to Lanie.

"Hey," I forced out.

My skin started burning and I was pretty sure it was pink top-to-toe as his eyes slid the length of me. When he made it to the top of the steps, he looked down at me and he didn't look happy.

"What're you doin' here?" he asked.

I stared at him, surprised. I mean, I'd told him on Saturday night I was his new office manager.

Didn't I?

So I said, "I work here."

"You what?"

"I work here."

His eyes did a top-to-toe again then he repeated after me, "You work here."

"Yes, Eloise hired me. I'm taking over for her. I'm your new office manager."

He stared down at me and he didn't look any less unhappy. In fact, he looked unhappier.

Then he stated, "You're shittin' me."

I fought against biting my lip again, succeeded and shook my head.

Apparently, Tack wasn't a big fan of working alongside women he'd loved and left. Or, in my case, loved and then kicked out of his bed.

I found this interesting, not in a good way but it was interesting nonetheless.

Then Tack announced, "You don't work here anymore."

I blinked up at him as my hand automatically reached out and grasped the railing beside me.

"What?" I whispered.

"Babe, not good," he growled. "What the fuck were you thinkin'?"

"About what?" I asked.

He leaned in and it hit my fogged, stunned, fired before

I even started brain that he was even unhappier than before and I had to admit, it was a little scary.

"I do not work with bitches who've had my dick in their mouth," he declared and that was when my skin stopped burning and felt like it was combusting.

"But," I started when I could speak again, "I thought I told you I was your new office manager."

"You did not," he returned.

"I'm pretty sure I did," I told him.

"You didn't," he replied.

"No, I think I did."

He leaned even closer to me and growled, "Red. You. Did. *Not*."

"Okay," I whispered because he was now definitely scaring me but also because I actually wasn't pretty sure I did, I was just kind of sure I did.

"I do not fuck anyone who's got my signature on their paycheck," he again made his opinion perfectly clear and my mind raced to find a solution to this new dilemma at the same time it struggled with fighting back the urge to run as fast as I could to my car and peel right the heck out of Ride Custom Cars and Bikes forecourt and get as far away from this freaking scary guy as I could.

I mean, what was I thinking? I thought he was beautiful. Perfect. My motorcycle dream man.

Boy was I wrong. Very, very wrong. He wasn't. He was a rough and ready motorcycle man, the president of a motorcycle club and he was downright frightening.

With effort, I pulled myself together.

Then I told him, "Okay, that works for me. Minor blip. We forget it happened and since it's never going to happen again, we move on from this and you don't have to break your no sleeping with employees rule in order to, um...employ me."

"We forget it happened?" he asked, looking even angrier.

"Uh...yeah," I answered.

"The rule's broken, babe, no unbreaking it," he returned.

"It's not broken," I told him.

"Red, it's broken."

"It isn't."

"It is."

"It isn't," I stated and he opened his mouth to speak again, his face hard, his eyes flashing and I quickly went on to explain my reasoning. "See, you said you don't sleep with anyone who's got your signature on their paycheck. Eloise hired me but I hadn't actually *started*. So, I didn't have your signature on my paycheck because I'd only had the job offer. I wasn't actually doing the job. I walk in that door," I pointed to the office door, "that's when I'm your employee and since we're not, erm...you know...and won't again, then, technically, you didn't break your rule and, um...won't."

"I know what you taste like," he informed me of something I already knew.

This was an odd and slightly rude thing to share so I had no response.

"And what you sound like when you come," he continued being rude.

This was not getting better and I clenched my teeth to stop myself biting my lip.

"And how fuckin' greedy you are," he went on. "Babe, you think you're around I'm not gonna want seconds, you're fuckin' crazy."

I blinked.

Then I asked quietly, "What?"

"Darlin', you're the greediest piece of ass I've had in

my bed in a long fuckin' time. I got a taste for greedy, you think I'm not gonna take it?"

Now he was definitely being rude.

"I'm not greedy," I whispered.

He leaned back. "Jesus, you fuckin' are. So fuckin' hungry, you nearly wore me out. And, darlin', that's sayin' something."

This was already not fun and it was getting less fun by the second.

"Can we not talk about this?" I requested.

"Yeah, absolutely, we can not talk about this. That works for me. It also works for me you showed since you didn't leave your number before you took off on Saturday. So give me your number, get your ass in your car and I'll call you when I got a taste for you."

Oh my God. Did he just say that?

I felt the blood stop rushing through my veins as my entire body solidified.

"Did you just say that?" I asked when I got my lips moving again.

"Red, give me your number, get your ass in your car and I'll call you when it's time for us to play again."

He did. He did just say that because he'd also just mostly repeated it.

I clenched my teeth again but this time for a different reason.

Then I asked, "Do you know my name?"

"What?" he asked back.

"My name," I stated. "I told you my name Saturday night and I know I did so don't tell me I didn't." And I did. I absolutely, *totally* told him my name. In fact, I'd done it at least three times when he kept calling me "Red".

"You're shittin' me," he said again.

"Stop saying I'm shitting you. I'm not. What's my name?" I demanded to know.

"Babe, who cares? We don't need names," was his unbelievable answer.

"Ohmigod," I whispered. "You're a jerk."

"Red—"

"Totally a jerk." I kept whispering and he crossed his arms on his chest.

"Two choices, Red, give me your number, get your ass in your car, get outta here and wait for my call or just get your ass in your car and get outta here. You got five seconds."

"I'm not getting in my car," I told him. "I'm waiting for Eloise to come and show me the ropes then I'm going to work."

"You are not gonna work here," he returned.

"I am," I shot back.

"No, you aren't."

"I am."

"Babe, not gonna say it again, you aren't."

That was when I lost it and I didn't know why. I wasn't the type to lose it. You didn't lose it when you planned every second of your life. Caution and losing it did not go together.

But I lost it.

I planted my hands on my hips, took a step toward him and lifted up on my toes to get in his face.

"Now, you listen to me, scary biker dude," I snapped. "I need this job. I haven't worked in two months and I *need* this job. I can't wait two more months or longer to find another job. I need to work *now*." His blue eyes burned into mine in a way that felt physical but I kept right on talking. "So you're good-looking, have great tats and a cool goatee. So you caught my eye and I caught yours. We had sex. Lots of sex. It was good. So what? That was then, this is now. We're not going to play, not again. We're done playing. I'm going to come in at eight, leave at five, do my job and you're going to be my scary biker dude boss, sign my paychecks, do my performance evaluations and maybe, if you're nice, I'll make you coffee. Other than that, you don't exist for me and I don't exist for you. What we had, we had. It's over. I'm moving on and how I'm moving on is, I'm… working… this… *job*."

I stopped talking and realized I was breathing heavy. I also realized his eyes were still burning into mine. I knew he was still angry but there was something else there, something I didn't get because I didn't know him and I couldn't read him. But whatever it was, it was scarier than just him being angry which, frankly, was scary enough.

When he spoke, he did it softly. "You think, Red, right now, I put my hands and mouth on you in about two minutes you wouldn't be pantin' to be flat on your back, legs wide open in my bed?"

At his words, I forgot how scary he was and hissed, "You're unbelievable."

"I'm right," he fired back.

"Touch me, you bought yourself a lawsuit," I retorted acidly.

"You are so full of shit," he returned.

"Try me," I invited hostilely though I didn't want him to. Not that I thought he was right, but because he was a jerk. A *huge* jerk. And I'd just decided I'd rather be touched by any man currently residing on death row before I wanted Tack to touch me again.

"Is everything okay?" We both heard and our heads turned to look down the steps to see Eloise at the bottom looking up at us with wide eyes.

I opened my mouth to say something to Eloise, what, I had no idea but before I could speak, Tack did.

"You tell her she wears that fancy-ass shit to work again, her ass is canned," Tack growled and I watched Eloise's body jerk in surprise.

She was in jeans, a tight t-shirt and high-heeled sandals and I was in a pencil skirt, blouse and high-heeled pumps therefore I had to admit I definitely made a mistake on the dress code but it wasn't worth termination.

I looked to him to see his eyes cut to me. "And you," he said, "I taste you again, *any* way I can taste you, and I will, Red, trust me, you're gone. Outta here. Get me?"

"You won't," I declared and he glared at me then his eyes moved over my face. They did this for a while and while they did this, they changed. I could swear I watched the anger leak clean out of them and something else, something curious, something warm, and therefore something far more frightening filled them.

His warm blue eyes locked on mine and he muttered, "We'll see."

Then he stepped away, jogged down the steps, sauntered to a bike, threw a leg over it, started it, backed it out and roared away.

"What was that?" Eloise asked, I jumped and turned to see she was standing at my side.

"I don't think I made a good first impression on my new boss," I answered. Eloise was staring after Tack but at my words she looked at me, eyes still wide, so I pulled my "I can do this" mask over my face, smiled at her and cried, "Oh well, never mind! He'll come around. Now, let's get crackin'."

And I turned to the office door.

# THE DISH

*Where Authors Give You the Inside Scoop*

♥ ♥ ♥ ♥ ♥ ♥ ♥ ♥ ♥ ♥ ♥ ♥ ♥ ♥ ♥

*From the desk of Jaime Rush*

Dear Reader,

DRAGON AWAKENED and the world of the Hidden started very simply, as most story ideas do. I saw this sexy guy with an elaborate dragon tattoo down his back. But much to my surprise, the "tattoo" changed his very cellular structure, turning him into a full-fledged Dragon. I usually get a character in some situation that begs me to open the writer's "What if?" box. And this man/ Dragon was the most intriguing character yet. I had a *lot* of questions, as you can imagine. *Who are you? Why are you? And will you play with me?* This is the really fun part of writing for me: exploring all the possibilities. I got tantalizing bits and pieces. I knew he was commanding, controlling, and a warrior. And his name was Cyntag, Cyn for short.

Then the heroine made an appearance, and she in no way seemed to fit with him. She was, in the early version, a suffer-no-fools server in a rough bar. And very human. I knew her name was Ruby. (I love when their names come easily like that. Normally I have to troll through lists and phone books to find just the right one.) The television show *American Restoration* inspired a new profession for Ruby, who was desperately holding on to the resto yard she inherited from her mother. I knew Ruby was raised by her uncle after being orphaned, and he'd created a book about a fairy-tale world just for her.

But I was still stumped by how these completely different people fit together. Until I got the scene where Ruby finds her uncle pinned to the wall by a supernatural weapon, and the name he utters on his dying breath: Cyntag.

Ah, that's how they're connected. [Hands rubbing together in anticipation.] Then the scene where she confronts him rolled through my mind like a movie. Hot-headed, passionate Ruby and the cool, mysterious Cyn, who reveals that he is part of a Hidden world of Dragons, magick, Elementals, and danger. And so is she. Suddenly, her uncle's bedtime stories, filled with Dragon princes and evil sorcerers, become very dangerously real. As does the chemistry that sparks between Ruby and Cyn.

I loved creating the Hidden, which exists alongside modern-day Miami. Talk about opening the "What if?" box! I found lots of goodies inside: descendants of gods and fallen angels, demons, politics, dissension, and all the delicious complications that come from having magical humans and other beings trapped within one geographical area. And a ton of questions that needed to be answered. It was quite the undertaking, but all of it a fun challenge.

We all have an imagination. Mine has always contained murder, mayhem, romance, and magic. Feel free to wander through the madness of my mind any time. A good start begins at my website, www.jaimerush.com, or that of my romantic suspense alter-ego, www.tinawainscott.com.

*Jaime Rush*

♥ ♥ ♥ ♥ ♥ ♥ ♥ ♥ ♥ ♥ ♥ ♥ ♥ ♥

## *From the desk of Kristen Ashley*

Dear Reader,

I often get asked which of my books or characters are my favorites. This is an impossible question to answer and I usually answer with something like, "The ones I'm with."

See, every time I write a book, I lose myself in the world I'm creating so completely, I usually do nothing but sit at my computer—from morning until night—immersed in the characters and stories. I so love being with them and want to see what happens next, I can't tear myself away. In fact, I now have to plan my life and make sure everything that needs to get done, gets done; everyone whom I need to connect with, I connect with; because for the coming weeks, I'll check out and struggle to get the laundry done!

Back in the day, regularly, I often didn't finish books, mostly because I didn't want to say good-bye. And this is one reason why my characters cross over in different series, just so I can spend time with them.

Although I absolutely "love the ones I'm with," I will say that only twice did I end a book and feel such longing and loss that I found it difficult to get over. This happened with *At Peace* and also, and maybe especially, with LAW MAN.

I have contemplated why my emotion after completing these books ran so deep. And the answer I've come up with is that I so thoroughly enjoyed spending time with heroes who didn't simply fall in love with their heroines. They fell in love with and built families with their heroines.

In the case of LAW MAN, Mara's young cousins, Bud and Billie, badly needed a family. They needed to be protected and loved. They needed to feel safe. They needed role models and an education. As any child does. And further, they deserved it. Loyal and loving, I felt those two kids in my soul.

So when Mitch Lawson entered their lives through Mara, and he led Mara to realizations about herself, at the same time providing all these things to Bud and Billie and building a family, I was so deep in that, stuck in the honey of creating a home and a cocoon of love for two really good (albeit fictional) kids, I didn't want to surface.

I remember standing at the sink doing dishes after putting the finishing touches on that book and being near tears, because I so desperately wanted to spend the next weeks (months, years?) writing every detail in the lives of Mitch, Mara, Bud, and Billie. Bud making the baseball team. Billie going to prom. Mitch giving Bud "the talk" and giving Billie's friends the stink-eye. Scraped knees. Broken hearts. Homework. Christmases. Thanksgivings. I wanted to be a fly on the wall for it all, seeing how Mitch and Mara took Bud's and Billie's precarious beginnings on this Earth and gave them stability and affection, taught them trust, and showed them what love means.

Even now, when I reread LAW MAN, the beginning of the epilogue makes my heart start to get heavy. Because I know it's almost done.

And I don't want it to be.

*Kristen Ashley*

♥ ♥ ♥ ♥ ♥ ♥ ♥ ♥ ♥ ♥ ♥ ♥ ♥ ♥ ♥ ♥

## *From the desk of Kristen Callihan*

Dear Reader,

In SHADOWDANCE, heroine Mary Chase asks hero Jack Talent what it's like to fly. After all, Jack, who has the ability to shift into any creature, including a raven in *Moonglow*, has cause to know. He tells her that it is lovely.

I have to agree. When I was fifteen, I read Judith Krantz's *Till We Meet Again*. The story features a heroine named Frederique who loves to fly more than anything on Earth. Set in the 1940s, Freddy eventually gets to fly for the Women's Auxiliary Ferrying Squadron in Britain. I cannot tell you how cool I found this. The idea of women not only risking their lives for their country but being able to do so in a job usually reserved for men was inspiring.

So, of course, I had to learn how to fly. Luckily, my dad had been a navigator in the Air Force, which made him much more sympathetic to my cause. He gave me flying lessons as a sixteenth birthday present.

I still remember the first day I walked out onto that small airfield in rural Maryland. It was a few miles from Andrews Air Force Base, where massive cargo planes rode heavy in the sky while fighter jets zipped past. But my little plane was a Cessna 152, a tiny thing with an overhead wing, two seats, and one propeller to keep us aloft.

The sun was shining, the sky cornflower blue, and the air redolent with the sharp smell of aviation gas and motor oil. I was in heaven. Here I was, sixteen, barely legal to drive a car, and I was going to take a plane up in the sky.

Sitting in the close, warm cockpit with my instructor,

I went through my checklist with single-minded determination and then powered my little plane up. I wasn't nervous; I was humming with anticipation.

Being in a single-engine prop is a sensory experience. The engine buzzes so loud that you need headphones to hear your instructor. The cockpit vibrates, and you feel each and every bump through the seat of your pants as you taxi right to the runway.

It only takes about sixty miles per hour to achieve liftoff, but the sensation of suddenly going weightless put my heart in my throat. I let out a giddy laugh as the ground dropped away and the sky rushed to meet me. It was one of the best experiences of my life.

And all because I read a book.

Now that I am an author, I think of the power in my hands, to transport readers to another life and perhaps inspire someone to try something new. And while Mary and Jack do not take off in a plane—they live in 1885, after all—there might be a dirigible in their future.

*[signature]*

♥ ♥ ♥ ♥ ♥ ♥ ♥ ♥ ♥ ♥ ♥ ♥ ♥ ♥ ♥ ♥ ♥

## From the desk of Anna Sullivan

Dear Reader,

I grew up in a big family—eight brothers and sisters—so you can imagine how crowded and noisy, quarrelsome and fun it was. We all have different distinct personalities, of course, and it made for some interesting moments. Add in a couple of dogs, friends in and out, and, well, you get the picture.

I was the shy kid taking it all in, not watching from the sidelines, but often content to sit on them with a good book in my hands. Sometimes I'd climb a big old elm tree behind our house, cradle safely in the branches, and lose myself in another world while the wind rustled in the leaves and the tree creaked and swayed.

Looking back, it's no wonder how I ended up a writer, and it's not hard to understand why my stories seem to need a village to come to life. For me, the journey always starts with the voices of the hero and heroine talking incessantly in my head, but what fun would they have without a whole cast of characters to light up their world?

The people of Windfall Island are a big, extended family, one where all the relatives are eccentric and none of them are kept out of sight. No, they bring the crazy right out and put it on display. They're gossip-obsessed, contentious, and just as apt to pick your pocket as save your life—always with a wink and a smile.

Maggie Solomon didn't grow up there, but the Windfallers took her in, gave her a home, made her part of their large, boisterous family when her own parents turned their backs on her. So when Dex Keegan shows up, trying to enlist her help without revealing his secrets, she's not about to pitch in just because she finds him...tempting. Being as suspicious and standoffish as the rest of the Windfallers, Maggie won't cooperate until she knows why Dex is there, and what he wants.

What he wants, Dex realizes almost immediately, is Maggie Solomon. Sure, she's hard-headed, sharp-tongued, and infuriatingly resistant to his charms, but she appeals to him on every level. There must be something perverse, he decides, about a man who keeps coming back for more when a woman rejects him. He enjoys their verbal sparring, though, and one kiss is all it takes for him to know he won't stop until she surrenders.

But Maggie can't give in until he tells her the truth, and it's even more incredible—and potentially explosive to the Windfall community—than she ever could have imagined.

There's an eighty-year-old mystery to solve, a huge inheritance at stake, and a villain who's willing to kill to keep the secret, and the money, from ever seeing the light of day.

The Windfallers would love for you to join them as they watch Dex and Maggie fall in love—despite themselves—and begin the journey to find a truth that's been waiting decades for those with enough heart and courage to reveal.

I really had a great time telling Dex and Maggie's story, and I hope you enjoy reading about them, and all the characters of my first Windfall Island novel.

Happy reading,

*Anna Sullivan*

www.AnnaSulivanBooks.com
Twitter @ASullivanBooks
Facebook.com/AnnaSullivanBooks